LEADERS

A Twin-bred Novel

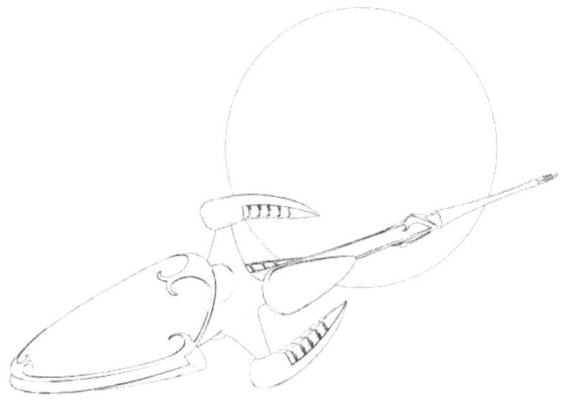

Karen A. Wyle

ISBN 978-0-9905641-7-1

Printed in the United States of America

Cover design by David Leek
Author photo by Alissa Lise Wyle

To my family
And to all families
With love

Once Again, an Introductory Caveat

As this series progresses, reintroducing characters and their relationships threatens to become a cumbersome distraction. I've included a few reminders, most of which I hope are on the subtle side. I welcome all readers!—but this book will be of most value and pleasure to those who see its characters as familiar friends (or enemies). So I recommend reading Book One, *Twin-Bred* (permafree online in all the usual places), and Book Two, *Reach*, before diving into this story.

Pronouns and Punctuation

Here's one of those reminders. Tofa are hermaphroditic, each sexually mature individual capable of emitting and receiving spores and conceiving and bearing young. Among the various English alternatives for representing this state of affairs, I chose to use singular masculine pronouns. Glider reproduction involves three Gliders, and their households are composed of three adults plus any children, but neither humans nor Tofa can readily distinguish one Glider gender from another. Rather than either employing three distinct pronouns for Gliders or inviting confusion with Tofa, I picked a combination of "it" and "one" for all Gliders.

This time around, I've tweaked the way I punctuate nonverbal communication between Mara and Levi and between Judy and La-ren. (Another reminder: in each case, a living person is communicating with a twin who now exists only in some undefined realm of psychology or neurology.) In this book, such communication is indicated by parentheses.

Chapter 1

(Tofarn)

JAK-RAD-TAN, the sole Tofa Twin-Bred remaining on Tofarn, walked home beside his oldest child Lan-sol in the waning light of dusk. Since completing his formal education in his mid-teens, Lan-sol often picked Jak-rad-tan up at the government-affiliated Dispute Reconciliation Office at the end of the day. Jak-rad-tan cherished the ritual while acutely aware that Lan-sol might, at any time, decide his parent was too ancient and uninteresting for the custom to continue.

As happened so often, a few passersby turned and looked after them, one pointing toward Lan-sol, several more speaking softly to each other in the hushed tones of awe. One bit of conversation, barely audible, reached them as they passed: "The first time they tried to kill him, he had not even been born!"

Lan-sol stiffened and walked faster. Jak-rad-tan hurried to catch up and laid an upper hand on his offspring's shoulder. "Must you let it trouble you?"

Lan-sol stopped abruptly, turned toward Jak-rad-tan, and waved his upper hands in frustration, fanning Jak-rad-tan in the process and sending an errant tree-seed dancing in his direction. "Can they never stop talking about me? And they can't even stop with the facts! 'The first time'—did I miss something? Did some hovering 'they' try to kill me after Ton-lal-set failed?"

Jak-rad-tan did not respond. He had no evidence that any hidden allies of the deposed Eminence had made such attempts. But Lan-sol's health, in his early years, had been less than robust. Not until his second year had he first divided his thicker arm in two. The doctors were unsure whether the prenatal attack had had lingering effects or whether something else was going on. Jak-rad-tan knew several of the scientists working on the reproductive spore protection project, and had asked one to test samples of Lan-sol's wastes, looking for signs of toxic substances. None were found.

Lan-sol had wandered over to the bank of the nearby stream and was leaning against a tree, tossing pebbles into the water, making short-lived geometric shapes with the splashes. Jak-rad-tan joined him. He could change the subject slightly while still conveying information of interest. "I have been talking with Henry Abuto, my former history professor, about the followers you have attracted."

Lan-sol snorted, an impressively close approximation of the human sound. "Followers! I haven't gone anywhere or done anything! Don't they care?"

"Professor Abuto reminded me that among humans, many religions and other legends featured infants with great destinies before them, infants who began life with a narrow escape from death. Tofa may be similarly attracted to this meme."

Lan-sol reached his upper right hand into the tree and plucked a golden blossom, twirling it in his fingers. "I may not know all the stories, but I thought the threats usually came from the tyrant, or whatever, that the baby was supposed to overthrow. Gen-tar-ten and the rest defeated Ton-lal-set and the others like him years ago, at the same time as they rescued me. Rescued us."

Lan-sol tossed the flower into the stream. Parent and offspring stood watching it float toward the choppier water where stream joined creek and flowed toward one of the many rivers.

Jak-rad-tan finally broke the silence once more. "It will be good to see Veda and Melly and Laura at your birthday party. I have not made sufficient effort in recent months to coordinate our schedules."

"That's another thing. I'll be glad to see friends, and even to have a party. But my birthday is part of the problem. All those people talk as if something momentous is supposed to happen when I turn seventeen. Just because the Twin-Bred—the rest of them—were seventeen when they left

Tofarn." Lan-sol turned toward Jak-rad-tan. "Were the Tofa this irrational and mystical before the humans came?"

Jak-rad-tan shrugged, before realizing that so human a gesture might be inappropriate at that moment. "My knowledge of Tofa history and tradition is still well short of what it should be. Eminence Gen-tar-ten will be attending your festivities as well. You could ask him. But it is hardly fair to apply such labels to the entirety of our people."

Lan-sol was pacing back and forth in a manner that reminded Jak-rad-tan, with a pang, of Dr. Mara Cadell. "But it almost seems as if they're right about me. I *do* feel as if I'm meant to do something. And it *does* feel as if it's time. But what am I supposed to do?"

Jak-rad-tan gestured for Lan-sol to come to a stop. "I have one comfort to offer as you ponder that question. Recall that I, when just a little younger than you, found a path I wished to follow. And that I did not allow the expectations of others to dictate what that path should be. I am sure you have the capacity to make your own decisions as well."

Lan-sol took a deep breath, and some of the tension in his posture melted away. Jak-rad-tan pointed toward the path ahead, and the two resumed walking. The green sky had darkened almost to black by the time they arrived at home.

* * *

Veda and Melly sat on a riverbank in Central Park, dabbling their toes in the water. Such a thing would never have occurred to Veda; but since the time Melly had pulled off her shoes one warm day and plunked her feet in, it had become a way for Veda to connect with her daughter and to demonstrate a capacity for informality.

Melly kicked a foot, splashing toward a beetle-biter. "Only four more days until Lan-sol's birthday party! Have you decided on a present yet?"

"Laura and I are joining forces—and you'll be surprised to know that I'm letting her decide. I think Laura has a better feel for what would please a member of Lan-sol's generation. What about you?"

Melly tilted her head. "I wouldn't assume that Lan-sol is completely in step with his 'generation.' Anyway, I'm giving him season tickets to my theater. Two season tickets, actually. He can take a friend, or go with Jak-rad—I mean Jak-rad-tan." She grimaced. "You'd think I'd be used to Jak-rad-tan's adult name after all this time. I guess I can blame Peer-tek and the other Tofa Twin-Bred on New Landing. When they decided to keep their birth names unaltered, the way their twins would be doing, they guaranteed I'd get confused."

Veda chuckled. "I know. I spend a few minutes saying 'Jak-rad-tan' over and over whenever I'm going to see him or talk to him. And in a couple of years, we'll have to do the same for Lan-sol. . . . I'm bringing a few little presents for Lan-sol's younger siblings, so they won't feel too left out. You?"

Melly smirked a bit. "I'll do my part by actually spending some time with them during the party. I can join them in playing with their new toys."

Veda twitched a well-groomed eyebrow. "Better you than I, daughter. Those children barely speak Terran. And I don't have your advantages where Tofar is concerned." The retroviruses used to keep human host mothers from rejecting Tofa embryos, combined with whatever genetic material Veda had absorbed from Peer-tek before the twins' birth, had had some unanticipated effects. Melly, born years later, could produce more of the telepathic component of Tofa speech than any human without that prenatal history.

Babysitting was all very well, but it should hardly be the sum total of Melly's activities at a party. "I hope you manage to get away from the little ones at some point. You should meet more of Jak-rad-tan's and Randy's friends." Even as an adult, Melly's social circle was less extensive than Veda would have liked. Lan-sol and Jak-rad-tan, plus Jak-rad-tan's twin Randy, provided Melly's only link to the fond foster siblings and stimulating environment of the long-gone Project days. Companions whom any of these found congenial might meet with Melly's approval as well.

Melly looked away, probably to roll her eyes at Veda's expression of concern; then pulled her feet out of the water and crossed her legs, rubbing her feet on her skirt. "I wonder if Stan will make the trip. Stan, Stan, the ladies' man! Maybe we can set him up with someone. Or a few someones."

Veda shook her head in disbelief. Stan had been Mara Cadell's faithful and diffident assistant through all the years of the Project. Even with Mara at such a distance of space and time, Veda would have bet money, or even jewelry, against Stan ever coming so drastically out of his shell. But his involvement in the insurgent Tofa takeover had lent him the requisite touch of glamour and intrigue, and he had taken full advantage. A few years after that revolution, he had even become a competitive ballroom dancer. Veda had made the trek to see that for herself. The man could actually dance! And to top it all off, he looked pretty damn good in the historical fancy dress—tuxedos, or some such word—that had come back into fashion.

Veda turned toward Melly to remark on Stan's transformation; but Melly's posture and apparently her mood had altered dramatically while Veda was woolgathering. She was hunched over, holding herself in the unsatisfactory auto-hug she had adopted during the dissolution of the Project so many years ago. "Melly, what's wrong?"

Melly answered with a sniff, then a sob, before finally choking out the words. "It's Jimmy and Peer-tek. They have ch-children now, some almost as old as Lan-sol, and I haven't m-met any of them. And I h-haven't s-seen my brothers in all these years. I haven't even talked to them—not really, not back and forth without the time lag in between."

Did people who suffered significant traumas in their childhood years revert more easily to childish ways? Veda could not imagine yielding to sorrow so conspicuously at Melly's age. But then, Veda had been a fundamentally political creature from childhood on. She should be glad Melly remained capable of spontaneity.

* * *

Jak-rad-tan relaxed against his favorite leaning post and reviewed the lengthy guest list for Lan-sol's birthday celebration. Had anyone been omitted who should be included?

He had invited all the members of his twin Randy's commune, as well as the former Project staff with whom either he or Randy remained in contact. He had of course invited Veda, her friend and fellow host mother Laura, Laura's husband Sapir, Stan, Melly, and any close friend whom Melly wished to bring. Gen-tar-ten would be an honored guest, along with many of those who had assisted him in displacing the previous Eminences. Lan-sol had submitted his own list of friends; Jak-rad-tan had suggested, without success, that the most socially prominent of those who viewed Lan-sol as a prophet-in-training should be added. Jak-rad-tan had considered asking his host mother to attend, but decided that she would probably prefer benign neglect.

Who was missing?

Siri, of course. Jak-rad-tan felt the constriction in his chest that could, if he allowed it, lead him to hum in sorrow. Siri's burden had finally become unbearable, three years since. The knowledge that she had saved countless Tofa lives, perhaps even the entire Tofa species, had not, in the end, been enough to overcome her guilt over the homicidal means she had used to accomplish that rescue. Jak-rad-tan and Veda and Stan had taken the lead in erecting a statue in her honor in Central Park, where Siri had often walked to remind herself of the Tofa she had saved from Councilman Kindall's and Dr. Bloom's xenocidal machinations. As for Kindall and Bloom, their burial sites had long since been rendered officially anonymous, but locations where they were thought to lie sometimes sported venomous graffiti in Tofa script.

The other omission popped back into Jak-rad-tan's mind, as it had done so frequently in recent months. Jak-rad-tan had carried Lan-sol, built Lan-sol's body from his own, protected him from assault, birthed him and raised him—but he had not created him without assistance. Somewhere must be the other Tofa, the one whose spore Jak-rad-tan had breathed at just the right time. To that Tofa, whoever and wherever he might be, Jak-rad-tan owed more than he could ever repay.

An answer should not be hard to obtain. The spore protection project would be winding down soon, its scientists at least temporarily idle. Surely he could find a willing volunteer.

But as much as the revolution had altered Tofa society, Tofa still resisted disruptive ideas at least as much as humans would. What would it mean to the Tofa if every child were seen as having two parents? What obligations might follow the revelation of spore-parent identity? Would assumptions as to custody and control be questioned and contested? And Tofa society retained some degree of social stratification. How would a high-status individual react to learning of a child whose carry-parent had a humbler station?

Jak-rad-tan was far from sure that he wished to be the center of political upheaval once again, after so many relatively quiet years.

He could approach some trusted member of the spore project in secret. He knew them all well enough to know which of them would find the question most intriguing, and which—an overlapping though not identical set—could probably be trusted to keep the inquiry confidential. At least for now.

* * *

Veda poked her head into the office Laura occupied when she visited the spore protection team. "Time for you to work your magic again."

Laura sighed dramatically. "And here I thought the time had come to hang up my cape. All the work is finished, isn't it? You've addressed all the vulnerabilities we could dream up. You've fortified the reproductive spores against any sort of hijacking—with the side benefit of protecting them from various diseases that could make them less potent. Your Tofa representatives have signed off on the work, and they're supposed to be organizing the immunization program as we speak."

"Well, somewhere along the political chain, someone isn't satisfied. They want more tests." Veda sat down in one of the few chairs that didn't dwarf her petite frame. "And they have what they consider the ideal test subjects."

Laura's face went as grim as her fundamentally benign nature could allow. "Prisoners?"

Veda made a check mark in the air with her forefinger.

Laura blew out a long, slow breath. "So they immunize the prisoners as per our protocols, flush out any problematic ingredients—and conceivably get rid of a few undesirables."

"Multiple motives: the Tofa signature."

Laura got up and closed, then locked, the door. Veda suppressed any sign of surprise and waited for the communication that required such precautions.

Laura sat down at her desk again. "I know you consider me awkwardly idealistic and inconveniently forthright. I would expect you and the other insiders here to protect me from details I might find it hard to conceal. So it's time to tell me: is there anything in the formula, or in our testing procedures, that would alarm the Tofa? Anything based on Bloom's research, or left over from earlier Tofa history?"

"Of *course* we didn't use Bloom's research!" And there was no point feeling hurt. Given the secrets Laura did know about Veda's past, she might hesitate to make comforting assumptions.

Laura relaxed only a little. "And?"

Veda braced herself. "There have been some experiments on the effects of various airborne gases on spores—including some tests with adult volunteers. The technicians administered antidotes almost immediately, which limits the utility of the results. And of course, they used chemicals more easily controlled than whatever the Tofa threw at each other before humans showed up."

Laura tapped her fingers lightly on her desk in an arpeggio wave, back and forth—a rarely exhibited "tell" indicating nerves. "And that fact wasn't shared with the Tofa authorities in case it appeared too sinister. But the censorship may have backfired."

"Then would you say the solution is to share the information, however belatedly?"

Laura sat up straighter and quieted her fingers. "I would say so. I can tell them, truthfully, that I only learned about it after their recent proposal came in." She looked Veda in the eye. "But there are only so many times I can go to them and say I've been excluded before I become completely ineffective. And while I'd hoped we had reached a point where that would no longer matter, it appears I was wrong."

*   *   *

Ton-lal-set, deposed Eminence of the Southern

Region, leaned against the corner of his cell, draped in chains, and pondered his chances. He had survived many panel reviews, but had never been informed what considerations led the panel to keep him alive on any or all of those occasions. This might be the day his execution was finally decreed.

Had Jak-rad even known that his fate was being discussed, and his possible execution deferred, during his periods of imprisonment? Had he realized he was being evaluated, not simply interrogated? If only the panel had eliminated that mutated menace as they could and should have done, all the catastrophes that followed would have been prevented, and Ton-lal-set might by now be leading his own, purely Tofa expedition to the stars!

Ton-lal-set vaguely recalled, from his days as host mother at the Twin-Bred project, that the humans had quite a different penal system. When panels met periodically to consider the fate of a human prisoner, they were deciding whether to release the prisoner before a maximum sentence had expired. How typical of humans, with their vacillating and sentimentality! But where his own fate was concerned, he could wish that the human-loving Tofa now running things had adopted such a procedure.

What little gossip he had managed to hear suggested that executions had become less involved and less painful under the new regime. Rumor had it that one recently condemned prisoner, another former host mother, had been given a drug that put him to sleep as it killed him. Dying in one's sleep! What sort of execution was that?

If Ton-lal-set did not follow his former colleague into slumber and death, was there in fact any purpose in continuing to live? Or were all the Tofa outside the prisons content to abandon their traditions and forego ambition, slurping up favors from the humans? Had the world changed so much?

Chapter 2

(New Landing)

MARA AND Fel-lar walked along a path at the base of a glittering crystal cliff, the omnipresent red ground cover stretching away across the valley on the level side. Both, in their ways, were accompanied by Mara's never-born twin Levi: Mara through their lifelong sharing of consciousness, Fel-lar by means of the rudimentary Tofa telepathic sense, amplified by physical and emotional closeness.

They could have driven to and from the concert, but New Landing's climate, relatively invariant, made walking a natural default for such distances. As natives of Tofarn, neither would have objected to a rain shower, if graced with one; but rain rarely occurred by Tofarna standards, and the evening remained dry.

Besides, Mara was in no hurry to arrive.

As the venue came into view, she took a deep breath and blew it out again. Fel-lar stroked her shoulder with an upper hand and patted her bottom with a lower, simultaneously reassuring and distracting her. "I know you find it disconcerting to be the subject of a musical epic, but like it or not, you have a history of redirecting the societies you encounter."

"At least I won't have to understand all of it." Mara's mastery of the Glider tongue remained incomplete, even after all these years; she used her ear-translator when, and only when, she wished to be sure of what was being said. Glider language had much in common with Glider music, which she found equally difficult to comprehend.

Levi threw out a comment. ("You know I can help. Just ask.") Levi's tone was smug as well as fond. Fel-lar's frequent communion with Levi included sharing the music which Fel-lar and several of the younger Gliders composed together. Levi, in his turn, could share with Mara at least a glimpse of what the music meant to those who appreciated it.

Mara looked up into Fel-lar's marbled eyes, once again appreciating their colors—green like the twilight sky on Tofarn, rich brown, pure white—and then turned toward the gathering crowd. Most were Gliders, fluttering and hoping about, with a very few humans, looking for places to sit, and rather more Tofa, standing or finding supports against which to lean. She turned back to Fel-lar. "Are your twins here?"

Traditional Tofa, of course, would always have known the whereabouts of immature offspring, and would in fact have been likely to dictate the same. But even for them, twins posed a challenge. (Other than those who had chosen to produce two-species Twin-Bred pairs, Fel-lar was one of the few Tofa Twin-Bred with twin offspring. Given the value all of them placed on twin status, several of the Twin-Bred persisted in claiming—in jest, Mara hoped—that her influence was somehow responsible.) Almost all the Tofa Twin-Bred scrupulously avoided commanding their unborn fetuses, so as to allow their young the maximum in free will once they emerged, but Fel-lar—warned by Tofa back on the home planet—had known to expect a special level of autonomy from twin offspring. It was seldom that either twin bothered to share an itinerary with his parent.

Fel-lar, with his height advantage, was able to spot the more musically inclined of the pair, towering over several Glider apprentice musicians. He caught Mara up in all four arms, so that none of his hands would exert a painful pressure, and lifted her just long enough to see. "No doubt he will regale us later with his well-informed criticisms of my work."

They had been standing around long enough to attract attention. Rides Above Danger, Fel-lar's co-composer, launched himself from the window of the concert hall and slanted gracefully down to land next to Fel-lar. As always, the Glider's belt of ornamented metal—the belt whose loss had triggered a crisis all those years before—circled its midsection, catching the afternoon light. The belt must be expandable: the Glider had grown sturdier and stouter over the years.

Some Gliders had lately taken up the human custom of makeup, and Rides Above Danger was evidently among them. He had ringed all three eyes with bright red liner, and highlighted his back wing with the same color. The claws on all three feet, in contrast, had been painted shiny black. Mara glanced around to see if Emily Wilson had shown up. Emily would no doubt want to note the composer's fashion statement as a data point. But the crowd was too dense for her to tell.

Mara turned back to Rides Above Danger and activated her translator in time to hear the Glider ask Fel-lar, "Are you ready for our debut?" The Glider hardly waited for a reply before turning to Mara, sweeping its left and right wings backward and dipping its head in the Glider equivalent of a most respectful bow. "Welcome, Benefactor."

Mara responded with a bow of her own. She could justify it as showing respect to an artist. And she had never yet managed to come up with an appropriate manner for receiving tribute.

The audience greeted the piece with enthusiasm. By the time Fel-lar and his fellow composer were done receiving congratulations from admirers and answering questions from music students, Mara was more than ready to return to their own settlement. The organizers, ever deferential to her needs, had provided a chair, sprouting all too visibly among the ubiquitous perches and cushions, but they lacked sophistication in the matter of comfortable human furniture.

The twins were spending the night with their spore-parent Mat-set, so Fel-lar and Mara headed home alone. The two of them walked along the crystalline cliffs, the ground cover dark red in the waning light, Fel-lar occasionally reproducing some musical thread under his breath. During a silent interlude, Mara took his nearest arm and squeezed it. "You know how I feel about all the perpetual fuss, but you should be proud. That was an ambitious and masterful piece of work."

Fel-lar widened one eye in approximate imitation of a human's raised eyebrow. "Did you engage your translator so as to follow any of the 'fuss'?"

"I do have some curiosity. I turned it on for the first

movement. Really, Fel-lar! Did Rides Above absolutely dominate where libretto was concerned?"

Fel-lar whistled his amusement. "To what particulars did you object?"

"Let me count the ways! I brought the ship through the wormhole by pure force of will? I personally invented the communications relays we planted there? I blessed the colony with fertility, for God's sake?"

Fel-lar put his left hands against her side to bring her to a halt. "As to the first point: the assertion is, in a nontechnical sense, essentially correct. The construction of *Star Seed*, the evasion of all schemes to obstruct her completion and departure, the process by which we determined to risk the wormhole's potential dangers: all these were primarily your accomplishment. As for fertility, you oversaw the reversal of the contraceptive regimen and helped educate a ship full of nubile youngsters as to what awaited them once they were able to reproduce."

Mara counted off one on her fingers and paused dramatically. "What happened to Item Two? The communications relays?"

Fel-lar whistled again. "How perplexing. Perhaps your translator malfunctioned during that passage."

Mara gave him a soft slap on the waist and resumed walking. "I may be less suspicious as I get old and fuddled, but I'm not yet that easily gulled."

The first of the two small moons had risen, its light reflecting off facets of the nearby cliff and making it easier to see the cluster of buildings at the cliff's base. Those buildings sheltered the small community Artemesia had founded for those who chose to continue the Twin-Bred legacy more directly: only three households, but eleven family units. Not content with producing a new generation of fraternal human and Tofa twins, some of the members also sought to recreate the communal atmosphere in which most of them had been raised. Mara looked at the nearest house and suppressed a shudder at the thought of carrying not only twins, but the larger Tofa fetus as well. At least one of the mothers had needed last-minute medical intervention for potentially dangerous complications.

Mara's pace had slowed, no doubt due to her

distraction. Fel-lar matched his pace to hers, and stroked a finger down her right arm in the familiar signal for introducing an emotionally challenging subject. She glanced at him, then looked away toward the path on which they walked.

Fel-lar hesitated, then spoke. "On the subject of your supposed great age: have you spoken to Harriet Gaho about the matter we discussed?"

Mara walked faster, a futile gesture given Fel-lar's longer stride. "No, I haven't. And I still don't see why I should consider bearing a child, even if I'm capable of it." She felt Levi's intention to join the conversation and wordlessly bid him hold his peace.

Fel-lar passed her and wheeled around to stand facing her, obstructing her forward progress. "The vehemence with which you reject the prospect comes from no rational considerations. It reflects, rather, the emotional state which in large part motivates me to persist. You do not believe that you could nurture and love a child of your own. Given all you have done for the Twin-Bred from the moment of our inception through our infancy and at every stage thereafter— given the affection you have maintained for Levi, despite all pressures to disclaim it—given that you opened your heart to me, despite all the profound differences between us—given the nurture and guidance you have given my offspring—the evidence strongly suggests you would make a mother beyond compare. In the positive sense."

Mara bit down hard on her treacherously quivering lip. Fel-lar lifted a lower hand and traced along her mouth with one long finger, then moved to her cheek and finally her hair. Mara intercepted his hand, pressed it, then clasped it and drew it to her side as she headed on toward home.

* * *

Jimmy lifted the pot lid and took a deep sniff, then turned to Anna. "What do you think? Is it ready?"

Anna leaned over the pot with a spoon and took a taste. "Yup. Call the horde."

Jimmy headed to the doorway and hollered. "Peer-tek! Kids! Come and get it!"

Jimmy's and Peer-tek's firstborn led the charge, the girl's left hand in the Tofa's lower right. The two were as close to Twin-Bred as offspring born separately could manage. Jimmy and Anna's younger daughter ran close behind; the remaining Tofa youngsters came pelting after, Peer-tek's middle child carrying little Sin-han. No doubt the toddler had been stumbling along behind the others, humming at being left in the rear.

Peer-tek appeared quietly and distributed spoons, while Jimmy dished out the stew and plunked the bowls down on the upper and lower tables. The firstborn "twins" loosed their hands reluctantly. Anna had laid down the law years before: letting either of the two eat at a table designed for the other led to spilled and wasted food. She had, however, allowed each of the youngsters to use condiments better suited to the taste of the other, as long as they kept the quantities small—and consumed most of the portions served to them whether or not they liked the result.

Over the rattle of utensils, Anna asked Peer-tek, "Are you taking Sin-han over to Dar-tan and Cindy's this afternoon?"

"I don't think so. Dar-tan's youngest carry-child is still recovering from that respiratory infection."

Jimmy, listening to the exchange, wondered whether any Tofa back on Tofarn used the process that had, on New Landing, seemed so natural and even inevitable. It was easy enough, with the technology available, to identify which member of the Tofa community had emitted the spore that fertilized a Tofa egg. Every Tofa child had two acknowledged parents, a carry-parent and a spore-parent, even though children generally lived with their carry-parent and visited their spore-parent. But it had been a human, Jimmy vaguely recalled, who came up with the notion of finding out.

* * *

Fel-lar stood looking over Mara's shoulder as she sketched. "Is that the last page of the current installment?"

Mara paused, her cartoon rendition of the Glider concert almost complete. "Unless something happens that inspires me before I send it to Veda." She looked at the drawing and shook her head, with a short grunt of disapproval. "I'm not sure we'll manage to keep up our regular correspondence without the spore project as a focus. Local gossip is rather less interesting to me and probably to her."

"Now that you are able to return your attention to more local scientific concerns, such as your research into flight-related Glider genetics, you could share some of the details, as you did with your work on blue intoxication."

Mara merely shrugged. "The work on blue had an obvious utility for Tofarn—though I gather some of the Tofa there view even that research as tainted by association."

Fel-lar tried again. "As for what you call gossip, I hope you will remember that what appears commonplace to us still retains some freshness for our friends on Tofarn." Fel-lar glanced out the nearest window, in case any usable anecdote should be developing within view. A trickle of humans and Tofa were heading toward the Glider village, most of them carrying baskets. "Have you featured the Glider market in any way?"

Mara checked earlier drawings. "Here's Elspeth, running errands for the oldest farmer—there she is, staggering along with a big armful of fruit—so she can compare the way older and younger farmers speak. And Emily, haggling with the Glider who sells yarn. Leave it to our diplomacy expert to come up with body language that means something to Gliders! When the dust settled, Emily ended up with two extra skeins."

"Perhaps, if you have not done so already, you should include a portrayal of the Tofa who also knit with Glider fibers. I am told that humans find our technique amusing, if somewhat enviable."

Mara chuckled. "Maybe if I had your quantity of arms and hands, I'd manage to learn to knit. That's a good suggestion—thanks."

Fel-lar had many years of practice at withholding observations. It was therefore easy to refrain from offering his opinion that Mara could in fact learn to knit, if she were able to recognize and banish her unconscious resistance to the activity. But any mention of Mara's mother and her near-constant knitting would darken Mara's mood for some time, possibly even hours.

He reached out his lower left hand to stroke her hair. She glanced up at him. "What just happened?"

He stroked once more before withdrawing the hand. "A train of thought reminded me of my fondness for my companion."

Mara pushed away her tablet and stood in front of him, placing her hands on his torso between his upper and lower arms. "I could use a break to express some fondness of my own."

Rounding the familiar turn in the familiar path, Fel-lar came to a vista that might have ranked as one of his favorites, were it not for the complex emotions it inspired. Crystalline cliffs both soared above and plunged below the level of the path, rimmed with crimson ground cover and set against the bluest of skies.

As soon as Mara and her team had perfected the genetic adjustment eliminating Tofa susceptibility to blue, Fel-lar had considered it appropriate, even necessary, to announce that all his offspring would undergo that adjustment. As a leader, he had needed to demonstrate commitment to their new home. Of course, adults could also receive the treatment; but whatever others might speculate, only Mara actually knew that Fel-lar himself had elected to continue with the less efficient chemical suppressant. For him, though not for his children, blue intoxication remained possible.

He had never, since their arrival all those years ago, allowed his immunity to lapse. But despite the anger that still burned, if well banked, at the thought of his and his fellows' treatment on Tofarn, he could not quite decide to set himself apart from his species in such a way.

And he had made sure, before his offspring received the genetic treatment, that it was at least theoretically reversible.

Almost all the original New Landing colonists, Twin-Bred and Project staff alike, recorded birthday greetings for Lan-sol's celebration, to be compiled into one long message and sent through the wormhole's communications relays.

Few of the colonists saw any need to consult with others about the contents. Jimmy and Peer-tek were exceptions. Older and more prudent than on a previous occasion, they arranged a meeting with Mara to explain their intentions in person before acting thereon.

Jimmy, more confident than in his youth, took the lead. "Mara, we all remember vividly how much you objected to the idea of visitors from Tofarn, especially Tofa visitors, during our colony's early days. Has enough time passed, and has the situation on Tofarn changed enough, to change that objection?"

As Jimmy explained their proposal, Peer-tek attempted to read Mara's body language and expression. Both were moderately encouraging. Her fists had not clenched, nor had her jaw. Rather than blasting them with her well-known glare, she seemed to be making an effort to remain inscrutable.

When Jimmy had finished, Mara twitched an eyebrow and just barely smiled. "Thank you both for allowing me to comment." She waited a beat, possibly to see whether Jimmy would blush, then went on. "I will discuss it with Fel-lar, who may choose to seek further input from other members of the leadership."

Jimmy and Peer-tek glanced at each other before Peer-tek replied. "The relevant calculations indicate that the composite message will need to be sent quite soon."

Mara surprised him by chuckling. "And both of you, I imagine, will be hoping for an even shorter period of suspense. I will do my best to keep it to a minimum. Now off with you."

Chapter 3

(Tofarn)

THE LARGEST island in Central Park was barely large enough to support the size of the gathering. Tables of the usual two heights, but more of the taller, were scattered not only throughout the central pavilion, but on every outdoor surface more than a Tofa's arm length from the water. Randy's commune had supplied much of the food; more refined delicacies for both species had been brought in from elsewhere. Jak-rad-tan had reluctantly allowed some of the wealthier of Lan-sol's admirers to defray the cost of the affair.

The rain came and went, as usual, but between the showers the sunlight sparkled in the leftover raindrops in a positively festive manner. Golden shrubbery all around the pavilion glittered in the intermittent sunshine; the brighter light revealed what clouds had hidden, the first faint traces of the purple that would shortly sweep throughout the landscape.

Given the guests' likely disagreement as to the value of either human or Glider music, a small auxiliary building confined the music and dancing, doors closed to reduce unwanted exposure to the sounds within. Even with ventilation, the dancers quickly grew uncomfortably warm; a steady stream of overheated party-goers passing in and out left the doors open long enough for passages of music to leak through.

Food was available from midmorning onward, but the more organized and lavish feasting began at midday. Once only the most voracious of the youngsters were still eating, it was time for the presentation of gifts. Not all were from human guests: many Tofa considering themselves progressive had adopted the human custom of giving birthday presents. Jak-rad-tan had placed a cap on the expense and extravagance that might otherwise have been likely, but had still allowed the guests' munificence to exceed what most young Tofa could expect. Within a few minutes, Lan-sol stood surrounded by everything from hundreds of scent sticks to stacks of metal books, compilations of Glider music and (to his gamely concealed dismay) artistic renderings of his famous prenatal ordeal. On one of the adjacent streams, two new sailboats bobbed on the water, their sails reflecting their respective human and Tofa origins.

Last of all came the most anticipated phase of the festivities: the message from New Landing, played on the largest screen available with the highest quality audio. The message would almost certainly be in Terran rather than Tofar, given the limitations of any recording of Tofar speech. Lan-sol's Terran would be up to the task; the same might not be true of some of the party guests, but there was little Jak-rad-tan could do about that state of affairs, short of inconveniencing other guests by asking them to serve as translators.

Seth Baruti began the message, his birthday congratulations followed by a somewhat rambling discourse on how much Lan-sol's parent Jak-rad-tan had contributed to the advancement of science on both worlds. Off camera, the party guests could hear muttering from a voice that some recognized as Mara Cadell's, after which Baruti wrapped up his message somewhat abruptly.

Next came Emily Wilson, former Diplomacy teacher, telling Lan-sol that the entire New Landing contingent considered him a member of their community, however distant, and expressing her delight at the progressive changes in Tofarna society since Lan-sol's birth. Harriet Gaho, who had been the Twin-Bred project's chief nurse, followed with a most heartily delivered Happy Birthday, as well as the expressed hope that Lan-sol was not currently eating himself into a stupor. An assorted group of Twin-Bred came next, expressing a babble of good wishes in which any individual speech was difficult to discern. Suzie, on the periphery, looked on with tears in her eyes.

A single Glider came on camera, its hisses and trills

reminding the Tofarna audience of the Glider music they had all heard on one or another occasion. A pleasant computerized voice translated the Glider's speech into an unremarkable birthday greeting.

Next Mara appeared, looking less thin and considerably more relaxed than in the Project days. She congratulated Lan-sol not only on his birthday, but on his good fortune in growing up with a remarkably brave and resourceful member of the Twin-Bred fraternity. Then she paused for a moment, a sterner expression returning to a face that had so often borne it. "Jimmy and Peer-tek—and two of their children—will speak last. The content of their message is their idea. None of us opposes it; but as for its viability and degree of good sense, we will *all* defer to Jak-rad-tan and those others—on Tofarn or in New Landing—whom he wishes to consult."

Lan-sol's guests turned to each other, and murmuring quickly grew to something of a clamor. Jak-rad-tan found himself holding his breath, and forced himself to release it. What surprise was in store? Mara's cryptic words suggested one possibility. He who had benefited in the past from Jimmy and Peer-tek's audacity might now be paying the proverbial piper.

Jimmy and Peer-tek took center stage. In front of them, as Mara had indicated, stood two youngsters, a human girl and a Tofa, holding hands. Peer-tek also used one of his upper hands to hold Jimmy's hand, while his lower hands rested on the heads of the two children. Melly, watching, took a deep breath and let it out with something between a sigh and a sob.

Jimmy spoke first. "Lan-sol, we hope you're having an absolutely terrific birthday!"

Peer-tek added, "We who know and love your parent, as well as others who are with you today, wish you all much joy. We hope that the following year will be especially fruitful and enlightening."

Jimmy again: "With that goal in mind, these children have an invitation to extend."

Then, in concert, the two younger voices: "Cousin Lan-sol, please come visit us!"

Peer-tek leaned forward slightly toward the camera.

"We hope, based on your accounts over the years, that the situation on Tofarn is reasonably stable. Our settlement here is thriving, and relations with both the original human colonists and the Gliders are friendly and mutually beneficial. We believe the time has come when the prophylactic effect of interstellar distance is no longer necessary. We propose to inaugurate the next stage of our joint story—and invite Lan-sol to be the first to take part.

"We can provide *Star Seed*'s complete schematics, material lists, and other information, if any of that information can no longer be located on Tofarn. We cannot, of course, know who among the humans who assisted in her construction may still be available, but we hope and expect that some of them will be."

Jimmy spoke next. "Of course, building another spacecraft will take time—and cost plenty. We're sending replicator codes for some foodstuffs and knickknacks that you might be able to market as oddities or luxury goods, in order to defray the expenses. If there are humans or Tofa on Tofarn who believe a closer connection between our worlds would be desirable, they might want to contribute as well."

The camera panned away to show the other video participants standing behind Jimmy and Peer-tek's contingent. Mara had the last word. "We know we've given you a lot to think about. Please don't let that overshadow your celebrations. One more time, from us all—" She and the entire crowd on camera shouted in unison: "Happy Birthday!" Then the screen faded to black.

Lan-sol looked at Jak-rad-tan. Jak-rad-tan was not surprised to see and feel the excitement that had seized him. Jak-rad-tan turned away, seeking Veda. When he found her, he looked her in the eye; Veda looked back, shaking her head a little, a wry smile twisting her mouth. Jimmy and Peer-tek had done it again.

As soon as the video had ended and the hubbub had diminished somewhat, Jak-rad-tan looked around for Laura. It took him some time to locate her: while his height allowed him to find clusters of humans immediately, the crowd was thickly packed and the various heads of hair difficult to distinguish. After a while, he stopped trying to identify her visually and listened for her voice, with its unique blend of warmth, good cheer, and authority. Then he extracted himself from the chattering group surrounding him and made his way to her side.

She saw him approach and excused herself in turn, coming to meet him and grasping both his lower hands. "That's quite a surprise they sprung on you—if it was a surprise."

Jak-rad-tan whistled briefly. "Very much so. Could I consult you for a moment?"

"Of course. Let's head out by that river. I think the rain has stopped for the moment."

Most of the guests were either eating once again or discussing the invitation. Jak-rad-tan and Laura had no trouble finding a spot with some privacy, as long as they kept their voices fairly quiet. There was nowhere to sit or to lean: he would have to keep this initial consultation brief.

Laura spoke first. "It's feasible. I don't know whether that's what you wanted to hear."

Jak-rad-tan shrugged as humans and Tofa-Twin-Bred did. "It would have been simpler if the invitation were impractical; but that result would have left me with an even more restless offspring."

Laura held up her right hand and began ticking off points on her fingers. "We'll have the necessary technical information. As for producing the materials, it's been done, of course, and some of the production equipment and facilities still exist."

Jak-rad-tan twitched in surprise. Laura smiled a little. "There were several of us on the Council who thought we should keep our future options open. And for the same reason, we've kept track of the folks who helped the Twin-Bred with the job, before the Tofa establishment of that time warned them off."

"That is . . . fortuitous, for Lan-sol at least. There is also another possible source of materials and expertise. Are you familiar with Ton-lal-set's space project?"

He had thought he might surprise Laura in turn, but no. "Yes. We had people keeping an eye on it. His design and construction were both seriously flawed, and most of the Tofa who worked on that project are, shall we say, no longer available . . . . But a few managed to ride out the governmental transition and might be persuaded to take part."

Who would be most suited for such persuasion? Laura, more than most humans; Lan-sol, perhaps more than most other Tofa. But of course, persuasion would be less crucial if Gen-tar-ten approved. And perhaps impossible if he did not.

"You ask me to resume, or copy, a project pursued by my predecessor?"

Jak-rad-tan hoped his odor did not carry any traces of emotional strain, as Lan-sol's would surely have done. "The circumstances are quite different. Although there may conceivably be benefits to—" He almost said "demonstrating," then substituted a safer term. "To reminding the community that your administration is more competent than his when it comes to ambitious scientific endeavors."

Gen-tar-ten let out a short whistle. "Such competence notwithstanding, I can hardly devote sufficient resources to such a task without affecting programs with more widespread impact and utility."

"We have sources of funds, with ideas on how to obtain more. And there are humans with substantial expertise who could assist." Jak-rad-tan explained the history of human involvement in the construction of *Star Seed*, then added, "Some of Lan-sol's young Tofa . . . acquaintances could provide assistance while receiving valuable training."

Gen-tar-ten buzzed in thought for a few moments. "I will not go so far as to treat the construction or launch of this ship as a governmental endeavor. There are too many imponderables attached. But I will allow it to proceed, and will assist, at least initially, in smoothing the way."

Jak-rad-tan bowed as far to the side as he could reach. "Thank you for your generosity." *And thank you*, he added to himself, *for leaving the project sufficiently independent that your own continued popularity will not be essential to its success.*

Jak-rad-tan, looking through the small high window of their dwelling, saw Lan-sol approaching at something close to a run. Behind and around him hurried a crowd of Tofa, mostly his age or up to a few years older, all of them talking and gesturing in chaotic combination. A few of the pursuers had divided their thickest arms in two, so as to have more hands available for grabbing at Lan-sol.

Within a few strides of the door, Lan-sol stopped short, whirled around, threw up all his hands, and shouted, "ENOUGH!" Those at the front of the crowd tried to stop; those farther back plowed into them, propelling them forward. Two in succession knocked into Lan-sol himself; he staggered, regained his footing, and gave a panicky glance toward the door. Jak-rad-tan flung it open and waved Lan-sol inside, then shooed the others away like a Terran farmer scattering barn fowl.

Jak-rad-tan closed the door and looked to see where Lan-sol had landed. He found the young Tofa leaning over the kitchen water spout, webbing his fingers and sucking water out of his hands without any such trivial accessory as a saucer. Lan-sol waited until Lan-sol paused, then offered him a woven cloth to dry himself. Lan-sol hesitated, took the cloth, then tossed it aside and lunged at Jak-rad-tan with all his arms spread wide, wordlessly begging to be held, as if he were half his present age and size.

Jak-rad-tan opened all his own arms and held his child tight, squeezing until he felt the youngster start to stir. Then he let go and stepped back. "Would you like another drink? Or are you ready to share the details of that unusual scene?"

Lan-sol looked over toward the nearest leaning post, then collapsed against the wall. "What I could use is some blue. Don't you have an unfiltered feed from New Landing here somewhere?"

Jak-rad-tan rotated the top joints of his upper left-hand fingers to one side and the other, a Twin-Bred variant on the human custom of wagging a reproachful finger. "As you said so recently: enough! Tell me what happened."

Though he imagined he could guess.

Lan-sol pointed a shaking lower hand toward the front door. "Some of them say that by leaving the planet, I'm running away from my destiny. That I'm supposed to tell Gen-tar-ten to step aside, thank you, while the next generation takes over and makes the world perfect. Or I get to discover the formula for immortality. Or is it a fountain, hidden in one special stream in one special forest?" Lan-sol turned toward Jak-rad-tan, radiating disgust and impatience. "Or else I'm supposed to find a way to make humans understand us. The way you and the other Twin-Bred tried to do, but somehow I'm supposed to know how to do it better. Or else I'm supposed to be the next great mystic and reveal some new variety of babble. Oh, and I'm supposed to add the third syllable to my name now, instead of waiting. Won't *that* get me plenty of new attention!"

Jak-rad-tan moved quietly over to the cabinet containing a small selection of alcoholic beverages. Their effect on Tofa was small compared to human intoxication, but might be just enough to soothe Lan-sol's nerves without inducing actual disorientation and loss of control as blue would have done. He poured a small quantity of his favorite, a chocolate liquor that pleased him more for its flavor than its somatic effects, into a saucer and held it out toward Lan-sol. Lan-sol looked up at him, startled: Jak-rad-tan had never before made such an offer. Then he stood up from the wall, his posture suggesting at least a transient swelling of pride, and held the saucer beneath his chin.

Jak-rad-tan waited for Lan-sol to ingest every drop before prompting him. "Are any of your would-be followers in favor of the expedition?"

Lan-sol let out a short and somehow jarring whistle. "Oh, yes. Some of them want to come along and help me take over the colony. Some of them want to head out in some new direction, and never mind seeing any of those uninteresting family and friends of mine."

"Are there none who have shown themselves content to let you explore your own path?"

Lan-sol held out the saucer in mute appeal. Jak-rad-tan fetched the bottle and poured him a second, smaller serving, then brought out another saucer and poured some for himself as well. Remembering the old human custom, Jak-rad-tan held his saucer upward in Lan-sol's direction. Lan-sol looked puzzled for a moment, then apparently remembered and clinked his own saucer against his parent's. Both drank. Finally, Lan-sol answered. "A couple of them want to support whatever I choose to do. But they tend to stay quiet when the others are shouting."

Jak-rad-tan collected Lan-sol's saucer, took it and his own to the kitchen, then returned and reclined against the leaning post near where Lan-sol stood. "Give me their names, if you would. We can invite them over and encourage them to speak. And if they—and their overlooked fellows—regard the invitation as an honor, perhaps that will have some salutary effect."

* * *

Once again came the footsteps, and the key in the lock. The door slammed open and two guards entered. Always two, when he left his cell; even after all this time, they must fear he would intimidate one guard unaccompanied.

Time to live or to die.

The nearer guard unlocked the shackles and gathered up the slack of the chain in his lower hands. The small, almost odorless candle given to prisoners flickered feebly. As the guards tugged him along, Ton-lal-set resisted for a moment and blew as hard as he could at the candle, snuffing it out. Then he swaggered toward the door to meet his fate.

It grew harder each time to keep up with the guards, maintaining a properly dignified posture despite the weight of the chains, throughout the long trek from cell to hearing room. The miserable rations provided to prisoners were not designed to maintain their strength. It had been years since Ton-lal-set had even managed to divide his thickest arm.

Ton-lal-set distracted himself from the screaming of his muscles by counting the doors of the cells they passed. He lost count when a door opened and two Tofa, a guard and a functionary with what looked like medical paraphernalia, emerged, the guard closing the door firmly behind him. It seemed as if the newcomers had joined their party, until the guard produced a key and stopped at the door of the next cell in order. Were executions by drug in progress at this moment?

It was very bright in the chamber, far brighter than the cell in which Ton-lal-set had spent the past few uninterrupted months; and the light had somehow been given a purple cast, to ensure (as if there were any doubt) that the prisoner would feel endangered and exposed.

Ton-lal-set stood in front of the panel of four Tofa, all leaning against well-padded posts. Even the guards, stationed on both sides of the door, leaned against the walls.

The apparent head of the committee looked pointedly about. "It appears that no witnesses have come to speak in your favor. How unfortunate."

Ton-lal-set made the gesture indicating that a would-be comedian had failed to amuse. Of course no one had stepped forward. No Tofa with the intelligence to find the prison in the first place would associate himself with so toxic a prisoner.

"We will proceed with your own testimony. Explain, if you can, how it would benefit the community for your life to continue."

The previous panels' questions had been less direct.

Ton-lal-set commanded his limbs not to falter. He rarely spent more than a few minutes unsupported and erect, and they had kept him waiting in the hall.

"I am one of a dwindling number of Tofa with a unique ability to comprehend human cognition and behavior. Many of the Tofa with such advantages have been executed, while others are unimaginably distant."

The shortest of the panelists hooted in anger. "You yourself, and your co-conspirators, deprived us of the Twin-Bred resource! There is no word sufficient to label your presumption in making such an argument."

Ton-lal-set suddenly remembered a discussion overheard many years before in the Project dining room. There was, in fact, such a word—although it came, originally, from a human language he had never heard spoken. The word was "chutzpah." He considered mentioning the fact, in the hope of embarrassing the panel member; but now the committee head was speaking. "How, exactly, do you imagine we could make use of this supposed ability?"

Ton-lal-set tilted his head back in the pose for confusion. "When some human activity proved baffling to the present government, I could be interrogated at the government's convenience."

"Oh, yes. But we have hardly forgotten your strength of will, which would give you a greater than average capacity for deceit—even if you had not had years of opportunity to study deceit from the humans, to whom it comes more naturally. The more crucial the need to understand the humans, the more perilous it would be to rely on your supposed interpretation."

One of the panel members who had not previously spoken now picked up the thread. "We might as well simply ask the humans to explain themselves. We would be as likely to learn the truth by that method as by asking you."

Ton-lal-set turned slowly toward the speaker. His glare had once had the power to make the strongest of his subordinates stagger backward. Even now, as undernourished and feeble as he had become, the fellow visibly twitched. "By all means, assume that the Eminence who made the Tofa a space-faring people, and commanded respect from human and Tofa alike, would just as soon deliver his people into the humans' power. I can only hope that some other force arises to protect the community from your foolishness."

The committee head beckoned one of the guards and clicked the fingers of his upper left hand against each other. Ton-lal-set knew the gesture well: he had used it often himself. The guard grabbed Ton-lal-set's torso with his lower hands and used his upper hands to strike two resounding blows simultaneously against the sides of Ton-lal-set's face. Ironically, the opposing forces canceled themselves out sufficiently that Ton-lal-set was able to remain upright.

The guards apparently needed no more explicit instruction to take him away.

When the territory of the government offices ended and the prison corridors began, the guards handed him off to a single unfamiliar Tofa wearing the armbands of a jailer, who led him toward his cell. Ton-lal-set had expected some new and final destination, but apparently the execution would be delayed.

For some reason the jailer chose to walk slowly. Ton-lal-set matched the jailer's pace, just as glad to conserve what remained of his strength. It took a moment for him to realize that the jailer was whispering, in a hurried and almost inaudible whisper.

"Do not despair. The order of execution, if issued, will not reach its destination, and no record of it will be found."

Was this some more subtle attempt at torture, or could he possibly have allies?

They had almost reached Ton-lal-set's cell. The whisper became even faster and more difficult to decipher. "We will find a way to tell you more."

The footsteps of a second jailer approached from around the corner. The first jailer gripped Ton-lal-set's upper arm tightly and dragged him to his cell, flinging the door open and shoving him inside. "Stay there and rot, then!" he shouted. The tone struck Ton-lal-set as unconvincing. As he stumbled into his cell, he hoped the other jailer lacked sufficient interest to investigate.

Chapter 4

(New Landing)

SETH BARUTI, peering through the telescope he had planted atop the highest local cliff, heard the soft sound of wings parting the air and straightened up with relief. His back was ever more inclined to protest when he spent too long peering at the stars.

As he had guessed, Wings Spread Wide was there circling around him, its wings briefly and beautifully echoing the starry expanse before taking on the night-dimmed warmer tones of the ground cover where the Glider came to rest. The faceted stones on the Glider's belt glinted faintly in the starlight. Not for the first time, Seth pondered the fact that despite the elder's position of respect, its belt was no more (and no less) ornate or complex than that of any other Glider. Of course, Gliders received their belts upon attaining adult status, before their future accomplishments or reputations could be a factor.

Wings Spread Wide made the sideways sashay that served the Gliders as a bow, then perched on a nearby ledge. The translator Seth wore spoke over the end of the Glider's greeting. "Open skies to you, Elder."

Seth had never quite brought himself to explain to the Glider that his own standing among the Twin-Bred colonists fell something short of the deference Wings Spread Wide received from its community. With the familiar blend of amusement and guilt, he bowed in the Glider's direction. "Open skies to you, Elder and my friend."

"Have you seen any new marvels through your star glass?"

Seth shook his head. "I wasn't really trying to. Sometimes I look at the sky as a sort of meditation." The two of them had discussed the concept before: Gliders had their own version, involving repetitive flight patterns rather than physical immobility. "I'm finding it hard to be patient, now that we're waiting to meet an emissary of the next Tofa generation. Talk about stars and marvels—I'm so hoping that young Lan-sol will succeed in making the observations I've come up with! I'll be sending the list to Tofarn in a few days, after I've gone over it another time or two."

It occurred to Seth that he was rattling on, rather. He looked toward his companion and found it looking up at the stars. "Is there some astronomical event I've managed to miss?"

"No, indeed. That would greatly surprise me." The Glider thrust its small head toward Seth, its bright central eye aimed squarely in his direction. "I come with other thoughts to share. Friend Seth, do you expect to die soon?"

Seth's jaw dropped, and he goggled at the alien, who appeared both literally and figuratively unruffled. *Different cultures*, he reminded himself. "No, friend, I expect to live and remain reasonably healthy for at least a few years to come. Why do you ask?"

"Our customs may be different. We begin preparing for our deaths when first we notice a decline in our bodies and in what our bodies can do. I have been preparing for some time, and my preparations are reaching the stage when I will be involving others in the process."

And Seth had come out here tonight to calm himself with the quiet of the stars. . . . "Please go on."

"Soon—perhaps after your young visitor has come and gone—I will compose my last song. It will be a long song, with everything I wish to remember or to have others remember about my life, from the egg to my final nesting place. And after I have made this song and have helped to perform it, I will sing no more. I will not speak. I will be silent for as long as life lingers within me."

Seth tried to imagine such a prospect and shuddered away from the thought. "Is this your choice? Do you have any other?"

Wings Spread Wide trilled its high laughter. "I need no other. I am content. But it would in fact be difficult to live on in silence, even for so short a time, if I had no one to speak or sing on my behalf."

That was better, if only a little better. "Who will that be? One of your students, or someone older and wiser than they?"

Another trill. "Indeed, older and wiser—though the one I would choose may find the job more difficult than a student would. There will be much I will have to explain ahead of time. But you are old and wise enough, I am sure, to learn what is necessary. I look forward to hearing you sing."

Seth trudged up the ramp to Wing Spread Wide's living quarters, grateful that a ramp existed and that he need not attempt to ascend via artificial air currents. Reaching the nearest window, he climbed in, thankful for the relatively low gravity, grunting only a little. Once safely inside, he looked eagerly around him. He rarely had occasion to visit any of the Gliders at home, and had never visited the elder before.

Glider homes rarely bothered with separate rooms for separate functions, and the single room was vast, which might reflect the Glider's exalted status. The ceiling sloped from relatively low to tall, well over twice Seth's height. Morning light poured in through three large windows (or rather, for Gliders, doors) in the higher wall, set flush against the face of the cliff. The wall decorations varied with the apparent functions of the different areas. What looked like sanitary facilities might, at need, have served for a human, but had nothing in the way of a privacy screen. Seth made a note to keep his visit short.

Seth's host had swooped in beforehand, and now sat on its perch, fluttering its wings in a curiously tentative way. "There is little I can offer you in the way of refreshment. But some of the humans enjoy this fruit." The Glider's hand appeared from underneath its wing, pointing toward a bowl in what must have been the food preparation area. "Please take some—unless you already know that the fruit would fail to please."

"I've had that fruit, and it pleases very nicely. Thanks!" Seth picked up one of the largest of the bulbous objects, its fuzzy peel a pale orange-pink color somewhere between the colors of ground cover and cliffs.

With the fruit halfway to his lips, Seth paused,

remembering a question about which he had been curious for years. "I've never seen anything green on this planet except the crops you grow. What makes them so different? Did they arrive with the human colonists?"

"Yes—along with several other plants. The others were not so useful. They crowded out some of our food crops unless eradicated often. We lost one variety of ground crop altogether. But the—" The translator stuttered the static indicating the lack of a plausible word choice. "—can be controlled, and makes excellent cloth."

"Cloth? I'd assumed the crop was edible!"

The translator's version of Glider laughter blended harmoniously with the actual sound. "Only to chicks young enough to gnaw on it and expect nourishment. And disappointing even to them."

"But what do you even do with cloth?" Belatedly Seth realized that he was standing on a woven rug, and that most of the walls bore similar covering, either embroidered or plain.

The Glider followed his glance. "It provides temperature control, as well as visual pleasure. We add or subtract layers as the seasons change—which also gives us aesthetic refreshment."

How exactly would Gliders manage weaving? Did they use only their hands, or also their wings, or their feet? Had they mechanized the process? He would have to find a way to inquire or investigate.

Seth recalled the fruit in his hand, took a bite, and licked his lips happily. Then he found a cushion that offered some possibility of comfort and with difficulty folded himself down into sitting position. "Did the human colonists even realize the problems their plant life had caused you?"

The Glider twitched its head in a manner suggesting surprise. "I had not thought to wonder. We all assumed so."

Seth had not premeditated his question, but the answer provided a useful segue to his proposal—or rather, his counteroffer. "There's so much we want to know about the history of this world, now that we're here and are hoping to remain. Some of it, of course, the humans can tell us. But there's a lot they won't know, and even more, maybe, that they'll think they know and have altogether wrong.

"What we need, the Twin-Bred community, is for one of us to spend some time with one or more of you, asking questions and learning. But most of our people, yours and mine, are pretty busy. So I had an idea.

"You've asked me—" Seth's voice shook despite his attempt to sound matter-of-fact. "You've asked me to hear your song, the song of your life. While you're composing it, or beforehand, we could meet sometimes, and you could tell me about the lives of your people, and about the humans and how they came here. I don't have all that much to do these days. Your plans suggest that—in your eyes, at least—your day to day duties are no longer a priority. So we both have the time. And my people and I would be most grateful for the knowledge you could give us."

And Seth would be in seventh heaven, gratifying his curiosity and spreading so many new tidbits to interested listeners.

Wings Spread Wide brought his wings slowly up and then down again. Seth had no idea what the gesture meant, but he found it somehow intimidating. "This is the price you ask for granting my request."

"Ah, um. Well. As for calling it a price . . ." Seth had neglected to prepare a fallback position.

The duet of Glider and translator laughter came again. "We have no objection to bargaining. And the price is fair.

"But I find myself growing tired." The Glider's wings and its head had begun to droop. "With your permission, we will begin another time."

Chapter 5

(Tofarn)

THE JAILER who brought Ton-lal-set's meal seemed ill at ease, anxious to deposit the tray and be gone. And the tray had a cover, unnecessary for the usual cold food. Could there be a message underneath from that other jailer, the one with the cryptic and exciting hints? Or could the meal be poisoned, a delayed result of the latest hearing?

Ton-lal-set waited to hear the jailer's key locking the door, then waited a few more seconds before lifting the lid.

He understood at once. There was a message of a sort, but not the kind he had imagined. Next to the limp slab of overcooked meat and the lump of vegetable mush sat a long thin fruit with a dull brown peel, almost the color of dried blood. Ton-lal-set grabbed the fruit and hurled it against the wall. It did not burst, but flattened, adhering to the wall for a moment and then sliding slowly down, pulp leaking from the splits in its sides.

There was only one occasion for offering this fruit, the only bitter fruit his people grew and harvested: the death of offspring.

He had received such a fruit—not at mealtime, but thrust into his hand on his way back from a hearing—four years since. He had no way of knowing, and still did not know, for which of his children the fruit had been given him. But now he knew that both of them were gone.

He had left two young and healthy offspring when he joined the Project as host mother. There were others to tend them, and the Project offered staggering opportunities for the future. As he carried Twin-Bred in his womb, and even more after he expelled the Tofa twin before its time, he had forced aside memories of carrying his own true young, birthing them, dripping nourishment under their tiny chins. Then, when he returned in triumph and took up his place as Eminence, his strong grown children joined him and served him, waiting for their own turns at power.

One of them had been present on that last day, part of the attempt to dispose of Jak-rad-tan's fetus, while the other scoured the city for the slanderous sheets the rebels had distributed. When the rebels dragged Ton-lal-set away, had he caught a glimpse of his child so close at hand? He could not remember.

How had they died? Death by poison, death by strangulation, death by projectile, death by knife, death by club? Had either of them died fighting, trying to escape? Had they simply given up and turned away from the tasteless, pointless meals?

Ton-lal-set found himself humming. He forced himself to reduce the volume. He would mourn his children quietly, that the jailers might not hear.

*   *   *

Veda's coffee cup froze in midair before she collected herself and lowered it carefully to the kitchen counter. "You want to do *what*? No, of course. I shouldn't be surprised. You wanted more or less the same thing when you were twelve years old."

"Mother!" Melly only addressed Veda with that label when highly indignant. "We're not talking about some childish fantasy!"

"On the contrary." Veda remained unruffled. "There was nothing childish about the desire at the time. Your brothers, your foster cousins, almost everyone you knew was about to leave you behind, and you didn't like it one bit. Given what the next few years turned out to be like, I'm not so sure we shouldn't have let you go."

Melly's eyes went wide, and her mouth gaped for a moment before she caught and closed it. *Score one for mama*, Veda thought. She could count on one hand how often she had rendered Melly speechless.

Veda scooted over and gave Melly a quick shoulder-hug. "Not that I have any regrets, at this point. I'd be devastated to be so far away from you. And in those first years, it was bad enough not to know what dangers the twins were facing and whether they'd survived them. If you'd been gone too . . . ." Veda cleared her throat of the inconvenient lump that formed there as she remembered those days.

"Let's both come back to the present," Melly commanded, with a briskness that gave Veda the feeling of looking in a mirror. "It'd be a pretty long trip, but I could be away for even longer if I went on a major island-hop or sailed all the way around Tofarn. I'd be going to visit family and friends. We could stay in touch—with a time lag, but still, you'd know more or less what I was up to. And I could give Jimmy and Peer-tek a kiss from you." Melly stopped short. "Unless you'd like to come with me, and do it yourself."

Now it was Veda's turn to be struck dumb. To blast off away from the planet, to see the stars so close; to experience the unparalleled strangeness of the wormhole passage, so vividly described by her twins and friends; to have Jimmy and Peer-tek lift her off her feet in their strong hugs; and to live once again, if only for a little while—or longer?—surrounded by those who had changed her into the woman she was proud to be. . . .

Veda shook herself as if shedding inconvenient raindrops. "I might consider it someday. But the second ship ever to leave Tofarn? That's rather too soon to be past the buggy stage. And I'm by no means ready to leave Jak-rad-tan and Lan-sol and the rest to their own devices. I may understand Tofa politics better than we all did back in the Project's day, but I'm far from sure I can predict when trouble is coming."

Melly's grin had a "gotcha" component. "So staying home isn't always the safest choice, is it!"

Veda allowed herself to sigh. "Come here, you. Let's sit down." She headed for the family room and beckoned her daughter to follow. "Come sit on my lap and squash me into the cushions. That'll remind me that you're all grown up and will do what you like—even more than you always did."

They settled on the couch. Rather than actually sitting on Veda, Melly lay down with her head in Veda's lap; Veda stroked her hair. "Please, my love, and in all seriousness: think hard about this. The ship hasn't even been built yet.

You have time to think it through."

*   *   *

Melly, waving goodbye to her mother, suppressed a twinge of guilt at allowing Veda to remain uninformed. Matters were proceeding more swiftly than Veda had supposed. The framework of the ship was more than half complete. Not that Veda was wrong on the fundamental point: it would be months before Lan-sol could depart.

She may as well go and watch the construction for a while before heading back to work. Rehearsals for the new play would start next week, and there was plenty to do, but the pace was not yet altogether frenetic.

She might or might not see Lan-sol at the shipyard. In preparation for his journey, he was studying harder than ever before: Tofarna history, Twin-Bred history, biogenetics, astronomy, not to mention specifications and repair protocols for every kind of computer or mechanical system the ship would contain. But he somehow found time for frequent visits to the construction site, even taking a hand in the welding and shaping and polishing.

On her arrival at the hangar she found not Lan-sol but Jak-rad-tan, standing at the elevated railing that ran around the inside perimeter, looking down at the growing skeleton of the ship below. She tried to assess his state of mind from the familiar subtle clues. From what she could guess, Jak-rad-tan was troubled and uncertain, but not in any acute distress.

She approached him and waited for him to notice her. It took longer than usual, but after several minutes he turned toward her and held up both left hands in greeting. He waited a moment to see if she would speak, then faced the construction floor again.

Melly had not yet confided her desire to Jak-rad-tan, or (until that morning) to anyone but Lan-sol. She did not know whether Lan-sol had told his parent. Jak-rad-tan's silence suggested that Lan-sol had not done so, nor did his manner invite such a revelation. For a moment Melly wished for the heedless confidence of her younger days. When they all lived at the Project, she would have flung herself at Jak-rad-tan (or Jak-rad, then), demanding his attention so she could unveil her scheme.

Of course, back then she would have had no chance to render Jak-rad-tan a service of her own. He might just need a confidant. She reached up and tapped lightly on his upper left arm. "You look like something's weighing on you. Could I help in any way?"

Immediately she felt his mood lighten as he turned once more in her direction. "Perhaps you can. You are particularly well situated to do so: older than Lan-sol, but not so much older that the concerns of youth have started to recede."

Melly suppressed a chuckle. Jak-rad-tan tended to put on the airs of an elder, when really he was not so very much older than Melly herself. She waited for Jak-rad-tan to reveal her assignment.

Jak-rad-tan glanced away for a moment, not at the ship framework but up toward the sky beyond. Then he looked her in the eye. "Since Lan-sol accepted New Landing's invitation, we have sent a number of questions to New Landing about various technical matters. Most have not been answered. I went to the astronomy department at the university, to make sure the latest message had not somehow gone astray. At my request, they tested the communications relays."

Melly stared up at Jak-rad-tan, willing him to mean something else; but he went on. "Something has gone wrong. I have not yet told Lan-sol. But the astronomers could tell me nothing about whether New Landing had sent us a message. It appears that the communications relays are no longer functional."

Chapter 6

(New Landing)

ON THE DAY, as close as they could calculate it, when the New Landing colonists' message to Lan-sol would actually be played, many of those who had participated in the taping gathered to watch it again. The same sort of calculations indicated the shortest interlude that would have to elapse before they might receive an answer.

Afterward the crowd, or most of it, headed off to one of the restaurants jointly owned by Tofa and Gliders and serving food for all three local species. Judy declined to go along; Mara shot a keen glance in her direction, then turned away and followed the others. Elspeth, Judy's current intimate companion, lingered, looking puzzled and a bit hurt. Judy gave her a quick hug and a kiss on the cheek. "I just need to walk and think a bit. I might join you in a few minutes." She waited, trying to hide her impatience, until Elspeth had caught up with the group. Then she headed in the opposite direction, walking fast enough that she could feel the welcome strain in her legs and thighs.

La-ren signaled for her attention. ("Would you like to walk and talk, or should I restrain my curiosity until you have worked off some of this restless energy?")

Judy slowed her pace and looked around until she spotted a particularly plush patch of ground cover, then headed for it and plopped down, lying on her back and gazing up at the sky. One of the mist clouds was passing overhead, partly obscuring and partly diffracting the glitter of the cliffs. She watched it until it dissipated, then closed her eyes and let the sun warm her eyelids.

("So you have questions?")

("First, let me say how much I like Elspeth. She could

be good for you, I think: strong and vital, creative yet sensible, not too startling but not too predictable. And her expertise in neurology might, if you ever wish, allow us to better understand my own somewhat ill-defined existence.")

Judy shuddered.

("I'm sorry if that is too sensitive a topic . . . . In any event, I hope you will resist the restlessness that has often driven you to move on.")

("I'll keep you posted. Can we talk about Jimmy's and Peer-tek's latest bright idea?")

She felt La-ren's momentary satisfaction. ("I was correct, then, in identifying what was troubling you. Why does a visit from Jak-rad-tan's offspring cause you such trepidation?")

("You can't imagine it'd be Lan-sol and nobody else. No one's going to build a spaceship to take one teenaged Tofa on a trip across the galaxy! Who else would come along?")

("Whom do you fear?")

("Let me turn that around, brother. Who would *you* fear? Among the not-too-unlikely possibilities, which would be trouble?")

("Hmmm. Let me ponder the question for a moment, while you attempt to relax and enjoy the sunshine.")

Judy did her best to comply. Indeed, she realized when La-ren next spoke that she had gone halfway to falling asleep. His words jolted her awake. ("The worst-case scenario would have Lan-sol accompanied either by hostile humans, or by Tofa affiliated with the displaced Tofa regime.")

("But how—why!—")

("I did not say this scenario was likely. I expect neither to materialize. And accordingly, I do not share your apprehension—which you have yet to explain.")

Judy sighed. ("I'm not sure what I'm afraid of. Tofarn and everything associated with it still feels like danger to me. I don't want anything bringing it closer.")

("Which is why you have had so little contact with our mother, all this time.")

Judy felt the tears well up and let them seep out through her squeezed eyelids and glide down her cheeks. ("I loved her so much. Love her. But I can't afford to think about her, or it'll hurt too much to miss her.")

("She might come. On this first voyage, or later. We might see her again.")

She caught the faint echo of humming. ("La-ren, are *you* crying?")

("All these years, I have never even spoken to her. I have not wanted to press the point, or to cause her pain with such an indirect and incomplete form of contact. But I, for one, am not afraid to miss her. And I am not, it seems, content to live—or exist, or whatever it is I do—for the rest of the years we share without some more substantial contact with our loved ones, and with our former home. And what is worse—" The humming grew louder. "We left, in large part, because I died. My fate hurled us here, and I feel the responsibility.")

The need to touch him, to hug him and drain away his sorrow with her flesh, burnt in her with a frustration not much short of fury. ("That wasn't your fault! None of this is your fault—or mine! And don't forget the others who died, and what the human community would have done with us if we'd stayed—enslaved us, or close enough. And the Tofa might not have let us live at all if we'd insisted on staying.")

("But things have changed. Our mother and Veda and Jak-rad-tan, and the Tofa who gave us knowledge, and the humans and Tofa who have helped them for so long—these are the people we could see again.")

Judy curled up on her side, in the self-protective huddle that had dismayed and saddened one after another of her lovers. ("But no matter what seems likely to us, we don't really know what's happening on Tofarn. Or who else might come.")

*   *   *

Kenneth might now be Secretary of Communications for the Twin-Bred community, but he still preferred hands-on signal processing to managerial duties. Or at least, he would have preferred it if the residents of Tofarn and New Landing would oblige him by having more to say to one another. Whenever he scheduled himself to handle communications traffic, he was likely to end up twiddling his thumbs for most of the shift. When he got bored, he got hungry, and his suppressed sweet tooth would threaten to rise up and send him in search of some gooey and sugary snack.

Today was one of the dull days. That surprised him: he had expected Lan-sol, or someone acting on his behalf, to send more questions about ship construction and the like. But it seemed Lan-sol was passively expecting information to be sent his way.

So Kenneth had been sitting there for hours with nothing to do, and had even dozed off for a while, to dream of the cinnamon buns aboard *Star Seed* . . . and the way Jimmy and Peer-tek had used them to lure him into trouble. The fearsome vision of Dr. Cadell's face that day jolted him out of sleep; he found himself panting.

He made himself breathe deeply and focus on the fact that he was no longer a teenager, and Mara Cadell was no longer so much older than he—at least, not in relative terms—and, more important, no longer in charge.

At least not officially. But she did live with Fel-lar, and Fel-lar and Anna were co-chairs of Congress. And Fel-lar, impressive fellow though he might be, could hardly be expected to ignore Mara if she got truly worked up about something. . . .

Finally, some work to do! There came Suzie down the street, no doubt with yet another letter to her mother. Of course she could have sent it to the communications center electronically, but she was a gregarious sort and liked the chance to chat.

Kenneth took and logged the message chip and listened with half an ear to the latest achievements and adventures of Suzie's two children. He checked the settings, sent through the test signal, waited for confirmation—

"The children helped me bake these. Would you like one?"

Kenneth hesitated, then reached out for the irregularly shaped cookie. It would be rude to refuse, and even assisted by her children, Suzie made good cookies. This one looked soft and chewy. He licked his lips, then glanced back at the instruments in front of him.

And forgot about the cookie he was holding, for something was wrong.

*   *   *

("But what *happened*?")

("Sis, I have the distinct impression you'd like to ask that question while grabbing someone and shaking him silly. I fear for our good friend Fel-lar. If we ask him to channel me, I can bear the brunt of your frustration.")

Mara paced back and forth as though she had never managed to break the habit. ("The relays check out remotely. The system tests as absolutely fine, except that the last message from Lan-sol cut off in mid-syllable and nothing's come through since!")

("The threshold question, then, is whether the message ceased, or the transmission of it.")

Something arrested Mara's passage across the room: the firm grasp of a Tofa hand above her elbow. Mara twisted to face Fel-lar, contemplating indignation; then she yielded to fatigue instead, stumbling toward him and leaning against his narrow chest.

In a moment came the comforting constriction of four strong arms . . . though one felt thinner than usual. Fel-lar must have split his largest arm for some reason. She sniffed. "You're holding something to drink, aren't you? But it isn't chocolate."

"I hope I did not miscalculate. I thought that tea might provide the most helpful balance of soothing and stimulant."

Mara took a deep, if uneven, breath. "All right, you can let go of me and give me my potion. Thank you."

She took the tea and headed for her standing stool. Loosely based on both Tofa leaning posts and Glider perches, it lessened the load on her feet while allowing her to spring into upright motion with the smallest possible delay. It had seen less and less use in recent years, and was in fact covered in glittering dust—but cushions on horizontal surfaces were no match for her present mood.

Fel-lar leaned on his nearby post and tapped his upper fingers together. "I have been meeting with various members of Congress. We discussed how long to wait for communications to resume before taking any serious investigative steps."

"Such as?" Mara took a gulp of her tea, then stiffened and leaned forward to almost vertical. "You're not considering—but of course you are."

"If our remote diagnostic procedures cannot identify the problem, what alternative do we have other than inspecting the array at a lesser distance?"

Mara put down the tea, sprang to her feet and began pacing once again. "And if in fact the array doesn't prove to be the problem?"

Fel-lar stood up as well and positioned himself just outside her path. "Then we will have to decide how much the state of affairs on Tofarn remains our concern. And what we might risk, in what the ancients referred to as 'blood and treasure,' to go back and intervene."

As a young woman, Mara would never have predicted that she would some day write regularly to her mother. But when the crew of *Star Seed* discovered the wormhole and decided to enter it, Mara sent Elizabeth what might serve as a farewell message; and in that message, she spoke openly to Elizabeth about Levi for the first time since her thwarted childhood attempts to do so. She did not, at that time, allow herself to think about how Elizabeth might respond. When Elizabeth actually thanked her for the drawings of Levi, Mara was more shaken than relieved. What had she started? What would Elizabeth expect of her now?

Once contact with Tofarn resumed, Mara sent a short, stiff note in reply. When Fel-lar asked what she had written, she found herself embarrassed, even ashamed, to show it to him; and when Elizabeth persevered, writing again and asking questions about Mara's new life, Mara managed to strike a cordial tone in her answer. The correspondence that developed provided Mara with little in the way of comfort or interest, but she had never quite brought herself to discontinue it. And Levi, for some reason they had not discussed, prodded her to write when she neglected to do so, and suggested topics and turns of phrase.

She had begun a letter before the communications failure, after a longer than average delay; and in one of her many abortive attempts to distract herself from her restlessness, she reopened and reread it. Fel-lar, passing by on his way to another meeting of Congress, paused to stroke Mara's hair and peer over her shoulder. "I am glad to see you preparing for the time when communication with Tofarn is restored. Please give your mother my regards." Mara caught his emanation of sympathy and reached out to briefly grasp one of his lower hands before he moved on by and went out the door.

Levi stirred. ("Well, go on, then.")

Mara gritted her teeth. ("Fel-lar was jumping to conclusions. Why should we bother with it now?")

("We can preserve our present thoughts in all their original sparkle. In fact, we could be somewhat less circumspect in this initial draft, to capture the current state of affairs for historical purposes, and then edit it later for her actual consumption.")

("And if the editing slips my mind? No, thank you.")

("Very well. Censorship it is.")

Mara looked at the message once more. ("You're the one who wants to write. Think of something to say.")

("You could tell her you might be dropping by sometime soon, along with a few shipmates.")

("You can't be serious. We don't know for sure that anyone's heading to the wormhole, let alone through it; and if it happens, why would I go along?")

Silence, then: ("Moving right along . . . You could tell Elizabeth about the concert. She might like to hear that her closest approximation of a son-in-law has immortalized your career for generations of Gliders to come.")

Mara snorted. ("I still haven't completely forgiven him for that foray into fiction.")

("Now, now. You must make allowances for poetic inspiration, not to mention romantic ardor.")

("You egged him on. I know you did. It must have been while I was asleep, or I'd have squelched it.")

She felt Levi's laughter. ("He offered me an acknowledgment. I declined. But you've found me out. Shall I bother to pretend to apologize?")

("No. And I'm not inclined to bother with this letter.")

Now Levi's tone was serious. ("Please, Mara. Just peck out a few words and get it over with. She'll appreciate it, when she finally gets it.") And then, again, the habitual—

though she thought it a bit forced—note of levity. ("And besides, you have Fel-lar's greeting to convey. You mustn't be the cause of in-law estrangement.")

*   *   *

Fel-lar strode to the front of the Congress chamber. (The older humans and the more historically inclined Twin-Bred had, after some debate, come up with the "Congress" label, after the community unanimously rejected the idea of setting up any body called a "council.") Seeing him approach the podium, the members gradually wrapped up their several conversations and found their seats and posts, except for his co-chair Anna, who joined Fel-lar up front.

When the members were more or less silent and attentive, Fel-lar grasped Anna's left hand with his lower right hand, and the two raised their clasped hands and lowered them again. Then Fel-lar completed the opening ritual. "This Congress is in session to consider the business of the colony." The thought crossed his mind, as it had several times before, that sooner or later they would need to refer to themselves as something else: a state, a nation, or some other such label, a political unit that stood on its own without reference to its origins.

Anna loosed her hand from Fel-lar's and spoke next. "We called this meeting in order to discuss the mission or missions on which *Star Seed* may be sent, after a suitable period of waiting, if communication from Tofarn does not resume. The nature of the mission will determine the composition of the crew."

Nathan raised his hand; Anna pointed to him in recognition, and he stood to address his fellows. "Whatever the mission, the crew must include engineers capable of diagnosing and resolving any problems that arise with the ship itself, from propulsion to meteor defense to life support to communications. To cover all these specialties and ensure some redundancy, I would suggest no fewer than three engineers, two of whom will be prepared to deal with not only the ship's communication systems, but with the wormhole array. I've already prepared a report with some personnel recommendations—and I've included myself in that list." He sat down again.

Hal-tet held an upper hand out horizontally; Fel-lar gestured for him to proceed.

"First, I have a question for my friend Nathan." A ripple of surprise passed through those present; Hal-tet waited for it to subside before continuing. "Nathan, you were always a gentle soul; and in our years on New Landing, you have become something of a pacifist. Is that not so?"

Nathan looked straight ahead for a moment, his expression one of thoughtful scrutiny, rather as if he were studying himself in a mirror. Then he looked back up at Hal-tet. "I suppose that describes me well enough. And I believe I know why you raise the point. You're thinking we may, if we go all the way to Tofarn, encounter a violent reception."

"It is a possibility. And I must therefore ask whether you could, in that event, defend yourself and your companions."

Nathan sat up straighter and squared his shoulders. "If I believe it to be absolutely necessary, I would fight for others. I can't promise I'll accept anyone else's assessment of that need, even our captain's. As for my own safety, I'll take responsibility for it. If that answer doesn't satisfy you all, I hope you still respect my skills enough to include me, and assign me to tasks where my questionable skills at combat won't be called upon."

Hal-tet walked closer to where Nathan sat and briefly gripped his shoulder with a lower hand, then returned to his original spot. "On a largely unrelated point: we have been somewhat negligent about maintaining our ability to pilot the ship. I would not exactly say that we assumed there would be no urgent need, as that we let the question slide out of our collective consciousness. The pilots who helped the ship to bring us here, and the programmers who provided the necessary software, are of course still among us, but their, or I should say our, skills will have suffered from disuse. Whether we should call upon this precise group or train others, including some from the younger generation, to supplement their ranks needs to be determined."

Fel-lar held out an upper hand to the side as Hal-tet had done. "If I may, I would like to join the discussion, not as co-chair but as a member of this Congress. Hal-tet's first comments raise a topic I wished to discuss in any event. The fundamental decision we have to make is whether to treat the mission as potentially two-fold, including a possible trip back through the wormhole to Tofarn. If events on our planet of origin have become tumultuous, we must ask what we would hope to accomplish by landing in the middle of the tumult. Would we expect to use our previously scorned mediation skills? Or to rescue and bring back to New Landing those friends we left behind, along with their families?"

Anna raised a hand and stepped forward. "I thank Fel-lar for redirecting our attention to this threshold issue. Hal-tet's comments suggest the possibility of some sort of quasi-military intervention into whatever may be taking place on Tofarn. Wouldn't even the largest possible crew for *Star Seed* be ridiculously outnumbered? Especially if we had to leave room for whoever we might want to rescue?"

Hal-tet waited for all buzzing and murmuring to die down before responding. "Not necessarily. We could deploy a probe to gather information about anything resembling troop movements before we arrive. That would allow us to direct our forces to any conflict in which they could be effective, or to abandon such intervention if it had insufficient chance of success."

Peer-tek raised his hands. "Any rescue attempts may at some stage require negotiations. If we send our best negotiators and politicians, we must weigh the cost of doing without their services here. We should all know by now that crises, especially those involving species-specific communities, can arise quickly and from unexpected directions."

Emily Wilson, who now taught Diplomacy to the children of her original students, raised a hand and stood once recognized. "I volunteer for the mission, if Congress or any committee it establishes think I would be useful. My more capable students, raised on this planet and with lifelong knowledge of all its inhabitants, could handle emergencies at least as well as I—and they would have various elders to consult if they thought necessary." She turned her gaze toward Fel-lar. "I suspect that many of us are at this point asking themselves the same questions: should we ask Mara to take on the responsibility of joining, or even leading, this mission? And if we do, is she likely to agree?"

Fel-lar laid his upper fingers across each other, widely spread, in the gesture for insufficient knowledge. "While I see advantages to the suggestion, I expect that whoever draws the task of persuading her will find that task daunting indeed. But I am not completely without hope."

Chapter 7

(Tofarn)

THE TEACHER on outdoor duty at the school let out the shrill warble that signaled the end of outdoor recreation, reinforcing it with the usual nonverbal command. Perhaps two-thirds of the children immediately responded, jumping down from climbers, catching balls and stowing them beneath an upper arm, abandoning efforts to chase or catch or outrun. As a neat line formed to reenter the classroom, the remaining children glanced at the teacher and hesitated.

The teacher signaled again, even more loudly, and followed the signal with words. "Cease your play activities immediately and line up with your classmates!"

Slowly, too slowly, they complied. One of the laggards—Jak-rad-tan's youngest—whispered something to the child in front of him, who whistled in response, then glanced at the teacher and pulled his arms closer to his torso.

The teacher had been only a few years older than his charges were now when the former Eminences fell, but he remembered his own school days. None of his classmates would have conceived of disobedience. None of them had any such capability. But Jak-rad-tan had introduced his peers, and those Tofa coming of age after the revolution, to the idea of limiting their control of their offspring. A minority, but one increasing in size, commanded their fetuses and infants only when doing otherwise would be a major inconvenience, and limited coercion of children past infancy to actual emergencies.

Had it occurred to them that when those emergencies occurred, especially when adults other than the parent were in charge, the coercion necessary to keep their children safe might no longer be possible? Would the parents find comfort then in the alien notion of "freedom"?

* * *

Jak-rad-tan had more reason than ever, now, to set in motion some project for identifying spore-parents.

Lan-sol was determined to head across the galaxy, and not even the loss of communications with New Landing had deterred him. Quite the reverse: what had seemed to some, and possibly even to Lan-sol, like a self-indulgent excursion had become both a more dangerous and a more important quest. Lan-sol could plant new communications relays, testing them before venturing into the wormhole, and with luck could restore the colonists' ties to their home world. That was the more optimistic scenario. Jak-rad-tan found it all too easy to imagine a chilling range of others.

Somewhere on Tofarn, most probably in this very city, was Lan-sol's other parent—and unless that parent was identified soon, he might never have the chance to meet his offspring.

Lan-sol's spore-parent could be anyone. He might even be someone they already knew, someone who could influence Lan-sol in the direction of greater caution. What if Jak-rad-tan's co-parent proved to be Gen-tar-ten himself? Gen-tar-ten might already be the only Tofa to whose opinion Lan-sol would conceivably defer. But so far, Gen-tar-ten had shown interest in Lan-sol's plans only insofar as they might affect his own. Knowledge of parenthood, even parenthood of a kind not previously contemplated, could nudge him toward a more personal involvement.

And what a thrill it would be for Jak-rad-tan himself, to share the pride of creation with one so eminent and respected!

Jak-rad-tan caught hold of his fantasies before they could carry him away. The odds were against such parentage, after all. Lan-sol had probably not been in Gen-tar-ten's proximity often, possibly not at all, during the crucial period.

But it was possible.

"And now you want me to be the first, the different one, *again*?"

Jak-rad-tan had made progress with Gen-tar-ten, who agreed to develop a procedure for any Tofa who chose to deposit genetic material for spore identification, and even (to Jak-rad-tan's slight dismay) to require such deposits from government workers and detainees. His own enthusiasm thus reinforced, Jak-rad-tan had foolishly assumed that Lansol would either share his interest in identifying spore-parents or prove genially indifferent—or at worst, dismissive. He should have known better. Why was it so easy to overlook the way a loved one viewed the world?

Lan-sol had by no means wound down. "It's not enough that I had free will. It's not enough that I was famous for not getting killed. It's not enough that everyone's parent practically fought a *war* over me. Oh, I know!" Lan-sol held up a lower hand to forestall the comment Jak-rad-tan had already decided not to make. "It wasn't about me. I was just the catalyst, and besides, it would have come soon anyway. Do you think my peers understood all that when I was growing up? Do they understand it even now?

"And my parent is the only Tofa Twin-Bred left on the planet—"

Jak-rad-tan could not help but flinch. Lan-sol paused, obviously struggling to suppress contrition. "You know I wouldn't want a different parent, but it set me apart even more. You know that. And you want to make everything *worse*? Promise me you won't!"

Jak-rad-tan's training in diplomacy had included instruction in the varieties and techniques of deceptive half-truth. It was all too easy to recall the tricks. "I will neither take nor submit any samples of your genes without your consent."

And after giving that assurance, how could he confess to his child that he had already, in careless confidence, done exactly that?

*　*　*

Melly suspected that all the clamor and activity surrounding Lan-sol's plans might be leaving his younger siblings less noticed and less supervised than was optimal. She made a point, therefore, of taking a personal day and scooping them up for an outing. One of the playgrounds in Central Park would do nicely.

The twelve-year-old and eight-year-old immediately headed for the swings—or, as some called them, the Wings, due to their Glider-style accoutrements. The baby of the family, little Ved-rad, seemed more interested in making the most of Melly's attention. He clung to Melly's hand and tugged her toward the concession stand. "Can we have ice cream?"

"Why not?" She purchased double scoops for both of them, sticking to fruit flavors for herself, foregoing vanilla for fear the odor would spoil Ved-rad's pleasure in his own chocolate and cinnamon. They found a human-height table where Melly could sit and Ved-rad, standing, would be at a convenient level for conversation.

Melly sat back and lost herself in the pleasure of fresh air and ice cream. In a few minutes, however, she noticed that Ved-rad was looking at her with a certain intensity in his stance. "What is it?"

Ved-rad brought the cone to his ingestors for another generous taste, then dropped it again. "Aunt Melly, why don't you have children of your own? Wouldn't anyone help you make some? I know humans need help."

Melly almost dropped her cone, then almost spilled it in the act of recovery. A moment of dismay yielded to the great temptation to laugh, but she managed to resist. "Well, now, I'm sure I could find someone to help me, if I wanted to."

"Don't you *like* children?" Ved-rad's change in posture suggested concern and insecurity.

Melly got up and gave Ved-rad a hug before returning to her seat. "Of course I do! And you and your sibs most of all."

"Then why?"

"I guess I'd like to be really sure of where I want to make a home, and with whom, before I have children. Then I won't be hauling them from place to place, or taking them away from people they know."

Ved-rad stared at her again. Melly half expected him to buzz thoughtfully and say, "Ah, yes. You wish to avoid inflicting on your children the trauma you suffered. . . ." But instead, he stuck his chin down onto his ice cream hard enough to squish it down his chest. Melly went foraging for a napkin to clean him up, and the subject was dropped. Indeed, Ved-rad said nothing more until Melly got up and looked around for the older children. She held out her right hand for his upper left, but instead he clasped all his hands together and stared up at her. "Melly? When is Lan-sol going away?"

"Not for a little while, sweetheart." The latest schedule, from what she had heard, involved a departure two months hence. She had not yet given Lan-sol a final answer about her own plans. Her initial desire to come along seemed childish, now that one of the many possible complications had manifested itself even before takeoff.

The child was shaking; in a moment he would start to hum. "I'm scared. I don't want him to go."

Melly, with some effort, picked him up and planted him between her knees, the closest she could get to holding him on her lap. "He'll be very careful, I know. And he'll have friends with him, to help if—" She must not plant ideas. "If he needs them."

"Aunt Melly?" The large marbled eyes searched her face. "Would you go along? To take care of him? I know he'd be safe with you."

Melly put her arms around the child and herself, hugging both of them together, feeling him tremble and wondering if she were trembling herself.

Chapter 8

(New Landing)

SETH BARUTI had assumed that all his history lessons with Wings Spread Wide would take place in the Glider's own living quarters, and had contemplated bringing a portable chair. But when he mentioned the arrangement to Mara and Fel-lar, his notions and preferences soon fell by the board.

Mara's eyes went wide at his announcement, but almost immediately her expression morphed into concentration, and then that intense and somewhat combative look she got when she was planning to push through some scheme she'd hatched. "Of course you could record and write up whatever Wings Spread Wide tells you. But why not take more immediate advantage of this extraordinary opportunity? Couldn't there be more people present?"

Seth bit his lip and then forced himself to smile. "What an interesting idea! But I don't think you've quite grasped the nature of the occasion. Wings Spread Wide has asked me for a very personal favor. I pushed my luck a bit asking for a change in—or rather, a precursor to—the ritual it described. I don't want to reward its flexibility with more demands, especially the injection of a whole crowd of people. Even if it agreed, it might not be happy about the change."

Mara looked up at Fel-lar; Fel-lar looked at Seth. "You raise an important point. But Mara's idea has significant merit as well. The key issue appears to be whether Wings Spread Wide would resent the suggested expansion of its audience, or welcome the same, or be indifferent. So let us ask."

Seth opened his mouth, but Fel-lar held up an upper hand to forestall him. "I did in fact hear what you said about the possibility that our friend might feel constrained to conceal its true feelings. It seems to me that such an accomplished diplomat would be able to convey its preferences in an appropriate manner. But if you are truly concerned, I could ask Judy and La-ren to assist me, as they did years ago. If I were to host La-ren and allow our consciousnesses to merge, we could reach beyond any polite dissimulation. I would rather not, as such telepathic eavesdropping constitutes an invasion of privacy, and I do not in fact believe it to be necessary."

Mara turned back toward Seth, the satisfaction on her face giving way to a somewhat annoying solicitous expression. "Would you like to make the inquiry? Or would you be more comfortable if one of us did so?"

Seth thought quickly. "I was already supposed to drop by tomorrow. One of you can come with me, and I can explain that you have a—a request." He may as well try for magnanimity. "I'll make clear that I have no objection, but that we want to proceed just as Wings Spread Wide would wish." And by being present, Seth could try to make sure that neither Fel-lar's size nor Mara's force of personality played too great a part in the Glider's response.

When, therefore, the Glider elder began to tell its stories, it did so in a small meadow with room for dozens to sit and dozens more to lean, before an eager audience of human and Tofa children. That had been Fel-lar's refinement of the plan, added just before he broached the subject with the Glider, and Seth had to admit the suggestion was a shrewd one. How many old people, of whatever species, could resist the role of storyteller to the young?

Wings Spread Wide had established itself on a promontory on one of the surrounding cliffs, not too high for its voice—or, for those who needed the assistance, the voice of its translator—to be heard below. Before settling themselves to listen, all the children took turns bowing to the Glider, front-ways or sideways depending on their species, and speaking their names. Or, in many cases, their nicknames: Glider-style names had become increasingly common as nicknames in the Twin-Bred communities, and even in the earlier human settlement. So now, Talks Too Fast sat on the ground cover, snuggled against the feet of Learns Glider Music, and so on.

When the crowd finally quieted down enough that he could speak without bellowing, Seth came forward and bowed as well. "I am Seth Baruti, also called Creaky When Bending." He was rewarded with human giggles and Tofa whistles. Wings Spread Wide poked upward several times with its beak in its own form of laughter; Seth hoped that the translator had adequately conveyed his jest, or that the Glider understood Seth's Terran, but the gesture might have been mere politeness. He forged ahead. "We come to hear whatever stories of your people you may wish to tell. Thank you for allowing us to listen. Please begin when you are ready." With that, Seth headed to the chair he had brought, a sturdier model than he had initially planned: two of the older Tofa children had carried it to the meadow.

Wings Spread Wide lifted its wings up and out as if in demonstration of its name, then folded them again. "Welcome, all. Since your parents made a long, long journey to come to this world, I will start by telling you about a journey my people made—not as long, but the longest we had ever attempted—when I was a fledgling the same age as some of you.

"This meadow, these cliffs—who knows how long they have been there, or how much they have changed? But for hundreds and hundreds of years, no Glider had beheld them. My people lived near other meadows, other cliffs. In that other place, the weather was colder, and all of us grew thicker fur. On the coldest days, our belts were so cold that it hurt to wear them, and we had to wrap our middles in cloth before fastening the belts around us. . . ."

The story went on, complete with hardships and heroes and ingenious ideas—the Gliders had built large artificial wings and fastened themselves together in teams so that some could sleep while the others steered and watched for predators.

"The little ones, I and my friends, were pulled behind like the kites you children play with, tied to our parents, bobbing this way and that. . . ."

A little girl climbed to her feet and waved her hand. "But how did they know where to go?"

"We were cold so often, we wanted to live where it was warmer. So we made shorter journeys, one after another, in every direction, looking for places a little warmer than where we lived. We could only go where the wind would carry us. In the end, we hoped for the best."

It seemed a very haphazard way of doing things, especially with children in tow. But then, what had the Twin-Bred and their elders done that was so much more prudent? Sailing through a wormhole, landing at the first planet on the other side: they could hardly point fingers, of whatever variety, and call themselves wiser.

Seth ended the call, stared at his phone, and seethed. Anna never meant to be rude, but like many of the Twin-Bred, even after all these years she had not quite mastered what normal humans expected in the way of tact.

Why shouldn't this planned *Star Seed* mission include astronomical observations? And they could say all they liked about waiting for some separate occasion, but they'd never yet got around to a purely scientific mission, had they? *Star Seed* would never have a chance to fly unless some emergency cropped up.

And yes, he was furthering the cause of human-Glider relationships by letting Wings Spread Wide tell story after story like some alien, avian Scheherazade. Not that the stories weren't fascinating, and Seth had enjoyed many a subsequent dinner conversation with his fellows, relating one or another tale (since only the children had heard the stories already). But astronomy was his abiding passion, and here was the first opportunity in what felt like forever, simply going to waste.

Suddenly the radiance of a brilliant idea filled Seth's head, all in an instant, dazzling him with his own creativity.

What if Wings Spread Wide were to ask to be included in the mission? The Gliders, after all, had never been to space. Surely they must be curious. The ship had no facilities for a Glider, but that could be remedied without too much trouble. And Congress would hardly insult the Glider's most revered local patriarch by refusing.

And to avoid disrupting the elder's ongoing retirement ritual, it would be essential, would it not, that Seth Baruti come along for the ride?

Seth glanced at his timepiece. He had about an hour before he was supposed to meet Wings Spread Wide at the meadow. If he hurried, he could meet the Glider at its dwelling instead, and while they traveled to where the children would be waiting, he could begin the process of unfurling the suggestion. But no, their different modes of travel made conversation too cumbersome. He would hurry even more, and arrive before they needed to depart.

* * *

Harriet Gaho sat on the exam table in the main Glider clinic. The Glider doctor, for want of a better term, perched on a built-in ledge jutting out from the opposite wall, smoothing its fur with its beak. Gliders did not consider self-grooming to be a private activity.

Harriet could only hope the Glider was paying attention. "I'm not saying I'd try to prevent Wings Spread Wide from being part of the crew. I just want to be sure that it, and you, know some of my concerns—both the unexpected possibilities and the expected ones."

The Glider removed its beak from its fur. "I would like to hear these concerns."

Harriet glanced at the list she had brought with her. "First of all, I'm not sure whether Wings Spread Wide is aware of Tofarn's greater gravity."

"How much of a handicap would that gravity present?"

Harriet shrugged. "Even if we make a whole series of calculations, all we'll have is a more educated guess."

The Glider resumed grooming itself. Harriet went on down the list.

"The ship has artificial gravity, which could conceivably malfunction or fail altogether. If it goes offline completely, the crew would all be weightless for as long as it took to get the gravity back. That means bobbing about and bumping into things—including other crew members as well as much harder surfaces. It also means not being able to get where you want to go. And while there'd be supplies on board for emergency waste disposal, there's the possibility of accidentally ingesting substances that stopped being food quite a while before. If the system gets out of whack and the gravity increases, that's bad news for joints and any delicate body systems, and for internal organs if it's severe enough.

"Then there are the essential life support features, heat and atmosphere. If those fail, or the meteor defense system misses something and a meteor punches a hole in the ship, then it's either a quick and heroic repair effort, or everybody dies—or both."

The Glider fluttered as it adjusted its position on the ledge, then settled down again and aimed its central eye at Harriet. "And the likelihood of all these failures?"

Harriet shrugged, then realized the Glider might not be familiar with the gesture. "It's hard to say. None of them happened on the way here. We'd do our damnedest to make all the systems failsafe, or at least robust."

The Glider turned its head to regard Harriet with its right eye, an indication of lessened tension. "Wings Spread Wide will die soon. When Gliders grow old and approach the time of their death, some of them take more risks. All they risk losing is the chance to sing their final song. This matters more to some than to others. I will need to talk to Wings Spread Wide about its level of concern.

"Even if it would normally consider this an unacceptable risk, there is another factor. You mentioned an expected danger. Did you mean the strange passage that, years ago, allowed you to travel in such a short time from such a great distance?"

Harriet nodded. (Surely the Gliders understood a nod by this time.) "The wormhole, yes. It has very curious and disorienting effects on human and Tofa. Neither we nor you have any way to know what those effects would be for a Glider."

"Exactly! Wings Spread Wide, if it goes with the ship, would be the first Glider ever to experience such a passage. For our most respected elder to sing of such a journey—how could it turn from such a chance and flutter away the rest of its days at home instead?

"But there is an issue of timing. If Wings Spread Wide finishes composing his life song before the ship leaves, the chance will be gone. When will the ship leave?"

"I wish I could answer you." Harriet slid down from the

table and headed for the window/door and the ramp beyond. "But I'll head back and see if my people are any closer to finding out."

* * *

Wings Spread Wide's youngest grandchild clung tight to its grandparent's belt and squealed with delight as they rode the air currents toward the child's home. Wings Spread Wide ignored the protests of various creaking joints. This might be the last time one's grandchild would ride on one's back; the ache belonged as a theme in that music.

Wings Spread Wide pulled up in front of the entrance to the dwelling; the child tumbled off with one last happy trill. The elder stretched its wings up and down in relief. The child hopped over and tried to smooth its grandparent's back fur, though it could hardly reach high enough to accomplish much.

Wings Spread Wide expected the child to hop and flutter its way inside at once, but it seemed inclined to linger, leaning up against Wings Spread Wide's side and running its hands along the edge of the elder's wing. "Are you really going away?"

"Yes, if the Travelers can make the ship fly well enough for a long, long journey." Many of the People still talked about "the Incomplete Beings," and a few still referred to them as "perverts," but Wings Spread Wide considered either term ill-mannered and did not wish a grandchild to use such language.

"Will you come back?" The tiny fingers traced along the wing. Wings Spread Wide almost laughed: the child's light touch tickled. But laughter during this conversation might be misinterpreted.

"I hope so. I would like to sing my final song to my people in person, if I still have the strength."

"Where will you go, on the ship?"

Wings Spread Wide reclined against the base of the building and beckoned for the child to climb up on its belly. The child scrambled up, curled into a ball, and grasped the elder's wrist. Wings Spread Wide used its other hand to groom the child's fur, combing in a slow, repetitive rhythm.

"First, we will go to a tunnel, a strange tunnel where everything happens backwards." That was probably not quite right, but none of the descriptions of what actually took place had made much sense, and this was as close as Wings Spread Wide could come in terms both it and the child would understand. "Then, once we go through the tunnel, we might fly to a world flowing with water, big and little rivers wherever you look, water and growing things covering up the rocks."

And if Seth Baruti had explained conditions on Tofarn before one had made one's decision, before others told one the truth? Had Wings Spread Wide known from the first that the air on Tofarn was so thin, and the ground so greedy, that one might be able to glide no better than a fledgling child, would one ever have consented to go? But now, to pull back would leave a hollow and echoing place where the end of one's song should be.

The child, half asleep, could still manage to ask questions. "Will there be Travelers there?"

"Yes, many Travelers. All the Tallest Travelers come from that world, and the Not as Talls that arrived with them."

"Will there be any of the People there?"

"No, little one. If I reach that world, I will be the very first one."

Wings Spread Wide's final song would have to confess the limits of one's courage. One longed to glide among the stars, and even to enter the incomprehensible tunnel; but one would rather that they found the communications problem without going any farther, and solved it, and came home again. One had no doubt that one's Traveler shipmates would do their best to keep one safe on that other world, but what could they do if the inhabitants overwhelmed them? Presented with such a curiosity, a new kind of singer, would the Travelers on that planet ever allow one to go home?

Chapter 9

(Tofarn)

NET-MO-SAN completed his summary of the Southern Region's crop production during this year's gold season and glanced toward the door with foreboding. He would be walking home past purple vegetation. Modern Tofa youth, and other Tofa who chose to interact extensively with the human community, made a point of showing indifference to the change of season, no longer minimizing the number of trees and bushes near Tofa offices and habitations. And they were right, in a superficial sense, that such caution had not been necessary for hundreds of years—not since the elimination of the predators whose camouflage had made them so dangerous in purple time. But what was the point of ignoring one's instincts? It could be a dangerous habit, when not all one's inborn warnings had become obsolete.

Net-mo-san gathered up the thin metal sheets of his report. He would scan them for digitized storage—another newfangled, human-derived innovation—and then head for some establishment serving the hot and foaming beverages that best dispelled the seasonal chill.

Several of the Tofa he passed in the halls greeted him cordially; only one or two made a point of ignoring him. He had survived the upheavals better than most of the former Eminence's staff. Most likely Jak-rad (Jak-rad-tan now) had been responsible, emphasizing the ways in which Net-mo-san had been Jak-rad's mentor and eliding his role as the lad's overseer. Jak-rad had never been one to hold grudges— except against those who had attacked Lan-sol in the womb. If Net-mo-san had not made a point of absenting himself whenever Ton-lal-set's rage approached its crest, he might have been one of those commanded to perpetrate the attack on Jak-rad's fetus. None of those Tofa had escaped unscathed.

Net-mo-san reached the room where the scan-and-store machinery sat with its disconcerting subliminal hum. He was about to feed his sheets into the scanner when he noticed that the machine was busy processing a file from some other location. Supposedly the machine could handle input and output simultaneously, but that had not been his experience. He waited, wondering idly what information had been sent and from where.

Wasn't there a panel that lit up according to the type of transmission? Ah, there it was. The incoming file was apparently audiovisual. But finally it had finished transmitting, and Net-mo-san could scan his crop report and head out for his drink.

* * *

Gen-tar-ten slurped at his first hot beverage of the morning and forced himself to stand at the window. This must be the room to which his human friend Veda had been brought, many years ago, to be released from detention. She had known enough about Tofa preferences, even then, to be curious about the existence of a room with so much exterior lighting. He did not know whether she had noticed the extensive garden, so full of color-changing vegetation, outside the window, next to the alley used for entrance from the outside. Artificially tinted lighting could not, as yet, achieve the same impact as the sight of actual purple plants.

He had never told Veda that the room was used for interrogation during purple season, but by now she had probably deduced it.

Political fortunes shifting as they did, he might be dragged into this chamber some day with secrets to conceal. If he could learn to conquer his instinctive reaction, so much the better.

But that was enough for now. He pivoted away from the window and strode out of the room toward his office.

* * *

Veda contemplated the contents of her medicine

cabinet. Should she take something to fortify her digestive system before meeting her father for lunch? He would almost certainly be riding his current political hobby horse, and she was, so to speak, quite fed up with it. But she should really have sufficient self-discipline to ignore his ranting and process her meal without chemical assistance. She closed the cabinet. Then, reconsidering, she reopened it, grabbed an almost empty pill bottle, and popped it into a convenient pocket. She could swallow a pill in mid-meal if necessary.

Stewart Channing, once and conceivably future member of the Council, gestured emphatically with his butter knife. "We've made the mistake before of assuming the best, or just refusing to think about the worst. We let the Eminences take over the Tofa leadership and did nothing to stop it. Who knows what they might have done in another few years? They hated humans! And they'd learned too much about us, thanks to that Project of yours. What have we done to make sure they don't regain power? Nothing! We've left it to the Tofa. Do you really think your friend Gen-tar-ten wouldn't form an alliance with that faction if it suited him for some alien, incomprehensible reason?"

Veda glanced at her purse. It might be worth taking the pill. If her father insisted on paying for the finest products the meat vats could produce, it would be a shame not to fully appreciate it. "How is the campaign going?"

Stewart contemplated his pasta and sighed. "It's an uphill battle, to be sure. It's easy for my opponent to throw my record in my face. But those were difficult times! These newcomers just don't appreciate what we had to contend with. And besides, I've woken up now, haven't I? I'm the one trying to puncture human complacency, aren't I?"

Stewart drained his water glass and interrupted himself to crane his neck conspicuously toward the waiter, giving Veda an opportunity to extract her pill without his noticing. She swallowed it just as the waiter arrived with the pitcher. Her father held up his glass with a hand whose tremor was just barely noticeable.

"Daddy, are you taking care of yourself? Eating well, sleeping enough, going to your doctor's appointments?"

Stewart smiled in what she found an unconvincing

manner. "Of course, my dear. Don't you start fretting over me."

She would make one attempt at addressing his concerns. "About the former Eminences. You know several of them are dead. And the rest are in prison and could be executed on short notice. Why in the world would the current leadership do anything to strengthen their political enemies?"

Stewart shook his head with a condescending expression she had not seen in some time, and would have been happy not to see again. "Veda, Veda. They aren't all in jail—that is, not all of their allies and sycophants. And what makes you so sure you understand their penal system, or their politics?"

Veda would have bet another fancy meal that she understood more of both, at this point, than her father did. But he did have some fraction of a point. She should stay vigilant—as a matter of principle, if nothing else.

*   *   *

Ton-lal-set heard the key in the lock at an unexpected time and went through the ritual he had developed for such events: hushing his internal monologue, allowing his senses to dominate his awareness, maintaining his muscles in a state between alertness and relaxation.

The door opened and a single guard appeared—the same guard that had reassured him of his safety after his last hearing. The guard unlocked Ton-lal-set's chains, but rather than gathering them up, left them on the floor of the cell. "It has been determined that your illness has rendered you sufficiently weak that the chains are unnecessary. It also requires a change in the conditions of your confinement."

Ton-lal-set suppressed all signs of surprise, confusion, or pleasure. He had never been sure, in all these years, whether the current regime had chosen to imitate humans with their omnipresent recording devices. He stood and awaited orders, slumping and dropping his shoulders in a manner he hoped reflected his supposed weakness. The guard grasped Ton-lal-set's right arms in the guard's left and led him toward the door.

Ton-lal-set took what he hoped would be one last glance at the tiny stone cube in which he had passed the last seventeen years. The rage that welled up in him took him by surprise, making him stumble. The guard grabbed his arms more firmly, pulled him closer, and whispered, "No need to overdo it." Ton-lal-set did not answer.

The new cell contained a much larger candle, a leaning post, and even a bed. Ton-lal-set could not know whether or how recently it had been inhabited, but the room smelled only of the candle, with no stench of unwashed prisoner or of waste. He looked in the corner for a bucket and saw—could it be?—an actual waste disposal unit.

The guard saw the direction of his gaze. "I will give you a few minutes to yourself before I return to complete your orientation."

Ton-lal-set flicked an upper hand in the gesture for skepticism. "Do I have more than the illusion of privacy?"

"Yes. Your privacy and ours is essential and has been carefully ensured."

The guard's phrasing reminded Ton-lal-set of their earlier exchange. The guard had made a similar reference that day—something about a "we" in which Ton-lal-set was not included. What did it all mean, the transfer, the luxuries, the cryptic hints? Impatience flared up in him as if he had never spent years learning to extinguish it.

But the guard had already slipped through the door. He must wait the projected few minutes, at least. In the meantime . . . Ton-lal-set hurried to the disposal unit and leaned into it with a pleasure bordering on ecstasy.

This time Ton-lal-set heard two sets of footsteps before the lock turned in the door. The same guard appeared with a companion, a Tofa perhaps half Ton-lal-set's age and with the air of a mid-level functionary.

The new arrival appeared nervous, shifting his weight and randomly waving the fingers on his lower hands. "We will not have time today for much substantive discussion. But the number of Tofa willing to assist you—and hoping that you will eventually be able to assist us in turn—is expanding, as your new quarters surely indicate."

Ton-lal-set made a very slight sideways bow, such as one could use to reward a subordinate, but gave no other response. This fidgety fellow would doubtless reveal information without Ton-lal-set needing either to exert or to commit himself.

"As you must have deduced, there have been few willing to take the risk of opposing the revolutionary regime. But the accumulation of subversive ideas this leadership has either generated or tolerated is at last provoking a reaction, though largely a clandestine one."

Ton-lal-set now allowed himself to show some interest. "What ideas have you and your colleagues found sufficiently offensive to stir you into action?"

The visitor first described the scheme to submit the entire Tofa population to inoculation with some supposedly protective substances. But at least—and this must be what he had seen on the way to the hearing—Gen-tar-ten had displayed some minimal caution by testing the inoculation on dispensable subjects. The irony! He whistled, then condescended to share his thought with the others. "If the usurper's lackeys had not been planning to execute me immediately, I would no doubt have been one of those subjected to experimentation. Their plans for vengeance became my protection."

The guard and visitor both whistled back. Then the visitor stood up straighter and threw all his arms out as if addressing a crowd. "There is more. I myself have taken the lead in opposing the proposal to subject offspring to special tests, no doubt developed by the humans, in order to identify the source of the spores that fertilized the parent. As if a child could have more than one parent!"

Ton-lal-set started backward. This was subversive indeed! Could the rebels leave no tradition untouched?

And yet . . . .

He had forgotten the tickling, tingling feeling of an idea fighting to be born. It had been so long since ideas could serve some purpose. He must not let further discussion drive it away or drown it out. He headed for the leaning post and positioned himself upon it. "You may have provided useful information. Now I will rest. You will return soon, and we will speak further of those political developments I may have missed."

The guard and his companion gave a somewhat

abbreviated version of the obeisance due to a superior; then the guard opened the heavy cell door, ushered the other Tofa through, and clanged it shut behind him, turning the key in the lock. That reality, at least, remained. Ton-lal-set found the hated sound somewhat reassuring. He had not drifted into some insanity of wish-fulfillment: he still knew himself to be imprisoned.

* * *

Lan-sol opened the door to the hangar containing the partially completed ship, edged inside, and turned on the lights. Once he could see his way through the obstacle course of scaffolding and machinery, he beckoned to his friend to follow him in. Gen-tar-ten's child Nin-til was one of the few young people of either species whom Lan-sol could honestly call a friend. Lan-sol could have wished that Nin-til were older than he, instead of slightly younger; and he would happily have treated his friend with some amount of deference, as Jak-rad-tan still treated Gen-tar-ten. But unlike his parent, even Nin-til was not entirely free from the effects of Lan-sol's legendary, pseudo-heroic status.

Lan-sol adjusted the lights for minimal leakage to the outside. If his followers learned that he had given one tour, they would badger him unceasingly to give more.

"Here's the main control center. There's an adjacent sleeping chamber so that the pilot on duty can attend to emergencies with the least possible delay." He pushed back the familiar worry about the training he and the alternate pilots were attempting. Lan-sol had been counting on recorded lessons from the Twin-Bred who had steered *Star Seed* to its safe landing—but unless communications were restored, he and his crew would have to keep relying on incomplete records from the original human colonists, and reinvent some aspects of the proverbial wheel.

Had the latest environmental features been installed yet? It looked like it. Without announcing beforehand what he was about to do, Lan-sol pressed a button on the appropriate panel. Then he waited for Nin-til to notice. It took a few moments before Nin-til started looking around, radiating puzzlement. "That sound—could we hear rain, in here? I did not think the sound would carry through the walls."

Lan-sol whistled. "That is not the sound of rain currently falling. My parent suggested that we make the sound available on board and play it occasionally to alleviate homesickness."

"That might help." Nin-til paused for a moment, then made the gesture for an unsolved problem before continuing. "My parent and I are still arguing about whether I can go along."

Lan-sol suppressed the urge to whistle. The matter was serious enough for his friend, and indeed for him: he would love to have Nin-til's company. But the situation had its amusing ironies as well. Ideologically, Gen-tar-ten approved of minimizing the coercion of offspring, and had gamely put the idea into practice with Nin-til and at least some of his younger siblings; but Jak-rad-tan had dropped hints that when the revolutionary leader began confronting the results of his enlightened policies, he found them somewhat unpalatable.

Lan-sol continued the tour, pointing out the areas designated for communications center, mess hall, and crew quarters. Nin-til grew quieter as the tour proceeded. As the two of them picked their way out of and away from the ship, Lan-sol was about to ask the reason for Nin-til's silence when Nin-til said, "The colonists on New Landing: more than half of them are humans?"

Lan-sol did a quick calculation. "Based on the offspring of both groups, I believe the numbers of human and Tofa are now close to equal, with Tofa in a slight majority. Since only half of the humans can become pregnant, and the Tofa gestation period is only a little longer than that of humans, the balance has shifted over time. But wait—I was forgetting the humans who arrived before *Star Seed*. Your estimate is correct."

"That is many more humans than you associate with at home."

"True. Why do you mention the fact?"

Nin-til, and therefore Lan-sol, had slowed to a stop. Nin-til buzzed for a moment, then said quietly, "I have been wondering what you truly feel about the humans. You seem so untroubled by them. Is that a deliberate . . . posture? Or do you understand them the way the Tofa Twin-Bred are supposed to do?"

Lan-sol was more than ready to turn off the lights and leave the hangar. It had been a long day in a series of long days; he wanted a hot drink, an hour of reading—maybe with an extra candle scenting the room—and then as much sleep as he could manage. It would take too long to answer his friend's question truthfully, even if the truth were something he could confide.

He put his lower left hand on Nin-til's upper right arm, an intimate gesture to substitute for the intimacy of more complete disclosure. "They trouble me less than they seem to trouble you. If you would like, I can arrange for the two of us to spend more time with some of the friendlier ones, like Melly. You may find that it gets easier."

As they left the hangar and walked toward Nin-til's home, the rest of the answer, the part he could not speak, played itself in Lan-sol's mind. Yes, humans could be confusing and even disquieting—but less so, significantly less, than the Tofa he had known all his life. The difference between those Tofa and Lan-sol's parent loomed almost as large as the difference between Lan-sol and humans, and it bothered him far more.

Jak-rad-tan had left the Twin-Bred community in order to know his own species. Lan-sol's quest would be an ironic reversal of his parent's. He had many reasons to accept the invitation from New Landing, but the one he kept secret, the one closest to his heart, was hope: the hope that in the Tofa Twin-Bred and their children, he would find his own people.

Chapter 10

(New Landing)

HARRIET GAHO watched one young Tofa finish bandaging another, then double-checked the work. "Good job!" She turned to the patient. "And you'd better consult one of Nathan's engineering students, if not the master himself, before you test another gliding frame. You could have bashed yourself up considerably worse. Don't try to web those fingers until I've told you they're healed enough."

Harriet's helper escorted his friend to the infirmary door, then came back in. "What other injuries might he have suffered besides lacerations and contusions, and what could we have done to repair them?"

Harriet snorted. "With a little bad luck, he could have got himself killed—which I can hardly teach you to fix! But short of that, he could have dislocated or sprained or broken an arm or a leg. And if he hit hard in an area with a lot of crystal dust, it could have abraded his membranes and breath tubes."

The young Tofa looked out the window at a flock of juvenile Gliders swooping from their classroom for mid-afternoon playtime. "But it looks like so much fun. Doctor Gaho, wouldn't you like to glide?"

"Sure, I would. And maybe I will. Now that you young folk are really paying attention to it, I'll bet we'll have reliable glide frames for humans and Tofa before I get altogether decrepit."

"Or else we'll do it the other way."

Harriet raised her eyebrows as high as they would reach. "You think building frames is tricky and a lot of work, just wait until you try playing around with two sets of genomes! And we don't even have samples of the Terran critters that had gliding abilities. Tofarn didn't have those, you know—maybe because of all the rain."

The Tofa shrugged, in the quasi-human manner the Tofa Twin-Bred had passed on to their offspring. He obviously didn't care to hear how hard his pet project would be. Well, why discourage him further? Young folk *should* have outsized expectations.

As her assistant cleaned up the work space, Harriet gazed out the window at the Glider children and thought about the genetic tinkering idea. It had first come up years ago, as soon as Tofa and human toddlers starting noticing that they couldn't flutter and glide like the native fledglings. Young parents, trying to field the endless variations on "Why?" and "Why not?", starting asking themselves and their elders the same questions.

It would take quite the commitment of resources: lots of time from lots of community members, lots of construction of gizmos that could produce and manipulate and refine lots of biological elements. But Mara had taken up the work for its scientific interest, which was a start. And while the goal of flying unassisted might seem frivolous considering the required investment, was it really? If these kids and the generations coming after them would be living next to beings who could more or less fly, what resentments and tensions might arise unless they could do the same?

Not that the human youngsters took it that hard when they found they couldn't split any of their arms. And none of the Tofa had got especially upset that they didn't have tongues to stick out.

But soaring through the air, from cliff-top to cliff-top . . . That spoke to something that sat deeper, in the human soul at least, and apparently in the Tofa as well.

Harriet looked out the window again, this time staring up at the blue, blue sky. The color still had an impact, after all this time. Talk about genes: human genes were made to look up and see blue, at least when the weather was fine. But lately, she'd been starting to miss the sky she'd been born under, that light, clear, vibrant green; and the darker green at the end of the day. . . .

What if some of these young folk wanted to return, some day, or their children did—back to Tofarn, to visit or even to stay? Humans and Tofa had trouble enough getting along back there. What would those on Tofarn make of humans or Tofa with Glider all mixed in? Likely enough, there'd be no going back, not for the ones that reshaped themselves.

"Doctor Gaho? Is everything all right?"

She turned round and smiled. "Right as rain—as they used to say on Terra, which is funny when it rained so much less there than it did on Tofarn. All's well and fine enough. Now you run along and tell Mara and Fel-lar what a good job you did in your doctoring today."

* * *

Elspeth returned from the market with two skeins of Glider fiber, a bulging bag of fruit, and flushed cheeks that the weather was neither hot enough nor cold enough to explain. Judy kissed her, took the bag of fruit to wash, and left Elspeth to stash the fiber with her weaving and knitting supplies. She would wait a few minutes to see if Elspeth volunteered an explanation.

To her relief, Elspeth appeared in the kitchen before Judy's self-imposed deadline had elapsed. "I know I shouldn't let it bother me, but it does sometimes. Maybe I'll dumb down my translator just enough that it forgets how to translate 'pervert'."

Judy grimaced. "Was it one of the older ones, or some young squirt?"

"Older. Almost as old as Wings Spread Wide—but *it* would never say anything like that. Though I wonder if it feels that way and is too gracious to say so."

Judy offered Elspeth a just-washed fruit. "I don't think so. It had an open mind, right from the start. It understands that humans don't naturally do triads—that we don't have the same biological reasons the Gliders do."

Elspeth bit into the fruit, turned it so the portion she'd sampled faced Judy, and held it forward. Judy took a bite just next to Elspeth's. "I had an idea on my way back. I wasn't sure whether to mention it to you, and it's not something I'd come close to insisting on. But there is something we could do that might get them to stop sneering at us."

Judy didn't much care whether the Gliders sneered or not. Though Elspeth spent more time and ran more errands in places where she'd encounter them. La-ren now and then asked why—

Was Elspeth proposing *that*? Judy froze, the partially eaten fruit still in her hand.

La-ren stirred. ("Elspeth's idea—if you've divined it correctly, and I believe you have—is intriguing. Though those Gliders inflexible enough to be hurling insults after all these years may not be likely to understand or appreciate the notion of a corporeal/incorporeal triad. You could begin by explaining to Wings Spread Wide, and consulting him as to whether to explain to others.")

Elspeth, fidgeting, took the fruit back and chomped away a larger chunk. "Do let me know when the two of you are finished."

Judy stared at Elspeth. Her lover had never before used such a waspish tone in reference to her and La-ren's communication. "What's going on? Is there something else, besides what happened at the market?"

Elspeth turned away. "I'm sorry."

Judy took gentle hold of Elspeth's shoulders and turned her back again. "Honey, I don't care about apologies. I want to know what's wrong." She steered the two of them to the couch and fell back into it, pulling Elspeth with her. "Tell me. Please."

Elspeth took a deep breath and sighed it back out before answering. "You know, don't you, about how Mara and Fel-lar and Levi are? How they're together?"

"More or less." In fact, Judy had done her best not to listen when either of the principals made their casual references to the arrangement. That same casual attitude had damped any gossip that might otherwise have flourished.

For the first time, Judy wondered just how Mara—so rigidly private back on Tofarn, and so used to keeping Levi a secret—had achieved, or learned to feign, such nonchalance.

And Fel-lar's leadership position, acknowledged and honored even more by the Gliders than by the Twin-Bred community: had the claim to triad status, even by such an unorthodox definition, been a prerequisite?

She had been silent too long. Elspeth was flushed again, and turning her head to conceal what might be tears. Judy grabbed Elspeth's hand and squeezed it. "Don't be upset. I'm thinking, that's all. Just give me a little time to think." Elspeth gulped and nodded.

Judy had never actually asked La-ren to lie low, to stay quiescent, when she and Elspeth made love. But of course he had known what she wanted. And after all the failed relationships, Judy had been determined, this time, not to let obtrusive thoughts of La-ren's presence keep her from accepting intimacy. Even so, there had been moments of distraction, passion derailed and opportunities squandered.

How much more difficult would it be—or could it somehow be easier?—if she acknowledged, even welcomed, La-ren's presence in such moments?

How did Mara manage? Older, raised in a purely human community, she must have internalized the incest taboo even more thoroughly. How could she allow her brother—her (in some sense) human brother—to take part? Or did they manage some other way? She could imagine no possible circumstance that could render her so bold as to ask.

("La-ren, what do I say? Where do I start?")

("We could undertake an indirect investigation. You could ask Fel-lar, on some occasion when Mara is not present.")

("But then he'd remember and she could find out. *No*.")

"Elspeth, how important is it to you that we—declare ourselves as three?"

The soft sound might have been a sniff. "It's not just about the Gliders and the triad thing. It's being on the outside. Never knowing if you're with me completely, or you're listening to your twin."

"But Mara and Fel-lar and Levi, that's different. Fel-lar's abilities make their rapport possible. We couldn't *share* La-ren that way."

"We could try. All of us have more telepathic ability than other humans. And I *knew* La-ren. That might make a difference."

("La-ren? How well did you and Elspeth know each other?")

("She was a member of Professor Abuto's literature

club. In fact, she was the first to read Anne Frank's diary, before I mentioned it to the professor. I enjoyed her contributions to our discussions.")

Elspeth sat in rigid expectation at Judy's side. If Judy drew this line and told Elspeth she could not even try to cross, Elspeth would leave. It might take days or weeks, but Judy would lose Elspeth as she had lost the others. And even if another took her place, Judy would still—Judy and La-ren would still end up alone.

"Come here. Come close." Judy put her arm around Elspeth and pulled her tight against her side. "Think of a book, a line from a book. Something you and La-ren both read, but not a line you actually talked about." ("La-ren, you heard. Tell me if you know what she picked.")

Elspeth closed her eyes; her face showed her concentration as she nodded.

("La-ren?")

Judy felt his support, his approval, his equivalent of a smile. ("Oh brave new world, that has such people in it!")

"Elspeth? Was it from Shakespeare's *The Tempest*?"

For answer, Elspeth laid her head on Judy's shoulder, and Judy could feel her nod.

* * *

Mara knew this feeling so well—and loathed it: the constant press of worries and decisions, with never enough information to address them. She would have thought, back at the Project, that being in charge made the pressure more intense; but that was before she had to stand on the sidelines, almost, while the one she loved suffered as she had once suffered.

Although he claimed not to be suffering all that much. ("Levi, how is he holding up? Really?")

("Sister mine, you need to stop projecting. He was raised to solve problems, after all. And he didn't grow up with anger and grief and self-doubt all stirring around inside him. Complicated situations don't make him want to explode—he finds them invigorating.")

Mara made her way back to the room where Fel-lar stood studying plans and reports and drawings. He was singing very softly under his breath, a passage from the epic whose premiere she had attended—how long ago?

If he was singing, then Levi was right, and she must make sure not to dampen Fel-lar's mood and interfere with his doing his job.

Besides, if she diverted his attention, he might dredge up the idea of her going along on whatever expedition might be forthcoming.

She turned around and made her way as quietly as she could to the front door. She would take a walk to the Glider market and hope to find some sort of distraction.

On the way, she passed within sight of the meadow where Wings Spread Wide was recounting his childhood to the current generation of children. Seth Baruti sat near him, tapping busily on his tablet, and looking at the Glider now and then with a proprietary, almost smug expression.

Movement caught her eye, and she turned to see several of the older Glider children swooping by, chattering to each other in great excitement. They were too absorbed to notice her, and that happened rather rarely, such was her unfortunate legendary status. What was going on? She let them get ahead of her and then followed.

Soon she was standing at the base of a fairly tall cliff. She had passed the spot often, and had never seen the roughly cleared path that now wound its way upward. The Glider children had scattered to various nearby promontories and were pointing upward toward something she was too low to see. She sighed and started looking for a way to climb higher. One of the children noticed and descended in a series of hops and flutters and short glides to render assistance. "Here, grab this rock, and then turn this way; a few more steps, and up, and back over, and up again. . . ."

They were directing her to a clearing thick with ground cover. Three teenage Tofa stood in the middle of it; they reached down and helped her up the last bit of the climb, then stood back as if unsure how to handle her presence. She thanked them briefly and looked over where the Gliders had been looking. Now she could see the flat top of a nearby cliff, and the cluster of human teenagers and a few Tofa of similar age. The humans were strapping each other, and some of the Tofa were strapping some of the humans, into broad and complicated contraptions whose purpose was immediately obvious. A bright yellow wind sock flapped gaily in the breeze.

How long had it been since the last casualty from attempted artificial gliding? Weeks or merely days? There was no time to summon any adult reinforcements. Even as she watched, a line began to form, with a tall girl—Anna's older daughter, it looked like—in the front. Mara could only hope these young people had done their work well.

She shook her head suddenly, annoyed at the too-familiar trend of her thoughts. Enough worrying! The youngsters were living as youth should live, pushing boundaries, extending themselves. She imagined herself standing at the edge of that cliff, about to spring forward, hoping, at last, to fly; how the crystal cliffs all around would glisten, how clean the air would taste, how every sense would almost crackle with intensity. . . .

She held her breath as the girl lifted the artificial wings, ran down the slope, and leaped.

The crowd whistled and clapped and cheered as the machine soared across the canyon in a perfect arc, reached the clearing where Mara sat clutching her hands together, and made a shallow descent, the girl moving her feet as if running before they touched the ground. As she touched down, some of the Tofa near Mara ran to grab the machine and steady it while the girl came to a stop.

Mara jumped up, clapping and beaming, and ran to join the girl, who was busily unstrapping herself with the Tofa's help. "Wonderful! Congratulations! *Mazel tov!*"

The girl turned, startled. "Oh, my! Doctor Cadell! I had no idea—I hope you—" Her pride and joy burst forth, wiping out the moment of diffidence. "That was *amazing!*"

"It certainly was! Did you have a hand in building this?"

The girl nodded vigorously, her windblown hair bouncing. "Mama Anna helped with the drawings, but I made the wings myself. We all worked together on the rest of the frameworks, assembly-line style, but we wanted to make our own wings."

Mara turned to look at the Tofa. One of them, she now noticed, was Li-sen's oldest child. She asked him, "Have you managed to make any for yourselves, or is that project still on the drawing board?"

He buzzed for a moment, then held up a finger in imitation of the human signal for discretion. "We want to surprise my parent. The model is almost ready for testing."

Mara tilted her head. "Surprise him how? Do you want to show him what you can do, or are you going to try to get him to use it himself?"

The young Tofa whistled gleefully. "Both! Do you think he'll do it?"

Mara found herself bouncing on her toes, then from one foot to the other. The wild, thrumming energy that had seized her demanded movement. "I might just know a way to encourage him." She turned toward the girl who had already flown. "You're about my height, aren't you?"

The girl stared at her with wide eyes. "Are you thinking . . ." Her face lit up, and she bounced up and down just as Mara had. "Would you? Would you really? Oh, I'd be so proud!" Then her expression grew anxious. "But are you, um . . . Can you?"

Mara let out a short bark of laughter. "I'm fit enough, never fear. I won't blame you if you don't want to risk your wings when you've only used them once!—but if it's me you're afraid of breaking, you needn't be."

The girl relaxed and smiled again. "Come on, then! We don't even have to go back over there—we had everything set up for a series of glides." She ran over to another wind sock, a green one, lying at the edge of the clearing and hoisted it upright. Then she pointed to two more Tofa climbing a path toward another clearing. "But we'll have to hurry, while the wind is still right."

The girl and her Tofa companions pulled Mara toward the machine and bustled about, strapping her in, checking, adjusting. Two Tofa seized the wings and guided Mara toward the edge facing the next landing site. The girl, standing near the edge, looked nervous again. "You saw what I did? You run, and then you push off and lift your feet with your knees together . . . And you saw how I landed?"

"Yes, yes, I saw it all!" Mara flexed her fingers toward the girl's hand, the closest she could come to reaching out; the girl, understanding, came up for an awkward but enthusiastic handshake, then stepped back to leave Mara sufficient clearance.

"Thank you so much! Wish me luck!" Mara stood up straight, nodding to her assistants. "And here I *go!*"

She ran for the edge, hollering in exaltation, and leapt into flight.

Chapter 11

(Tofarn)

THE YOUNGER, more progressive Tofa prided themselves on adopting a few useful human inventions. While few of them had gone so far as to use the cybernet, and no Tofa equivalent had emerged, these Tofa no longer limited themselves to publishing material worth the effort and investment of folded metal books. Instead, many of them used paper to distribute humorous or topical material. One of the less desirable variations, Lan-sol reflected glumly, was the recent development of gossip rags. Of course the purveyors were desperate to find any new tidbit or angle on Lan-sol's plans and intentions.

The latest pest, dogging Lan-sol's steps as he headed from hangar to home, had no concept of privacy. "What if one of the crew gets pregnant on the voyage? What would space flight, and especially the wormhole, do to a fetus? Aren't you *concerned*?"

Lan-sol had various mental tricks for ignoring mobile nuisances. This time, he imagined the fellow as a Terran creature he had seen only in old footage: a donkey, braying as close to his ear as the beast could manage. If any of the animal's noises resembled Tofar, that would be only a coincidence. . . .

He had not needed some random busybody to bring the issue to his attention. Bad enough to have been attacked in utero during a political upheaval. What ceaseless curiosity would await a fetus—one already born into a famous family— who had been subjected, before birth, to the uncanny and possibly mind-altering experience of neural reflection?

The limited Tofa openness to human inventions did not extend to the idea of Tofa contraception. Lan-sol had no intention of explaining to the general public what he and the other members of his crew had discussed in confidence. There would be no edict from him, but Lan-sol had consulted with former members of the Project staff, and he would most reluctantly be inhibiting his own reproductive capacity until he reached the Twin-Bred colony. After that—well, if the Twin-Bred were indeed his people, he would not have to wait any longer.

* * *

Melly, leaning on the hangar railing in her usual spot, was not surprised to be approached by a stranger. It happened more and more often, as word spread that she would be accompanying Lan-sol: the only human so far to have volunteered, or at least (she could not know which) to be accepted.

Or was this in fact a stranger? The woman standing next to her, shifting uneasily from foot to foot, looked somehow familiar. But Melly had the oddest feeling that the woman should look younger—not actually young, but not so close to old.

"Excuse me. You're Melanie Seeling, aren't you?" The woman's voice, even more familiar than the face, added to the unreality of the meeting. Then suddenly, as the woman started to speak again, Melly made the connection and gasped. The stranger looked and sounded like Mara Cadell!— older, and without the electric, restless energy that Mara radiated, but now that Melly had seen it the resemblance was unmistakable.

Melly stared at the woman and nodded.

"I'm sorry to disturb you." Had Doctor Cadell ever spoken so softly? "I'm Elizabeth Cadell. My daughter started the Twin-Bred project. And now—" The woman had tears in her eyes, and made no effort to wipe or blink them away. "She's out there, where you're going."

Melly finally shook off her confusion and reached out her hand. "I'm pleased—honored—to meet you."

The woman hesitated, then accepted the handshake while shaking her head. "I've earned no credit for my daughter's accomplishments. Except, maybe, by leaving her so alone that she made her own community, and then found her own world."

It was awkward to be pulled into the woman's story of regret. "Is there something I can do for you, or answer for you?"

The woman smiled a little without looking any less sad. "One of those, at least, and possibly both. When you go on the ship, can you take anything with you? Anything— nonessential?"

The ship would have some limited cargo capacity. They would be bringing upgrades of various useful devices, along with other less practical gifts: the brand of chocolates that had been Mara's favorite, a generous supply of aroma sticks, recordings of some of Melly's plays, Tofa attempts at Glider-style musical compositions. . . . "Did you want me to take something to the colony? I might be able to, if it isn't too bulky or heavy."

The woman leaned over and picked up a shopping bag that had been sitting nearby. "It isn't—they aren't heavy; and they can be compressed somewhat without coming to any harm." She pulled out something woven, a sweater, loosely knitted from fuzzy yarn in muted warm colors. "I make these sweaters. I always did, and now I sell them. But I'm not sure—I don't know if Mara had any to take with her, when she went away. I'd like her to have this one. And—" She pulled out something longer and thinner, a scarf with a bolder pattern in dark gold and darker purple. "This—it could be for a woman, or a man." The woman stopped and bit her lip for a moment before she went on. "And it would remind her—remind them—of the colors of home."

Melly reached out to touch the sweater. It was soft and springy, a pleasure to touch. Surely Mara would be glad to have it. And if Mara didn't want it, Melly would ask if she could take it—but she would have to be careful never to wear it where Elizabeth Cadell might see.

Mara's mother slid the sweater and the scarf back into the bag. Melly reached for the handle. "I'm sure it would be fine."

Melly took the bag, hesitated, then put out her hand again. The older woman grasped it for a moment, then turned and walked slowly away, turning back just once to gaze at the bag before disappearing out the hangar door.

* * *

Over the years since Veda first approached Gen-tar-ten with a proposed alliance, the two had discovered unexpected similarities in their world views and tactical talents. They stayed in touch, despite the very different circles in which they generally moved. Once Veda had decided to follow her son Peer-tek's lead and master encryption technology, the Eminence sometimes enlisted her services as a consultant. For a while, each provided the other with an opportunity to improve their knowledge of and comfort with the other's language; though Gen-tar-ten, to the surprise of neither, eventually surpassed her in that competition, and they usually conversed in Terran. Gen-tar-ten occasionally dropped by Veda's home and took some refreshment; but more often the two would take a stroll through the intermingled Tofa and humans frequenting Central Park.

Their current excursion must be something of a treat for the Eminence, who would probably have avoided any unnecessary outdoor promenades during purple season. Short as the season seemed to humans, even as privileged a Tofa as Gen-tar-ten no doubt suffered from some degree of cabin fever before the gold returned. But by now, only a very few plants, well away from the footpaths, retained a tinge of purple.

Though some careless gardener had missed that tiny shrub—

Veda glanced over at her companion. He was not looking at the offending foliage, but his pace had slowed, and his posture suggested discomfort: he held his upper arms close to the torso, while his lower arms pointed out slightly in different directions. She stopped and turned toward him. "Is something wrong?"

Gen-tar-ten let his lower arms drop, but changed course toward a path that led away from the clearing they had been approaching. "It is nothing, really. I sometimes find the intermixture of human and Tofa voices disconcerting. It renders both human and Tofa speech close to incomprehensible."

His complaint reminded Veda of how much greater a variety of speech her ancestors would have considered normal. "When you were at the Project, did you ever happen to hear about Terra and all its different languages? In some regions, even a short journey could mean a Terran would understand nothing the locals were saying."

Gen-tar-ten emitted a discordant buzz of distaste. "How unpleasant."

"We even have a myth about it. The story goes that humans used to work so well together that they built a tower reaching far up into the sky. And God—you remember my stories about God, I trust?—God found humanity's progress threatening, and decided to hinder it by making it harder for them to understand each other." She searched her memory for the sonorous phrasing her father had often quoted. "God decided to 'confound their language, that they may not understand each other's speech.'"

Now it was Gen-tar-ten's turn to stop in his tracks. "The Terrans attributed such wickedness to this God?" His upper arms were clenched close to his trunk again, the elbows actually digging into the flesh.

Veda's hand twitched toward the Tofa's nearest lower arm; but she had never ventured to touch Gen-tar-ten, and had no idea whether it would make matters better or worse. "I'm sorry. I didn't expect an old Terran story to upset you."

Gen-tar-ten made an obvious effort to relax, loosening the muscles of one arm after another. "It was not the story itself, but its resemblance to an episode of my people's history, that caught me by surprise."

Veda's mind raced. Gen-tar-ten was rarely indiscreet. What would keep him talking? Skepticism, perhaps. . . . She raised an eyebrow. "How could that be? Did there used to be many different languages in some area of Tofarn?"

Gen-tar-ten made one of the gestures signifying annoyance. "I refer to an episode, as I said. An incident. In one of our wars."

"We've talked before about the war where chemical weapons were used, but I don't see—"

"Not that one. Much earlier. We did not, so long ago, have the level of technology needed for chemical weapons, but not every weapon requires such sophistication. It was thought, afterward, that the belligerents might have discovered the technique by accident."

Gen-tar-ten fell silent and started walking again, his long legs soon leaving her behind. Veda resumed walking as well, at a comfortable pace. Sooner or later, Gen-tar-ten would probably fall back to accompany her if she failed to keep up. And she could use the interval to think.

Years ago, when Ton-lal-set was still Eminence and Gen-tar-ten led only a group of dissidents, that group had defied Ton-lal-set's policies and taught the Tofa Twin-Bred much of the history of their species. Had that history been incomplete, or had Jimmy and Peer-tek simply failed to mention this ancient conflict? Veda thought the former more likely.

Why would those who compiled the information have found this weapon more threatening than chemical warfare? Given what had triggered the revelation, the "incident" must have involved some unprecedented disruption of communications. What primitive, serendipitous, yet dangerous technique could possibly—but of course! "Somehow they stumbled on a way to disrupt the telepathic component of Tofa speech."

As if echoing her epiphany, Gen-tar-ten stumbled on the smooth footpath, then caught himself and forged ahead. She had pushed her luck: clearly, she was correct, and just as clearly, she had upset and possibly offended her very powerful acquaintance. She would have to retrieve the situation quickly. She switched from Terran to Tofar. "Eminence, please forgive the trespass of your erring servant."

Gen-tar-ten halted again, stood still for a moment, then turned slowly around. He stared at her for a moment and then, to her considerable relief, whistled loudly. "Your accent is acceptable, but your humility is unconvincing. You are no one's servant, and certainly not mine."

Veda sighed and smiled, hoping Gen-tar-ten would recognize the expression. "I did mean the apology. I shouldn't have pursued the subject once you dropped it."

Gen-tar-ten spread the fingers of his upper left hand as if launching a tree-seed into the breeze. "It is my responsibility to watch what I say. Particularly in the presence of a human.

You are a species much given to curiosity." Then he held out a lower hand, cupped Veda's elbow, and escorted her toward the path leading out of the park. Neither of them spoke until they had almost emerged from the wooded path closest to the exit. Before they could leave the shelter of the trees, Gen-tar-ten exerted a firm pressure to turn Veda towards him. "We have been of much assistance to each other in the past. I hope we will always remain on good terms. Which could not be the case if I were ever to learn that you had spoken to other humans about the history I mentioned."

"I understand completely. I will never disclose it without your explicit prior authorization."

There did not seem anything else to say, after this ultimatum and submission. Veda waited for Gen-tar-ten to release her arm, bowed slightly, and then turned to walk away.

Chapter 12

(New Landing)

WINGS SPREAD Wide had not yet chosen to share with its audience the Glider's-eye version of how humans arrived on the planet. Seth was reluctant to probe, despite his curiosity. The Glider elder seemed somewhat less friendly since Mara and Harriet had met with it, explaining the limited mobility with which it might have to contend if *Star Seed* reached Tofarn. Seth had taken to sitting behind the children when the Glider told its tales. If Seth took one more wrong step, the Glider might cancel their special final-song arrangement—which would obviate the need for Seth's presence on *Star Seed*, even if the Glider still made the trip.

As an alternative, he could try pumping former Administrator Macauley for information. The old man might welcome a visit, especially from a human near his own age. Seth could offer in implicit exchange his own account of Tofarn, the Twin-Bred project, and *Star Seed*'s voyage.

Seth did a bit of investigation and was able to arrive bearing gifts: Macauley's favorite local liqueur, derived from one of the fruits both humans and Gliders could consume, as well as some Tofarna aroma sticks. Seth had not taken the chance of being refused, but arrived unannounced. Fortunately Macauley was home and even outdoors, sunbathing on the uncovered portion of his large porch. Seth introduced himself and offered his tribute. Soon the two men were sharing the liqueur, while Macauley sampled the various aromas.

"I haven't a clue about this one . . . . Oh, this one is easy! Nothing like the smell of fresh-brewed coffee! But what's that other smell mixed in?"

"That's hara nut, Mr. Macauley. Our best guess is that

it's similar to Terran hazelnuts, but less likely to trigger allergic reactions."

"Oh, call me Alvan. No standing on ceremony for two old-timers like us! That is, if I may call you—what was your name again?"

"Seth Baruti. Of course, call me Seth. Here, try the pipe smoke. It goes nicely with the liqueur. Alvan, I don't know if you've heard about how I'm recording some history of this planet from the point of view of the elder, Wings Spread Wide. I was wondering if you've written any memoirs yourself." Seth already knew that as far as anyone in the community knew, Macauley had not. "It'd be very useful to have a human account for purposes of comparison. For fact-checking, as it were."

Macauley shook his head. "I've thought about it, naturally. After all, there's so much of our history that'll vanish with us old folks if no one preserves it. But after all the years of having people demand things from me, I find it's rather difficult to demand things of myself. I'm glad you came along to boost my willpower a bit. Perhaps I'll get started after you leave!"

Seth took a small sip of the liqueur. (Palatable, at best.) "What a good idea! And you could warm up for the task by remembering out loud, here, with me. For example, there's the period your descendants will most want to hear about, when their ancestors first arrived. You must have so many memories of those days."

Macauley took a large sip of his drink and rolled it around in his mouth, then swallowed and sighed in satisfaction. "You know, I didn't touch a drop from the day we sighted the planet until the day I retired. Oh, I'd have liked to, either to celebrate the good times or to escape the cares of the anxious ones, but I needed to stay sharp. Everyone was depending on me."

"That's very admirable. Your colony was lucky to have such a dedicated leader. Were you in charge throughout the journey?"

Macauley tensed and sat forward, his sudden change in posture making the lightweight lawn chair teeter for a moment. "No. When we went through the wormhole . . . Our captain found the effects too much for him. We had no idea what to expect, you see. I gather you somehow knew more about it?"

Seth would have liked to explain how he had predicted the basics of the wormhole experience and prepared his comrades, but he wanted to get Macauley past this part of the story before it spoiled the mood. He simply nodded.

"Well, the captain had a nervous breakdown. He didn't recover very quickly, so quite a few of the colonists found out about it. He lost their confidence. I was one of the younger officers, and more resilient. The crew turned to me."

"How soon after leaving the wormhole did you find the planet? Or did you know about it already, before going through?"

Macauley chuckled and relaxed. "Oh, we knew where we were going! We could see the planet through the wormhole almost three weeks before we went through it." Seth mentally chalked up a second tally mark: *Star Seed* had once again done better. But he did his best to look impressed.

"When did you find out about the Camos?" Seth was gambling that Macauley would appreciate his use of the first colonists' original term for the local inhabitants. Macauley looked a bit startled, and Seth feared he had miscalculated, but the moment passed: Macauley shrugged, took another swallow of the liqueur, and sat back in his chair. "We saw them flying around on our scanner footage, but even after we saw those belts of theirs, we weren't sure what to think. I— we assumed at first that there was some other sentient species that put the belts on them for their own purposes. When we reached the planet, we orbited several times looking for that species." He leaned forward and lowered his voice. "In fact, there are still some of our people who claim to believe that there's another species, a humanoid one, hiding somewhere on the planet, and that they trained the Camos to make those belts and build the cliff dwellings and so on."

That went some way toward explaining how clumsily the first human settlers had managed their human-Glider diplomacy. If Seth's own parents and their fellows had not settled on Tofarn and been a minority species for several generations, they might have been just as ill-prepared to assess and deal with a planet full of nonhuman inhabitants.

Although . . . Seth reached for the liqueur and took a

larger swallow, almost a gulp. It might not be his favorite, but it would wash away the sour taste in his mouth as he remembered just how difficult and perilous human-Tofa relations had become, before the Project. And how little they knew, even now, of what might be happening between the two species, back on Tofarn, since communication had been lost.

* * *

("Well, that's another fine mess you've gotten us into. Unquote.")

("Don't joke right now! I'm scared and frustrated and in pain. And if I laugh, it makes everything hurt more.")

("My apologies, Sis. How long do you think it'll be before someone finds us?")

Mara tried to reach her tablet to see if it could by any chance still send a message. The effort sent a sharp stab through her free arm, her side, and her hip. She shouted a curse, then gritted her teeth and tried again. This time she was able to snag the corner and tug the device out from under the mess of shattered wing and entangled limbs. Scooting it up toward her head, she assessed the bent case and broken screen. "Here goes nothing." She hit the wakeup button and was not in the least surprised when nothing was indeed what happened.

("Well, I won't be able to call anyone, or to check when the next fliers are due. But I think Anna and her daughter are supposed to show up in a couple of hours. By the way, go ahead and say it.")

("No need. We both know what I said. But I will, with your permission, do a little psychoanalyzing about why you ignored my advice, and your own knowledge of basic safety, to go gliding without a buddy.")

("The hell you will.") Mara punched the button again, with the same result.

("Your childhood and adolescence were singularly lacking in adventure and spontaneity. Your peers—well, they were hardly that, but the larvae you grew up with—made sure you were aware of the fact. Now, after decades and light-years, you surprised yourself—")

("And you.")

("Oh, no. I knew you had it in you.—Surprised yourself by jumping off a cliff and enjoying it, and now you're determined—Damn!")

("What is it?")

("Seems that when you're in this much pain, I can't keep it out, not completely. Ouch! *Shit*! What's so great about risk again?")

("Now you're scaring me. You never grumble. Think about something else, like how to get us out of this.") Mara pushed herself up on her relatively uninjured arm, enough to turn her head. At least she hadn't managed to break her neck.

("Levi! Is that a Glider on that rise over there?") All she could see was movement, two reddish tones moving in relation to each other.

("Maybe. Try yelling again. Something scandalous, to get their attention.")

The hope of rescue was reviving Mara's sense of humor. Craning upwards as far as she could, she hollered, "MARA CADELL IS A CRAZY OLD IDIOT WHO SHOULD HAVE WAITED FOR A FLYING BUDDY!"

She collapsed again, groaning.

("Yup, that hurt. But it was worth it. Look.")

A dot of red was definitely moving, moving closer, up and down, kicking up shimmering dust. Then came others, just behind; and now she could hear, faintly, the trills of excited Gliders.

While she waited, she took stock of her injuries. ("Arm, shoulder, leg, ribs. What about insides? Did I damage anything major?")

("I'm a little concerned about how things feel in your abdomen. But we'll know soon enough.")

"What did Fel-lar have to say?" Harriet Gaho finished strapping a bandage around Mara's ribs.

Mara started to shake her head, then halted as the motion reawakened various discomforts. "I've never seen him so angry. Well, not in quite a few years. And never at me. You should check me for frostbite." How long would it have taken for him to relent, if Mara had not been feeling so uncharacteristically fragile? He must have been almost as surprised to see her cry as she had been to see his fury. Artemesia had told her once about the odor, like a poisonous gas, that had rolled off of Hal-tet after he rescued her from attempted rape. It might have been the chemical, however emitted, that first brought tears to Mara's eyes. But she had cried; and crying had eroded, as if washing away, what little energy she had left. She would have collapsed if Fel-lar had not rushed over to catch her. But she had not allowed him to apologize. He had every right to be angry.

"Well, you won't be flying again for quite a while, so carelessness brings its own punishment. Just be glad we can help the bones and muscles along, instead of waiting for them to heal in their own sweet time."

"And there's nothing worse? Internally?" But she already knew. Harriet was too cheerful, in a businesslike way, to be waiting with any dire tidings.

"Nothing to worry about. Mind, you came a mite close to perforating your uterus with that big splinter. That might have made up your mind for you about having kids someday, if it didn't heal up right." Harriet helped her down off the table. "I'm sorry you have to give up your fun for now. It's been good to see you play, after all this time. But next time, don't push your luck."

* * *

("Levi?")

("She's asleep, Fel-lar. We can chat a bit—if there's something you wanted to say.")

("Only that I am sorry.")

("You were hard on her. You should know that she's been kicking herself already. And with a broken leg yet.")

("What happened? Was it really an accident?")

("I think so. We're still at the trial-and-error stage with this gliding game. You're imagining conspiracies?")

("I am always concerned for Mara's safety. And complacency did not serve us well in the past.")

("Ahem. You younger folk may have been oblivious, but Mara wasn't—Mara and I weren't—complacent. We knowingly took risks, starting with creating you lot—risks a good deal more worthwhile than jumping off mountains strapped to a tinker-toy.")

("A what?")

("You played with them, back at the Project. These.")

("Oh, yes. None of the teachers used that name. I hope the wings are considerably sturdier. . . . Mara will not allow me to apologize. But I will bring her hot chocolate in bed, tomorrow morning.")

("You might miss the chance if you don't go to sleep. Which will let me do the same, more or less. If one of you is awake, then so am I.")

("Then sleep, my friend. Go to Mara in her dreams, and help me hold her close.")

Chapter 13

(Tofarn)

JAK-RAD-TAN read the pamphlet with a blend of amusement and dismay. Apparently the more reactionary elements had begun to adopt their opponents' methods and spread their screeds on paper. But written Tofar, generally used for scientific and historical purposes, was not ideally suited for propaganda. Emotional content could be conveyed only with blunt ideographs.

Alert [alarm]! Did you know your parental authority may be threatened [alarm] by the latest ideas [ridicule] of those who compulsively imitate humans?

Your children look to you as their parent [pride], and society looks to you to control and guide them. But what if another adult [alarm] can claim to be their parent as well? To whom will your children look then for direction and nurture?

Jak-rad-tan skimmed the rest to ensure that the pamphlet was indeed talking about his own idea of identifying spore-parents. He started to crumple it in his strongest hand, then paused. Were the concerns expressed so different from his own?

How would he feel if Lan-sol's spore-parent, once identified, had ideas about Lan-sol's future incompatible with Jak-rad-tan's own? And Lan-sol at least was near adulthood. Was he willing to share the duties and decisions involved in parenting the younger children? Especially little Ved-rad. What if Ved-rad's spore-parent tried to exercise control, the coercive techniques that had for so long been accepted child-rearing practice? Would a spore-parent have greater control over a child than any other Tofa adult?

Jak-rad-tan smoothed out the paper and examined it

further. It closed with notice of a rally, to be held across town this very afternoon. He would clear his schedule and attend.

The site of the rally had been chosen to accommodate considerably more Tofa than those actually present. That might be the downside of the pamphlet approach: those most receptive to the message would never bother to look at paper in the first place. But the speaker did not let the relatively small audience dampen his ardor. He declaimed and gestured with a passion just short of parody.

The speech and the pamphlet differed little in content, but Jak-rad-tan had to concede the speech's impact. Of course the telepathic components of Tofar would be more effective than any writing. The pamphleteers had used a two-step technique Jak-rad-tan would have to remember: use paper or other nonpersonal media to attract attention, then direct the consumers to an occasion where they would receive more potent propaganda.

And now the speaker was explicitly addressing human "contamination" of Tofa social values. "These attempts to contort Tofa society into an alien shape have gone too far! Will you at last see what is happening and take warning? ..."

The speech ended; the crowd dispersed, with many of its members in conversation with each other. Jak-rad-tan drifted here and there in an effort to eavesdrop. He did not manage to hear much, but among those he heard, pamphlet and speech together appeared to have made an impression.

Jak-rad-tan walked slowly back to his office. If spore-parent identification was to remain an option, he and other proponents would have to come up with some safeguards to limit the societal upheavals that might result—and the political upheavals that might follow them.

* * *

Ton-lal-set heard the key in the lock, presumably heralding the arrival of food, and realized that he must decide how to use his new freedom of movement on such occasions. Should he be ostentatiously relaxed against the leaning post, or in some posture from which he could more easily defend himself if necessary? The latter would be prudent. But the door opened before he could do more than take a step away from the door.

The guard who had brought him to this new cell entered with a tray and set the tray on the bed. He glanced toward the open doorway and muttered, "I cannot stay long on this occasion. But if you have any urgent questions, I will try to answer them."

Ton-lal-set ignored the tray and reclined against the post. "Tell me about any allies you have in other regions, and how they are assisting any other Eminences similarly situated."

The guard looked over his shoulder and back at Ton-lal-set, radiating nervousness. "We have little information on such matters. Inquiries would be dangerous, and gossip is unreliable."

Ton-lal-set suppressed his displeasure at the response. He might not have completely succeeded: the guard took a step backward and stammered, "But once our efforts on your behalf prove fruitful, no doubt our example will inspire others elsewhere." He did not wait for a response before giving a short and jerky sideways bow and slipping back through the door.

*　*　*

Tofa rarely expected humans to understand their speech.

Veda would have enjoyed walking in Central Park in any event. The park designers had done a fine job with the paths and the plantings, the play areas and the picnic tables. She particularly liked the alternation of spiny and feathery trees, and the clever way the dining areas were hidden until one suddenly came upon them. But she might have visited the park less often if not for the chance to eavesdrop. She could understand Tofa better than she could speak it, and she never knew when she might pick up news that the human leadership needed to know, or gain new insight into Tofa customs. Or she might simply happen on a piquant anecdote or two.

So when the path led her toward a tall table at which three Tofa were standing, leaning toward each other with some intensity, she made what she hoped was a subtle transition from striding to strolling. And as she came within earshot—easy to do, given the volume and intensity of the conversation—she found a nearby bench, sat down, and pulled out her tablet as if reading. She would have liked to take notes, but the idea struck her as imprudent. With luck she would remember any essential points.

" . . . blue, from that planet the mutants live on! And he *denied* it! I had to force him to tell me that he even possessed the recording, and then where he had hidden it. It had been so long since I needed to enforce his obedience, I was almost unable to do so. What if I had failed?"

The Tofa closest to the speaker pressed two left hands together to express sympathy. "Scandalous! But it may not have been his age, or the passage of time. I have heard that repeated exposure to blue can coarsen a youngster's temperament and make him less responsive to authority."

"Where are they obtaining these recordings?" The third Tofa glanced around as if searching for blue dealers. Veda bent her head over her tablet and relaxed her neck and shoulders. Never mind me, I'm just sitting here reading . . . .

"Where do you think?" The first Tofa, the aggrieved parent, was practically shouting. "That planet is overrun with humans! And they want to undermine Tofa society, in revenge for our having resisted human tyranny here!"

The third Tofa pulled all his arms inward and curled his torso. "It's not just the humans. They have allies. Allies all around us. Tofa who can't see what's going on. The kind of Tofa who believe all that about the spore project, and how it's *protecting* us."

Veda almost looked up, catching herself just in time. Was this sort of talk what had spurred the demand for additional testing? Did the leadership know about it?

The first Tofa spoke again, but this time barely above a whisper, leaning so far toward the others that he looked likely to overbalance. "Do you think—is that why the young people are so defiant, so absorbed in unwholesome pleasures? Is it something they've done to the spores?"

The sympathetic Tofa gave the almost inaudible hum for a polite expression of sorrow. "If only our former Eminence had retained his position. . . ."

The third Tofa recoiled, shoving himself rigidly upright and stepping back from the table. "You mustn't say such things, not here!" But his calmer companion reached out an upper hand to forestall any abrupt departure. And now all three Tofa left the table and clustered together, muttering so quietly that Veda could no longer hear.

Veda sat up and stretched, languidly, putting her tablet away and rising casually to her feet. She let her gaze pass with obvious disinterest across the incomprehensible aliens as she returned to the path and walked away.

Now what?

So the deposed Ton-lal-set had sympathizers. She had no idea, and the Tofa she had overheard might not even know, whether Ton-lal-set was still alive. And Gen-tar-ten might know all about the rumors she had heard, and the nostalgia as well. For all she knew, one of the three Tofa had actually been one of Gen-tar-ten's agents.

She should get word to Gen-tar-ten, all the same. But how best to do so? Most likely he had little desire to hear from her at present.

But no one, as far as she knew, had ever flatly refused an overture from Laura.

*   *   *

Laura sighed. Of course she understood why Veda had asked her to serve as messenger; but how to accomplish this without appearing to act on behalf of the Council, involving her fellow members in whatever uproar might result? Her role in the spore project, including her list of contacts, had been carefully defined to avoid such difficulties.

But Veda would realize all that. Her making use of Laura in spite of these complications underscored the importance of the information to be conveyed.

Perhaps it was time, finally, to retire from the Council. Sapir would probably like that, as much as he claimed that the public benefits of her demanding work schedule outweighed the drawbacks for him personally. And Gen-tar-ten could be one of the first to know, which he might conceivably appreciate.

Gen-tar-ten summoned Laura after only a ten-minute wait. Laura entered the inner office and tried to conceal her tension as she waited to see whether Gen-tar-ten would close the office door. He did not always bother to do so, and she could hardly insist. Nor did she want to give any audible hints of her mission while the door remained open. But whether by good fortune or by a surprising skill at reading human body language, Gen-tar-ten looked in her eyes briefly and then pushed the door closed.

Gen-tar-ten generally provided human visitors with a chair, and while less luxurious than Gen-tar-ten's leaning post, it was reasonably comfortable. Laura sat and prepared to exchange opening pleasantries; but Gen-tar-ten faced her and held up an upper hand to cut her off. "We need not waste time. It is my impression that you have something of importance to discuss. Please proceed."

Gen-tar-ten stood beside his leaning post, stiff and immobile, as Laura gave her report. Nor did he speak immediately once she was done. She would have liked to stretch her arms and legs, releasing the tension of the last few minutes; but Gen-tar-ten might find the process puzzling, even impolite.

Finally, Gen-tar-ten took a visible breath, leaned back against his post, and looked at Laura. "I thank you for coming. Did Veda explain why she preferred to send you in her stead?"

That was not so simple a question. Veda had offered as little explanation as Laura would allow, referring only to some unexpected friction between Gen-tar-ten and herself at their last meeting. Should she admit even that much? Years of government service had much improved Laura's ability to lie. But given how difficult it would be to foresee the impact of her words, she would rather that any unintended consequences spring from the truth, or a diplomatically phrased version of the truth, rather than from falsehood. "She said she had been so unfortunate as to displease you in some way."

"And she thought it likely that my displeasure would distract me from important information? No, I am quite able to put aside such trivialities." He buzzed briefly under his breath before going on. "This information is not altogether surprising. But it is worth knowing, nonetheless. Did our friend Veda say how old these Tofa appeared to be?"

Had she? Laura had been afraid of such followup questions, most of which she would be unable to answer. "I think I told you that one of them, at least, was a parent. And if Veda's phrasing reflected the actual conversation, one of them said something about 'our' former Eminence."

"As if he had been a cognizant adult during that era. Yes." Gen-tar-ten tapped his upper fingers together in an arpeggio sequence back and forth. "Have you shared this information with the rest of your Council?"

"Not yet. I will probably find it necessary to do so at some point, although I am open to requests about—about how to characterize the situation."

Gen-tar-ten gave the quietest of whistles. "I have little intrinsic interest in how humans conduct their affairs, as I hope the Council has little interest in interfering with ours. My sole concern is to avoid such interference. I may need to take certain measures in response to incipient insurrection or subversive activities. Should these come to the Council's attention and provoke any degree of consternation, I would ask that you explain their cause."

Chapter 14

(New Landing)

SUZIE HAD been the first human Twin-Bred to marry a member of the earlier colony. Now, his untimely funeral brought the two colonies together once again, gathering in the valley near the Twin-Bred settlement where years before the couple had said their vows.

Fel-lar and the retired administrator Macauley presided together over the brief ceremony. At its conclusion, Suzie's twin Mat-set helped her climb the path to the nearest ledge and cast her husband's ashes to the wind. An escort of Gliders followed the drifting ashes for a moment, then returned to the valley floor.

The crowd of humans and Tofa drifted slowly away, leaving the widow and her children to mourn further in private. Suzie clasped her daughter to her side, while Mat-set watched over Suzie's young son as the boy toddled about, curious about the gathering and oblivious as to its meaning.

Fel-lar looked on as Anna came over and held out her arms to the widow. Suzie ran into them, letting go of her daughter, who clutched at her leg and stumbled along beside her. Jimmy came to stand beside Anna, but backed away at Anna's warning expression. This was not the time and place for exemplars of spousal devotion.

Fel-lar approached in his place, adding a lower hand to the embrace and using an upper hand to stroke Suzie's hair. Suzie had earlier seemed too stunned to cry, but now she broke down and sobbed on Anna's shoulder, with the little girl soon following her mother's example.

Mat-set came over, toddler in tow, and tapped the girl on the shoulder. "Your brother is missing his sister, I think. Would you look after him for now? I would like to consult

Fel-lar about something." The girl wiped her eyes and held out her hand to her brother, who clutched it and stared up at her with wide round eyes, then tugged her away to examine the view from the nearest cliff. Mat-set found his and Fel-lar's twins, standing close together and silent amid the mourners, and murmured something inaudible; the pair moved within grabbing distance of Suzie's children.

Fel-lar detached himself from Anna and Suzie, where he appeared to be accomplishing little in the way of comfort for the bereaved, and followed Mat-set to the periphery of the dwindling crowd. "With what can I assist you?"

"You can tell me whether to dissuade my sister—if I can—from joining the crew of *Star Seed* and leaving us all behind."

"The ship? Why would Suzie do that?" As soon as he asked, Fel-lar knew the answer. "To see her mother."

"Even before the accident, Suzie was struggling with sadness and guilt about Tilda. Family has always been so important to Suzie. Tilda would never really know her grandchildren, Tilda would never sing her grandson a lullaby, Suzie would not be there to care for Tilda when she grew older . . . and so on."

Fel-lar looked back over at Suzie, now sitting on an outcropping of stone and staring across the canyon while Anna looked after the children. "Do you share any of these feelings? After all, Tilda was your host mother as well."

Mat-set shook his head in the Tofa Twin-Bred manner. "I was, of course, grateful for her participation in the Project, and I appreciated her nurturing. But Suzie's and Tilda's personalities meshed remarkably, though not necessarily in a way that gave Suzie the greatest chance of developing an independent spirit. They share a certain vulnerability, and a great need to give and especially to receive affection."

Fel-lar looked around at the landscape, so utterly different from the forests and rivers of their former home, different even to the color of the sky. "And now that her family here is incomplete, the contrast with her memories becomes ever more painful."

He looked back at Anna, holding the hands of Suzie's children as they strained toward their mother. "But would she take the children on a journey so full of uncertainties and possible danger?"

Mat-set clasped three hands together. "She may prove unwilling to confront that aspect of the situation. I fear her grasp on reality is becoming tenuous."

Who, in Tilda's absence, could get through to Suzie and halt her emotional deterioration? But of course! Not the soft and yielding foster mother, but the Mother of them all. Fel-lar quickly took leave of Mat-set, promising that they would talk again soon, and strode away to find Mara.

Fel-lar spent the rest of the afternoon with Mat-set, babysitting Suzie's children. By evening he had gained new respect for the many community members who managed to keep up with human youngsters. Even Suzie must have undreamt-of reserves of strength to manage it.

He made his way into the living room to find Mara collapsed in an armchair, eyes closed, face haggard with fatigue. Clearly, dealing with the mother had been even more exhausting than his own task. He stood behind the chair and massaged her temples with his lower hands. "What did you say, and how well did you succeed?"

"Ohhh. Don't ask me questions while you're saving my life. That feels wonderful."

Fel-lar whistled softly and continued his efforts. After a few minutes, Mara sat up and stretched. "All right, back to life and its godawful tangles. . . . I laid down the law. It was her turn to be the parent, and so on. I ran through a few scary scenarios about what the ship might encounter, and asked her how Tilda would feel about her grandchildren disappearing into a wormhole or drifting forever in space."

Fel-lar flinched. "That is what I supposed you would need to say, but the details are harrowing. How did she respond?"

"At first I thought I'd overdone it. She curled up in a ball. Well, by then I couldn't really reverse course, so I just sat there and waited. When she started to uncurl a bit, I put down the stick and picked up the carrot. I told her that we—which of course really means you and Anna and the rest of the leadership—*would* re-establish contact with Tofarn, come what may. And that once we'd done so, one of the first orders of business would be working out the protocols for occasional travel between our planets for those who wanted it."

Fel-lar leaned against the post opposite Mara's chair, watching and admiring the play of thoughts and feelings in her face. "I presume the combined approach was more effective."

"Oh, yes. All I had to do was promise the quite-possibly impossible, and she sat up and wiped her face and apologized. Then she was off to tell the children that if they were patient, they'd all get to go with her someday soon to see Granny." Mara shook her head, then pressed the heels of her hands into her forehead. "Remind me to run the other way the next time you ask me to play the tribal sage."

*   *   *

"I thought you would be singing your final song once and only once." Seth Baruti strove for a matter-of-fact rather than an injured tone.

Wings Spread Wide peered at him with a bright side eye. "That has certainly been the custom until now. But that custom assumes the elder will remain on the planet while composing and completing the song. What if some misfortune, one of the many possible misfortunes, prevents me from returning—or weakens me so that I would be unable to sing so long a work? I have discussed the question with several of the Twin-Bred, and one of them told me about the archaic human art form, Previews of Coming Attractions." (Seth bit his lip to keep from smiling, even though the Glider might not have noticed.) "Since my waning days are already suffused with change, I will embrace this novelty as well."

There were no children in this audience. While Seth could not call himself an expert in assessing Glider ages, he had the impression that most of those in attendance were elderly or close to that status. Was that part of the custom for the final song? Or had Wings Spread Wide thoughtfully invited those who might no longer be present for the ship's return?

And Seth was the only human guest. He did not bother to suppress or conceal his pride.

Rides Above Danger swooped in, holding an instrument for which the translator had so far failed to find a suitable name. Wings Spread Wide, possibly having realized Seth's dislike of last-minute surprises, had already explained that final songs included an accompanist. The instrument resembled a Glider's wing, abstracted and curved in an attractive though anatomically unlikely shape. The younger Glider took its perch and began to tune up or warm up, tapping the thinnest struts with its beak, running a finger or a wingtip along others.

The usual pre-concert mutter and jangle subsided as Wings Spread Wide emerged from an inner room and, with visible effort, assumed the high central perch. The elder waited for perfect silence before it began to sing.

Seth enjoyed Glider music more than did many humans. (He had never cared greatly for percussion instruments, the most conspicuous omission.) While scholarly debate continued, there might be a correlation, among humans at least, between appreciation of complex music and mathematical ability, although Mara's disinterest in the music varied from that pattern. Tofa were almost all enthusiasts where Glider music was concerned, adding another datum in support of the hypothesis that Tofa had an innate capacity for science and technology greater than their progress to date would suggest. If their society ever began to reward innovation and experiment, then the humans on Tofarn had best look to their laurels.

Seth recorded the concert for later translation and analysis, a choice for which he hoped Wings Spread Wide's permission was implied. He preferred, on first hearing, to appreciate the song purely for its musical qualities, but the historical information it contained must be preserved as well.

It was, naturally, a splendid composition. Wings Spread Wide had likely attained his present social stature not merely from age or even diplomatic achievements, but from a lifetime of artistic predominance. The clamor of appreciation at the end gave Seth a headache in short order. The elder spread its wings over and over as if confirming the appropriateness of its name, but as the applause went on, the breadth of the Glider's wingspan began declining little by little. And even when the applause subsided, the audience crowded around the singer, their wings surely reducing the amount of fresh air reaching Wings Spread Wide from the open window.

Seth sought out Rides Above Danger. "The master appears weary. How can we bring this evening to a close?"

Rides Above Danger, in response, extracted itself from its own admirers and pushed through to the elder's side, placing one wing behind its teacher's back. The crowd immediately receded and cleared an exit to the window, but Wings Spread Wide turned back and gestured toward the inner room from which it had earlier appeared. "I will rest there for a while before I go home. Thank you all."

Seth turned to the younger Glider. "I'd be glad to go with him and make sure he's comfortable. You have fans here still hoping to congratulate you."

Wings Spread Wide rested on a perch placed in an alcove lined with woven tapestries, so that the Glider would not injure itself should its grasp on the perch give way. It had tucked its head under one wing; the wings rose and fell slightly, not quite fluttering, with each slow breath.

Seth watched his friend sleep with a tenderness paradoxically bordering on paternal. It must, he mused, be an evolutionary adaptation to feel protective of sleepers, or their vulnerability would have posed too great a peril. Did the Tofa share this tendency? Or did their failure to dream arise from the need to wake more swiftly, so as to confront any approaching Tofa who might prove hostile? Did they in fact wake more easily than humans? The Twin-Bred would know, and those humans who lived with them, but Seth had never attained that level of intimacy with any of the species.

And yet here he stood, watching an alien sleep.

* * *

Mara finished packing up the remains of the picnic she and Fel-lar had just shared, then lay down on the blanket with her head on her arms and her knees in the air. "I still don't understand it. Why would anyone want me on the mission? I'm no longer a leader, thank God. We have no reason to expect my scientific training to be of use. I'm hopeless as a diplomat. And if there's any sort of rescue mission involved, a skinny middle-aged lady hardly makes the best soldier material."

Fel-lar promptly undid Mara's efforts by digging down into the picnic basket and retrieving a somewhat ragged hunk of cheese, then leaned back against the cliff side to grind away at it. "You persist in ignoring your unique place in Twin-Bred psychology. When Jimmy and Peer-tek experimented with Doctor Cadell worship in their younger years, they were not being entirely facetious. You created the Twin-Bred, in the sense of imagining them and causing your imagination to become reality. And then, you led the exodus that saved them from slavery or extinction. To borrow elements of the Terran Judeo-Christian legend, you combine key attributes of Jehovah, the Creator, and Moses, who led his people out of Egypt. Your presence would be profoundly reassuring on a level beyond immediate practicality."

Mara reached out for a many-faceted pebble and raised herself up just enough to hurl it toward the cliff at a safe distance from where Fel-lar was lounging. "If there's any truth to that analysis, we should start weaning the lot of them from this bizarre dependence. And, contrariwise, if the Twin-Bred find me so comforting to have around, what about the vast majority of them who'll be staying right here?"

Fel-lar ignored the question. "As for needing your scientific capabilities, the expedition is more likely to encounter unprecedented scientific dilemmas. You remain one of our finest scientific synthesists." Fel-lar finished ingesting the cheese and looked down at his empty hand. "There is also another factor." He hesitated, then moved to where Mara could see him without changing position. "If I go with the ship, I would like to have you there."

"*You* go?? What brought this on? Why you?"

Fel-lar turned and took a few steps, then reversed direction, then repeated the pattern. Mara sat upright. "Are you *pacing*? What's got into you, that you're picking up my bad habits?"

Fel-lar halted and faced her again. "I am profoundly suspicious of this communications failure. I suspect intentional interference. And while I have not managed to conceive of a likely motive, I have what we may call a 'hunch' that our original enemies are involved. If any of the Eminences survive, they may have set yet another scheme in motion."

Mara hauled herself up, managing not to wince at the twinge from her ribs. She walked over and took Fel-lar's lower left hand, massaging it gently, then more vigorously as she felt the tension in it. "This didn't start with the communications failure. I'm guessing that just validated a fear you had already."

Fel-lar lifted their joined hands and blew gently on the back of Mara's. "I wonder at times whether my connection with Levi helps you know me so well, or whether you would find me an open book regardless."

"Damned if I know. But you're not itching to back to Tofarn because you're afraid. Tell me more."

Fel-lar twitched away as if to start pacing again. Mara held his hand firmly, and he desisted. "Returning to Moses. He grew up a prince of Egypt. And in the end, his greatest victory was to run away, with all his people. They, unlike him, had been raised as slaves. But what if all of them had shared the same princely goals and expectations?" Fel-lar was humming now, with that uniquely Tofa ability to hum and speak at the same time. "How much pride could any of them take in leaving all those dreams behind—no matter how long or short their journey to some substitute promised land, some distant Canaan?" The humming grew louder, and she had to strain to understand his words. "Would he not wonder whether he should have stayed to fight? To strike at least one blow?"

Mara searched the cliff face and found uneven stone on which she could step. She climbed up, working to maintain her balance, and reached a cautious arm around Fel-lar's neck. He stopped humming and grabbed her arm with an upper hand to steady her and draw her close. That left her other hand free to stroke his cheek. "So recent events have jarred all these feelings loose. And that's why you've been— different lately. Less calm. Less patient."

"Less patient, and easier to anger. Which is why you should allow me, after all, to apologize for directing that anger at you, when you were hurt."

"All right, if it'll make you feel better. Now enough of that. Fel-lar, are you really thinking of flying back across the galaxy because you're spoiling for a fight?"

Fel-lar unwrapped Mara's arm from around himself, grasped her carefully under the arms, and lifted her down from the ledge. Then he moved the picnic basket aside and picked up the blanket, folding it rapidly with all four hands. "I may not have mentioned that I have been studying military history and tactics from time to time."

Mara reached for the blanket without looking Fel-lar in the face and put the blanket in the basket. "No, you didn't."

"I do not want a fight to be necessary. I would prefer that all this proves to be 'much ado about nothing.' But if anyone must fight to protect our friends on Tofarn: well, I am no longer too young, if I was then. I am a leader, by my people's choice. And I am ready to do battle."

Chapter 15

(Tofarn)

FINALLY, the familiar guard put in an appearance other than his brief mealtime visits, this time accompanied by two strangers. The previous visitor did not appear. Ton-lal-set asked, rather sharply, why not; the guard assumed a submissive posture Ton-lal-set had not seen in far too long, and explained that the gatherings must be kept small enough to be easily concealed. "It mattered most that today's companions have the honor of meeting you."

Ton-lal-set had put the intervening time and solitude to productive use. "I have considered the attempts being made by our enemies to identify the sources of spores. The matter has more aspects than our absent associate had grasped." He paused for effect, running his left fingers along the edge of the leaning post, then continued. "The humans, of whom I learned so much in my years at the Project, have several useful aphorisms dealing with conflict and war. One of these is the advice to 'Know Your Enemy.'

"By all means, we should oppose the widespread use of this human technology. But if we are able, through pressure or purchase, to obtain this information concerning the origins of our more important foes, it may prove fruitful. Perhaps one or more will prove to have lowly or otherwise embarrassing connections."

His listeners buzzed appreciation of his cleverness and foresight. The taller of the newcomers ventured to speak. "That Lan-sol upstart would be worth investigating. There are too many young people eager to imitate his every move."

Ton-lal-set put a lower hand back to grip the leaning post, then deliberately relaxed the hand. How many years since he had heard that name? Of course, during his thwarted effort to eliminate Jak-rad's fetus, he had no idea that the rebellious young Tofa had gone so far as to name the creature in his womb. But the charges leveled at Ton-lal-set had prominently featured the name, and the mobs through which he was led to prison had chanted it over and over. . . .

He must not appear emotionally affected. "Toward what destination is this Lan-sol leading his followers?"

To his surprise, the others seemed to find his question somehow embarrassing. After much shifting about, the two new visitors turned toward the guard, who stared back at them, then looked off toward an unoccupied corner of the room and said, "At the moment, Lan-sol is planning to lead a small number into space. They are building another ship."

Ton-lal-set jolted upright, the post teetering back and forth behind him. "A ship? *A SHIP?*"

All three of the visitors jerked their heads toward the door, and the guard ran to it and put his head against it, apparently listening for any reaction to Ton-lal-set's outraged bellow. He must not forget his present circumstances. Majestic roars of displeasure belonged to his former state. He must not indulge himself in any behavior that could return him to the solitary and stinking cell from which he had been delivered, or deter those who might be willing to assist him further.

Neither the jailer-conspirator nor any others reappeared for ten days—Ton-lal-set had resumed keeping track of time—after the meeting that ended with his intemperate outburst. Ton-lal-set thus discovered that there was, after all, something worse than utter tedium and hopelessness. The revival of hope followed by uncertainty constituted a more acute form of torture.

When the guard finally returned, bringing with him the same Tofa as had appeared when Ton-lal-set received his new quarters, Ton-lal-set's relief was such that he had to suppress an impulse to express gratitude or appear overly welcoming. He attempted to make his greeting somewhere between gracious and imperious. He must have succeeded well enough: their response was deferential, and not unduly relaxed.

After that initial exchange, the guard's demeanor

became almost smug. "We will have less time pressure than on previous occasions. There is a pregnancy celebration for the senior jailer's deputy—who is one of our number. He and I have feigned antagonism recently, which now acts as my excuse to absent myself from the festivities."

The other visitor also seemed pleased with himself, but in a more excited key. "I have been waiting since before our first encounter to tell you about a clandestine project, prepared years ago by one of our operatives and now in progress. It should reduce the Twin-Bred influence on our society, especially our young people, and allow us to concentrate on our local adversaries."

He paused dramatically, then glanced in annoyance at the guard when the latter interrupted. "Eminence, you may not be aware that the Twin-Bred expedition encountered a separate human colony, as well as a third sentient species, at its destination."

"What was that?" The title of Eminence, so long withheld, had distracted Ton-lal-set momentarily from what the guard actually had to say. The guard repeated his statement, then continued. "The Twin-Bred therefore pose an even greater threat of alien influence on our society than they would otherwise have done."

The visitor moved in front of the guard, shoving him backward, and resumed his account. "We have succeeded in cutting off communications from the Twin-Bred colony to Gen-tar-ten and his allies, as well as the reverse. The messages from both locations have been diverted and stored for our—" He glanced at Ton-lal-set. "—For your future perusal."

The lessons of the last ten days had been well learned. Ton-lal-set did not explode in wrath. Instead, he stood at his tallest, then leaned very slightly forward in the other's direction and said nothing at all. Predictably, the visitor began to manifest surprise and discomfort, and finally asked in a less confident tone, "Is there some adjustment you command?"

Ton-lal-set finally allowed himself the luxury of sarcasm. "If you or your clandestine operative have managed to locate or invent a machine for traveling in time, I will give you yourself the mission of going back to countermand the operative's instructions. Otherwise, we must direct our efforts toward minimizing the damage you have done."

The fellow was not sufficiently cowed to accept this assessment without protest. "Perhaps your confinement has made it difficult for you to keep abreast of developments and properly assess the desirability—"

"Perhaps," Ton-lal-set hissed, "my many years' exposure to both the Twin-Bred and the humans who created them has enabled me to predict their likely reaction to the possibility that their friends, allies, and relatives on Tofarn have been attacked."

The visitor stepped back, then stepped forward again, though by a lesser distance. "As valuable as your knowledge and experience must be, it should not matter greatly how the Twin-Bred community reacts, when it can no longer communicate its reaction."

Ton-lal-set tensed his upper fingers together into points and shook his hands in the other's face, while the guard shrank backward toward the corner. "Idiot! *They can build ships!* They already have one, and they can build others! And their numbers have grown—not only by their own increase, but by who knows how many additional humans!"

Ton-lal-set relaxed his upper hands and waved them at the conspirators in contemptuous dismissal. "I assume you have not actually rendered the communications system permanently inoperative?"

The guard replied from his corner. "No, Eminence. It can be re-engaged when you require it."

"We must send a message purporting to come from Gen-tar-ten, or Jak-rad-tan, or Lan-sol—I will consider which would be most credible. It will explain the communications failure in some innocuous way, and describe how peaceful and quiescent the Tofa community has remained. I will, of course, compose the message. Bring me writing materials."

The guard hesitated. "It will be easier to do so unobserved if you will accept paper rather than metal as the medium."

"Very well. Make sure the sheets are small enough to conceal." If he had been in his old, barren cell, he could never have managed it. "You may inquire in two or three days whether I have completed the message."

Had he, as the game-loving humans used to say, overplayed his hand? Would the visitor, who after all had no current objective reason to fear Ton-lal-set's anger, acknowledge his dominance? It appeared so: both Tofa departed with repeated apologies and thanks, promising to return as per his dictates. He may as well assume he had prevailed.

What message could he send? What would convince the humans and half-breeds? He must allow himself—force himself—to remember everything he could of his Project days, and the behavior he had adopted to survive and function in that alien environment. He would call upon his past self to revive and assist him in this most delicate task.

Chapter 16

(New Landing)

MARA COULD not remember the last time the congressional leadership had asked her to attend a Cabinet meeting. They all knew—certainly, Fel-lar and Anna knew—that she preferred not to be dragged back into politics; and at least some of the Cabinet members shared that preference, viewing her as a relic who would be likely to push obsolete notions. When Fel-lar wished to consult her, he usually did so in the privacy of their home, the confidentiality of the discussion presumed and occasionally stated aloud to remind them both.

It was almost as seldom she bothered to consult her mirror, but she looked herself up and down, considering. She'd be damned if she abandoned comfort, but some level of formality would be appropriate to the setting, which would matter to Fel-lar whether or not he admitted as much. Her attire would provide the less friendly elements of the Cabinet no reason to sneer. She traded the somewhat shapeless sweater she had been wearing for a jacket, ran a comb through her hair, and headed out.

Fel-lar rose and greeted her at the door, ushering her in without any intimate gesture, but with enough warmth to remind his colleagues that disrespect shown to her would constitute disrespect to their co-leader as well. Then he made his way to the front of the room near the large display screen, on which nothing was currently displayed.

The meeting room contained a table curved in an arc, with chairs for the human members, and leaning posts flanking it on either side. A seat had been added next to Anna's; Mara took it and folded her hands on the table, looking around, nodding greetings equally in all directions, then looking back at Fel-lar. Once Mara was settled, the Secretary of Infrastructure pressed the button to bring the screen to life.

Mara scanned the image up and down—and gasped, clasping her hands together and gripping tightly. "A message came through! From Lan-sol and Jak-rad-tan!" She looked around the room again. She could see no signs of relief or relaxation, let alone joy. "Or didn't it? What am I looking at?"

Anna flashed a brief smile that left concern in its wake. "That's what we're trying to decide. We hoped that with your experience, and your knowledge of the parties involved, you could help us do that."

Mara frowned. "My knowledge of Lan-sol is no greater than yours, and derived from the same sources."

("A fact known to anyone who cares to consider the subject.")

Of course Levi had something to say. In fact, she had probably been invited as much for his cynical perspective as for any contribution of her own.

Mara looked at Kenneth, Secretary of Communications. "The message is addressed to you. Were you the signatory on the messages we sent after we started to think something might be wrong with the relays?"

Kenneth nodded.

She read the text again. It began with the news that the communications problem had been found and fixed, then went on to express Lan-sol's continued determination to make his visit, some rather bland accolades about Gen-tar-ten's latest policies, and a glowing report of the progress of ship construction. "This explanation about the technical issue: it looks a little vague. Am I missing something?"

"Not really. But Lan-sol could just be passing along the gist of someone else's assessment."

Mara tilted her head, considering. "Kenneth, how well did you know Jak-rad? And Randy, for that matter?"

"Fairly well. We all knew each other—you know that. We used to speculate about what sort of communications technology the Tofa had come up with on their own, before we showed up."

"So he'd expect you to be curious about the details of

what went wrong. And he'd be inclined to tell you, in this message or in another." She turned back to address the group at large. "When did this message come in?"

("You mean, was Fel-lar sitting on it without telling you?")

("Hush. You know perfectly well that's not the reason I'm asking.")

("Not the only reason. All right, I'm hushing.")

"We received the message only this morning, approximately two hours ago."

"So others could show up soon. We may as well hold off on jumping to conclusions."

Peer-tek, Secretary of Defense Planning, tilted forward from his leaning post. "We may refrain from conclusions, but we can, in the meantime, list some possibilities."

Anna pressed a control, and the message was replaced by a blank screen. She nodded toward Peer-tek. "I assume you have a few to get us started."

Fel-lar raised an upper hand to interject. "Before we discuss the nature of the message, let us for a moment focus on the fact that it was received. Kenneth has already confirmed that it did not originate anywhere on New Landing. While he cannot completely exclude unknown sources in the direction of the wormhole or of Tofarn, he considers it highly likely that someone on Tofarn sent it. Which means that the necessity of examining the wormhole's communications relays may be far less than we had supposed."

Peer-tek waited to be sure Fel-lar had finished, then proceeded, holding up successive fingers of his upper right hand as he did. "Assuming, then, that it came from Tofarn. First: the message is genuine, and may be followed by others. Second: the message is a forgery. This alternative branches off into several more." He switched to his lower hands. "I start with what I regard as the least likely: the message is a practical joke, or a media stunt of some kind. This alternative depends on the prankster or media source having access to repaired communications before Gen-tar-ten or any other government agent, and before our other friends as well.

"Now to the more plausible possibilities. Some hostile agent obstructed communications so as to buy time for a plot to unfold. The hostile forces could be human, or Tofa. The plot could be against the current Tofa regime, or against Lansol and his crew—with the ship as a possible object—or against the human community of the capital city, or against humans as a whole." Peer-tek returned to counting on his upper fingers. "Another set of sub-possibilities concerns the fate of our allies on Tofarn. They could be oblivious; imprisoned; or dead."

There had been no background conversation while Peer-tek spoke, but the silence as he finished seemed somehow more complete.

("Levi—any ideas on what we do now?")

("We mustn't be rude. Of course, we reply to the message—and send others, to various recipients. And without explicitly quizzing them, we ask questions designed to provoke answers containing information that those recipients are more likely to know.")

Mara hesitated, then relayed Levi's suggestion, giving credit where it was due. A few Cabinet members stirred in surprise: Mara almost never spoke of Levi in public, despite the community's knowledge of him.

"Thank you for your assistance, which has been as helpful as I expected." Fel-lar's tone had a special warmth, not so rare in public as her own statement had been, but still unusual in this official a setting.

Anna looked at all those present in turn. "Everyone, please submit your suggested messages to Peer-tek. Before we actually send them, we should ponder and discuss whether he should encrypt them, and if so, to what degree. Peer-tek can also screen the draft messages for information we would not want any foe—human or Tofa—to obtain." She glanced at Fel-lar, then announced, "This meeting is in recess."

* * *

Fel-lar paused on the threshold of Rose's dwelling, adjusting his grip on the large portfolio in his left hands, and listened to the clamor within. It sounded like a game of keep-away, with the human children trying to anticipate the erratic ups and downs of one or more of their Glider "siblings." He heard nothing that sounded like Tofa speech or whistling; the Tofa children's greater height and reach must have disqualified them as likely to win too easily.

When the noise receded from the front door, Fel-lar felt safe in opening it and calling to his twin. As she did not immediately respond, he ventured further inside and headed for Rose's study. She could often be found there, writing or editing her accounts of her family's ongoing communal experiment.

Passing a room from which shafts of light slanted down into the hallway, Fel-lar was not surprised to see Rose's Glider co-parent swoop through the door and alight a little way ahead of him. The Glider swept one wing toward the interior of the house in a sign of welcome and trilled a message to the same effect, echoed by the translator attached to its belt. "Good to see you! You're on the right track. Rose will be glad to see you as well."

Fel-lar made his way up the stairs to the second floor. He looked around for signs that any of the various nonresident co-parents were visiting at the moment. The two Gliders who had completed the reproductive triad rarely braved the interspecies chaos of Rose's household, preferring that the children come to them, but the human children's father and the Tofa children's spore-parents dropped by with some frequency. Today, however, he saw none of them. His visit would not constitute an undue burden on Rose's hospitable resources.

Li-sen had an office of his own near the top of the stairs. Fel-lar poked his head in, hoping to greet his friend, but the room was empty. Fel-lar headed on down the hall to Rose's sanctum.

The door was closed, as usual. Rose had declared herself unable to concentrate without shutting out the yells, whistles, trills, hisses, buzzes, wails, and hums of her assorted charges. Fel-lar knocked high and low on the door with his right hands. In moments he heard the squeak of Rose's chair on the floor and then her rapid footsteps. She flung open the door and stood on tiptoe to kiss his cheek. He assisted by bending over, hugging her with his lower right arm, before straightening up and holding out the portfolio. "Mara and I finally finished those drawings of the children, the ones we started at your last harvest party."

Rose beamed. "I can't wait to see them! But I will wait, after all, so the whole household can admire them at once. Just lay the portfolio on that table, and I'll bring it down at suppertime. Can you stay?"

"I would be happy to stay. I would enjoy seeing the children's reactions to the drawings. And spending some time with my oh-so-busy twin."

"You should talk, Mr. Co-Chair of Congress!" Rose looked behind Fel-lar, into the hallway. "Couldn't Mara come?"

Rose always made the same polite inquiry when Fel-lar visited on his own, as if to deny any preference for her twin's undivided attention. Fel-lar played his accustomed part, though on this occasion there was no need to stretch the truth. "Mara is resting. The process of regrowing and strengthening the damaged bones and ligaments has sapped her overall energy."

Fel-lar put down the portfolio as instructed and leaned against the wall near Rose's desk. "Tell me the latest in the continuing adventures of the Woman in the Shoe."

Rose stuck out her tongue at him. "I know perfectly well what to do with all my children, thank you. Except this morning, when my youngest brat chased all the Tofa kids through the house with a vanilla aroma stick, and one of them rounded a corner and knocked over two Glider perches—occupied perches, may I add—and they all ended up explaining and complaining at top volume simultaneously. Fortunately Li-sen stepped in and conducted an impromptu mediation." Rose paused and shook her head. "You know, sometimes I forget that we all spent so much time learning and practicing those skills. It's like another lifetime, or even a dream."

"Another lifetime, on another planet. And yet that life and that planet can still reach us with reminders—and possibly more."

Rose looked up at him, eyes narrowed. "Li-sen said you were talking about going with *Star Seed*, and going all the way back. . . . I can guess some of the reasons why. But it's not something I can let myself think about."

Fel-lar glanced around the room at the walls, on which

hung several of his and Mara's previous drawings of the children, as well as paintings of the local landscape. For the first year or two of their time on New Landing, Rose had displayed a different series, paintings Fel-lar had made of her with *Star Seed*'s virtual reality chambers set to various Tofarna scenes. Rose had never explained why she took those paintings down and (as far as he knew) hid them away. But he inferred that as a remedy for homesickness, the paintings had been incomplete and may have come to act as the reverse.

Rose had built a life here, perhaps a more complete life, more fully integrated into the world they had found, than most of the Twin-Bred could boast. Her roots were not as shallow as Suzie's, nor as easily disturbed. If her longing for Tofarn ran at least as deep, Fel-lar could not fault her for avoiding any subject that could lead to thoughts of returning.

He had come hoping to confide in her, to unburden himself, spilling out his turbulent emotions for her to examine and analyze and help him put in order. He should have known that this burden was not for her to share.

Fel-lar left the leaning post and retrieved the portfolio, pulling the contents outward a few tantalizing centimeters. "Come and have a preview. A private showing, by special appointment. Shoe Mother's Eyes Only."

Rose pulled back her unfocused gaze from some distant destination, stood up, grinned in an almost natural manner, and ran over to pull the drawings the rest of the way into the light.

Chapter 17

(Tofarn)

IN ANNOUNCING that he would compose a message for New Landing's consumption, Ton-lal-set had not thought through all the consequences and ramifications. Not until several days later did he realize that a single message would not suffice. Indeed, he might be forced to carry the Tofarna end of an extended correspondence. He would perhaps have come to this realization sooner if his diet had improved as much as his accommodations: he was still somewhat malnourished. He would have to instruct his followers to remedy the problem immediately.

His first message had purported to come from Jak-rad-tan and Lan-sol. He would produce a second message, this one from Gen-tar-ten, which would allow him to use more unadulterated Tofa symbology and style. But what would the usurper have to say for himself?

Would he assure the Twin-Bred that Ton-lal-set remained in prison? If so, would the point be to emphasize that Ton-lal-set was in no position to make mischief, or that the benevolent current leadership had kept their enemy alive?

Gen-tar-ten had been one of those chiefly responsible for providing the Tofa Twin-Bred (and thus, inevitably, the humans) with historical background about Tofa society. He could express hope that all the younger Tofa born since the voyage were being taught this material. And delightful thought: he could even supplement that material with new tidbits—which could be as counterfactual as Ton-lal-set pleased.

Some of his followers might possibly object to promulgating a distorted version of Tofa history. But the visitors had remained subservient, despite his occasional excesses of temper at their earlier meetings. It was unlikely that they would balk at such a detail.

He could have wished that human aphorisms did not still float into his mind, even after all these years. But at least this one was appropriate: Fortune did favor the bold.

He was growing impatient by the time the guard next appeared with two familiar supporters. He waved the latest message at the group as it entered, only to realize that the guard was carrying some writing of his own, on proper sheets of metal.

The guard made the proper respectful gesture, echoed by the others, and approached. "We received this reply to your message, Eminence, as well as a message directed to Jak-rad-tan. Both communications include questions whose answers we are not sure how to obtain. We require your wisdom."

Questions! Was this coincidence, or had his message been less than fully convincing? And had this possible failure occurred to the others?

Ton-lal-set took the messages in his upper left hand and began to read. Someone had marked the problematic portions. The letter to Lan-sol, from some Tofa Twin-Bred healer named Poo-lat, asked for a reminder of just what commands Jak-rad-tan—while still Jak-rad, of course—had given Lan-sol in the womb. Ton-lal-set could make some educated guesses. Any pregnant Tofa, for example, would order the fetus to be still when the parent wanted to sleep. The eccentric Jak-rad would no doubt have come up with some atypical commands, but the letter—possibly for the sake of subtlety—did not explicitly demand those.

The message to Jak-rad-tan from one Peer-tek could be more troublesome. It mentioned, and requested specifics concerning, conversations between the young Jak-rad and a Twin-Bred named La-ren—why was that name familiar?— concerning one of La-ren's favorite books. There might be no way of finding those answers, short of capturing Jak-rad-tan, if they had any allies capable of doing so; and even then, there would be no way to verify his answers.

And why were these questions, referring to long-past

events, coming from Tofa too young to have added a third syllable to their names? Or did the Twin-Bred cherish youth so much that they refused to acknowledge full adulthood in the time-honored manner?

Then Gen-tar-ten noticed something else, something no one had marked. He jabbed the message with the pointing fingers of both lower hands. "Look at this! This Peer-tek refers to another message, a third one, from someone called Fel-lar to Gen-tar-ten himself. Where is that message?"

The others looked at each other, their bodies taking on almost comically similar postures of dismay. One of them pointed to the guard. "Find it at once!"

Ton-lal-set gathered the metal sheets and looked around for a place to hide them. Finding nothing suitable, he thrust them at the nearest visitor. Then he turned away in dismissal and waved an upper hand behind him. "All of you, go in search." He did not look back at them before the door swung shut behind them.

* * *

Gen-tar-ten, striding toward the day's first meeting and mentally running through its agenda, was at first annoyed to have his thoughts interrupted by an adolescent Tofa. The youngster ran up and then stopped, chest heaving, between Gen-tar-ten and his destination.

As part of his plan to enlist the next generation in his coalition, he had been finding—or more often, inventing—minor jobs for them to perform at headquarters, where their well-meaning efforts often seemed to cause more work for their elders. This youngster, a new arrival, handled some sort of busywork involving the scan-and-store machine. What was he doing here?

"Eminence! I found something! At least I think I did— could you come with me and see?"

Gen-tar-ten had a short time to spare, and granting the request would probably be quicker than asking questions and trying to make sense of the answers. "I will come."

Soon they were standing in front of the machine, the young Tofa pushing buttons and pointing, his words tumbling out quickly. "I'm supposed to make a list every morning of what files went into the machine the day before. And this morning there was one from outside the complex. When someone puts a document directly into the scanner, they put a description of it in this field, here, and that's where I get the information—but for a file sent from outside, all that shows is where it came from and who should receive it. I have to open it and look through it so I can describe it."

Gen-tar-ten buzzed for a moment, then caught himself as the youngster looked up, startled. He had not known about this procedure. Anyone wandering in could review incoming messages? He would have to assign someone to draw up a plan with better security precautions. He gestured for the lad to continue.

"*This* came in last night!" The youth bounced on his toes in excitement and pointed to the lighted screen on the upper surface of the scanner.

"From Fel-lar?? From *New Landing*?" Gen-tar-ten stared first at the readout, then at the excited Tofa before him. "How much of this did you read?"

"Only the beginning, Eminence. Then I came and told you, right away. Because I knew . . . ." He trailed off. Evidently the gossip had reached even the junior employees, and this most junior of them all had the wit to realize that his knowledge might be unwelcome news to his superiors.

Gen-tar-ten vaguely recalled that there was a way to put files off limits to any but designated personnel—but he did not remember how. He made himself relax and assume a casual demeanor. "Thank you for showing me this. Now you can show me what other skills you have mastered. First, produce a printout for me. And next, you can demonstrate the use of the security settings."

Gen-tar-ten postponed his meeting and locked his office door, then read the printout twice from beginning to end.

It was a curious message. It did not, as he might have expected, explain what had happened to interrupt communications between New Landing and Tofarn, nor how they had been restored. Instead, it referred to a supposed message from Lan-sol and Jak-rad-tan, somehow transmitted and received in the recent past. He would send for one or both at once and find out how this had been accomplished.

And the message had an odd, rambling structure, with questions tossed in almost at random. Why would Fel-lar, now a high government official with as much business to occupy him as Gen-tar-ten himself, be concerning himself with reconstructing the order in which Gen-tar-ten and his associates had once visited the Twin-Bred complex, and what lessons they had taught on each of those visits? It made no sense. But perhaps Lan-sol or Jak-rad-tan would be able to explain it.

*   *   *

The adolescent Tofa on Jak-rad-tan's doorstep, standing very straight with an air combining nervousness and self-importance, bore an armband that Jak-rad-tan knew he should recognize. After dredging his memory, he had it: the youth was one of those serving the Eminence's administration in an essentially menial capacity, what some early Terran societies would have called a "page," and at least one later one a "gofer."

Jak-rad-tan invited the youngster to come in and take some refreshment. He refused with a somewhat shocked expression, stirring not a step before delivering his message. "The Eminence of the Southern Region, to whom all respect is due, would like to speak to Lan-sol, Renewer of Hope, at his headquarters. Immediately. I am to escort him."

Lan-sol, hearing his name, had joined his parent at the door. Jak-rad-tan turned toward him. "I know your past preference. Has it changed, in general or in connection with this special invitation?"

Lan-sol had never wanted to set foot in the complex where his parent had been forced to work and he himself had so nearly perished before birth. Jak-rad-tan had sometimes regarded this aversion as superstition, sometimes as paranoia, but he had never insisted on overriding it.

Lan-sol stepped forward; Jak-rad-tan stepped back so that Lan-sol could face his young peer directly. Lan-sol looked the visitor in the eye for a moment, then shrugged in the human manner the Tofa Twin-Bred had passed on to their children. "For what purpose does the Eminence ask to see me?"

The young Tofa flicked a startled hand, and Jak-rad-tan suppressed a whistle, at Lan-sol's characterization of what Gen-tar-ten no doubt intended as a command rather than a request. "I am not permitted to say. But it is important." The youngster managed to stand even straighter. "I myself was involved in the discovery about which he will consult you."

Lan-sol stepped back. "I would, of course, be honored to meet and converse with the Eminence, but I do not wish to go to his headquarters."

The visitor flicked both upper hands. "You do not expect *him* to come to *you*?"

Jak-rad-tan inserted himself between Lan-sol and the scandalized emissary. "I will accompany you and speak to the Eminence myself. I will explain that I insisted on doing so." And if Gen-tar-ten chose to retaliate by withdrawing government approval from the Dispute Reconciliation Office, then so be it.

But he need not unnecessarily court that outcome. "If I cannot answer the Eminence's questions, he can give me whatever commands are then necessary."

It might not be wise to leave Lan-sol alone when some unknown new developments, involving several levels of the government bureaucracy, were apparently in process. "We will, on our way, escort Lan-sol to—" He turned to his offspring. "Where would you like to go where you will be surrounded by well-wishers?"

Lan-sol hesitated a moment, then stood very straight. "I will go to the shipyard. I was expected there in any event, and so are most of the crew." He reached out to touch the back of Jak-rad-tan's nearest hand. "I had meant to invite you as well. The ship—except for some unimportant details of crew comfort, the ship is completed."

Jak-rad-tan gripped Lan-sol's right hands tightly with his own left hands. "What wonderful news! I would have very much liked to be there. By all means, go and celebrate. Let us not—" Jak-rad-tan glanced back at his escort, now buzzing faintly in nervousness. "Let us not keep any of those expecting us waiting longer than necessary."

"Are you sure? Absolutely sure?" Gen-tar-ten took back the printout he had shown Jak-rad-tan and gripped it tightly in an upper hand while drumming his lower fingers together.

Jak-rad-tan ran through all his and Lan-sol's recent discussions about New Landing and the projected journey. "Eminence, you also have offspring. You know that parents, especially in this era, must retain a certain humility as to their knowledge of offsprings' activities. But Lan-sol possesses an expressive temperament. I do not believe he has much skill in concealment. And from everything he has said and done since communications originally failed, I am close to absolutely sure that he does not believe communications to have been restored, and has sent no message on that assumption."

"He could have tried again, even while believing the attempt would fail."

"Possible, though I believe it unlikely. But the message to Your Eminence—"

"We have known each other too long for these formalities. You may address me by name."

Jak-rad-tan made a carefully calibrated sideways bow, and determined to avoid using any form of address when possible. "This message is, as you say, peculiar. While it has been many years since I last saw Fel-lar, and we have had few extensive communications in that time, I suspect the message is in the nature of a test, to see if someone is communicating with the New Landing residents under false colors." Gen-tar-ten stirred in annoyance; Jak-rad-tan made haste to rephrase. "Using an assumed identity."

Gen-tar-ten continued to drum his fingers, then dropped the printout on a nearby table. "Come with me."

Jak-rad-tan soon found himself in a room he had never seen, containing one large machine and little else. Gen-tar-ten studied the controls. "I would rather not rely upon my staff for this . . . Ah." He punched a long series of buttons. A screen lit up, showing a list of entries. Gen-tar-ten let loose with an impressive string of Tofar curses. "They are here, hidden. All of them! All this time!"

Jak-rad-tan hesitated, then asked, "May I approach and see what you have seen?"

Gen-tar-ten barked an affirmative. Jak-rad-tan moved just far enough forward that he could read the display. It was clear enough. This machine, if the readout was accurate, contained transmission data, at the very least, for months of messages received from New Landing, with varying members of the Twin-Bred community listed as the senders. Almost at the end, with a time stamp only days before that on the printout Gen-tar-ten had shown him, was a single message sent in the opposite direction.

Gen-tar-ten wove the fingers of his upper hands together as he punched more buttons with his lower left. "If I recall the procedure I recently saw used, these messages cannot now be seen by anyone but me. Though whatever traitor or traitors intercepted the messages and sent another may well know how to override that protection."

Jak-rad-tan burned to see the messages. Not only would they contain news of his distant friends, but there might be urgent news that would somehow affect those left on Tofarn. He glanced over at Gen-tar-ten. This was not the time to ask. He must tread carefully.

"Eminence—" Jak-rad-tan risked using the title, guessing that Gen-tar-ten could use its reassuring ring. "Is there anyone on your staff, anyone in whom you have full confidence, who could eliminate whatever program is capturing these messages and interfering with direct transmission of your own?"

Gen-tar-ten muttered a few more curses. "If there are members of my staff with these capabilities—capabilities of which I have had no occasion to become aware—they are as likely as not to be the perpetrators."

"May I offer a suggestion?"

Gen-tar-ten, to Jak-rad-tan's considerable surprise, let out a short whistle. "I can hardly invite a member of the Twin-Bred into my presence and expect to escape without a suggestion or two. Go on."

"Former host mother Veda Seeling, whom you know as well as any human, is not only accustomed to political intrigue, but technically and scientifically adept as well. It is possible she might have some useful thoughts on how you could approach this dilemma."

Gen-tar-ten did not react as positively to the proposal

as Jak-rad-tan had expected. Instead, the Eminence stood very still for several moments, apparently deep in thought, the odor of emotional strain just barely emanating from him. Then he threw his head back and punched hard with a lower finger to power down the machine. "Contact her at once."

*   *   *

Veda had hoped something would happen to restore the amicable tenor of her relationship with Gen-tar-ten. When Jak-rad-tan sought her out and explained (in rather cryptic terms) why Gen-tar-ten now sought a meeting, she could only reflect on how often the universe insisted on reminding her to be careful what she wished for.

Given Gen-tar-ten's and Veda's longstanding acquaintance, it would be nothing remarkable, Jak-rad-tan suggested, for the Eminence to drop in on her. "Such a visit should attract minimal attention."

Veda gently suggested that he moderate such hopes. "If Gen-tar-ten has such active enemies as you've been cryptically suggesting, they'll be watching his every move—and may have been keeping an eye on his known human associates as well. But there's no point in fretting about it."

"Lan-sol and I will at any rate be there to protect you during the meeting itself."

Veda refused the offer as likely to make the meeting more conspicuous, hoping she had done so without raising Jak-rad-tan's suspicions. If Gen-tar-ten was seeking Veda's political expertise, she might need to suggest measures more duplicitous or coldblooded than Jak-rad-tan—let alone his even younger and (most likely) more idealistic offspring—could stomach.

And there was one more matter, even more potentially explosive, that she could raise with the Eminence. But she would wait and assess how dangerous he considered his situation before venturing onto that ground.

Gen-tar-ten's guards had remained outside. Peeking through her living room window, Veda saw that the rain had begun again. The guards ignored it. One turned constantly from left to right, surveying the approaches to the house; the other faced the front door, presumably alert for any sign of tumult within.

Gen-tar-ten finished his hot chocolate—almost all Mara's friends had picked up her custom of including chocolate in their hospitality—and settled back against the leaning post, placing his saucer on the small attached platform. "Now that I have brought you up to date, rather than asking you particular questions, I would prefer to hear you extemporize as to the elements of this dilemma and how I should prioritize them."

Veda drained the last drop of her own hot chocolate and set down her mug. "I'm not sure which of two tasks is more important: identifying the hidden adversary on your staff, or finding an expert to try to undo the alterations in your communications equipment."

Gen-tar-ten's torso went stiff, suggesting displeasure. Veda affected ignorance of the fact, pouring both of them a second serving of chocolate; Gen-tar-ten relaxed slightly, retrieved his saucer, and slurped a sip before responding. "I take it you are suggesting a human expert. I cannot allow humans to interfere with our office technology. Particularly at present."

Veda blew on her chocolate and took a sip. "Hmph. All right. Then let's think about how to find your—well, your traitor, as no less inflammatory word occurs to me at the moment."

Gen-tar-ten stiffened the fingers of the hands not holding the saucer, in what Veda had learned to be the equivalent of a human clenched fist. "The term 'traitor' will serve admirably."

Veda allowed herself another swallow of chocolate, then abandoned it as too much of a distraction. "I'm not sure I know enough, or understand enough, about how your government works, or about how Tofa workplaces work, to be of much help. But Jak-rad-tan knows much more. And either he or Lan-sol or both of them might just know if someone on your staff is more technically savvy than he's demonstrated on the job."

Gen-tar-ten buzzed for a moment. "Jak-rad-tan himself did not mention this possibility."

Of course not. Had he truly failed to think of it? Or . . .

This was going to be exceedingly tricky. A misstep could land either Veda or her friends in dangerous waters. "Perhaps his modesty about his own knowledge and abilities prevented him." She could stop there and let Jak-rad-tan take care of himself. After all, he had thrown her into this mess.

Damn maternal instinct. It interfered with proper self-preservation. Not that raising the difficulty in advance would necessarily be any better; but her instincts urged her on. "While I am sure Jak-rad-tan and Lan-sol have the strongest desire to assist you, it is possible they will have some concerns about how you will use any information they provide. Both of them have some experience with how, ah, rigorous Tofa governments can be in dispensing what they regard as justice."

Gen-tar-ten buzzed again, more loudly, put down his saucer with a clatter, and took a step in Veda's direction. "You equate my government with the regime from which we rescued your friends?"

Veda resisted the urge to scoot her chair backward. "If I did, I would hardly have dared to make such a comment. But you hold the same office as Ton-lal-set held, and neither Jak-rad-tan nor Lan-sol is likely to be sure of just how dramatically you have transformed it. . . . Let's consider what you could do with any leads they provide. I doubt either Jak-rad-tan or Lan-sol could identify the spy—there, now, a less loaded word—for certain. One time-honored human technique for handling spies is to keep them in place and feed them false information; and that wouldn't hurt the innocent suspects. But . . . that wouldn't be quite enough, would it. We're talking about one or more Tofa who can out-tech most if not all of your staff. You can't leave them free to operate."

"Not indefinitely, at least." Gen-tar-ten returned to the post and leaned back, ignoring what was left of his chocolate and placing all his hands on their opposite elbows in what might have been an unconscious pose of self-protection. He said nothing more, and Veda saw no point in guessing the direction of his thoughts. She pulled her tablet toward her, trying to be unobtrusive about it, and checked her messages. There was an update from Lan-sol, announcing that the ship could be ready for launch fairly soon, with the final determination of its crew the most likely cause of delay.

Veda pushed her tablet to one side and addressed Gen-tar-ten. "Lan-sol's trip itself might solve the communication problem. Once he gets to the array, he can probably find a way to send and receive messages directly. Though we would still need to figure out how to avoid their interception."

Gen-tar-ten unfolded himself and spread all his fingers wide. "Then, after Lan-sol's safe departure, I will place the spy, if found, where he can do no more harm."

"Lan-sol and his parent will guess as much."

Gen-tar-ten stood up from the leaning post and took a step toward the door. Clearly, the audience was almost over. "Let them. I will make some concessions as to how the spy is to be treated. That should suffice to let them do their duty to their people and their leader without obstruction or hesitation."

Hesitation. She could, indeed, hesitate no longer: she must share her thought and take the consequences, or live with the consequences of remaining silent. She stood up and craned upward to meet his eyes. "Eminence, please wait a moment longer. There is an idea I wish to explore with you—but only as much, and for as long, as you permit."

Gen-tar-ten flicked an upper hand toward her in a peremptory gesture of permission.

"Eminence, I have not mentioned to anyone, in any way, the history we discussed in the park." Gen-tar-ten jerked his head backward; she flinched in response, but continued. "Now, however, the potentially grave situation you describe leads me to wonder whether you would consider authorizing any—research into the technique involved. There may be a way that such research could be conducted without the slightest word of it reaching your enemies."

Gen-tar-ten stood very still for a moment, then said, "Continue."

Veda took a moderately deep breath before she went on. "The Tofa Twin-Bred are already your allies, and they would have every reason to guard your secrets from supporters of the former regime. Nor would those supporters be canny enough in the ways of Twin-Bred, or of humans, to deceive either into betraying such secrets. If you allow, I will send the information you shared, and any additional details you choose, to my own twins. As the Tofa twin, Peer-tek, is skilled in cryptography, I can encode the message for additional security."

Gen-tar-ten stared down at her. "Message? How could you send a message without alerting those who have sabotaged communications?"

"Eminence, we will have no need of any remote method of transmission. We will use that most ancient form of sending a message—the messenger. My daughter Melly has joined Lan-sol's crew. Nothing will appear more natural than that her mother ask her to convey greetings to her older siblings."

Gen-tar-ten returned to the leaning post and covered his eyes with his upper hands, conveying the need for the utmost in concentration. Veda, holding off the beginnings of exhaustion, edged over toward a bookcase and leaned there. After a few very long minutes, Gen-tar-ten opened his eyes and straightened up once again. "As always, and as expected, you have provided me with new ideas, and with the challenges that new ideas so often carry. I am grateful, and I would rather not repay your service by threatening you as I did at our last meeting. Yet I must, to this extent: during the current crisis or at any time thereafter, so long as either of us may survive, I will hold you and yours responsible for the use of this information. If my indiscretion sows the seeds of an attack against my people, they will not be the only ones to suffer for it. Do you still wish to send your message, on these terms?"

Veda took a deep breath, hampered somewhat by the tension that filled her chest. Did she still wish it? A very good question: what did she owe Gen-tar-ten and his faction, after all, to place herself and her children in peril on his behalf?

Too much, in the end, to ignore. Without his help, her Tofa child would have fled the planet in almost total ignorance of his heritage. And what harm might Ton-lal-set and his ilk have contemplated or succeeded in doing to Tofarn's human population, with so many more years in power?

She clasped her hands together tightly as she looked up at Gen-tar-ten and replied, "Yes. I do wish it. And I accept the terms."

Chapter 18

(New Landing)

FEL-LAR LOOKED around at the members of Congress and the guests Congress had invited for the occasion. The initial chaos of greetings and logistical shuffling had died down. He may as well begin.

He kept introductory verbiage to a minimum and jumped to the heart of the situation. "We have received no replies to the messages we sent upon receiving the purported communication from Lan-sol. With every passing day, the likelihood decreases that this communication was genuine. If it was indeed a forgery, we cannot escape the inference that the regime we consider our ally has either been overthrown, or is directly or indirectly under attack.

"In this case, Jak-rad-tan and Randy and their families, as well as mothers Veda and Laura and our benefactor Gen-tar-ten, may be endangered, imprisoned, or dead."

The uncompromising words visibly startled several of those listening, but he continued without pause. "Unless we manage to overcome the existing communications obstacles, obstacles probably erected by those who bear us or at least our friends considerable ill will, a journey to Tofarn will likely be perilous. And as we have previously discussed, we cannot send sufficient numbers to overwhelm any large enemy force."

Peer-tek raised his upper hands, requesting a chance to speak. "I would add that this limitation derives not only from *Star Seed*'s limited capacity, but from the need to ensure that sufficient community members remain behind to confront any threatening situation that may arise."

Fel-lar nodded. "Indeed. But as I was saying: if there is anything we can do to affect the course of events in what was once our home, we will learn as much only by proceeding, peril or no.

"I propose that we hear from any of our guests who wish to speak, and then discuss who will make the decision, and after that, what the decision is to be."

Anna took over, pointing first to Suzie. Her choice surprised Fel-lar for a moment, but then he acknowledged its shrewdness. Suzie would only grow more nervous if kept waiting.

Suzie stood, cleared her throat twice, and then spoke. Her first words were so quiet that Fel-lar doubted many of those assembled could make them out; evidently Suzie realized the same, and started over, just loud enough for him to hear. "I wasn't initially invited to be here today, since Dr. Cadell told me I wouldn't be allowed to take my children on the trip, and I wouldn't go without them." Fel-lar tried not to show his chagrin. The members of Congress might not approve of his impromptu use of Mara as an enforcer. Suzie, meanwhile, was gaining both speed and volume as she spoke. "But I asked if I could speak to you. Because I don't think I'm the only one in our community that needs to maintain ties with our home world." Several Tofa—all of whom, Fel-lar noted, had declined to adjust their children's genetics as to blue intoxication—buzzed to each other in what must have been agreement. Suzie went on. "I'm not saying anyone should take risks right now. But if we don't, we need some other strategy." She stopped, swallowed, and looked around the room with a resumption of her initial timid air. "That's all." She sat down and slumped in her chair.

The remaining guests had all asked to join the crew and been provisionally accepted. Neither Mara, whose possible crew status remained uncertain, nor Wings Spread Wide, whom Fel-lar had not wanted to seem to summon, was present. Other than the engineer Nathan and former diplomacy teacher Emily Wilson, all were Tofa; and all of those Tofa came from the first generation of Twin-Bred, except for Can-til, a protege of Kenneth, trained by him in communications. Fel-lar had deflected inquiries from a few other restless youngsters: he would be in no position to shepherd such, nor to cope with their shock or disillusionment when they encountered the realities of conflict.

Fel-lar reconsidered his earlier suggested procedure and turned toward the group. "I for one assume that all of you are in favor of the proposed mission. If that assumption is incorrect as to any of you, please stand and explain why."

At first, none of them stirred. Then Emily Wilson rose slowly to her feet. "I am willing to go in case my presence has a chance of reducing the scope of any unfortunate results our arrival might have. I have so many conflicting thoughts as to whether the ship should take off that I may as well be counted as having no opinion." She sat down again.

Nathan raised his hand. "If I may, I'd like to address the question Fel-lar raised about how the decision will be made." Anna nodded; Nathan stood. "You've given us a chance to make our views known, which makes sense. But our community has chosen all of you to represent us and make decisions on our behalf, and I'm inclined to get out of here and let you do it." He cocked his head. "So do I need to sit down again, or can I go and get back to work?"

He looked around at the other would-be crew members. They in turn drew toward each other in an impromptu circle; after a few minutes of rapid muttering, they fell back and left Artemesia's twin Hal-tet to be their spokesman. Hal-tet made a short sideways bow toward Nathan, then turned back toward the members of Congress. "Some of us are needed to continue preparing the ship. But as for the rest of us, if we care enough to make this journey, we care enough to do whatever we can to make sure it takes place. We will stay, if you allow it."

It was soon moved, seconded, and agreed that those prospective crew members who wished to remain would be allowed to take part in the discussion and the vote on this one issue, on this one occasion. Nathan and a few others filed out, and the chamber grew silent again.

But not for long.

* * *

Fel-lar stumbled in the door hours after Mara had expected him, obviously exhausted. Mara moved quickly to his side, to act as a portable leaning post if needed. "Do you want to eat or to collapse?"

Fel-lar patted her head, rather feebly, with an upper hand as she steered him in the direction that would serve for either kitchen or bedroom. "First, I will report while I eat. Then I will be very glad to collapse. And I hope you will not be too busy to join me, though I expect I will make rather passive company."

Mara planted him against the kitchen leaning post and put together an easily consumed, energy-restoring snack. She handed it to him and sat at their small kitchen table. "So—report. Is *Star Seed* heading to the wormhole?"

"Ah, food. Food is wonderful. Remind me not to take it for granted—especially when heading off for momentous and contentious meetings of Congress. Yes, the ship will go to inspect the communications array, and make further recordings and observations of the wormhole itself—not to mention according Wings Spread Wide material for his final composition, assuming he survives the experience."

Mara absorbed the news for a moment, then got up to fetch herself a double chocolate muffin. "Do you want one?"

"To be sure. If you are not too displeased to give me one."

She handed him his muffin and sat down again, holding her own in both her hands. "Which means you're still determined to go along."

Fel-lar ground away at the muffin. "You are not eating."

She shrugged. "I thought I wanted it, but I might have indigestion."

Fel-lar pushed himself forward off the leaning post, came over to the table and put down what remained of his muffin. "I will wait until we can enjoy chocolate together."

"Sentimental tonight, aren't you? Or trying to soften me up? How long do I have to decide?"

"The tentative schedule for departure is in twenty days' time."

Mara put down her muffin and pushed Fel-lar's half-eaten muffin away from her. "I don't even know whether I'm hungry, let alone whether I'm game for this insane expedition. Do the others really want me to be part of it?"

Fel-lar reached down a hand to pull her from her chair. "I was correct in predicting the attitude of the majority of

Congress, as well as of the crew. Those who did not affirmatively favor your presence had no objection to it."

Mara followed Fel-lar to their bedroom, then changed quickly into a lounging robe and joined Fel-lar, who had in the meantime lowered himself onto the bed. Fel-lar patted the mattress next to him. "We can talk a while longer, if you are willing. Eating has restored me somewhat."

"Maybe in a minute. Let's just lie here, first, while my stomach settles and my mind clears."

They lay together in silence until Fel-lar spoke. "I have also spoken to Mat-set about the twins. He would be happy to include them in his and Suzie's household until our return. He must speak to Suzie, but expects no objection from her. She will probably be glad of their assistance with the children."

Mara just barely twitched an eyebrow. "You had better make sure the twins are as enthused about that idea."

Neither of them spoke again for some time. Then both of them stirred simultaneously, Mara muttering, "What?" just as Fel-lar asked nonvocally, ("Friend Levi? Did you speak?")

("I'm glad to see the two of you are listening. Not that either of you has bothered to consult me.")

Mara had no immediate response—was, in fact, internally tongue-tied. Had she really ignored Levi's share in this decision?

Fel-lar relieved her of the need to answer. ("My profound apologies, brother. What do you want Mara to do? Or should I ask, what do you want to do, to go or stay?")

("About time. Both of you can hush up, now, and let me speak my piece. First, let me place on record my opinion that this whole notion is—to borrow my sister's recent phrase—sentimental in the extreme. The odds of more people we like, ourselves included, being alive and well at the end of it are lousy. And your Glider elder will probably get seasick.")

Mara's stomach was roiling even more by now. If Levi didn't want to go—if he was, even, afraid to go—where did that leave her? And was her reaction a sign that for whatever unfathomable reason, she really did want to make the trip?

("Whoa, Sis. You're racing off in the wrong direction. Who said I didn't want to go?")

Mara sat up and pressed her hands against her forehead. ("I don't understand.")

She could feel his chuckle, and Fel-lar whistled faintly in a reflection of it. ("That's because you're doing a lousy job of listening. Yes, it's crazy—but we've lived long and interesting lives already. We can afford to take a crazy risk now and then, if we get the notion.")

Mara took a deep breath and slowly lay down again, this time close to Fel-lar's side where she could feel his warmth. ("Why would you want to take this particular risk?")

Fel-lar lay still, listening to them both.

("It's simple enough, really. If we go back—if we go all the way back—you and I and Fel-lar, then I may get a chance for a meeting that never took place. A meeting, you could say, that was aborted through mischance.")

Mara stopped breathing for a moment. Fel-lar stretched out an upper arm to pull her close as he responded. ("I would be happy to facilitate this meeting. And to introduce you to your mother.")

* * *

Rose sat on a blanket near the edge of a short cliff overlooking the ship. Fel-lar leaned against the smooth, sun-warmed side of the cliff, lower left hand reached downward to clasp Rose's upraised right hand. Rose had packed a picnic, but most of it remained, somehow forlorn on the blanket.

Rose wiped her eyes on her sleeve. "We may not see each other that often, when either of us is busy, but I've always known you were near. That's always, as in all our lives. And now you'll be too far for us even to sense each other. Anything could happen to you, and I wouldn't know." A sob escaped her. "Not until later. Maybe not at all, not ever."

Fel-lar turned so that his lower right hand could reach and wipe away a tear Rose had missed. "I would reassure you if I knew some truthful way to do so." He whistled softly. "Or, perhaps, if you were likely to find comfort in a lie."

Rose used her free hand to pick up her sandwich and take a minuscule nibble. Then she put it back down and looked up at him. "Thank you for not taking Li-sen."

Fel-lar buzzed briefly. "For that you should thank Li-sen. Or possibly Nathan, who could have made the choice more difficult for his twin."

"If you would thank him for me, if the moment ever seems right . . . . Li-sen and I will be some comfort for each other. More than usual, I mean. We'll understand what the other is going through."

Fel-lar moved closer so that his lower right hand could more easily stroke Rose's hair. "Any Twin-Bred would understand. Will understand. You and Li-sen will have more than each other for empathy."

Rose grabbed the hand stroking her hair and gave it a kiss, then sat up straighter, let go of Fel-lar's lower left hand, and handed him one of the fruits the colonists informally called apples. "Here, eat something."

"Yes, mother," Fel-lar replied gravely, taking the fruit and evading the half-hearted swat Rose aimed at his leg. Rose returned to her sandwich while Fel-lar devoured the apple. Then he gazed at the landscape surrounding the ship, the red ground cover, the sunlight reflecting off the many facets of the crystalline cliffs.

Rose echoed his thought. "It'll be strange, seeing the golds and greens of home—or will it be purple season?"

"I should attempt calculations to find out, so the Tofa members of our crew will not be caught unprepared."

They fell silent again, a silence Rose finally broke. "When you see our home again, brother . . . try not to leave it with blood staining the streams, or soaking into the paths."

He shared her wish, but could make no promises. So he said nothing.

After a while, they packed up the picnic and headed back down toward Rose's house, Fel-lar glancing at the ship as they descended, Rose looking away.

* * *

Almost everyone assembled to watch *Star Seed*'s departure. All the children attended who could cajole a parent into bringing them, or could bring themselves. Those with parents in the crew came to enjoy the splendid sight, or to show their pride, or to give themselves and their parents the sight of each other for a few more minutes. Almost all those with spouses or the equivalent managed to suppress their fears, or to show those fears in a way they found acceptable in public. Only one crew member, the communications engineer Can-til, had parents to consider; his birth parent and spore-parent stood next to each other with their adjacent arms intertwined.

The ship would carry only one Glider into space; but Gliders filled the meadows all around, and lined every cliff.

Mara had decreed, and assisted with, one final administrative task before launch, drafting authority figures from all the communities involved. Every human, Tofa, or Glider who might conceivably be present was assigned two buddies to ensure that no one strayed close to the blastoff area. There would be no careless flight into a disastrous path.

A few Gliders had been allowed on board to shepherd Wings Spread Wide and inspect its quarters. Rides Above Danger was the last to leave, trilling in tones that a careless human might confuse with laughter. The elder Glider drew its right wing along the right wing of its protege. "Time for me to go. If Seth Baruti and I both fail to return, you may sing the song I have entrusted to you. Soar high and smooth."

This time the trill mixed true laughter with sorrow. "I wish you the same, and know those wishes will be realized. Soar high, indeed!"

*   *   *

Mara buckled herself into her takeoff seat. ("I still can't believe I let you talk me into this.")

Levi chuckled. ("You give me too much credit. Fel-lar had a great deal to do with it, as I recall. Especially as I recall a certain night, not too long ago. . . .")

("I think I'm going to designate some part of my body as yours, so I can swat it when you misbehave.")

("I apologize. A bit. But please. As if you'd be content sitting at home and missing all the action. You've been needing this for years. So—you're welcome.")

Chapter 19

(Tofarn)

THE APPLAUSE continued for a few moments after the house lights rose; then it broke into separate strands and died away, in a pattern Veda suspected would have interesting mathematical qualities. Veda peeled her raincoat off the seat, looked about to be sure she had no further belongings to collect, and filed out of the front row toward the lobby to congratulate the director.

But the crowd around Melly was too dense, and its members too tall, for Veda to reach her daughter without effort and the use of elbows. She turned instead toward the bar in the corner, now pouring the final few orders into covered cups suitable for carrying out into the rain. By the time the bartender filled her order for two glasses of crisp white wine, the group around Melly had thinned enough for Veda to approach and be seen.

Veda caught Melly's eye, smiled, and raised one of the glasses in a toast. Melly grinned back. It took her only a few minutes to extract herself from her remaining admirers, join Veda, and take the proffered drink. Melly nodded toward the theater's office wing. "Would you like to go to my digs and sit down, or to take a walk?"

"Let's go to your office for a bit. I'll get wet enough heading to the boat-bus." Veda paused. "Unless you'd like to come back with me and spend the night."

Melly squirmed, then visibly caught herself. "Thank you, but I've barely done any packing. I'd better make the most of my down time, with the ship leaving only a couple of days after our final performance."

Veda used a sip of wine to assist her in clearing the lump in her throat. "So, no second thoughts?"

Melly turned and moved off toward her office; Veda followed, but could not see Melly's face as Melly answered. "Oh, I've had second thoughts, and third ones. But I'm going. I studied up on communications technology so I'd actually be useful. Oh, and I'll be playing courier as well! Elizabeth Cadell showed up, out of nowhere, and asked me to take a present to Mara from her."

"Elizabeth—Mara's *mother*?" Veda chided herself for feeling surprise. Mara might have stubbornly avoided mentioning the woman, but that hardly negated her existence. "Is she much like her daughter?"

Melly shoved open the door to her office and sank into her oversized desk chair, swinging her feet up on the desk as she did so. Veda settled more daintily into a chair in the corner as Melly took a gulp of her wine and plunked it down on the desk. "Like Mara? Hmmmm . . . . Superficially, yes. But she doesn't have that—that core of strength." Melly picked up the glass again, turning it this way and that. "I think Elizabeth looks the way Mara might if she were ever finally . . . defeated."

Veda suppressed a shiver and brought the conversation back to something Melly had said earlier. She had thought the idea would have to come from her; Elizabeth's poignant gesture had smoothed the way. "So you're bearing gifts, are you? How would you like to take something else, something from me to the boys?"

Melly bit her lip. "I'd love to—but would it take much space?"

"Oh, no—just a little something I can put on a chip. It's been too long since I've been able to send them my love."

Melly relaxed. "That'd be fine. You don't have it with you, do you?"

Veda could hardly explain that she had not yet finished the elaborate encryption necessary. Time for a white lie. "I hadn't thought of it until now." At least she could follow up with a truth. "And I'm just as glad. It'll give me a reason to drop by once more before you go—no matter how busy you are."

* * *

Gen-tar-ten had allowed Veda to convey his command that Jak-rad-tan and Lan-sol attempt to identify likely spies within Gen-tar-ten's work force. In retrospect, he had to admit that she had manipulated him with some skill. She had managed to imply, without so stating, that if he confronted parent and offspring directly, their reaction might force him into a confrontation that would alienate some of his younger supporters.

Jak-rad-tan eventually provided a few names, though emphasizing the likelihood that some or all of those named were entirely innocent. Gen-tar-ten would find ways to assess their innocence. In the meantime, he repaid Lan-sol's cooperation by taking steps to confuse those hostile to the young Tofa's voyage: he circulated a rumor that Lan-sol's departure would be delayed, while allowing Lan-sol to inform his crew otherwise.

* * *

Jak-rad-tan recalled a human phrase: "trying to keep one's head above water." He had never encountered any serious problems wading or swimming in stream or river, but the metaphor vividly conveyed what it felt like to handle the various cross-currents of local politics and of Lan-sol's plans. Now, more than ever, he would have welcomed a co-parent to share his responsibilities. But the laboratory to whom he had entrusted Lan-sol's genetic sample seemed to be under some sort of pressure to put its work on hold. At this rate, Lan-sol's spore-parent would not be identified until after Lan-sol was hurtling through space.

He somehow made the time to go to the lab and confront those who had promised him results. His visit left him troubled by more than the delay of the promised revelation. Something about the laboratory director's excuses, and a certain unified tone to his cryptic mutterings, put Jak-rad-tan on alert. Whatever conspiracy was at work at Eminence Headquarters, it might have reached out an arm long enough to touch the director.

Jak-rad-tan managed to extract a grudging promise to resume work on Lan-sol's sample, and to deliver the information by special courier as soon as it became available.

* * *

"So you really can't come?" Lan-sol stared at his friend in dismay. He had let himself believe that Gen-tar-ten would relent and allow Nin-til to take part in his adventure.

"I think he would have. But something's come up that has him nervous. He wants people he can trust to stay close, and stay ready." Nin-til radiated sudden self-consciousness. "I'm sure he would have wanted your help as well, if you weren't so committed to your mission."

Lan-sol silently translated Nin-til's words into political terms. Canceling the mission, which the public associated with Gen-tar-ten's regime, would look like weakness and thus do more damage than Lan-sol's actual assistance could be expected to prevent. In case of trouble, Gen-tar-ten could always rally Lan-sol's supporters by invoking their absent hero.

* * *

Jak-rad-tan assisted the crew in bringing the gifts and supplies on board, then stowed packages here and there at Lan-sol's direction. The complicated tangle of his emotions included sorrow and even dread—but he could also rejoice to see Lan-sol's excitement, and his confident competence, as he instructed his shipmates in the final preparations.

Seeing Melly ascending the ramp, Jak-rad-tan remembered his recent and uncomfortable exchange with Veda. For both Veda's and Melly's sakes, as well as his own child's, he hoped that his fervent assurances to her concerning Lan-sol's maturity and prudence were not exaggerated. Likewise, he would have to trust Melly's and Lan-sol's assessment of Melly's recently acquired expertise at communications engineering, since Lan-sol had put her in charge of that function.

Lan-sol escorted him back to the viewing platform. All around were families saying goodbye; the multitude of varying hums reminded Jak-rad-tan of a Glider musical composition. If all went well, Lan-sol would be hearing such music direct from the source.

Lan-sol gripped Jak-rad-tan in a fierce hug. "Thank you," he murmured. "You could have stopped me. Or you could have made me feel guilty about going. Thank you for letting me go."

A sudden image, like a human nightmare, seized Jak-rad-tan's imagination: himself, months from now, wishing with a corrosive bitterness that he had used all the means he apparently had possessed, and kept Lan-sol safe at home.

But even home might not be safe. Lan-sol might in fact be safer flying between stars than caught in whatever was to come.

Jak-rad-tan squeezed Lan-sol once more, then let go, slowly, one arm at a time. "Convey my love to all my friends and teachers. And keep as much and more for yourself, as you journey on."

Lan-sol stepped back, looked at his parent for one long moment, then turned, ran to his ship, and disappeared inside.

Jak-rad-tan stood watching, keeping his distance from the others watching with him, as the engines roared to life. As clouds of fiery gases formed along the rocket's base, as they filled the slowly growing gap between the ship and the charred Tofarna surface below, Jak-rad-tan felt someone tapping insistently at his lower left elbow. He snapped, "Not now! Wait!" and did not turn round.

Only when the glowing comet of the ship's trail was hiding the ship itself from sight did Jak-rad-tan look to see who had intruded. Standing beside him was a short, thin Tofa, standing in a posture of annoyance and holding a package. "I was told you wanted this delivery as soon as possible!"

Jak-rad-tan reached slowly out to take the package, fighting back an inappropriate whistle so that he could thank the messenger and send him on his way. Now, after his child was gone beyond recall, came the information that might reveal what other parent would also be bereft.

Alone once more, Jak-rad-tan looked down at the package. Should he take it home and open it there? No, he had waited long enough. He pried up the lid and extracted a sheaf of papers in no discernible order. He held them in his lower hands and paged through them with his upper right, searching for anything comprehensible. Searching for a name.

But when he found it, his fingers went slack, and he only just managed to tighten them again before the papers could fall and fly in all directions.

The report identified Lan-sol's spore-parent, with a qualification of 97.9 percent certainty, as former Eminence Ton-lal-set.

Chapter 20

(Aboard *Star Seed* and *Winds of Home*)

Log of Captain Fel-lar, *Star Seed* (excerpts)

Launch Day plus 1: Our initial gravity setting is equal to that of New Landing. My original plan was to increase it by slow increments so that Tofarna gravity would be attained if and when SS reaches Tofarn. Preliminary steps in that direction met with some dissension. Seth Baruti in particular expressed concern about inflicting stress on Wings Spread Wide before we know for certain that we intend to travel from the wormhole to Tofarn. I am likely to yield: the time from the wormhole to Tofarn would allow for a sufficiently gradual increase of gravity. Personal note: I am, however, curious about how I will adjust to the gravity I took for granted in my youth.

Launch Day plus 4: Seth Baruti has inquired as to whether SS' suspended animation facilities are operational and would be able to accommodate WSW. I have consulted Poo-lat, our medical officer, who informed me that the facilities had been placed in readiness for use in a medical emergency, but that there had been no testing or other preparation for their use in any species besides human and Tofa. Poo-lat will attempt to conduct appropriate testing to the extent ship facilities permit.

Launch Day plus 7: Emily Wilson has somehow persuaded Mara to take knitting lessons. I did not know enough about knitting, nor about human acquisition of nonverbal skills, to anticipate the peculiar and interesting result.

At first Mara found the required fine finger motions utterly beyond her power to imitate. I was soon called upon to provide a sounding board for her intense frustration, and to comfort her as best I could—a task made more difficult by Levi's mischievous enjoyment of her discomfiture. I went so far as to rebuke his attitude, which has happened very seldom over the years. I believe both Mara and Levi were somewhat startled, but Levi apologized, and Mara—after vacillating between gratitude for my support and defensiveness on her twin's behalf—settled on the former.

Mara naturally persevered, and by the second lesson she began to acquire the knack, but in an unfamiliar manner fascinating to us both. Her fingers proceeded with their work without Mara's conscious direction, and also without her having gained the ability to describe or remember the sequence in either words or images. Of course there were no equations involved.

Mara has had little occasion to use kinesthetic memory for any task more complex than climbing a tree, and learned that before my birth. (One possible exception is the use of laboratory equipment; but the scientific context may have led her to take her growing expertise for granted, as well as distracting her from the process.) She has been attempting to describe the nonverbal experience, a somewhat paradoxical effort, in her communications with Harriet Gaho back home.

Launch Day plus 11: Wings Spread Wide gave a concert presenting a portion of what he intends to be his final song, with Seth Baruti in attendance and hovering about the performer in a somewhat intrusive manner. Afterward, Baruti cornered Poo-lat and questioned him about his progress in testing the SA facilities for Glider use. I eventually intervened on the ground that Poo-lat could hardly make progress on that front or in his other duties while Baruti continued to detain him.

Launch Day plus 17: Once again my entry concerns Seth Baruti. I will admit to some annoyance when he suggested another conference, but if his concerns have merit, both the conference and his inclusion in the crew—which he arranged with impressive cleverness—may prove worthwhile. As soon as I understood the subject matter involved, I asked for and received his permission to record our discussion. (video file attached)

(Transcript of video file)

FL: Professor, now that we are recording, please repeat and continue what you told me previously.

SB: "Professor"? Really, my lad, aren't we past such formalities? But as I was saying: during my frequent hours of leisure, when Wings Spread Wide is resting or composing, I have been catching up on my reading. There are astronomy texts I haven't read for years, and others I had only consulted here and there without reading straight through.

FL: And?

SB: I came upon some information that was new to me. I feel somewhat remiss in not having found it before, so that I could brief you and the rest of Congress on the matter during the period when you were weighing the pros and cons of undertaking this mission.

FL: Am I to understand that this information would have weighed against our proceeding?

SB: Well, I suppose, at least for the more nervous among us. But we're in no danger at this point. And I hope to be able to assess the risk pretty well once we get closer to the wormhole.

FL: Professor, please explain the nature of this risk.

SB: It concerns the wormhole itself. We have no idea of its longevity or history, nor how many other ships—or comets, or rogue asteroids—have passed through it during its existence. Once I identified the issue, I contacted New Hope and confirmed what we have all assumed, that the New Hope colonists' ship reached New Landing through this same wormhole.

Patience, my young captain! I'm getting to the point. The total quantity of mass that has passed through a wormhole may, according to the speculations of some theorists, correlate negatively with the future duration of the wormhole as a stable astronomical feature. In other words, it may be possible to, ah, "use up" a wormhole's capacity.

FL: And when the capacity has been exceeded?

SB: Well, that's hard to predict with any confidence. It could collapse inward, which would probably destroy whatever matter was inside it at the time. Or it could dissipate, leaving a ship—damaged or undamaged—in the region of space the wormhole had occupied, or in some other unpredictable location. Or it might twist in some new direction, so that the ship would exit into unfamiliar territory—though in that event, it might be possible to turn around and go back to this side.

FL: And you expect to be able to ascertain, once we arrive, which of these possible fates if any would await us?

SB: Ah, not exactly. I could take extensive measurements and compare them to what I took years ago. If the numbers haven't changed much, we can probably proceed without too much worry. If they're different . . . Well, we can all put our heads together and try to come to some conclusions. Or in that event, we could decide to be prudent and abort the passage.

(end of transcript)

I find myself wondering whether the professor was in fact entirely ignorant of these dangers, or whether he forbore to mention them in order to indulge in the additional measurements and observations he will now be able to make.

Launch Day plus 23: New Landing has forwarded to us a supposed reply to the message I attempted to send Jak-rad-tan before our departure. It is far from satisfactory, and does nothing to rebut our suspicions. Rather, it supports the supposition that something is amiss.

Log of Captain Lan-sol, *Winds of Home* (excerpts)

Voyage Day 1: Today is the first day in my seventeen years that I have had no contact with either my parent or anyone of his (or an older) generation. I had to fight to exclude all such from this expedition, but I saw no other way of ensuring that I remained in control of its mission. I anticipated some anxiety once I was actually this isolated. So far, I feel nothing but delight.

I have resurrected an old Terran custom from seafaring ships, that of the "captain's table." On such vessels, invitations to the captain's table were either confined to high-status individuals or used to confer a particular honor. I will be rotating those assigned to my table in order to get to know them better. Given Nin-til's inability to join us, I have been left with no close friends with whom to relax or in whom to confide. I would, and we all would, be better off if I can fill this gap.

Voyage Day 5: I could wish that our ship had the entertainment facilities that I understand *Star Seed* to have contained. Virtual reality, for example—I would have liked to spend some time immersed in the landscapes of our destination, seeing its inhabitants at close quarters. Which brings to mind an interesting dilemma. The Tofa inhabitants of New Landing either take a drug to prevent blue intoxication or have been genetically modified to resist it. Due to the interruption of communications with New Landing at an early stage of our preparations, we will arrive without even the drug. Should we hide on board until our friends on the planet can supply it, or should we don some sort of protective lenses for our first forays? And once we have the option of experiencing the vast expanse of blue and remaining unmoved, must we really be completely consistent and disciplined about doing so?

(One of tonight's guests at the Captain's Table suggested that we generate some blue items and gradually increase our exposure to the color during the voyage. I told him there was no evidence of any habituation effect. He replied that we could test the hypothesis ourselves.)

Voyage Day 7: When will we see the wormhole? I hope we are on course. Our navigators worked with the same astronomers who analyzed *Star Seed*'s initial data, and eventually received all the information *Star Seed* collected. The navigators have assured me that wormholes do not travel, except in the same direction and at the same speed that the surrounding space is itself traveling. But the astronomers did not expect a stable wormhole to exist at all.

What if we have another surprise in store? None of us is expert enough to go hunting astronomical phenomena.

Voyage Day 8: Wormhole sighted and course fine-tuned to approach it.

Voyage Day 12: We have spent much of our spare time watching old messages from New Landing, as well as recordings of human, Tofa, and Glider daily life on New Landing—all, of course, sent before the communications blackout. I have reminded my fellows that we will need to look upward at frequent intervals, in case either a Glider or one of the local predators is approaching. (I suspect that after seventeen years with the Twin-Bred community on site, the predators will be nearing extinction. If one does not grow up with unpredictable peril from above, one is unlikely to tolerate it.)

Voyage Day 13: I must find ways to discern and ameliorate any homesickness on the part of my crew. I was concerned earlier today that Melly remained in her quarters through midday, singing songs to herself; but she informed me that the songs dated from the Twin-Bred project, and that she was rehearsing them for the pleasure of the friends she would soon be seeing again.

Voyage Day 15 (*designation: private*): I am homesick.

Voyage Day 16: One of my shipmates is skilled at drawing and is spending his off-duty hours making a series of drawings of Tofarna scenes as a gift for the Twin-Bred. I hope the colony has adequate facilities for scanning—I would like to retain stored copies. (*designation: private*) (Looking at his sketches may have had something to do with my emotional difficulties yesterday.)

Voyage Day 18: I have been spending time each day studying human customs and behaviors, and have come upon a small number of references to tickling. My parent may have mentioned tickling once or twice as something the Twin-Bred engaged in with each other. I believe, but am not sure, that the twins tickled each other—but did Tofa tickle humans, or humans tickle Tofa, or both? Nor am I clear on the precise actions involved, although it seems to involve the fingers of one or both participants.

Voyage Day 21: I have had to defuse or settle several small conflicts among the crew. I seem to be the only one on board (with the possible exception of Melly, whose intervention would not be easily accepted) who received some training as a child in mediating disputes—a benefit of my Twin-Bred heritage. I look forward all the more eagerly to meeting the other Twin-Bred and seeing what we have in common, and what I have still to learn from them.

Voyage Day 24: We should reach the wormhole in approximately 10 days. In the meantime, I cannot forget how much time has passed and how swiftly events may occur at home. Once, Ton-lal-set imprisoned my parent. Later, my parent's allies imprisoned Ton-lal-set. Now Ton-lal-set has somehow acquired allies once more. Will the two change places once again, before I return and with me so far away? Has it happened already?

Chapter 21

(Tofarn)

HAD THE conspirators become more cautious? Of late, they would visit Ton-lal-set only in the middle of the night, when the prison was lightly staffed. Perhaps any nervousness derived from the news they had shared. Despite their supposedly reliable information, Lan-sol's ship had left on schedule, and the intercepted messages from New Landing had become inaccessible.

Ton-lal-set found it hard to sleep when he knew he might be awakened at any moment; and lack of sleep had the predictable enervating effects, which could interfere with seizing any opportunity that might arise. He finally ordered his supporters to refrain from visiting, unless and until they had major news to report.

With less interrupted sleep, Ton-lal-set found himself recovering not only strength but patience. If he had supporters sufficient to bring about a significant change in his fortunes, he would hear as much sooner or later, and their work would proceed at whatever pace they deemed necessary. In the meantime, he would grow stronger still, in body and mind, and prepare himself for whatever chances might someday come.

Exercising mental agility posed a challenge in an unchanging environment with no appropriate materials. He could, however, use his memory. He called up heroic sagas he had learned in his youth, accounts of great Tofa leaders of the past, reciting them in as close to their entirety as he could manage. He even tried to remember some of the logic and arithmetic games the Twin-Bred had been taught, but he had been too successful at banishing those memories once he could put the Project behind him.

The sympathetic guard seemed to have vanished, and the guards assigned to him now seemed to change frequently. Even if his ally somehow managed to regain the position, he would hardly be able to trust the circumstances that allowed it, and would have to begin, at least, by pretending ignorance of all that had passed between them before.

When the lock turned at mealtime, Ton-lal-set looked up as usual—and almost hissed in surprise: the Tofa carrying the tray was no true guard, but the conspirator who had mostly recently visited his cell at night, before he had discouraged such visits.

Once again, as on the day he had learned of his last child's death, the tray carried a cover. But what evil news could it possibly contain? His own imminent execution? He watched his own lower hand lift the lid, proud that it did not tremble.

Then, almost at once, he had to force down a whistle. The tray bore two adjacent slabs of bread covered in some sort of grayish jam—with the jam inscribed with rows of symbols, almost too small to read.

The supposed guard was the one to whistle. "Not too appetizing, is it? I guess it'll take you a while to choke it down." He paused a moment, staring. Ton-lal-set gestured his submission. If their encounter were recorded, and the record somehow failed to show the writing, he would have an excuse to dawdle over his meal long enough to read the message.

Nibbling around the edges, then consuming each symbol after he had deciphered it, Ton-lal-set absorbed the meager news the message provided. It could certainly have been worse. None of the other conspirators had been arrested or questioned, though one had been assigned to duty in another region. Gen-tar-ten had played into Ton-lal-set's hands by collecting large amounts of genetic data for spore evaluation—while the laboratory sat largely unused, with few Tofa eager to venture into such uncharted waters. If Ton-lal-set found an opportunity to list those whose spore-parentage he wished examined, at least some of that information could be obtained from this resource.

Ton-lal-set sucked up the crumbs of the last bit of

bread and prepared to wash them down with the stale, tepid water. But the drink in his cup made the day's next welcome surprise: an infusion of herbs known to fight off illness and stimulate mental processes. If his diet was finally improving, it might be worth allowing himself to hope for better things.

*　　*　　*

Gen-tar-ten rarely offered hospitality. Jak-rad-tan gestured his thanks for the saucer of hot water and reflected that the political situation must be dire indeed.

Gen-tar-ten wasted no more time before demanding, "Are you presently in communication with any of Lan-sol's circle of acquaintance?"

"There is one young fellow who visits every few days, full of solicitude, to see if Lan-sol's aged parent needs assistance in conducting the activities of everyday life. Otherwise, no."

Gen-tar-ten drummed his lower right fingers up and down along the gleaming surface of his leaning post. "Your offspring's journey has proved ill-timed. We are left without those young Tofa most likely to prefer the current administration, and also most likely to hear whatever rumors and memes are spreading in the local population."

Gen-tar-ten obviously assumed, as Jak-rad-tan had let him assume, that Lan-sol had played some role in identifying those who might be spies for Ton-lal-set's faction. Jak-rad-tan had in fact done his best to keep Lan-sol from realizing Jak-rad-tan's part in that process. Most likely, his efforts would have eventually proved futile if not for Lan-sol's departure.

Time for a partial change of subject. Jak-rad-tan extracted his tablet and called up a file. "I can at least perform some part of the service you require—which will temper my regret at bringing unwelcome news. I have been hearing some familiar themes in the conversations around me. Stories that Ton-lal-set and his adherents once circulated about the Twin-Bred, grossly distorted and calculated to trouble Tofa sensibilities, have been revived with new and timely details. I have also been confronted with accusations linking your leadership with dissatisfactions ranging from crop growth to various human activities."

Gen-tar-ten reached for the tablet; Jak-rad-tan handed it over and waited while the Eminence reviewed the contents. Gen-tar-ten did not appear to read the entire list before thrusting it back. "Scurrilous, yes; but not so unusual as you may suppose."

Jak-rad-tan made haste to take the tablet before Gen-tar-ten disposed of it in some less careful manner. "Your Eminence, you may recall from your exposure to the Twin-Bred's training that we learned to notice certain methods of manipulation. There is a similarity in the wording I have picked up from quite different sources, leading me to believe that some single agency is distributing and fomenting them."

Gen-tar-ten did not immediately respond, instead taking a slurp of his drink and then jabbing at the intercom. An aide soon appeared; Gen-tar-ten beckoned for him to take the saucer. "Remove this waste product immediately and bring me some intoxicating beverage." The aide grabbed the saucer and backed out of the room.

Jak-rad-tan had never seen Gen-tar-ten so imperious. His manner suggested he felt himself seriously beleaguered; and Gen-tar-ten's political instincts were keen enough to have maintained him in power this long. However aggrieved Gen-tar-ten might feel about Lan-sol's absence, Jak-rad-tan might soon have reason to rejoice that his offspring had escaped whatever was to come.

If the allies of the former regime somehow managed to unseat Gen-tar-ten after all this time, what would become of him, and of those like Jak-rad-tan who had supported him? Would they be kept alive, as Ton-lal-set had been? Why had Gen-tar-ten allowed an undoubted enemy, also suitable to serve as a rallying point for opposition, to live this long?

Gen-tar-ten's thoughts were apparently running along similar lines. "Ton-lal-set should have been dispatched long since. In fact, I had believed the most recent hearing resulted in the decision to execute him; but there is some sort of administrative confusion on that point. By now, with his sympathizers apparently so active, I hesitate to energize them further by offering them a martyr of his prominence."

Gen-tar-ten knew of the obvious threat that Ton-lal-set posed to both Jak-rad-tan and himself. But Jak-rad-tan knew another. What would Ton-lal-set do if he should ever learn of his connection to Lan-sol? The arch-reactionary would no doubt consider it a scandalous secret, to be suppressed at all costs. And he would deem Lan-sol's life a small price to pay for that suppression.

Jak-rad-tan strove for an even, almost casual tone as he spoke. "Ton-lal-set's death could only serve his allies if they come to know it. He could be moved to a cell in some isolated location, with full administrative documentation of the same. He could then be dispatched with no such notations." Jak-rad-tan fought back the attempt of his conscience to intrude. "Or if that required entrusting the task to those whom you are hesitant to trust, the duty roster could be adjusted to avoid providing that cell with the necessities of life."

Gen-tar-ten leaned forward and stared. "I had not thought you quite so pragmatic in political matters. There are risks in the plan you suggest. But I will seriously consider it."

* * *

Ton-lal-set noted with amusement that the guard carrying his meal was once again a co-conspirator. But his mood shifted to concern almost at once: the Tofa gave every appearance of agitation. The tray bore no illicit message; instead, the guard came near him and spoke in a rapid whisper. "You are to be moved again. None of our party instigated the move, and the location is one we have not infiltrated. The files of your most recent hearing have also been accessed at the highest levels. You may be in danger."

Ton-lal-set examined the contents of the tray. The meal resembled those that had barely sustained him during most of his imprisonment, with none of the recent amenities. "Have you any proposal for responding to this threat?"

The visitor's right hands fluttered in agitation. "A desperate one. We have prepared an escape plan. We had hoped to use it when our numbers were greater, but we can hide you while we attempt additional recruiting. It is, of course, for you to decide whether to take this risk. We are at your command."

Ton-lal-set swung his lower arms and sent the tray flying into the wall, clattering against the wall and then the floor, the food falling underneath it. "Then I command you to free me. Tonight!"

Chapter 22

(Aboard *Star Seed* and *Winds of Home*)

DESPITE HIS decision to study military tactics, Fel-lar did not regard himself as violent by nature; but standing at Seth Baruti's side as Baruti studied his calculations, and reread them, and muttered inaudibly, and studied some more, he could imagine grabbing the elderly professor and shaking an answer out of him. Baruti may have sensed the rising tide of Fel-lar's emotions: he glanced nervously up at his captain and shuffled the printouts together into a pile. "I wish I could be more certain."

"As do I." Fel-lar gripped his lower hands and upper hands behind his back. "But you are our expert, and whatever tentative conclusions you can reach, we need you to reveal them."

Baruti swallowed and cleared his throat. "Some of the readings have changed. Not very much. And there are fluctuations in a few spectra, while others remain more constant. Unfortunately, I didn't measure all of them on our last visit, so I can only compare past and present readings on some."

Fel-lar sensed a presence behind him and turned to see their youngest shipmate, Kenneth's student Can-til, standing in the doorway of Baruti's cabin. Once the young Tofa could see he had Fel-lar's attention, he waved a lower hand in a broad arc and asked, "Can you hear that?"

Fel-lar relaxed his hands and listened, but heard nothing beyond the ambient hums and creaks that had accompanied their entire voyage. He looked at Baruti, who shrugged. Fel-lar turned back to the waiting youngster. "Apparently I do not. What do you hear?"

Can-til repeated his gesture. "There is a very faint hum

that I only began to hear when I awoke this morning." He shuddered. "It makes me think of the far reaches of the universe, crying."

Fel-lar flicked an upper hand in a stern gesture. "That is poetic and imaginative, but not excessively helpful. I take it you have no explanation of this new sound?"

Can-til hesitated as if racking his brain one more time. "No, captain."

Fel-lar tried to remember his first encounter with the wormhole. Had he heard any such sound? Would he have noticed it if he had, not being so attuned to sound in general as a communications engineer might be?

And if he ignored what might be a possible warning, would that be his final mistake, dooming all those for whom he was responsible?

Fel-lar and Mara stood facing each other, Mara holding Fel-lar's lower hands, in the posture they had long since adopted for intense conversation. Fel-lar finished recounting everything he could recall of Seth Baruti's statements and manner. He had already told her about the faint sound that he could not hear, but in whose existence he was inclined to believe.

Mara waited for him to finish, then took a deep breath before speaking. "Shall we try to sum up what we have to gain by heading through? It's obvious what we have to lose."

"Please give me your summary. We will see whether I disagree with any element or have anything to add."

Mara's face was turned toward his, but her eyes had the fixed quality that denoted concentrated mental activity. "First, we'd need to approach very close in order to test the communications array in a way we couldn't do from home. If it's functional, we'd want to try again to reach our friends on Tofarn—but if we can't, then the only way to know what's happening would be to go there, if we can. Of course, we won't know until we show up whether we can help." She paused, pondering. "It's perfectly possible that our presence would make things worse. By underlining Gen-tar-ten's and Jak-rad-tan's association with the Twin-Bred, we could tip the scales in favor of whoever's trying to undermine them."

Fel-lar buzzed to signal his desire to interrupt. "On the

other hand, there is at most one spaceship on the planet, so far as we know. The appearance of *Star Seed* might intimidate opponents of Gen-tar-ten's regime, assuming that regime is still in place. And while the Glider weapons we carry are not especially sophisticated, they have a certain visual impact. They could be used to bluff any belligerents."

Mara raised an eyebrow. "Briefly." She waited a moment, then squeezed his hands more tightly and went on. "Fel-lar, my dear, you wanted this expedition partly because you felt you had missed your chance to do battle with our enemies. You should perhaps—to use a human idiom—bend over backwards to ensure that you do not let that desire outweigh your more usual caution."

A tap on their open door interrupted their conference: the young engineer once again. Fel-lar released Mara's right hand and turned toward the door. "Has the sound you reported changed in some way?"

"No, Captain. But something else has happened. We have received a message. Through New Landing—but not originating there. It came from another ship. On the other side of the wormhole."

Fel-lar stood before the assembled crew, printout in hand. Mara faced him at the front of the crowd, ready to assist.

Fel-lar waited for the mingled sounds of human and Tofa excitement to subside before speaking. "Most of you will remember Jak-rad-tan—Jak-rad, when we knew him—who left the Project before the crises that led to our emigration, and survived great perils thereafter. New Landing has forwarded to us a message from his child, Lan-sol, whom we invited to visit us before communications with Tofarn became somehow impossible. Lan-sol did not contact us from Tofarn. Determined to accept our invitation, he and his comrades built a ship and have reached the other end of the wormhole we are approaching.

"Lan-sol was able to contact New Landing by using that portion of the communications array positioned just beyond the entrance from that side. He has thus demonstrated that the communications problem did not arise from the array itself—but as you will hear, he knew as much already."

The noise level rose again. Mara turned, two fingers in her mouth, and blew a loud and piercing whistle. The crowd fell silent immediately. Fel-lar gestured his thanks. "And all of you will learn how he knew, and what else has occurred to justify the concern that brought us here, if you will give me your attention."

He waited another moment, to ensure that he had it, and then began to read.

Lan-sol had been admirably concise in recounting both the events on Tofarn before his departure and his ignorance of, and fears concerning, what might have happened since. The crew waited to be sure Fel-lar had finished reading, then erupted into conversation. Fel-lar held onto his patience: a spontaneous exchange of views might be more efficient than any formal procedure.

After a few minutes, he looked at Mara in inquiry. She nodded; he raised his upper hands and called out, "If I may have your attention once more!" The noise subsided quickly, with a few crew members glancing apprehensively at Mara to see if another shrill whistle was in the offing.

Fel-lar had intended to lead the discussion, but remembering Mara's advice, he reconsidered. "Emily Wilson, please come forward. I would like you to serve as moderator as we decide whether to risk passing through the wormhole, despite our uncertainty about its stability, in order to join Lan-sol and return to Tofarn. I am in favor of doing so; but it is not my choice to make, unless the tally of views is so evenly divided that a tie-breaker is called for." He did not wait for Emily to make her way to the front before joining Mara and taking her hand.

The crew did not achieve complete consensus, but no tie-breaker proved necessary. A clear majority voted to proceed.

Fel-lar resumed leadership of the meeting. "Those of you who voted to turn back: some of you, at least, have an option besides the course you hoped to reject. The ship has a few escape pods with suspended animation capability. They would not suffice to accommodate everyone who voted Nay, but we could use random choice methods if necessary to

assign them. We can program the pods to return to New
Landing. They cannot attain the speeds with which we
traveled on the outward journey; but eventually, and
assuming no unlikely mischance, you would return to tell our
community of where the rest of us have gone, in case we have
not returned in the meantime to tell the tale ourselves.

"The choice is yours—but choose soon. Lan-sol's ship
could enter the wormhole at any time, if it has not done so
already. We ourselves will reach the wormhole in two days'
time. We will try to send Lan-sol's ship a message asking
them to await us on the other side; and we will attempt our
own passage as soon as we arrive. If there is a purpose to our
mission, it admits of no delay."

In the end, the pods went unused. Those easily
deterred by uncertainty or hazard had not joined the
expedition; nor did the pods necessarily offer an escape from
either.

Establishing direct contact with Lan-sol's ship proved
more time-consuming than Fel-lar had hoped. Can-til had no
training in ship-to-ship communications, nor in isolating the
origin codes for a relayed message. While the young engineer
worked the problem, Fel-lar ordered him to relay the
message through New Landing as well—but the latter would
not reach Lan-sol until after *Star Seed* reached the
wormhole.

The direct message did not go out until the wormhole
was almost at hand.

*   *   *

Winds of Home had hovered close to the wormhole
since sending its message to New Landing. The crew spent
the time playing and replaying the various accounts *Star
Seed*'s crew had recorded of their own passage, imagining,
anticipating.

As they entered the wormhole, a reflection of the port
side of the ship would be visible from starboard, and of the
starboard side from port. *Winds of Home*, like *Star Seed*
before it, had two distinctly different designs emblazoned on
its hull. Lan-sol had chosen two planets: one golden, with its

surface rippling to represent the waters of Tofarn, and the other red, its outline jagged to convey the crystal cliffs of their destination.

As for the more profound effects they could expect, a few crew members planned to experiment: if they practiced recognizing various words backwards, would they be able to think more clearly, even when the wormhole sent their neural impulses careening back and forth? To reduce complications, each of these Tofa would spend the passage alone. Others formed various groupings. Melly asked whether Lan-sol wished her to go through the wormhole in his company, but he gently declined: it might look like weakness for him to stay close to the oldest individual on board.

Lan-sol's attention to such details appeared to have been well worthwhile. The bold eagerness with which his fellows approached the challenge of the wormhole filled him with pride. But if they waited much longer, would that enthusiasm and dedication waver? Why, indeed, should they wait any longer? They could hardly be certain that the message to New Landing would even arrive, let alone when they might expect a reply. Whether New Landing responded or no, *Winds of Home* would fly onward, New Landing the goal and the wormhole the road.

Lan-sol activated the ship-wide intercom, his whole body buzzing with excitement.

"Prepare to enter!"

* * *

The last time he had passed through the wormhole, Seth Baruti had had Mara and Emily and Harriet at his side. All but Harriet were on *Star Seed* once again, but this time Seth had other duties.

He had suggested that Wings Spread Wide might more safely make the passage strapped in as if for takeoff, lest its reaction to the disorienting experience send it careening into walls or ceiling or furniture. But the Glider would have none of it. "I did not leave my nest so far behind and come these distances in order to huddle like a chick in its egg. I will meet these wonders as my name implies."

Seth alternated between dizzying elation and the wish that he himself had somewhere to huddle effectively. He had thought he was getting old, all those years ago. How young he had been by comparison! Soon he would once again see himself receding in infinite refraction, and find himself unable to understand his own thoughts. Could his mind, his nervous system, still recover from that assault?

* * *

No complete pair of Twin-Bred had joined *Star Seed*'s second expedition. Neither Nathan nor the Tofa Twin-Bred on board would relive the blurring of boundaries between twin and twin. There had been much discussion among the unaccompanied twins about how they should arrange themselves. In the end, most chose to enter the wormhole as a group. Some felt uneasy about what almost seemed a kind of infidelity; but curiosity, as well as the need for mutual support, outweighed such qualms.

Fel-lar consulted with Mara about how best to ensure his readiness to cope, as a captain must, with any crisis that arose. "Should I remain in isolation, to reduce the complexity of the distractions?"

Mara would never forget that first passage through the wormhole, the first time in her life she had seen Levi's face: in her mind, to be sure, but with a clarity beyond mere imagination. Now she examined other aspects of that memory. ("Levi, I didn't just see you that day. I heard you. And you made sense. It should be the same this time; and if I understand you, Fel-lar probably will too.")

("I bow. Captain Fel-lar, sir, I submit that you should remain in Mara's and my company, as between the two of us—if you will grant me status worthy of counting—we may be the only members of the ship's company who remain coherent. Though in any emergency, even if my thoughts remain comprehensible, they may or may not be worth comprehending.")

The visible reflection phenomenon would very slightly precede the more disorienting mental impact. Once again

Star Seed had prepared its hull, differentiating port from starboard so the crew could more easily observe the eerie effect. Instead of a silhouetted chain of humans confronting a similar chain of Tofa, they had (after much discussion) chosen to base both designs on the theme of flight. On the port side, three Gliders converged on a waiting pair of Twin-Bred; to starboard, a human with artificial wings followed a similarly equipped Tofa off a cliff.

Once again, as years before, the calm voice of the computer announced, "We are entering the wormhole." (Fel-lar and Mara had united to slap down Levi's suggestion that the computer speak for the wormhole and proclaim, "Welcome back.") In common rooms and in private cabins, the ship's company stared at the viewscreens in expectation.

Fel-lar stood behind Mara in the cabin they shared, encircling her in his lower arms, his upper hands resting on her hair. The viewscreen showed a tri-part view. Straight ahead, the concentrated cluster of stars loomed before them.

Last time, it had been his twin Rose there with him, holding his lower hands tight as their boundaries blurred, senses and identities interweaving. Would the same happen with Mara? He half hoped it would, as a confirmation of the closeness they had striven toward through the years, and half feared it, as somehow diminishing the unique importance of that earlier bond.

Suddenly the intercom squawked an interruption, a voice strained and halting, forcing out words. "Fel-lar—Captain—it's Nathan. Look! Starboard—two shapes! Look—the designs!"

Fel-lar could still, on some level, understand the words, though he found it difficult to grasp their meaning. He was supposed to look at something. The viewscreen? Starboard—that would be the right-hand portion of the screen. It should show the port side design, mysteriously reflected. But the screen showed two different images, overlapping. On the left, the port side, was a single reflection of the starboard design. Fel-lar looked back to the right. How could there be two reflections? And why did he only recognize one?

Just when he most needed to think, the full impact of the neural reflection overcame him: not a blurring or blending of identities, but a chaotic multiplication. Many Fel-lars, many Maras, milling about, engaged in some intricate and ever-shifting dance, vanishing and reappearing, and which of them, how many of them, was he? . . .

Mara was speaking, her tone urgent; but he could not understand her. They had prepared for this moment. What had they done?

Then, loud, clear, and almost shrill, came the voice of Levi: ("Nathan's right! Off to starboard, ahead of us—that's not *Star Seed*, not a reflection. The design is different! That's *another ship!*")

And finally, drowning out all other signals and voices, came the blare of the proximity alarm.

* * *

Lan-sol leaned against the corner of his cabin, trembling. Strange syllables echoed in his mind. Some trace of meaning lingered behind them: soon? Through?

The center of the viewscreen showed a dazzling field of close-packed stars. To the sides hovered the two planets, gold and red, red and gold, in ghostly escort.

But the empty planet of his design was acquiring occupants, winged creatures somehow approaching, crossing the orb . . . Coming closer . . . .

And then the creatures swerved in their flight, away from the ship.

* * *

Fel-lar/Levi/Mara barked orders to the ship's navigation system. Were they speaking in any recognizable tongue? Could the system follow such commands unassisted?

Somehow, the ship was turning. . . .

* * *

As *Winds of Home* emerged from the wormhole, captain and crew took long and shuddering breaths, looking around themselves, welcoming and wondering at the return of simple, normal sight and sound and thought. Lan-sol switched the viewscreen to the rearward view. The dazzling cluster of stars looked just like the wormhole as they had entered it. Were they indeed on the other side? What had happened? How could he find out?

Of course—the computer! It should be responsive to voice commands by now. "Summarize journey since last report."

"Astronomical discontinuity traversed. One vessel encountered. Collision avoided by maneuvers of other vessel."

"Identify vessel!"

"Markings unfamiliar. Dimensions and radiation signature similar to *Star Seed*."

Lan-sol rocked backward on his heels. "Location of ship tentatively identified as *Star Seed*?"

"Location not known. Extrapolation: within the discontinuity."

Lan-sol slapped the control to open the door to his cabin, turned back to the computer, and shouted a command. "Full stop!"

Log of Captain Lan-sol, *Winds of Home* (excerpts)

Voyage Day 40: We have survived not only the wormhole, but a most unexpected brush with catastrophe. We came close—we cannot say how close—to a fatal collision with the very ship on which the Twin-Bred left Tofarn. Apparently, *Star Seed* entered the wormhole en route to Tofarn, to offer assistance to those whom the Twin-Bred still consider friends. They sent us a message first, and if I had waited a little longer, we would have received it. But the message asked us to wait for their arrival; and I cannot say with any certainty that my crew and I could have endured halting on the threshold of that adventure.

Star Seed managed not only to move out of our way, but to reverse course, following us to what for them was the "home" end of the wormhole. We have established two-way symbolic communication, as fully intelligible speech in our own language requires physical proximity, and my command of Terran language is not what it could be. I am eager to actually meet, converse with, and touch the legends of my childhood. (I suppose I should now be more understanding of how my crew, and others like them back home, act in my presence. . . .) However, I am embarrassed to suggest what would probably be seen as an unnecessary nuisance.

Now a new choice awaits me, one I must make in concert with *Star Seed*'s captain (my parent's old friend Fellar). Should *Winds of Home* proceed to New Landing, while *Star Seed*, perhaps, goes on to confront our possible enemies on Tofarn? Or do we turn right around, traverse the wormhole as soon as we feel fully competent again and have checked all ship systems, and take part in our own defense?

I attempted to consult with Melly, as the closest I can come to availing myself of the shrewdness and common sense of her mother. But Melly pointed out that any threat to Jak-rad-tan might encompass Veda as well, making it impossible for her to serve as an objective counselor. It is, however, plain that her appetite for the outward journey—to the extent it was genuine, and not the result of entreaties from members of my family—has waned considerably while matters on Tofarn remain so unsettled.

Captain Fel-lar has made a few vague allusions to some hazard that might or might not be lurking in the wormhole itself. He will be sending a message shortly with more information, after Seth Baruti—still alive! And apparently in charge of an actual Glider!—makes some more measurements for *Star Seed*'s computer to analyze.

Log of Captain Fel-lar, *Star Seed* (excerpts)

Launch Day plus 36: After gathering our courage to enter the wormhole, we have almost immediately retreated to the New Landing side. Our difficulties in establishing communication with Lan-sol's ship (named, with surprising nostalgia, *Winds of Home*) proved too much for the patience of its captain. They plunged on through, nearly colliding with us in the process. Had we, journeying to Tofarn, crashed into the ship we left New Landing partially to assist, the irony would have been so exquisite and classic that I could feel some dismay at having averted that fate. What an epic poem, in the ancient Terran mode, it could have made! But of course, there would have been no survivor "escaped alone to tell" some possible poet.

Nathan, engineer extraordinary, realized the danger and somehow overcame the effects of the wormhole enough to override the previously programmed navigation instructions for a few crucial seconds. Then he apparently collapsed; but the guidance systems were by then in a position to take us away from *Winds of Home* and back toward the wormhole entrance. It is unclear whether the ship's programming or Nathan's intervention acted to prevent an even more catastrophic encounter with the wormhole's inner horizon. He is still weak and disoriented, so I have not been able to learn more about his role. (I could wish for Harriet Gaho's expertise, though not even she has any experience in treating the after-effects of undue mental strain during a wormhole passage. However, I suspect her well-developed medical intuition would provide some starting point.) I may invent some sort of honor to give him, like the medals awarded for courage and tenacity in the armies I have studied.

Now I must decide—or rather, we must decide, for I am sure Mara will have an opinion worth considering—whether and (if at all) how strongly to urge Lan-sol and his young companions to head for New Landing. Why should they risk another passage through the wormhole, in order to return to where they started? If some crisis has erupted, how much could they contribute in confronting it?

But then, one could say the same of our own motley collection of would-be saviors. We have a few weapons and a few mediators—hardly a force likely to turn any tides. Yet we have already determined to try. Lan-sol, if he wishes, has the right to do the same. I can, at least, tell Lan-sol about the option we offered any of our number who might not wish to pass through the wormhole. I have not yet ascertained whether *Winds of Home* has its own escape pods, but given the extent to which the ship is based on our own, as well as the desirability of such an emergency measure, it seems likely.

I could try to contact Jak-rad-tan and, if he managed

to respond, to learn his views. But in view of what has already happened, we could hardly be sure the message would not be intercepted, nor confident in the origin of any reply.

Seth Baruti is comparing the energies measurable inside the wormhole during our brief foray with those recorded on our original journey. I doubt we will learn from that comparison whether either or both of our ships would be at risk upon venturing back inside.

On a lighter note, Wings Spread Wide has apparently emerged from the wormhole full of unprecedented musical inspiration. It has, in fact, decided to rewrite the already completed portions of its final song, using its new musical insights. If it were up to our venerable Glider, we would without question be plunging back through—despite the fact that the wormhole has left the elder visibly weakened.

Launch Day plus 38: I have now had several exchanges with young Captain Lan-sol. I believe we can modify one of our escape pods to bring Lan-sol aboard *Star Seed*, and intend to do so. He would no doubt enjoy the opportunity, as he seems fascinated with every aspect of Twin-Bred history. And I would like the opportunity to more accurately assess his state of mind. I have the impression that he feels somewhat torn: loathe to postpone his arrival at a new world he regards as a Promised Land, but also duty-bound to return and confront a political upheaval for which he seems to feel irrationally responsible.

Lan-sol's crew appears willing to follow his lead. Indeed, "follow' is the appropriate term: his status has a quasi-religious aspect that, to his credit, he finds unpleasant and frustrating. It makes for quite a contrast with my own independently minded cohort.

The more I ponder the question, the more I am convinced that wherever *Winds of Home* chooses to go, we must go also. I cannot abandon Jak-rad-tan's child, here in the space between worlds, even if giving him escort requires that I abandon Jak-rad-tan and his fellows. But I believe Lan-sol will decide to return to Tofarn (wormhole willing), with the meager reinforcements we provide.

* * *

As *Star Seed* prepared to enter the wormhole one more time, almost all her Tofa crew availed themselves of a new distraction. This time, they would have musical accompaniment. Wings Spread Wide had led the way, resolving to play a recording of his rewritten song during the passage. Music inspired by the unique sensory and neurological distortion the wormhole provided, filtered through that same distortion, might be exciting indeed to aficionados of the art.

*   *   *

Log of Captain Lan-sol, *Winds of Home* (excerpts)

Voyage Day 42: I gather that *Star Seed*'s gravity is in transition between New Landing and Tofarna levels; but it is still less than I have ever experienced. Perhaps the physical sensation of buoyancy is contributing to the elation I am feeling—what Melly once referred to as "walking on air."

No matter what happens, I have achieved one of the desires that brought me here. I have boarded *Star Seed* and walked her corridors. And while I did not manage to meet everyone on board, I have met at least a few of the Twin-Bred.

Fel-lar is gracious and kind, but there is a power in him that I would hesitate to challenge. He and Jak-rad-tan may have been peers in their youth, but Fel-lar has grown into a Personage in a way my parent has not (perhaps through lack of opportunity).

As for the Founder, Mara Cadell: perhaps my emotions have been predetermined by her role in Twin-Bred history, but I found her more than intimidating—closer to terrifying. No small part of my admiration of Fel-lar derives from the ease with which he parries her thrusts and then meets her arguments head-on.

Fel-lar offered to escort *Winds of Home* to New Landing, but has acquiesced in my and my crew's desire to join with him in confronting whoever is behind the disturbing events at home. Fel-lar mentioned that he had offered his shipmates the option of avoiding the wormhole and returning to New Landing, albeit slowly, via escape pods. I am sure this constituted a tactfully oblique suggestion that I make a similar offer to my own people, and I intend to do so.

* * *

Melly could almost have wished that *Winds of Home*, like *Star Seed*, offered suspended animation. Then perhaps she could escape—if only for a while—the imagined voice of her mother, urging cautious avoidance of whatever battle might follow the ships' arrival on Tofarn.

On the other hand, that voice might well have followed her into what would have been inescapable dreams. She shuddered. Better to be free to answer back, when she was unable to ignore the voice altogether.

You didn't board that ship to end up in a crossfire. You wanted to see Twin-Bred again, and now you have, even sooner than you expected.

"But not my brothers!"

Doesn't the ship have escape pods? I'm sure Lan-sol would be more than willing for you to use one to get to New Landing. You could sleep away the journey, so it'd feel like no time at all.

"I wouldn't even know what was happening around me. And Lan-sol and everyone else here might be in danger, and I wouldn't be able to help."

Please be realistic, Melly. How much help could you be? Have you become an expert marksman since you took ship?

If only *Winds of Home* had a virtual reality chamber! They could have used it as a shooting range. But she was getting more used to handling the weapons they had on board, hefting their weight when loaded, aiming and dry-firing them when not.

And don't forget, you promised to bring the boys my gift. You promised!

Had there been something odd about Veda's oh-so-casual air, when she mentioned that data chip? That message—she should have realized it might be more important than Veda would confide. When had her mother had only one agenda at a time?

Well, Melly could keep that promise without abandoning ship. *Star Seed* was in touch with New Landing; it would be easy for Melly, as communications engineer, to get the necessary contact information. She could transmit Veda's message and send her greetings, and her love, at the same time.

Darling, you have a chance to be safer than those of us at home, safer than I'll be. Please, won't you take it?

But the voice had grown faint, and easier to ignore.

Lan-sol was too busy to see Melly about her sending Veda's message. Naturally. But there should be nothing problematic about ship-to-ship communication, which had been going on for some time now. She left him a note and headed to the communications center.

If Melly had delivered the chip to Jimmy and Peer-tek as originally planned, it would have been bad manners (however tempting) to take a peek beforehand. But now, she needed some minimal description for the ship's communications log.

She had had no clear idea of what to expect, but she had not expected an audiovisual clip, about five minutes long, of a once-familiar scene: the interior of their own family cabin back at the Project, as recorded by one of the various hidden cameras of whose existence she had then been unaware. It showed Jimmy and Peer-tek playing a game, probably hide and seek. Peer-tek, when the recording began, had the role of seeker: he stood with his upper hands covering his eyes for some seconds, before he dropped his hands and began surveying the living room in a methodical fashion. Then he passed out of view, only to return chasing Jimmy through the maze of furniture, Veda's voice from somewhere out of view adding a sharp warning to be careful. And there, glimpsed through the doorway to the kitchen, she could see her toddler self, in a high chair, ignoring a bowl of some orange-colored mush, banging with her spoon on the built-in tray in wild excitement. (What had that mush been? Yams? One of the first Tofa grains the Project had cultivated?)

Melly ejected the chip and sat back, puzzled. Had the imminent departure of Veda's youngest child triggered some uncharacteristic mood of general nostalgia?

Well, if Veda had some other motive for this message, there was no knowing what, and no point in wondering. She opened the communications log, noted the sender and recipients along with the time of transmission, and for nature of the message, wrote simply "home movies." Then she sent the message on its way and returned to her quarters.

Chapter 23

(New Landing)

JIMMY BURST into Peer-tek's study, eyes wide. "*Melly*'s on that ship! Lan-sol's ship!"

Peer-tek looked up from the puzzle he had been creating, observed Jimmy's distress, and thought how much his twin had changed over the years. Once, he would have been beaming in delight at the prospect of seeing their little sister. The perils and uncertainties that sprang instantly to Peer-tek's mind would have been slow to occur to the sanguine youngster Jimmy had been. Peer-tek felt a brief pang of regret for lost innocence, then pushed it aside to concentrate on the problem at hand. "How did you hear of her presence?"

"She sent a message." Then, to Peer-tek's relief, he smiled faintly. "And she attached a message from Veda. It'll be good to hear from her again."

"Indeed it will." Glad to see Jimmy's mood lighten, he declined to dampen it by remarking that Veda's communications had been known to impose their own burdens. If the message should prove to be encrypted, he would know to expect a problem to be addressed. He could only hope that this time, there would be no need to place himself in opposition to Mara, which would almost certainly entail defying Fel-lar as well.

Peer-tek managed to divert Jimmy's attention from Veda's message until Jimmy and the various children left to fly kites that afternoon.

Opening the file, he was at first bemused to find an audiovisual clip from his and Jimmy's childhood. In a moment, however, he realized that Veda, with her current expertise, might well have gone one layer beyond cryptology and employed steganography as well, hiding the actual message in a seemingly innocuous file. And he had best proceed on that assumption.

Taking one more look at the video before beginning his analysis, he whistled faintly as he realized the hint the video itself contained: hide and seek, with Peer-tek as the seeker.

It took more than one session for Peer-tek to solve Veda's conundrum, and Peer-tek began to fear causing family discord as he absented himself from several outings and activities to continue his work. Just when the domestic politics of the situation threatened to become problematic, he broke through to the extensive text concealed in the audiovisual file. By that time, he was not in the least surprised that the text was encrypted as well, and posed at least as many challenges as the files Peer-tek had examined so many years before. Of course Veda would be even more cautious than the xenocidal Annabelle Bloom.

And once again, he eventually discovered, Veda was inflicting upon her Tofa offspring the knowledge of a weapon dangerous to his species. But this time, use of the weapon would not mean utter catastrophe; and this time, it might be his friends who sought to use it. . . .

Veda did not explain how she had obtained the information about centuries-past disruption of Tofa communication abilities; but Peer-tek could imagine no possible explanation that did not subject Veda to some degree of peril. And indeed, her instructions suggested as much: "I know that you two will work together and help each other, as you always have. Please, boys, think twice and twice more before you share this knowledge with someone new. Consider not only whether you trust that person, but whether you trust everyone that person trusts. Record only what you must, and transmit less than what initially seems necessary. It should go without saying, but I'll say nonetheless, that any message you find a way to send must be encoded with all Peer-tek's admirable skill. Whatever method or methods you use, please do your best to ensure that only someone intimately familiar with the Twin-Bred project will be able to make the first crucial insights necessary to begin the decryption process. . . ."

Rereading the text, Peer-tek noted Veda's use of the technically obsolete term "boys." He suspected it showed some subconscious concern about the burden such urgent secrecy would place on them both, and especially on Jimmy. Peer-tek shared that concern to some extent, and Veda had not been in a position to witness Jimmy's maturation.

In the end, Veda and Peer-tek were alike in this: whatever the contrary arguments, neither could accept the emotional cost of erecting a wall of secrecy between the twins. So he would continue the task Veda had begun, the task of ensuring that Jimmy keep the secret and bear up under its strain.

Peer-tek stood beside Jimmy's chair, his lower right hand on his twin's shoulder, as Jimmy finished reading the message. He waited through Jimmy's moment of silence and pallor; then, when Jimmy looked up at him, he said, "While I awaited your return, I have begun organizing my thoughts as to how to direct our investigation, and whom to recruit—"

"Elspeth. Linguist, neurologist, smart, level-headed." A smile flickered briefly across Jimmy's face at Peer-tek's start of surprise. "Whoever else we approach, she should be one of the first."

"I may be inclined to agree, but we must consider the ramifications of including her. Either we include Judy as well, or we risk damaging their relationship."

"Don't you trust Judy?"

Peer-tek hesitated, choosing his words carefully. "You have emphasized that you consider Elspeth level-headed. Should I create a description of Judy, that is not the adjective that would first come to mind. She is passionate and somewhat emotionally volatile."

Jimmy sighed and tipped his chair backward, balancing it by stretching his long legs forward; Peer-tek glanced through the doorway to see whether Anna, who found this one habit especially aggravating, was anywhere near. Jimmy saw the direction of his glance, correctly divined its import, and asked, "When are we going to tell Anna? She'll have to know."

"Indeed—which may help us solve the dilemma we

have just been discussing. I would greatly value Anna's opinion on Judy's ability to cope with so stressful a secret—and on whether La-ren's influence is sufficient to counter any instability on her part."

* * *

In her initial delight over La-ren's ability to catch Elspeth's thoughts, Judy had never imagined how exhausting the process could be for her as a conduit. But then, she could hardly have foreseen that the three of them would use this means of silent conversation so intensively, for such a serious purpose.

At least Peer-tek had been satisfied with the security of the arrangement. No one could overhear, as long as both women remembered not to speak aloud about anything of substance; and they took special care to cut short any discussion if other Tofa approached the house.

And it didn't hurt that the process worked better if Judy and Elspeth sat *very* close to each other.

So now, Judy and Elspeth shared one of the curved stone benches around their crystal-topped breakfast table, thighs mashed warmly together. The morning sun had slanted through the kitchen window and warmed the table top, but by now it had moved on: Judy had slept late and was fortifying herself with both protein and caffeine, even as Elspeth provided La-ren with her morning update and La-ren relayed it to Judy. ("I've almost finished going through the Project's neurological research . . . Electrical activity is crucial in both human and Tofa brains, but the details are quite different . . . and Tofa have an area devoted to receiving and analyzing such signals, very close to the main language processing centers. . . . Nobody did any research about disease or other malfunction in either area, let alone deliberate disruption.")

Judy sipped her coffee, found it lukewarm, and gulped down the rest before refilling her mug. ("Maybe we can extrapolate from ways that humans sometimes lose language capacity—or at least, with causes that occur suddenly.")

La-ren relayed the comment to Elspeth, while Judy seized the moment to breathe in the steam from her fresh cup of coffee and to try to relax her shoulders. All too soon, La-ren was ready with Elspeth's response. ("Aside from physically damaging Broca's or Wernicke's area, there might be some sort of electrical attack possible—a way to induce artificial epilepsy . . . .")

("Whoa. Primitive methods, remember?")

Elspeth slumped forward, elbows hitting the table and sloshing the liquid in the mug Judy had just set down. ("Right. Damn.") Then she straightened up and spoke aloud. "Look, we all need a break. I'll be back in a minute." She turned to brush a kiss against Judy's shoulder, slid off the bench, and headed down the hall.

Judy swiveled around to lean her back against the table, stretched out her legs, and massaged her temples with her hands.

("Headache, twin?")

("A bit. It's a relief to talk just to you for a moment. Especially if we talk about something else. Did I have any interesting dreams last night? I can't remember.")

("There was one—perhaps not interesting, and rather familiar, but pleasant. Your first drum solo, on our seventh birthday.")

Judy bit her lip and fought back tears. ("It was so sweet of you to give me those drums, when you loathed human music as much as any Tofa. Talk about headaches! You must have had one that morning, the way I was banging away.")

("What I remember is how happy you were. And how smug I felt in consequence.")

("I wish I'd brought those drums with us. I was trying to be all sensible and mature, leaving them behind. Someone should have told me that when we get older, we don't care so much about what's mature. Or maybe we just get more sentimental.")

She twisted back around to face the table. ("How did it go again?") She tapped tentatively at the table with her hands and found a familiar rhythm, then sped it up until her hands were a blur and her palms stinging, La-ren's whistled laughter forming the accompaniment.

Elspeth ran into the room, staring, her mouth open. Judy laughed and stopped drumming. Had she ever told Elspeth about that birthday? "When La-ren and I turned seven—"

But Elspeth was pointing at Judy's now-motionless hands. "That—could that be it??"

La-ren buzzed for Judy's attention. ("Bring her closer!")

Judy beckoned to Elspeth and then put her finger to her lips. Elspeth flushed and hurried to Judy's side. Judy hugged Elspeth's waist as she sat down, then let go so as not to distract her and delay the coming revelation.

The seconds still seemed long before La-ren began to relay Elspeth's thoughts. ("In humans who have trouble with their speech . . . Some therapies involve the use of rhythmic sounds . . . such as songs and metronomes . . . but other background noises can make the problem worse.")

Abruptly, it was La-ren speaking for himself—and Judy had not heard that tone of excitement in many, many years. ("Elspeth, are you suggesting that human and Tofa brains are just different enough that what enhances language processing for humans may disrupt it, or at least the telepathy/language interface, for Tofa?")

Elspeth somehow combined a nod and a shrug. A few seconds later came La-ren's transmittal of her response: ("Well, it's primitive enough, and could have been discovered by accident. . . . And it might partly explain the Tofa dislike of human music! . . . But the rhythmic noise can't be just like what we find in human music, or the Tofa Twin-Bred would have noticed it . . . .")

("And Glider music has nothing like human percussion.") Judy stretched her suddenly tense muscles as best she could without elbowing Elspeth. ("So now we have to find some way of testing this hypothesis—without anyone knowing what we're up to. And we'll need at least two Tofa—") She stopped short and fought off tears. ("At least two corporeal Tofa. We'll need to talk to Peer-tek about who else to include.")

The three of them fell silent for a moment. Then La-ren spoke for himself again, soberly, all excitement gone: ("I have an idea for a way to keep the risk of exposure to a minimum. And it might be said, with justice and some irony, that it falls thoroughly within the Twin-Bred tradition.")

* * *

Jimmy had seen Peer-tek concerned, nervous, disturbed; but he could not recall ever before seeing Peer-tek outright angry. On a few occasions, when around other Tofa, he had smelled the sharp chemical odor Peer-tek was now emitting, but never from so close a distance, close enough to make his eyes water. The realization underscored both Peer-tek's essential good nature and the nature of the trap in which Peer-tek considered himself caught.

Not having seen Peer-tek angry, Jimmy had no experience with how to speak to his twin under such circumstances. He cleared his throat and made the attempt. "Um . . . Gen-tar-ten doesn't even know we got the message. Veda shouldn't get in any trouble if you don't answer. Or if you wait for a safer way to investigate."

Peer-tek swiveled his head toward Jimmy, then pivoted and grabbed the nearest leaning post in both left hands, shaking it back and forth. "Gen-tar-ten would find out eventually. Or if he did not, that could be because the uprising of former Eminences succeeded. I cannot increase the chances of that outcome, even by inaction." He thrust the leaning post away from him; it fell against a wall and slid down to clatter on the ground. "Not even to protect my child."

"Couldn't you just confide in someone else? Another adult Tofa?"

"Our community is too interconnected. Recall Veda's warnings."

Jimmy glanced at Sin-han, happily building a tower of blocks in the next room. "How do you know that Sin-han won't give the secret away somehow—by imitating the sounds he hears, making a game of it?"

Peer-tek let go of the leaning post and stood up straight and rigid, facing away from Sin-han. "If the experiment succeeds, Sin-han's experience is likely to be . . . unpleasant. It is unlikely he would base a game on it. And he has no malicious tendencies that would lead him to inflict such unpleasantness on a sibling or playmate. Besides . . . ."

Jimmy waited for Peer-tek to conclude his thought, but for a long time he said nothing more. Finally, he continued:

"You may be forgetting that with a Tofa child, especially my own, I have the means to prevent any such disclosure."

Jimmy knew his face must show his dismay, and that his twin would recognize the expression. Coercion of offspring was so thoroughly taboo among New Landing's Tofa that the generation now reaching adulthood might not even realize the possibility existed.

Peer-tek had started to hum quietly. Jimmy closed the distance between them and gripped his twin's lower hands; Peer-tek stopped humming and then said, almost as quietly: "If I decide such measures are necessary, I will have to hope that Sin-han does not understand what I am doing—why he is overcoming any impulse he might otherwise have to talk about or mimic what occurs here today." He squeezed Jimmy's hands and disengaged his own. "We may as well begin."

They began with a normal back-and-forth dialogue. Peer-tek told Sin-han a story and periodically asked Sin-han what should happen next. A human toddler his age might have had difficulty in answering, but Sin-han, as expected, did not, though his contributions were simple in form and substance. Peer-tek made periodic notes, maintaining as much visual contact with Sin-han as possible.

Then Jimmy, on Peer-tek's signal, pulled out his tablet and began to play the recording Elspeth had prepared.

Elspeth had been admirably methodical, including every conceivable variation, combination, and permutation of tone, amplitude, spacing, length, and regularity; every available instrument or improvised object that could, to any degree, resonate or otherwise sound when struck; human music, Glider music with percussion added, chaotic cacophony.

They were about two-thirds of the way through the recording, and Sin-han was narrating the encounter between Hero Sin-han and the Giant Flying Monster, when Peer-tek swayed backward and put an upper hand to his head, and Sin-han began to hum, wrapping all his arms around his torso. The always disconcerting toast-and-jam odor of Tofa trauma filled the room. Jimmy jabbed at the recording to stop it, jotting down both the point they had reached and the time at which they had reached it. Then he looked back at his twin, hoping he appeared calmer than he felt.

Peer-tek opened his arms and beckoned Sin-han with a lower hand. Sin-han ran to his parent, clutching him tight and burrowing his head into Peer-tek's torso. Peer-tek hummed for a moment before visibly forcing himself to stop. He looked up at Jimmy and loosened one arm to point toward the tablet. "When we have recovered, you must resume the playback. There may be other segments remaining, even more effective than this one."

Jimmy tried to steady his breathing as he nodded assent. "Can you describe what happened—what you felt, what you're feeling now?"

"As we surmised, I began to have difficulty understanding what Sin-han was saying." He paused. "I am also, at this moment, finding it hard to produce words and to keep my train of thought. There is also—" He looked down at Sin-han, and paused again before continuing, the burnt-and-sweet odor growing stronger. "—There is also some pain."

Elspeth frowned in concentration. "It seems that the disruption goes beyond the telepathic component of Tofar. That's not too surprising."

It took fifteen minutes for Sin-han to regain his placid demeanor, and for Peer-tek to declare himself able to continue. Jimmy forced himself to restart the recording, and the playback and the storytelling continued.

But they could only bear Sin-han's distress one more time before calling a halt.

Peer-tek leaned against the wall as Jimmy, this time, attempted to comfort Sin-han. On his knees, holding the loudly humming child, Jimmy looked up at his brother. "It was worse this time, wasn't it?"

Peer-tek pushed away tentatively from the wall, then collapsed back again. "Significantly." He massaged the area around his eyes with both upper hands. "Tomorrow, we must attempt to duplicate that final sequence with some live instrumentation, and compare the effect. As soon as the effect dissipates, I will—instruct—Sin-han not to disclose any details of today's proceedings."

But the minutes passed, and while the intensity of Sin-han's distress appeared to lessen, he continued to hum in quiet syncopated bursts. And even after Peer-tek was able to speak to him and receive a response suggesting comprehension, the attempt to command immediately triggered louder humming, the child thrashing about in Jimmy's arms.

The brothers stared at each other in dismay. Again they waited for Sin-han to calm down; and again, they reached only the equilibrium of quiet misery. Finally Peer-tek said quietly: "Please explain to Sin-han, as best you can. that he must not tell any of his siblings what happened here. We will keep him at home, and deflect any would-be visitors, until— until two days from now, when we may hope to complete the experiment.

"And please tell my child that I am sorry."

It took four days, not two, before Peer-tek decided that both he and Sin-han had recovered enough for a final test. And even then, he would only substitute live sound for the less effective of the two recorded passages. Jimmy took the recording and a few improvised instruments into a canyon out behind the house and practiced until he felt his imitation came close to the original. Elspeth, when summoned, concurred. They were ready to see whether the live version was as disruptive as the recording, or less so, or worse.

It was worse. Enough worse that according to Peer-tek's and Elspeth's newly educated guesses, it would be seven days or more before Peer-tek would be able to compel Sin-han to conceal what had happened. And to isolate Sin-han so long, even from his siblings, might raise so many questions as to possibly prove counterproductive. Nor would it help Sin-han himself recover from his ordeal.

Three more days passed.

* * *

Anna usually heard the approach of visitors and opened the door in welcome before they could knock. Today, however, Judy and Elspeth had to knock twice before Anna appeared, her older daughter at her side. Anna's expression was studiously neutral; the girl, in contrast, scowled at the visitors before she stepped out of the way just far enough for them to enter.

Elspeth gripped Judy's hand and turned toward Anna. "How is Sin-han?"

Anna took a deep breath and began moving toward the interior of the house. She spoke over her shoulder: "Worse than Peer-tek. But neither is doing well."

Judy felt La-ren's intention to speak and pulled Elspeth closer so that she could hear as well. Elspeth looked at her, startled; Judy held a finger to her lips.

("Peer-tek asked most urgently for our assistance; and Peer-tek, knowing the risks, chose to involve Sin-han. If Anna knows as much, then she knows she is treating you unfairly; and if she does not know, then to her pain when she learns of it will be added the fact that she has treated you so.")

Neither of the women had any comment to add. Silently they followed Anna through the corridor to Peer-tek's combined sleeping room and study. Anna knocked gently; in response, to the visitors' momentary surprise, came the fretful whine of a toddler. Anna pushed the door open, revealing Peer-tek lying on his bed and Sin-han tugging at Peer-tek's nearest hand. From the room came the burnt-and-sweet odor of a Tofa under physical or emotional strain.

Anna entered, stooped, and grabbed Sin-han around the waist, hoisting him up and kissing the top of his head. Then she leaned over somewhat awkwardly to tap Peer-tek on the shoulder. "Can you rouse yourself? Your—fellow experimenters are here."

Peer-tek opened his eyes, stretched his arms and legs, and pushed himself off the bed. Anna, shifting Sin-han so that she could hold him with one arm, steadied Peer-tek when he wobbled on his way to standing. Peer-tek made his way slowly to a leaning post, then beckoned Judy and Elspeth with a slightly tremulous upper hand. "Thank you for coming here. We will, if you please, speak only in Terran for the present."

Judy studied her Tofa friend, trying to figure out what was different about him besides his apparent frailty. In a moment she realized it: he was not, as he normally would upon greeting her, projecting the telepathic equivalent of a smile. Was the choice deliberate, or was he simply unable to do so? She shuddered; Elspeth squeezed her hand.

Anna reached out as if to stroke Peer-tek's cheek, but hesitated and pulled her hand back. "I'll send Jimmy in." She shifted Sin-han's weight and carried him out of the room, closing the door behind her with an emphatic click.

Peer-tek looked after her for a moment, then back at the girls, shrugging his upper arms in a less energetic version of the typical Twin-Bred gesture. "She is more concerned than angry; and her concern will reinforce rather than threaten her discretion."

Elspeth looked toward the door through which Anna had carried Sin-han. "What about the child?"

Another small shrug. "So far as I know from Anna's and Jimmy's reports, he has not wanted to talk to them or to the other children about what happened. I have thought it unwise to question the older children directly. . . . He seems to take some comfort in the fact that we are both feeling unwell at the same time. I doubt we have ever spent so much time together—though I am unfortunately not able to make the most of that time."

Elspeth slid her tablet out of her bag. "What are you, and aren't you, able to do?"

Peer-tek waved a lower hand toward the door through which Anna had gone. "I knew we would need to record as many details as possible. Anna has been assisting me; we have made entries several times a day, tracking the gradual recovery of my normal faculties. She will give you the records before you leave. To summarize today's situation: as far as I can tell without an actual attempt—which is a significant limitation—I could not yet speak to another Tofa in Tofar with full fluency. If my rate of improvement continues at its present rate, I expect that another two days will see me recovered to the point where my fellows would consider me weak or distracted rather than linguistically impaired."

They were interrupted by some sort of minor commotion outside the bedroom door; moments later, Anna opened the door again. Jimmy entered, his manner subdued, followed by Sin-han, who stumbled in holding two pale green frozen treats in his upper hands. Anna smiled at Sin-han, then turned to the others and let her smile drop. "These seem to make him feel a little better, somehow. So he wanted Peer-tek to try one, in case it helped him too."

As Peer-tek reached out a lower hand to accept the gift, Judy stepped closer to Anna and spoke softly in her ear. "Peer-tek has told us about the records you've been keeping. Do they cover Sin-han's condition as well?"

Anna gave a short nod.

Judy glanced at Elspeth, hoping for a moment of moral support; but Elspeth was jotting down notes on her tablet, and did not see. Judy suppressed a sigh and turned back to Anna. "If Peer-tek is up to it, we'll be discussing what to do with . . . with what we've learned; what to send, and where to send it. Do you want to be part of that discussion?"

Anna shook her head. "I've already told Peer-tek and Jimmy what I think."

"I think Elspeth and I would still like to hear it from you."

By now the other adults had noticed their conversation and fallen silent. Anna glanced around the room and gave a short huff of exasperation. "In summary: this is a weapon that hurts Tofa, and it's for Tofa to make the final decision. But I would be inclined to tell Veda and Gen-tar-ten that you tried, so sorry, and you can't figure out what those old legends were going on about." And with that she held out a hand for Sin-han and led him out again, banging the door a bit more loudly than before.

Those left behind stood silent for a moment, looking at the door and at each other. Then Peer-tek waved his left hands toward his bed. "Feel free to sit there, if you like."

Judy and Elspeth accepted the offer, while Jimmy stood with one hand on a bookcase near Peer-tek's leaning post. Jimmy forced a smile and said, "I hereby call this conspiracy to order. . . ." His smile faded and his voice trailed off.

Peer-tek spoke next. "Whatever Anna's manner may have suggested, I have by no means decided to reject her suggestion. Perhaps we may begin by listing the options we deem unacceptable. And I will provide the first: we cannot entrust this secret to anyone who would seriously consider using it when Tofa children are present."

La-ren stirred. ("Remember Veda's message, and its warning about trust. The same principle applies here.")

("I know.")

Elspeth turned toward Judy with eyebrows raised in inquiry: she was not sitting close enough to have caught the substance of the exchange, but must have noticed that it occurred. Judy dutifully repeated La-ren's observation for the others.

Jimmy clenched his fists. "But is there anyone on Tofarn that we could trust that thoroughly?"

"I think not." Peer-tek slumped more heavily against the post. "I believe this knowledge must remain in Twin-Bred hands—with the possible exception of Mara and Harriet. Indeed, even if we do nothing else, it might be wise to inform Harriet. Perhaps she and her medical team could work on devising better defenses against, or methods of treating, this effect. As for Jak-rad-tan, we do not know enough about his current relationship with Gen-tar-ten; and it is all too likely that Gen-tar-ten has potent means of coercion at his disposal. Jak-rad-tan must not be informed."

Peer-tek paused, leaned his forehead into his upper left hand, and continued. "But there are Twin-Bred on their way to Tofarn. We must weigh the importance of their mission, the likelihood that its success or failure will hinge on increasing their offensive capacity, and the danger that they would fail to prevent the Tofa of Tofarn from learning their secret."

Judy sighed. "Most of which it's almost impossible to predict. . . ." Then an idea struck her, and she sat bolt upright on the bed. "Maybe we should bring Fel-lar, or Fel-lar and Mara, into the preliminary loop—get their thoughts on whether we should tell them. And whether they even want us to."

Elspeth put her hand on Judy's. "But how, without saying too much?"

Peer-tek stood up from the leaning post and caught Jimmy's eye. "We can tell Mara, to begin with, that we have learned of new ways to harm Tofa. You may believe, all of you, that it will not be the first time that Mara has had to cope with the implications of such knowledge."

Chapter 24

(Aboard *Star Seed* and *Winds of Home*)

Log of Captain Lan-sol, *Winds of Home* (excerpts)

Voyage Day 60: We have survived our second passage through the wormhole. *Star Seed* emerged intact as well. Both ships, however, have self-diagnosed a reduction in margins of safety in two key systems. We will have to make repairs on Tofarn before *Star Seed* returns home, and before this vessel can reach the goal we have for now deferred.

Log of Captain Fel-lar, *Star Seed* (excerpts)

Launch Day plus 54: Neither we nor *Winds of Home* has received any message, either direct or relayed through New Landing, from Jak-rad-tan or Gen-tar-ten. Whether the absence reflects inability or discretion, we cannot say. After much discussion with my closest advisers, I have decided to refrain from sending updates of our own, and have suggested that Lan-sol do the same.

Captain's log, *Winds of Home*

Captain Fel-lar would prefer that I do not try to send messages to those at home about our unexpected return or about *Star Seed*'s approach. If there were some reliable way to coordinate our movements with those of our friends on Tofarn, I would respectfully decline this suggestion. But as things are, I will learn from the past tactics of the Twin-Bred, and of Mara Cadell in particular. I will maintain what Terrans once called "radio silence."

*   *   *

As Fel-lar left the mess hall, Can-til, the young communications engineer, followed him out. Fel-lar stopped and turned toward the youth, who seemed both self-conscious and excited. Fel-lar projected encouragement. "Is there something you would like to ask me, or to inform me?"

"The latter." Can-til stood very straight and immobile, a posture that Fel-lar's studies had taught him to call standing "at attention." "I have news. Even if that were not the case, I would have had a report to deliver, but it would have been of less importance."

"Come with me, and tell me as we go." Fel-lar headed off again toward the command center, the young Tofa close behind. In a moment he realized that Can-til was not talking. "We are going. Please do the telling."

"Yes, Captain. Before we left the communications array behind, I examined the system. It occurred to me that if anyone managed to send a message from Tofarn, the only destination the sender would know to use would be New Landing, and a good deal of time would pass before we could know its contents. So I instructed the array to send a copy to us of any message from Tofarn to New Landing."

Can-til paused. Glancing his way, Fel-lar saw that he appeared uneasy or embarrassed. "Yes?"

"I planned to report on these refinements at our regular technical meeting."

Fel-lar buzzed a brief wordless comment. "With all the thoughts occurring to you, you did not think to seek permission before adjusting crucial communications equipment? You seem to have learned more than technical expertise from my old friend Kenneth." The youth projected bewilderment. "Never mind. When we return, you may ask your mentor to tell you the story of the cinnamon buns. And consider yourself confined to quarters after this conversation, until I tell you otherwise. Now: why are you making this confession before the technical meeting, after all?"

"Captain, a message has come in. From Tofarn."

Fel-lar pulled to a halt so abruptly that the engineer bumped into him, then jumped back, stammering apologies. Fel-lar pivoted and strode toward the communications bay, leaving Can-til to keep up as best he could.

Fel-lar read only the header of the message before turning away. "This message is from Jak-rad-tan to Lan-sol. Apparently he sent a copy to New Landing as a backup, and it is that transmission that we have intercepted."

Can-til hesitated, then blurted, "Aren't you going to read it?"

"Not without Lan-sol's permission, certainly. And I have devised a more fitting penalty than confining you to quarters. You, in particular, may *not* read the message, nor any other messages that arrive. You will look only to ascertain the intended recipient. Now kindly establish communications with *Winds of Home*."

Can-til began pushing buttons, then looked back at Fel-lar, startled. "Captain Fel-lar, *Winds of Home* is contacting us."

"This message, you may read—at least unless I tell you to stop. Proceed."

"Captain Lan-sol is forwarding a message to us . . . ." The engineer stuttered to a stop.

Fel-lar suppressed a whistle. "Yet more temptation! Is it the same message you arranged for us to receive?"

It was.

"Direct it to the consoles in the command center and in my quarters. And do not read it!" Fel-lar left as rapidly as he could without running in the youngster's presence.

Fel-lar read the message through twice, then went in search of Mara. He found her with Emily Wilson, sitting in the smaller lounge and knitting, with less hesitation than the last time he had seen her at the task. Some long and unidentifiable strip of material lay wound up beside her.

Mara looked up at him and held the needles in his direction. "Whatever part of my brain has taken over my fingers seems to be managing nicely. But I could use an interruption." She looked closer, and the expression he knew so well, inquiry blended with intense concentration, took over her face. She laid the knitting aside without looking at it, stood up, and turned to Emily. "Thank you, once again. I believe our captain needs my more accustomed skills." Then she took Fel-lar's nearest lower hand and accompanied him, stretching her legs to their farthest reach to match his stride.

Back in their quarters, he pointed to the console. "Tofarn is once again sending messages. At least this one. You will soon understand why."

Mara sat down and read.

Lan-sol, eldest child:

Until now, Gen-tar-ten has forbidden the sending of messages in order to reduce the chance that they would fall into improper hands, and also to leave possible conspirators in doubt as to whether we have uncovered their communications sabotage. I agreed with his assessment. I also agree with the conclusion he has now reached: that events have rendered such precautions obsolete.

Ton-lal-set has escaped. Whoever, and however many, his covert sympathizers, they have accomplished what Gen-tar-ten would not have believed possible. What else they may succeed in doing remains to be seen.

I will, in case of interception, reveal no contemplated countermeasures. Nor would I cheer the allies of our old enemy with any intimations of despair, even if I felt such an emotion. But I will take advantage of this basically undesirable upheaval to send you my love and greetings— and to say that, considering the uncertainties of the time, I am very glad to know (what would otherwise be painful to contemplate) that you are so far away, and will soon be surrounded by my long-lost friends and others who also wish you nothing but good. I have sent your younger siblings to stay with acquaintances of mine who live in a primarily rural area where political ferment is unlikely to reach, at least not as soon as it is expected here.

I see no reason to assume that this message must serve as any kind of farewell. But it would be foolish to rule out that possibility. So I will say what would be worth saying in any case, and what I hope to say on many a future occasion.

You transformed my life from the moment I knew you existed—and even before, though I did not yet know the cause of my enhanced senses and my feeling of contentment. Other than my twin, you are the first being outside myself for whom I was willing to fight; and, without even that limitation, the first to whose survival and happiness I dedicated myself entirely.

Like your siblings, and for longer than they, you have given me an unending series of surprises, challenges, and joys. I have been privileged to enrich the universe by introducing you into it.

As events unfold, I will send whatever updates are feasible. And you are welcome to respond—though I ask discretion, given the possibility of eavesdroppers. I look forward to being able to tell you when that danger has passed.

Proud father and proud Twin-Bred, Jak-rad-tan

Mara looked up at Fel-lar, tears running down her cheeks. "It's beautiful. And he's being so brave. . . . You aren't crying."

"I am too angry to cry. I will need to control my anger before we reach Tofarn. I may have need of what military strategy I have managed to acquire, and applying that knowledge to possibly chaotic conditions will require an unimpaired intellect."

Mara stood up and came to nestle against Fel-lar's side. She did so only when profoundly troubled, and thus it was never an appropriate time to tell her that she made him think of an infant Glider taking shelter under a parent's wing. The thought refreshed him like the well-remembered showers of home.

"Mara, do you know what season will it be when we return? I meant to consult the computers, but have not yet done so."

She stepped back so that he could see her shake her head. He reached out a lower arm to draw her close again. "I hope it is well into gold season. If we survive the hour of our landing, I would like to see the rain bathing the foliage and making the flowers dance."

He felt the beginning of some comment from Levi, and

then a withdrawal. ("Friend and brother, what is it?")

("I started to say that all this unaccustomed lyricism, first from Jak-rad-tan and then from you, was making my head spin. But that would be rude. So in an equally uncommon moment of tact, I refrained.")

Mara shrugged in exaggerated helplessness. "What can I say? My twin does know how to puncture a moment."

Fel-lar gazed at his companion, then ran a forefinger slowly down along her face, to her neck, and paused at her shoulder. Mara shivered and gave a faint moan; he moved the finger in a circle, lightly touching the space beneath her collar bone. "Since the mood has in fact changed, I suggest we revive ourselves by celebrating the moment in which we find ourselves." He almost added, before he thought better of it: *And then, your unsentimental brother and I can make some plans.*

Levi, if he heard, made no compromising comment.

*　*　*

Can-til appeared in the doorway of the command center and buzzed softly to attract Fel-lar's attention. As soon as Fel-lar looked up, the young Tofa proffered two printouts, one in each lower hand, looking over Fel-lar's right shoulder rather than in his eyes. "Two more messages have arrived, one immediately after the other. They arrived only moments ago, and are addressed to the Captain and Dr. Cadell jointly. The message field itself indicates that they are urgent."

Mara suppressed her amusement at the engineer's conspicuous compliance with Fel-lar's earlier instructions. "Thank you for bringing them so promptly."

Fel-lar took the printouts with his own lower hands. "You may go."

Mara moved to Fel-lar's side and examined the printouts: a single sheet, and a somewhat thicker sheaf. "May I?"

Fel-lar handed her the sheet of paper. "This presumably came first. It instructs the communications engineer, most sternly, to transmit the longer message to us without reading it first. . . . It is fortunate, perhaps, that my earlier discussion with our young engineer reinforced that instruction." He placed the sheaf of papers on his standing desk, picked up the first sheet—and hissed.

Mara took an involuntary step backward, then caught herself and moved toward him again. He had gone rigid with tension, fingers clenched tight around the batch of papers. "What is it? Who sent it?"

Fel-lar handed her the thicker printout. "Peer-tek."

Mara waited for more; when no more came, she put her arm through his lower right elbow, squeezing gently. "I'm guessing that's an answer to both questions. That Peer-tek has some new bombshell to lob at us."

Fel-lar dropped his upper right hand down to stroke the top of her hand, once, lightly, then withdrew it again. "Indeed. But that is almost all the information he has provided so far. Read and see."

Mara stood at his side and began to read. She forced herself to keep reading until the end, her chest tightening so that she could feel every breath, so that breathing seemed like some difficult and unfamiliar task.

She turned toward Fel-lar's standing desk and reached up to drop the papers on its slanting surface. Her aim was imperfect: one of the sheets fluttered to the floor. She looked down at it for a moment, then walked stiffly to the chair that Fel-lar kept ready for her use. She thought Fel-lar might follow, to stand behind her and hold her shoulders in his lower hands, but he stayed where she had left him, looking down toward the papers remaining on the desk. He began to speak, so quietly she had to strain to hear him. "This weapon, whatever its nature, is dangerous only to Tofa, and especially dangerous to our children. By disrupting enemy communication, it confers a great tactical advantage on the users. But once observed, it would be relatively easy to reproduce, so that it could not thereafter be contained. Do I summarize accurately what we have both read?"

Mara nodded; but he was not looking at her, so she made herself breathe again, and said, "Yes."

Fel-lar's lower hands, and then his upper hands, clenched slowly into fists, as a human's might. "I would very much like to know: did Peer-tek realize the solution to the problem he has posed us? Would he have sent this message, with that solution in mind?"

She should rise and go to him. She should do

something to break the trance into which he seemed to be casting himself. But it was all she could do even to speak. "What solution is this?"

Now, finally, he looked at her. And the odor that came to her was neither the ammonia smell of Tofa rage, nor the burnt-sweet smell of Tofa pain, but some terrible fusion of the two. "There is one safe way, and only one, to deploy the weapon whose key elements Peer-tek has listed. The dangers it poses are too great if the knowledge of its nature is allowed to spread. To use this weapon—" The odor shifted toward wrath. "To use this weapon against our old enemies, to prevent their triumph without a cost greater than even their defeat would justify, there must be no possibility that they will one day wield it themselves. If we use this weapon . . . If we use it, we must use others as well, while its effect is at its peak. If we use this weapon, we must leave no survivors."

Mara stared at her lover, her mouth agape, her eyes wide. And as she stared, he turned on his heel, swiveled like a soldier in some long-ago army, and marched out of the room.

*   *   *

(New Landing)

Jimmy and Peer-tek had sent their warning; they had tried to share the burden of decision. Now they must prepare for what that decision might require of them.

The files they might be sending would have to be as thoroughly encrypted as possible—or at least, as was feasible while leaving it likely that Mara and Fel-lar could decrypt them. Fortunately Mara, never one to relish dependence on others, had insisted years ago that Peer-tek give her lessons in cryptology, until she was close to his level of expertise. Whether she had shared that knowledge with Fel-lar, they could not be sure; but surely Fel-lar would not try to exclude her from the process . . . .

Peer-tek was still constructing the necessary layers of encryption when they received a very short message from Fel-lar.

Thank you. Please send.

* * *

Judy and Elspeth had been seeing a good deal more of Peer-tek and Jimmy since their recent collaboration. There was no need, in each other's company, to explain away preoccupation or absence of mind. They quickly established common customs: when their qualms and concerns should or should not be explicitly discussed (not while eating, unless the food had been mostly consumed); how often to revisit a topic with no true resolution available (no more than once per gathering).

This togetherness had its costs.

Peer-tek had recovered full use of his telepathic abilities; but whether due to other residual effects or to their shared anxiety, he found it harder than usual to control his temper. If only the others would stop looking to him as an authority on Fel-lar's mental processes! They were all Twin-Bred, even if Judy had lost her twin and Elspeth, a singleton, had never known hers. The humans had grown up with their Tofa counterparts. And Peer-tek and Fel-lar had not been especially close in recent years. How could he predict in what manner the co-chair of Congress, now the captain of *Star Seed*, would discharge the responsibilities Peer-tek had never had to bear? And with Peer-tek changing his own mind from day to day, even moment to moment, about whether he had made a fateful error, how could he predict what Fel-lar would decide?

As the time drew near when *Star Seed* would reach Tofarn, Peer-tek could no longer stand to hear his own concerns and misgivings echoed and rehashed. He would not forbid Judy or Elspeth the house, or ask Jimmy not to invite

them; but when they came, he absented himself. Later, when they knew what had happened, he could make amends. Later he might need their understanding, or even their absolution.

Chapter 25

(*Star Seed*)

IT WAS pure chance that brought Can-til to the command center when Mara was present and Fel-lar, momentarily, was not. Would Fel-lar have told her at once about the new messages? She thought so, she hoped so, but she could hardly be certain.

"It's two messages again. I printed out the short one. The other's much longer." Can-til held a printed page in one hand and passed a data chip restlessly back and forth among the other three.

A human, looking at Mara's expression, would have already given her the printout and the chip. "I'll take them. Thank you. Tell no one but the captain."

"Should I go find him, to report as soon as possible?"

Fel-lar would be busy for some time, meeting with Lan-sol and with the most trusted lieutenants of both captains, reviewing topographical and population maps, evaluating possible landing sites. "It might be better not to disturb him at present."

This time Judy, not Peer-tek, was the sender. And compared to the earlier messages, the printed note was suspiciously lacking in important content. Its tone was closer to nostalgia. "Fel-lar, old friend: with so much distance between us, I'm glad I can still remember all that you and I have had in common, ever since we first visited the original human colony together . . . ."

The chip must be encrypted, and somewhere in this incongruous message lay the key.

" . . . It's too bad Rides Above Danger didn't know more about those early days . . . ."

If she—she and Fel-lar—failed to discover the key, she could use the massive power of the ship's most powerful computer in a brute-force decryption effort; but it would take far longer. Perhaps too long.

("Levi, help me with this! What did Judy and Fel-lar, in particular, have in common that had some connection to that first visit?")

She heard something like a sigh. ("I don't know why you expect my memory to be better than yours. But settle down somewhere, and we'll both try to remember.")

Mara had been standing, pacing, then standing again as she read the printout. Now she made herself sit in the room's single chair, closed her eyes, and called forth what memory she retained of their arrival. That first time she left *Star Seed*—had Fel-lar or Judy been present? No, their first foray had been later, the carefully orchestrated tour in which Administrator Macauley had tried to persuade them all that humans and Gliders lived in harmony . . . .

Who had noticed the flaws in that pretense? Judy? No—not Judy, not exactly. It had been whatever lingered of La-ren. And rather than pass on his observations secondhand, Judy had asked . . . .

("That's it, Sis!")

Of course! Judy had asked Fel-lar to open himself to La-ren's consciousness. On that day, Judy and Fel-lar had had La-ren in common. So either La-ren's identity or his report must be the key, or at least some component of it. But had that report been recorded? She could not remember. Even if it had been, Judy could hardly count on *Star Seed*'s computer records retaining a copy. So the reference was less likely to be that report's exact words than simply La-ren's name.

But "simple" was too apt a term. Judy must be working with Peer-tek, and Peer-tek would never entrust so important a secret to so short a key.

Back to the rest of the printout. Rides Above Danger. What difference did it make, what difference would it have made, if Rides Above Danger knew more about that early encounter? What use had he made of the knowledge he did possess?

Levi started humming a passage of Glider music. And

not just any passage. Fel-lar's collaboration with Rides Above Danger! That composition, or at least the portion of the composition dealing with *Star Seed*'s arrival and its aftermath, would be a complex enough key to satisfy even Peer-tek—even more so if combined in some way with La-ren's name. And anyone who knew Fel-lar, or even composers in general, would expect him to remember the music note for note. ("You're right! You must be.")

Levi chuckled. ("Naturally. Now get to work.")

But she would have to wait for Fel-lar to leave his meeting—or would have to interrupt him—before she could really get to work. . . . Or did she?

Hadn't Fel-lar, from some combination of authorial pride and teasing impulse, sent her a recording of the piece?

The name, the recording: that should be enough for her decryption programs to work with.

Mara's stomach had been growling for some time, but she had neither time nor patience to attend to its demands. Finally, finally, the program had completed its task. The contents of the message lay open to her.

She could wait for Fel-lar, now. Peer-tek had probably intended as much, or even left it to Fel-lar whether Mara should be included. But there might be no time to waste. Until she could read and evaluate the data, there was no way to estimate how long it would take to produce the weapon itself.

("And that's all you're concerned about, the available time. Really.")

("Please, Levi—not now.")

She could skim through the data, at least, to make such an estimate possible.

She had, of course, expected grim reading, after all the preliminary obstacles. If anything, the weapon was less fearsome than she had feared—far less devastating than what Kimball and Bloom had conspired to create. Even the greater vulnerability of Tofa children hardly compared.

But she must put aside that perspective. Comparing every threat to species extinction would leave her cognitively and ethically incapable of assessing still-serious threats.

What she read surprised her in quite another way as well. She respected the blend of commitment and caution that had driven Peer-tek to use only himself and his child as experimental subjects; but as a scientist, she could not ignore the effects of that decision on Peer-tek's results, which must be viewed as incomplete. When he could no longer bear to involve Sin-han further, and was perhaps incapable of continuing to participate himself, the experiments had ended, with certain key avenues unexplored.

She had assumed that whether to deploy a weapon dangerous only to Tofa should be, in the end, for Fel-lar to determine. Not because he held the rank of captain—not after his insistence on dragging her along for her expertise and judgment—but a Tofa, she had thought, should make that decision.

But . . . Fel-lar had been changing. Long-buried bitterness, and anger, and even shame, had risen to the surface; and how would he weigh the daunting choice at hand? Not all their years in all their shifting relationships could give her confidence in any prediction she might make.

Would he listen when she explained what Peer-tek and his collaborators seemed to have missed? Or would he push forward, grimly satisfied with an excuse to finish off old foes?

("Levi? Any insights, or advice?")

("All I've got—and it may surprise you that I can offer it—is hope. Hope that he'll listen. He's good people, our Fel-lar. But take all that history, all that hurt, and then throw the responsibilities of leadership into the mix . . . . Hope is as far as I can go.")

Could she delay the confrontation, start work on her idea, perhaps have an alternative further along before showing him what Peer-tek—

She jumped, startled, at the chime from her tablet, an interruption followed moments later by Fel-lar's voice. "We have finally finished. Would you like to meet me in the mess hall for a drink or snack, while I devour a belated lunch?"

Mara drew a deep breath, and hoped Fel-lar failed to notice the sound or, at least, thought nothing of it. "I skipped lunch too. I'll meet you."

She had never before thought the distance from the

command center to the mess hall too short.

Mara's bond with Fel-lar had been rooted in honesty, always. At the very beginning—as soon as she realized that something had begun, despite all the differences that made it so unlikely—she had risked revealing her most dangerous secret, Bloom's death, rather than allowing him to assume her past or her soul to be untainted. And never in all the years since, as best she could recall, had the thought of lying to him even crossed her mind.

Whatever sophistry she might indulge in, it would be a lie to conceal that Peer-tek's weapon was within their grasp.

The changes that frightened her, that made her question her trust in her friend and lover: how much further might those changes go without her influence? For if she lied, and he discovered it, that influence would end. To the great loss she would suffer in the loss of his companionship would be added the greater guilt of what he might then become.

The mess hall was nearly empty. As she entered, Mara spied Lan-sol at a table with several older Tofa. A slab of vat meat diminished rapidly beneath his chin as he fired question after question at his elders, who listened and responded with genial amusement. (Back in the first years of the Project, it had not been easy getting the human Twin-Bred to accept that their Tofa twins had an advantage at mealtimes; that humans should not eat and talk at the same time, for fear of choking . . . .)

("Focus, girl.")

Levi was right. She must not escape into memories of the past.

Fel-lar was waiting across the room, standing beside one of the small adjustable tables, standing very straight and still.

He had already lowered half the table to a height she could reach, but the table bore no food. She could delay, leading the way to the serving line; or she could tell him now, before she had the chance to change her mind.

She reached out and gripped the edge of the table in both hands.

"Peer-tek's next message came."

The tension in Fel-lar's torso grew less, and he reached

out his lower hands, trailing his forefingers across both her knuckles. "I know."

Mara staggered, thankful she had anchored herself to the table. "How?"

Fel-lar brought his hands back to his sides. "I crossed paths with young Can-til as I left the meeting. I do not, however, know the contents of the message, nor whether it included any obstacles to comprehension."

She looked up at him; he looked back, waiting.

"The message was encrypted." She allowed herself a brief moment of pride. "Quite thoroughly. But I managed to decrypt it."

Could any human smile carry the warmth a Tofa Twin-Bred could emanate without one? "Well done."

Of course he would take time for kindness. Why had she thought that he would no longer be kind?

But she remembered his words, and his look, when they received the last message; and she feared for him.

"My dear, I have something to ask of you. I ask that you let me do some investigation, before you see what Peer-tek offers you. I believe that he—that his circumstances did not allow him to explore all options. That there was a better option he failed to try, and maybe failed even to consider. Will you give me a little time, what little time we have to spare, in order to test that option?"

Fel-lar was looking beyond her now, staring over her shoulder. "There is little enough time left."

"I'll be efficient. I'll binge on stimulants if I have to. Levi can help me stay awake. And if I fail, I'll let you know immediately."

Fel-lar came round the table, took Mara's shoulders between his upper hands, and steered her toward the serving line. "I will, at least, let you begin this attempt; and I will not interrupt you until I believe it necessary. So now you must eat. Eat as much as you can. You will have little time for food as you proceed."

Peer-tek and the others had prioritized. With limited time, they had seized upon their first plausible hypothesis and tested it. Given first an unknown effect on possible test subjects, and then an effect they saw all too well, they had not explored any more variations than seemed essential, let alone gone back for other hypotheses. They had functioned not as scientists, but as engineers.

But Mara, scientist, looked for causes and explanations; and even without the opportunity to delve deeply, she had seen another possibility.

She had been afraid that possibility would evaporate as soon as she gave it further study; but ten hours later, her nerves buzzing with stimulants, her stomach on the verge of cramps from snatched and inadequate food, she had enough confidence to talk to Fel-lar about the next essential step.

"I need some test subjects. It would be best—I need a minimum of three, to do this properly."

Fel-lar immediately called up a file on his tablet and handed it to her. "I anticipated your request and have identified those crew members who come closest to . . . dispensable. You may interview them in the hope of finding volunteers."

Mara scanned the list. "I see Hal-tet isn't here. Are all those you've omitted as—as militant as he?"

Fel-lar did not answer.

Mara tried to ignore a wave of nausea, defying it by retrieving an energy bar and bottle of water from the cabinet, biting off a chunk of the bar, and washing it down with a gulp of water. She managed to swallow the bar without choking, then asked: "And if none of them volunteers?"

Fel-lar buzzed for an instant, then cut off the sound. "We will discuss that situation only if it occurs."

Three ship's days passed. Mara slept twice, for five hours and for three. Now, time had run out. She must share her results, however preliminary, with Fel-lar. They would reach Tofarn the day after tomorrow.

Her three volunteers were already in the infirmary, in drugged and restless sleep. If Tofa could dream, she would have supposed them to be dreaming. Were they in some intermediate and distressed state between sleep and waking?

She left them and headed for the command center, tablet in hand. She knew Fel-lar would be ready: he had summoned her.

The door stood open. She entered, and they stood silently, at first, each assessing the other.

They had barely seen each other these last three days; and she had never seen Fel-lar like this. During the greatest crisis of their shared past, she had been in charge, and he had been one of her charges, precious and irreplaceable as they all were, but not distinguished by any special status. Whatever distress he had then endured, she could not remember taking note of it. Now it was his turn to bear the burden of responsibility without the knowledge or leverage that could ensure control of the outcome. He stood very straight, but close to his leaning post; the fingers on his upper hands were trembling in a way she had rarely seen, a sign of true exhaustion, and his normal odor was barely perceptible through the scent of strain.

Finally he spoke. "We must prepare the weapons we have. There is no more time for study. Whatever you feared for me to see, I must see it now, unless you have found something better. Indeed, even if you believe you have done so, I must review both options and make my own decision. Lan-sol and members of his crew will be here in an hour to learn the details, and I will then designate a team with the skills necessary to prepare the actual materials."

Mara closed the door, pulled out her tablet, and approached Fel-lar. "I'm ready. I could of course use more time, but I know enough to offer you some alternatives, as well as my view on them. Shall I begin?"

Fel-lar let out a barely audible whistle. "Please."

Mara gave him a faint smile in return, then sat in the chair and called up the presentation she had just assembled. It began with a graphic of sound waves.

"The weapon uses certain specific sequences of sound. We should be able to direct the sound forward, enough that our people following some distance behind would be safe; but based on my limited research, I do not think a Tofa actually deploying the weapon can be adequately protected from it. There are only three humans available to your combined forces: Nathan, myself and Melly. We both know that Nathan, even if the events in the wormhole had not affected his health, would not take part in an offensive operation." Mara paused and took a deep, shaky breath.

("Are you there, Levi?")

("Of course. You can do this. Go on.")

Mara forced herself to look directly at Fel-lar. "Of the three options I'll be showing you, I am willing to deploy only one. What Melly would or wouldn't do, I can't say."

Fel-lar looked back, with the inevitable lack of expression, but without the usual telepathic substitutes. "Please proceed."

Mara bit her lip, then released it. "You will see the visual of three different types of tests. In the first two instances, you will see first the recording of the tests Peer-tek conducted, and then my own. I will wait until you have seen them all to reveal the audio components accompanying each—and I trust you will believe my description of those components." Without waiting for a response, she started the recording and tilted the screen to give Fel-lar the best view.

The playback began with the recorded sound sequence's effect on Peer-tek and Peer-tek's child Sin-han. She had not dared to predict Fel-lar's reaction, and was deeply relieved at the increased intensity of Fel-lar's burnt-sweet odor. The odor remained as the recording moved on to the test with Fel-lar's colleague, her first volunteer, whose results were essentially indistinguishable from the similar test Peer-tek had conducted on himself.

The odor intensified further as the recording moved on to the test of live percussion; and when Sin-han recoiled, and flailed, and obviously cried even though they could not hear his humming, she saw from the corner of her eye that Fel-lar flinched beside her, and heard his own faint answering hum.

Mara paused the recording for a moment. "The corresponding test on my own volunteer proved similar to that involving Peer-tek. Should I proceed to the test Peer-tek did not conduct?"

Fel-lar hesitated before replying. "For now, yes. I may consider it necessary to review the recording more fully at some later time."

Mara took a deep breath as she fast-forwarded to the test of her own innovation. With only the visual track, it was almost indistinguishable from the first test on Peer-tek, the one using recorded sound. At its conclusion, she paused the recording again and turned to look up at Fel-lar. "Shall I tell you, now, the nature of each variation of this weapon?"

Fel-lar let out a short hiss of impatience. "Of course."

Mara ran the recording back to the first test. "This one uses recorded sound. If I had more time and a larger pool of volunteers, I could experiment with different volume settings. For now, suffice to say that the sound is easily discernible to those affected by it."

She moved on to the second. "This version—obviously the most effective—uses live production of the sound sequence. It would take some practice to duplicate it, but not a great deal." A thought came to her, a most welcome difficulty with that approach. "It would, however, be difficult to control the volume precisely, and we don't know how much difference that would make."

Finally she returned to her own test. "For this test, I used subsonic vibrations only, with no audible stimuli."

The two watched the recording in silence. At its conclusion, Mara put the tablet on her lap and said, "As you see, it is similar in effect to the first—"

Fel-lar interrupted her. "Slightly less effective, in my view."

She looked up at him again and strove to speak in an even tone. "We may disagree in our assessments, or our current definitions of 'slight' and 'similar' may differ. In any event, the key distinction is that those on whom the weapon is used are unlikely—at least on first exposure—to realize what is happening." She reached out for his nearest hand, then thought better of it and returned her hand to her lap. "In this mode, the weapon can be used without disclosing its nature."

Fel-lar reached out a lower finger and tipped the tablet closed. "Or so you surmise."

Mara gritted her teeth, then willed her jaw to relax. "I do more than *surmise*. I made sure my final test subject had no idea what was coming, and then interviewed him afterward. He told me that he'd had no idea what was happening, and that his ignorance may have added to his disorientation and confusion. I have a recording of that interview, if you don't want to rely on my summary."

Fel-lar tapped the closed tablet with another finger. "I do not doubt your summary—of an interview with a single test subject. We both know, because you made sure that I and my fellows learned it, that a single test subject provides less than reliable data."

This time Mara could not keep both her jaw and her fists from clenching, and did not even try. "What can I do? Do you really want me to disable more of your crew in pursuit of a more reliable result? And even the audible alternatives— three test subjects isn't enough for any assurance of validity!"

"It is, however, considerably better than conclusions based on only one." Fel-lar put his lower hands on Mara's shoulders, gripping her more tightly than he normally would, and turned her to face him. "You seek to change the conditions that led me to declare how I would treat survivors of this weapon. You may overestimate my ambivalence as to such treatment." He held up an upper finger to silence her as she started to respond. "No, I will not mince words. You may overestimate my reluctance to kill as many of Ton-lal-set's adherents as stand in our way."

Mara forced herself to nod. Fel-lar held her shoulders a moment longer, then released her and waved his right hands toward the tablet. "Leave this with me. I will review the footage again, and ponder the alternatives. Please wait for me in our personal quarters."

Mara slumped in her armchair, hoping to doze off; but her fatigue was not enough to overcome her nerves, and she jumped up again, pacing back and forth across the small cabin. Turning back a nose's length from the wall, she caught sight of a mess of yarn and needles: her neglected attempt at a scarf for Emily. If she could pick it back up again, it might serve as a distraction . . . .

Some unknowable time later, she felt Tofa fingers stroking briefly through her hair, rousing her from sleep. She looked up, disoriented, yarn and needles in her lap, to see Fel-lar, his lower left hand retreating from her scalp, her tablet in both upper hands. His odor had returned to normal; he appeared resolute, solemn, but not so cold as before. He laid the tablet on Mara's desk. "Are you alert enough to hear my decision?"

Mara laid her knitting on the arm of her chair and stood up. "Yes. What have you . . . decided?"

He waited a moment that felt much too long, then continued.

"Despite its apparent power, the live performance alternative has too many variables to be reliable. Nor am I satisfied that the operator could remain sufficiently alert, throughout the performance, to respond to surprise or to danger. That leaves the audible recording and the subsonic equivalent.

"Whatever you may fear, whatever I have intimated, I am not completely oblivious to either the ethical or the tactical drawbacks of attacking first with sound and then with lethal force. But I will not stake our safety or our success entirely on one untried weapon.

"We will prepare to use your subsonic broadcast." Mara held her breath as he went on. "But whoever deploys it will be equipped, as well, with the audible version. And in the latter case . . . ." His odor shifted again toward the metallic. "There will be suitably armed Tofa following after, at a safe distance but able to reach the enemy before they recover enough to resist."

Mara let her breath out and closed her eyes. "I understand. And I can't argue with your decision." She felt herself wobble, and grabbed at the arm of the chair, knocking the knitting to the floor. Fel-lar grasped her arm to steady her, then released it. For a moment she imagined the comfort of his arms around her hips and shoulders, imagined loosening her muscles against that support; but that would have to wait. "Shall I contact Melly?"

"Please do so as soon as possible. I know you need rest, but contact her first. Discuss which of you is better prepared, physically and emotionally, to perform this task. And if Melly is the one chosen, I will speak to her myself—to ensure that she realizes what may be required of her."

Chapter 26

(Tofarn and aboard *Star Seed*)

AFTERNOON outdoor recreation at Golden Path Primary Academy should already have concluded. Some of the children simply kept playing; others clustered together talking. A few drifted toward the area where they would normally be lining up, but as these same students were those most accustomed to parental control, they did not remain long in their usual order without the catalyst of a command.

Two adults finally emerged from the building: the mathematics teacher whose turn it was to monitor outdoor recreation, and the Academy principal. The principal commanded the children to form a semicircle facing him, and to be silent. Even those who tended to disregard such instructions were eager to hear what the principal might say, and the arc formed quickly.

As soon as the last murmur died away, the principal stepped forward and spoke. "School will be dismissed early today. There is a possibility that several criminals who have escaped from the Eminence's prison may be in the vicinity, as they have brazenly announced a gathering tomorrow. While this foolhardy move means that the prisoners will be quickly apprehended, the process may be dangerous to bystanders. Members of your households will be coming to escort you home. We will send word to your families as to when school will resume."

Several of the children squirmed, as if questions were attempting to wriggle out of them. The mathematics teacher took pity on one of those nearest to him, pointing to the child and saying, "You may speak."

The child stopped squirming and stood very still. "Teacher, why would the escaped prisoners announce their whereabouts?"

The teacher looked around to ensure the other children were listening. "The escaped prisoners, whose opposition to our Eminence's leadership demonstrates their weak understanding and unbalanced minds, are unrealistically optimistic. They may be seeking to embolden any hidden supporters, to bring them to a location where the existing conspirators may identify them. This will, of course, merely ensure that the Eminence can identify them as well."

Some of the children, mainly the younger ones, buzzed in confusion. The principal reasserted himself, brushing the mathematics teacher aside and turning toward the children. "That is enough. Your parents will explain anything you need to know."

One of the older children raised a lower hand as if answering a question in class. No question had been posed, of course, and the principal's words should have been enough to discourage any. The principal flicked three upper fingers in a gesture of rebuke; the child dropped his hand and looked away, but the student standing next to him, child of one of the modern free-thinking Tofa, leaned over and whispered. The first child started, glanced at the principal, then whispered a few words in reply. The bolder child faced the mathematics teacher and said, "If our parent allows us to observe the rally from a discreet location, would a report of what occurs satisfy our Community Engagement requirement for this term?"

The mathematics teacher might have responded, if only to discourage the idea; but in the principal's presence, he could hardly acknowledge a question asked without permission. So he turned away and walked to the gate to see if any of the children's family members were in sight.

* * *

For security's sake, Mara had said as little as possible to Melly about why she and Fel-lar wished Melly to visit *Star Seed*. So Mara tried to put aside her fears and her fatigue, to greet Melly as if this reunion after many years had no darker purpose; and then walked with her down the corridors, noting and remembering the enthusiasm and physicality in

Melly's stride, concealing her impatience as Melly stopped to exchange excited greetings and embraces with each Twin-Bred she encountered.

And then they reached Mara's and Fel-lar's quarters, though it was not yet time for Fel-lar to join them; and Mara had to watch as the joy faded and the situation sank in.

Melly rested her forehead on her hand, shoulders slumped. "What a mess."

("Mess: a key attribute of battle.")

("Please, Levi.")

Melly dropped her hand and looked up at Mara. "Dr. Cadell—"

Mara snorted. "Don't be absurd. You're no child any longer."

"Mara, then. What do you think about all this—if you can tell me?"

Mara heaved a sigh that seemed to drag her weary limbs down toward the floor. "I almost wish your mother hadn't sent her message. But we don't know what forces we'll be facing—and if we can keep the secret without drastic measures, we'll probably do less harm than if we relied on the weapons we had already. And we're a lot less likely to take casualties."

"And it really works."

Mara winced, remembering her latest short visit to the infirmary. "Oh, yes. It works."

"Which makes it really, really important that Ton-lal-set and his followers don't learn how to use it."

Mara pressed her lips tightly together. "It goes beyond that. They can't have any idea what we're using. They may not include many good scientists, not with their world view, but it only takes one to connect what's happening to the old legends . . . . They'd be big on legends, I'd guess." Her next thought was chilling. "They may even have more detailed versions of the legend to draw on."

Melly wrinkled her forehead; then her eyes lit up, and she bounced to her feet. "Well, then. We'll give them something else to think about. Has anyone told you what I do for a living nowadays?"

Mara tried to think. "If they have, I'm afraid I've

forgotten."

Melly's smile brought back other memories, of a confident, energetic little girl sure that people and events would do as she demanded. "I'm a theatrical director. My life is all about spectacle, drawing people in, creating a world and making them live in it." She laughed outright. "And I'm sure I can give Ton-lal-set's minions plenty to get, and hold, their attention."

* * *

The ships could have spent more time in orbit around Tofarn, collecting and assessing information as originally planned. But now that communication was possible once more, Fel-lar had already learned enough to know that a crisis was at hand. Ton-lal-set and his supporters, flaunting his escape from custody, were planning a public gathering of some kind. If Gen-tar-ten's regime had any substantial opposition, this gathering might lead to unrest at least, and at worst, a broader rebellion. And even if Gen-tar-ten succeeded in suppressing the insurrection, Jak-rad-tan or his family might be in danger until that was accomplished. The crews of both ships, few as they were, might make a critical difference at this early stage.

If the ships could have landed within sight of the rally, the unprecedented spectacle might have eclipsed it completely and driven politics from the minds of the locals. But the available landing sites could not be seen from the rally's announced location, in what the human population called Founders Square; and in daylight, the light of the landing jets would not carry so far.

Gen-tar-ten had been a discreet dissident when Fel-lar knew him, providing the Twin-Bred with knowledge of their heritage, but doing nothing to alert the ruling Eminence of his activities. Jak-rad-tan and Veda and even Stan had somehow teased and tempted him into spreading anonymous sedition, but only the instinctive outrage triggered by Ton-lal-set's attack on Lan-sol had made the revolution possible in so short a time. Gen-tar-ten had never, since taking power, faced and surmounted open opposition. From what he had heard, Fel-lar sensed uncertainty beneath

Gen-tar-ten's bluster. Would he send forces to do battle, and risk the humiliation of losing the combat?

The captains and crews of *Star Seed* and *Winds of Home* did not exactly constitute trained reinforcements. But both captains put out the call for volunteers.

*   *   *

"Why would you want to do *that*?"

Seth Baruti had had no intention of setting foot outside the ship until any confrontations were over and done with. Whatever the definition of combat age, he was well beyond it. The only being on board *Star Seed* less likely to be useful would be Wings Spread Wide, handicapped not only by age but by Tofarna gravity. Since the ship's gravity had approached that of Tofarn, the Glider had seldom stirred from its cushioned niche. Yet it now insisted on being allowed to disembark—which amounted to a demand for an escort.

Seth would just as soon not be the one to deliver bad news. He could deflect the request. "You had better talk to Captain Fel-lar about this notion."

Wings Spread Wide furled and unfurled his wings. "I have already done so, and he has approved my request. Please bring your communications device with you. There may be much worth recording." The Glider cocked its head, one bright eye toward Seth, and made the warbling sound that meant laughter.

Seth's jaw dropped. Could the Glider have misunderstood the captain? Did the last days of Gliders typically include dementia?

Seth made sure the Glider was comfortable, and that it had water and a snack within reach. Then he left their quarters and, once out of earshot, attempted to contact Fel-lar. But the captain failed to answer the call. Seth stood in the hallway for a moment, then squared his shoulders and headed for the command center.

Fel-lar was leaving as Seth approached. Seth fell into step with the Tofa, or as close as his shorter legs could manage. "Fel-lar, my lad—"

"Professor, if this concerns your companion's request

to leave the ship on our arrival, I have no leisure to discuss my decision."

"Then you *did* approve? I thought . . . ." But Fel-lar was moving away, and Seth's left hip chose this moment to complain at the pace he was attempting. So he slowed down, turned around, and limped back toward his quarters.

* * *

Mara had offered to make herself scarce during their approach to Tofarn. Fel-lar would have the landing procedures to oversee, while still fine-tuning various alternative scenarios and backup plans for what would come after. And after their recent confrontations about Tofa casualties, would he view her presence as scrutiny rather than support?

Fel-lar responded by taking firm hold of her shoulders with his upper hands and steering her in front of him as he faced the viewscreen. "If the computer calls for my attention, I know you will allow me to respond without distraction. Otherwise, I prefer to have you close at hand, literally and metaphorically."

"Did I hear Seth Baruti outside when you left for your latest planning session? What did he want?"

Fel-lar twitched one of the fingers resting on her shoulder. "I did not stay to hear the details, but it appears he found it hard to believe my decision concerning Wings Spread Wide."

Mara put up a hand to cover Fel-lar's. "I'm not surprised. I gather you didn't share your own qualms about that decision."

Fel-lar just barely whistled. "Are commanders not usually enjoined to suppress all suggestion that they have qualms, or doubts, or any attitude short of firm and confident resolution? . . . But on balance, my misgivings are few. The Glider wishes to contribute to our mission. And its proposal for doing so fulfills certain prerogatives of its own. I will not protect it from its own decisions."

They both fell silent for a moment, watching the image of their home planet grow larger in the viewscreen.

("Go ahead, Sis, if you think it's worth a try.")

Mara removed her hand from Fel-lar's and cleared her throat. "Speaking of protecting people who are perfectly capable of making their own decisions: you don't really expect me to stay on the ship?"

Fel-lar's hands gripped her shoulders more tightly. "You and Melly have agreed that she, rather than you, will accompany our forces—and I must confess, now, my relief at that decision. The friends and allies you undoubtedly still possess are unlikely to be in evidence at this Tofa gathering. If you are recognized at all, it will be by our enemies."

Levi stirred. ("Filled as I am by the utmost in martial ardor, I say you should listen to our captain—and not just to save our collective skin. The expedition needs someone capable of handling emergencies here on the ship. All Fel-lar's Tofa contemporaries will be with him. I'd rather not entirely trust the ship itself, or its contents, or our communications center to the triumvirate of an invalid, a mild-mannered diplomat, and an adolescent engineer.")

Fel-lar whistled again, and his hands relaxed. ("As always, my friend, your reasoning is irreproachable. And I am sure your sister will concede as much.")

Mara sighed and leaned her check against Fel-lar's hand for a moment, then stood up straight. "I'll concede this much. I'll stay with the ship to start with. But if I decide the situation calls for it, I'll go where I think best."

* * *

Star Seed landed first, around two hours after sunrise, between two tree-lined rivers, in a field that usually grew grain. Fel-lar had been quite prepared to damage crops if necessary, but fortune smiled on at least this first phase of their endeavor, for the field lay fallow. Once the landing jets had fallen silent and the ship's surface had cooled sufficiently for the hatch to open, the landing party began to emerge.

Melly had remained aboard *Star Seed* in preparation for this moment. Now she descended the ramp with an escort of two Tofa Twin-Bred looming beside her. She had swathed herself in a hooded cloak that hid her almost entirely; her hand, barely showing where she held the cloak together, yet oddly colored, bore a band strapped across her palm with two large buttons. The Twin-Bred beside her swiveled left and right as they moved, maintaining a lookout. Just behind them came Fel-lar, wearing a backpack and carrying a grenade launcher, the largest weapon he could feasibly carry. He stepped onto Tofarna soil without breaking stride and beckoned for the others to follow.

Down the ramp after him came almost all the ship's complement of Tofa Twin-Bred, most carrying two weapons each of human or Tofa manufacture, but a few carrying Glider projectile rifles instead. Behind this group came two more Tofa Twin-Bred carrying Wings Spread Wide between them, the lower arms near the Glider serving as its perch, while the upper arms provided support behind its back. They carried one weapon each in their outside upper arms.

Last of all came Seth Baruti, eyes wide, almost twitching with nerves.

All the Tofa wore vests whose pockets contained additional ammunition as well as smaller weapons, knives or short-range laser pistols that could be wielded with a fifth arm if it became necessary to deploy it. All humans and Tofa had communication devices strapped to one or another wrist, with channels that could reach each other, *Star Seed*, or *Winds of Home*.

* * *

As soon as all had disembarked, Melly and about a third of the Tofa gathered to one side, while Fel-lar collected the rest, including the Glider and its escort, in a separate group. Fel-lar spoke quietly to the latter group for a moment, then crossed over to Melly and the Tofa with her. He waited for their complete attention before he asked, "Do you all understand your various instructions?"

He looked pointedly from one to the next, watching for any hesitation, confusion, or defiance. One after another looked back at him: some excited, some stern, Melly vibrating with the energy of a performer before the curtain rises.

He should have some final word for them; but his mind was suddenly blank. He raised the grenade launcher in an improvised salute, then returned to the troops he would lead.

The two groups set forth in different directions: Fel-lar's toward the spot where *Winds of Home* would land, and Melly's through the woods between *Star Seed* and Founders Square.

Fel-lar fought back his own distraction and reminded himself of the need to watch for the same in the Twin-Bred marching behind him.

Even purple vegetation would have been more welcome now, after such a long absence, than in the past. But when *Star Seed* approached Tofarn and the viewscreens showed expanses of gold threaded with green, the tangled emotions of gratitude, pleasure, nostalgia, and homesickness that swept through him had been almost overwhelming.

And now, here he was, passing through columns and arches of golden vegetation rustling in the breeze, with tree-seeds bobbing and drifting past or landing gently on the streams. If he could stop and watch for a while, he might see a water beetle touch down as well.

And he might see a beetle-biter rise from beneath the water and swallow the water beetle whole.

He paused and turned back to address his troops. "Stay alert, all of you! We may face danger at any moment, and with little warning."

* * *

Melly strained to hear and understand the muttered conversations behind her as she led the column of Tofa into the woods. She should have moved over to *Star Seed* earlier, so that she and the Twin-Bred would have more time to renew their acquaintance—or rather, to update it: they would remember her as an unruly child, not as an adult accustomed to something like command responsibility. But they knew a human must lead this mission, and that would have to suffice.

And it would take someone familiar with the territory to find the right spot. An error could prove catastrophic.

* * *

Leaving *Star Seed* behind, Fel-lar led his forces to the only other open space in the area where a landing was possible.

The park had two sets of play equipment, and for the most part, the children had gravitated to the sets designed for their species, although some of the older human children were clambering about on the structures meant for Tofa. Fel-lar halted at the edge of the clearing. Per orders already given, four of the Twin-Bred handed their weapons to their fellows and moved slowly forward. Speaking Tofar or English as appropriate, they went from one adult to the next, quietly explaining that they and the children must at all costs stay clear of the adjacent games field. Meanwhile, those assigned lookout duty climbed to the tops of various climbing structures.

Fel-lar began to direct a comment to Levi about the incongruity of soldiers using playground equipment, then remembered Levi's absence. He had not fully realized how much missing Mara included missing Levi as well.

* * *

Melly turned and held up her hands, directing the Tofa Twin-Bred behind her to hold their position. They seemed glad to obey, taking advantage of the halt to gaze at the golden vegetation all around, some pointing at favorite shrubs and flowers. A gleam of sunshine came and went, followed by a soft drizzle. Melly, to her surprise, found herself blinking away tears; one escaped to join the raindrops on her cheek. She had not thought to see the gold of home again so soon.

She was not the only one giving in to nostalgia: several of the Twin-Bred, with far more excuse, were humming as well. She tried to be discreet in identifying two who were not, and beckoned Hal-tet and Dar-tan forward.

Hal-tet stepped toward her immediately; Dar-tan, more distracted, followed a moment later. She waited for Dar-tan's full attention, then gave her orders. "Please survey the terrain in that and that direction. If there are any paths wide enough for three Tofa side by side to pass through these woods, other than this path here, come back as quickly as you can and let me know."

While the scouts headed off, she deployed the remaining Twin-Bred so as to remain unseen by anyone approaching on the path. If enemy forces came through on their way to either landing site, it would be time for her performance.

*   *   *

The exclamations of the families alerted Fel-lar that while he had been following errant thoughts, *Winds of Home* had appeared in the sky overhead and begun its final descent. The intense heat and roar of the landing jets overwhelmed some of the children: loud humming and human wails arose from several corners of the park, and even a few shrieks. But Fel-lar had no leisure to console the fearful. The ship was now settling into place.

*   *   *

"Eminence!"

The young Tofa burst into Ton-lal-set's temporary headquarters without asking permission, without even a preliminary knock on the door. But the youth's parent was the most socially prominent of Ton-lal-set's current supporters, so the display of deplorable manners would have to go uncorrected for now. Ton-lal-set contented himself with stiffening his torso and leaning toward the intruder, radiating reprimand. The young Tofa stopped abruptly, waving all his arms to keep his balance, then folded his arms behind him and looked up at Ton-lal-set, wordlessly begging permission to speak.

Ton-lal-set looked down at his lower fingers, tapped them together in an intricate sequence, and finally looked back at his visitor. "You have an errand of some kind? A message, perhaps?"

"Yes, Eminence! A message from my father! He said— he saw—on the edge of town, Eminence!"

A few weeks before, he would hardly have imagined that any repetition of his long-withheld title could grow wearisome. "*What* did your father see? Get to the point!"

"A *ship*, Eminence! A ship from space, getting ready to land!"

With a heroic exercise of self-control, Ton-lal-set kept his stream of curses from becoming audible or otherwise perceptible. Had the accursed Twin-Bred come back, just when Ton-lal-set's counterrevolution was gaining momentum? But at least—"One ship only?"

"I have told you all I know, Eminence."

Surely, if the idiot's parent had seen more than one ship, his message would have said as much. The world the Twin-Bred had been forced to inhabit must be sufficiently hostile to make surviving, rather than conquest, a priority.

Ton-lal-set would need to send forces to contain the crew of that ship until he had leisure to decide whether political expediency would in any way be served by keeping them alive. He would send as many of his followers as he could spare without depleting the forces required at the rally. If there had been more ships, he might have been forced to cancel . . . .

Ton-lal-set moved to leave the room and almost tripped over the young messenger, still hovering uselessly near the door. "Be off with you! And—summon your parent. If he makes haste, he may take part in the assault."

Chapter 27

(Tofarn)

MELLY CHECKED the settings on her earplugs. Subsonics had been known to induce feelings of fear or awe in humans; and while Mara had not had time to confirm that earplugs would reduce any such effect, they seemed a prudent precaution—unless she carelessly left them adjusted to block too much sound when she needed maximum awareness of her surroundings.

Melly heard footsteps and held her breath, her thumb poised over the buttons on her control unit. But in a moment came the whistled sequence of tones with which she had instructed her scouts to identify themselves. No normal Tofa would use whistling as an identifiable signal . . . unless, in this brief time, her scouts had been captured and interrogated? She would remain ready, just in case.

But there they came, unharmed and unaccompanied— and excited about the news they announced. "Tofa coming—" "Friendly ones!"

Melly allowed her hand to relax slightly. "And we know this how?"

Dar-tan radiated surprise and pleasure. "Because Jak-rad-tan is leading them!"

Melly stood on her toes, craning in the direction from which the scouts had come. She could see nothing; but surely, those were more footsteps, faint but coming nearer?

"Did they see you?"

"No. Hal-tet said we shouldn't let them, not without talking to you."

"And right he was. But you'll have your chance soon, though you'll have to keep it short. If we don't let them know we're here, Fel-lar will wonder what became of us."

* * *

One of Fel-lar's lookouts shouted and pointed in the direction of their march. A group of Tofa was running toward them. Fel-lar gave the arranged signal, and his troops brought their weapons to the ready position—until the lookout announced the identity of the Tofa in the lead.

With difficulty, Fel-lar restrained himself from rushing forward to meet his friend, waiting for Jak-rad-tan to reach him. And however much he yearned to embrace Jak-rad-tan with all his arms, he grasped him with lower arms only and kept hold of his weapon.

Jak-rad-tan spoke as the two stepped back from each other. "Our old friend Melly greeted us. She asked me to tell you that she is in position. She behaved somewhat strangely, shrouding herself in a peculiar cloak, and claiming it would be inadvisable for me to touch her. Is all well with Veda's youngest?"

Fel-lar buzzed for a moment, then temporized. "Depending on how events develop, you may see at least part of the answer for yourself. Any real explanation will have to wait for less public surroundings."

The sound of *Winds of Home* deploying her ramp—the ship almost forgotten in that moment of reunion—interrupted their colloquy. Fel-lar gestured to his troops, and they lined up to form a protective corridor for those disembarking. Jak-rad-tan looked around the site, then arranged his own Tofa in an arc facing the ship.

Lan-sol was first to emerge, armed much as those awaiting him were armed. He spotted Jak-rad-tan almost immediately; Fel-lar caught the start of surprise, the beginning of movement toward Jak-rad-tan, and then the remembrance of duty and occasion. The lad maintained a steady pace down the ramp, then stepped to one side and covered the descent of those following. Not until all had left the ship did Lan-sol allow himself to approach his parent.

Fel-lar missed the moment of greeting, distracted by movement behind him. Wings Spread Wide and the Tofa carrying it had made their way to the foot of the ramp. As Lan-sol turned from Jak-rad-tan toward Fel-lar and the rest,

Wings Spread Wide trilled a long melody of greeting. Lan-sol stared, then bowed deeply to the side.

Seth Baruti stepped forward. He must have realized that Lan-sol bore no translator capable of properly handling Glider speech; or perhaps he simply wanted to lay claim to a momentous occasion. Beaming, his chest puffed out, he began: "Captain Lan-sol, I presume? I did not have the honor of meeting you during your visit to our ship, but I now have a greater honor as well in making this introduction. May I present Wings Spread Wide, honored elder and premier composer of the Glider people, who expresses its delight at meeting so bold an explorer." As Lan-sol turned uncertainly back and forth between Baruti and the Glider, Baruti added: "Wings Spread Wide's translator is equipped to process Tofa speech—imperfectly, of course, but adequately for present purposes. You may address it directly."

Lan-sol bowed again. "You offer me a compliment more fitting for yourself. Welcome to Tofarn, pioneer of your people. And may I, in my turn, present my parent, Jak-rad-tan."

Jak-rad-tan bowed also, then moved closer to Fel-lar and said softly, "These courtesies are all very well, but time is short."

Fel-lar thought quickly. They had come to assist Jak-rad-tan, but chiefly to offer him protection. "My friend, are you determined to confront the rebels? There is room on our ship. You could summon those of your acquaintance who are now in danger. We could transport Gen-tar-ten and those loyal to him to any destination on Tofarn; and we could offer you, and any others who wish, passage to New Landing instead."

Jak-rad-tan paused only briefly before he turned his upper right hand in the gesture for respectful rejection. "Gen-tar-ten will not relinquish his position so easily. Depending on the fortunes of the day, he or his followers may yet accept this offer . . . if nothing happens to prevent it. As for me—" Fel-lar almost stepped back from the sudden overpowering odor of his friend's anger. "I will not leave the fray while Ton-lal-set remains alive and free."

*   *   *

Once again, Melly heard footsteps, more this time, and from the direction of *Winds of Home*'s landing site. It should be her people—but she made ready once again, shoulders back and finger poised, until Fel-lar appeared at the head of a long column of Tofa, with Seth Baruti, the Glider, and the Tofa carrying the Glider bringing up the rear. Fel-lar had, she saw, integrated Lan-sol's young crew into his own Twin-Bred. Fel-lar waved her toward a position in the very front of the column. "Take point, if you please."

She complied; then, after a deep breath, she led their combined forces along the path between a river and a stream, the path that led toward Founders Square.

"Halt! And be silent!"

The command was no less imperative for being softly spoken. Melly stopped and swiveled around to face Fel-lar; he gestured toward the point up ahead where the path curved to the left behind a dense grove of trees. She heard it almost at once: Tofa footsteps once again, at least as many as had heralded the arrival of Jak-rad-tan earlier.

"Melly." Fel-lar had bent down to whisper in her ear. "We will retreat to a suitable distance, but we will be watching. Wait until all the approaching Tofa have rounded the turn and are well within the estimated range of your device. Then question them as I instructed you—but do not wait long for an answer."

For a moment she felt the firm grip of a lower hand on her shoulder, before Fel-lar turned to direct his forces to their hiding place.

Melly stood by herself on the path, hearing the tramp of approaching Tofa. Of course Fel-lar and the others could not stay too near: Mara had had no chance to test whether the device directed the subsonic waves as well as it was meant to do, and there could be unexpected spillover, especially with the volume turned up higher than in any test. Of course they would have stayed with her if they could . . . .

Enough of that! Those approaching would be here any moment, and she must make sure she had everything ready.

Melly opened her cloak slightly, glanced at her arms, still coated in smoky purple makeup, and hoped her face remained thickly covered as well. The sparklers on each side of the contraption on her chest could be triggered with one quick squeeze apiece, as soon as the cloak was safely discarded; and the aroma sticks the sparklers would ignite, the wholesome and appealing odor of vanilla, would have quite a different effect on Tofa sensibilities.

And then, all she need do was push the button on her palm, and stand facing the enemy—and, recalling her days as actress rather than director, declaim one more monologue.

* * *

Tet-lit, warrior of the Tofa, strode boldly forward at his parent's side, with those less favored following behind. The latest shower had ended, and the sunlit golden fronds along the path glistened with water, water that scattered and refreshed him as the plants brushed against his legs and lower arms. How fitting, as Tofa society achieved a glorious rebirth, that the cold and dreary purple season had given way to gold!

It had been a near thing: if his father had hurried any less after receiving Ton-lal-set's summons, Tet-lit would have been bringing up the rear with the others his age. But now, Tet-let and his parent would vanquish the foe, and the other soldiers would report their valor, and the new Eminence, his position now secure, would . . . .

Well, it was difficult, even after such short acquaintance, to imagine Ton-lal-set showering praise on anyone. But surely, once Tet-lit had proven his worth, he would be given other important tasks, even trusted with secrets of state. It would all begin today.

He rounded the turn, and there, directly in his path, stood—what? The figure was small, small even for a human, and hidden by a cloak. And no one else, human or Tofa, was anywhere to be seen. But they must be nearby.

* * *

Fel-lar had kept Lan-sol by his side, and now asked softly: "Do you recognize any of them?"

Lan-sol hissed, more loudly than Fel-lar would have

wished. "The older one in front has never supported Gen-tar-ten. I think he was in prison at first, but from what I heard, he had friends Gen-tar-ten wanted to befriend as well, and he went free."

But there was no way to warn Melly without the risk of provoking an attack before she was ready.

*   *   *

The cloaked figure spoke—in Tofar, not in the human language, yet he was sure the figure was human.

Tet-lit's parent drew himself to his full height as he exclaimed, "We come to repel invaders, and to protect the true Eminence, now that he has been restored! Surrender and beg his mercy!"

Tet-lit turned to his parent to ask whether he might have the honor of taking this creature prisoner. But before he could speak, sudden motion caught his eye. The figure had thrust out its arms—only two, he had been right—and thrown off the cloak. But no human had skin of that disturbing shade, the smoky purple of dark forest in the cold season. And now sparks were flying around the creature, flying toward Tet-lit, and the most appalling smell seemed to follow them. And the creature was speaking again, declaiming, almost shouting—still in Tofar, Tofar more fluent than any human should speak—and its words made his blood chill in his body.

He had always known the words, or so it seemed. He had heard them again and again, first from his parent and then at school: the legend of a long-ago traitor and the curse laid upon him for his treachery.

"*And your legs will bend beneath you, and your arms will tremble and fall, and your thoughts will wander in darkness, for you have betrayed your rightful lord . . . .*"

And it was happening, it was happening here and now, just as the legend foretold! Tet-lit's head swam and throbbed, and his limbs grew faint. The creature was still shouting, but he could no longer understand what it was saying. His parent was speaking to him, urging some action, but he could not tell what he was supposed to do, and no command echoed in his mind. All around him came gasps, groans, hums growing louder and louder, and noises like words, and he could not understand the noises, did not know if they were curses or demands or pleas for mercy. . . .

Tet-lit threw himself down on the forest floor and howled.

*   *   *

Melly stood staring at the Tofa stumbling in circles, and the others—the younger ones, it seemed—who had already fallen. Some lay twitching and flailing on the path in front of her; two had fallen across the stream, living writhing bridges, and one had slid halfway into the river, his head perilously close to under water.

She had done all this; and she longed to grab her fallen cloak and huddle beneath it, hiding from the pitiful sights and sounds of what she had wrought. But the victory was not yet complete.

She jabbed at the button that shut off the subsonic waves, then turned to beckon Fel-lar and the others. They emerged from the forest, moving cautiously at first, edging closer, until Fel-lar reached Melly's side and called to them: "Quickly! They may not be helpless for long. You, on this side: go there, and there, and watch in case more are coming. The rest of you: follow Protocol Alpha."

Melly held her breath and waited. She knew the alternatives Fel-lar had considered. She could only hope her assessment of the situation matched Fel-lar's: he had not told her the meaning of his cryptic command.

Half the Tofa Twin-Bred raised their weapons . . . and handed them to their companions to hold, as Melly gasped in relief. Fel-lar opened the backpack he had been wearing and pulled out short lengths of strong plastic rope. The Twin-Bred who had two hands free descended on Ton-lal-set's followers in teams of two, one to bind the prisoners' lower arms behind their backs, the other to bind the upper. Once that was accomplished, they pulled out stretches of cloth and tied them around the prisoners' speech membranes. It would not work as well as gagging a human, but it would at least reduce the volume of any incoherent cries for help.

Fel-lar examined the result, buzzing; then he rummaged

again in the backpack and drew out some longer lengths of rope. He passed them out to a few of the tallest Twin-Bred. "Tie these Tofa to the sturdiest trees you can find, one to a tree, and not too close together. Confiscate their weapons. If you cannot carry them while remaining able to use your own, then find a place to conceal them on your way to Founders Square. Follow the rest of us there as quickly as you can."

He turned to Melly. "Have you suffered any ill effects from this encounter?"

She shook her head, as lost for words as the stricken Tofa.

He set his lower hands on her shoulders and turned her back the way they had come. "Then return to the ship. Report to Mara. And—thank you. I would say more of my thanks if we had time."

Then he made his way to the forefront of the waiting Tofa, and led them around the bend in the path.

Chapter 28

(Tofarn)

TON-LAL-SET stood within a circle of armed guards, surveying the growing crowd. He had stretched his principles so far as to adopt modern methods of publicizing the rally, with gratifying results. But if the crowd somehow became unfriendly, he would need greater numbers for his protection. Where were the rest of his followers? They should have returned by now, except for those left to guard prisoners.

He put aside the question—there was no way to answer it at present—and continued his perusal of those gathering to hear the speeches. With his retentive memory, Ton-lal-set recognized several Tofa who had escaped the purge and had presumably been lying low. If all went well, he would soon be able to reward them for emerging from hiding, even to the limited extent of appearing among the unfamiliar majority of the curious.

Ton-lal-set would be the second speaker. The first, one of those who had often visited him in prison, stood muttering to himself nearby, practicing his oration. Ton-lal-set assessed the crowd once more. Its size should suffice for them to get started; if they delayed, some might grow restless and drift away. Indeed, any greater numbers might put those on the edges of the crowd outside the range of full comprehension.

He made his way to the first speaker's side, tapped him on the nearest arm, and pointed to the clear space at the foot of the square's largest monument. Fortunately the monument, abstract in design, did not include any human figures, and his followers had pried loose the plaque at its base, covered with Terran lettering, and tossed it aside.

The crowd greeted the speaker first with an increase in chatter and exclamations, then with subsiding noise and finally with silence.

Ton-lal-set devoted only a fraction of his attention to the speaker, mentally rehearsing his own address. The crowd was reacting well to the comparisons between his own regime and that of Gen-tar-ten. When the speaker listed Gen-tar-ten's degrading imitations of human conduct and policies, a gratifying number of those listening shrilled their anger and derision.

But now the speaker was straying from the speech Ton-lal-set had approved. What was that about preserving Tofa tradition "for the children"? He certainly endorsed the sentiment—but mentioning children could be a serious misstep, reminding them of Ton-lal-set's reputation on the subject. Was that a whistle he heard from somewhere in the crowd?

One of Ton-lal-set's guards broke his concentration, ushering a Tofa who looked familiar. Of course—it was his contact from the laboratory conducting spore-parent identification. The Tofa made a hasty gesture of respect and handed Ton-lal-set a list on a long metal plate. "Eminence, these are all the Tofa whom we have studied to date. You will find two columns, children on the left and spore-parents on the right. If you review the names, you may find some whom you would wish to mention in your speech." Then he melted away into the crowd without waiting for a reply.

Ton-lal-set prepared to interrupt the speaker before he strayed further off course. Was there time for a quick look at the list? It might provide some potent distraction to help the crowd forget the speaker's unfortunate topic. He held up the list and scanned it as quickly as he could.

Ah, yes—that could be an embarrassing connection! And on the other hand, this young Tofa's connection to an honored elder could be most useful. And there—a most important name indeed!

Ton-lal-set paused before allowing his eyes to drift from Lan-sol's name, on the left, to the right-hand column. If only he found some disreputable connection that would tarnish the legend's luster, and allow their young people to find better role models to follow!

He looked at the list on the right.

What?

This must be falsehood, some malicious corruption of the data!

But the timing . . . Jak-rad-tan had certainly been in Ton-lal-set's vicinity, often, during the crucial period.

Ton-lal-set stood immobile, the list clutched in his upper left hand, as the speaker went on, now struggling to be heard over increasing whistles and chatter.

He could look once more, in case his eyes had somehow deceived him. He raised the list again.

There, still there! In the column on the right, neatly printed next to Lan-sol's name, he again read the name of Lan-sol's spore-parent.

Ton-lal-set.

Lan-sol, the hated emblem of his own defeat, misleader of youth, living child of the Tofa who had done so much toward Ton-lal-set's defeat: Lan-sol existed only because of Ton-lal-set's contribution?

Ton-lal-set looked back at the column on the left, titled "Child."

Ton-lal-set's children were dead, dead and lost to him.

Child?

His child?

A child of his, alive?

*　*　*

Seth Baruti stood next to Wings Spread Wide and its escort at the back of the crowd, clutching his tablet and wishing he had the Glider's higher vantage point. Then he could at least see, if not hear, what was happening. At first he had been able to hear the speaker, but the crowd had grown unruly, the speaker's supporters arguing with those less impressed at a volume that periodically drowned out the speaker entirely.

Seth squirmed forward to a less densely occupied part of the crowd. Now he could see the speaker glancing repeatedly off to one side, where a circle of armed Tofa surrounded another whom Seth could not quite see. Ton-lal-set, former Eminence, was set to address the crowd; the guards most likely were his retinue. What was delaying his appearance?

Suddenly the Tofa all around Seth seemed to be turning toward something behind him, emitting a host of startled exclamations. Seth turned as well, only to see the Tofa carrying Wings Spread Wide plowing their way forward. Seth ran to catch up, waving one arm to attract the Glider's attention. "What are you doing? Stay back!"

The Glider turned toward him. "There you are! I feared we had lost you. Please do not wander away again, or you might find yourself too far away to record my song." The Glider reached out and clasped Seth's hand, its wing covering their joined hands in a way that made Seth think of prayer shawls and blessings. "And thank you, my friend, for all you have done."

"*Singing*? Have you lost your mind? These Tofa have never even seen a Glider! Who knows what they'll do?"

The Glider reached out its wing to brush Seth's shoulder, in what he dimly recalled to be a gesture of reassurance. "Whatever they do, they are likely to pay attention in some manner. That is the point." It clucked at its escort, who resumed their forward progress.

"The point? Did Fel-lar put you up to this? Wait!" But the escort continued pushing through the crowd, leaving Seth to stammer, then to curse, and then to stumble forward in their wake.

* * *

Fel-lar hovered near the front of the crowd, clutching his weapon, as Wings Spread Wide and its escort reached a corner of the square containing a second sculpture, currently more accessible than the central monument. The Glider's helpers set it down within the sculpture itself, resting upon the figure's outstretched upper arms, and then stepped back toward the crowd. The speaker glared at them in indignation, sputtering to a halt.

The Glider stretched its body upward and its wings out to their farthest reach, and began to sing.

Fel-lar had considered appointing some Tofa to introduce and explain the Glider, but Wings Spread Wide had earnestly requested that the plan proceed with as little risk to others as possible. And perhaps no introduction could be as effective as the uniquely strange sight and sound of the Glider itself. While many young Tofa could have identified what the crowd was hearing, the audience Ton-lal-set had been able to summon contained few so well informed. Most of the listening Tofa were exposed for the first time to the tantalizing, seductive complexity of Glider song, the only music to which Tofa had ever been attracted.

As Fel-lar and Wings Spread Wide had hoped, the confusion and clamor that had met the Glider's first appearance subsided as the music took hold. Almost no one faced the main monument beneath which the speaker now stood, ignored. The speaker let out a wordless shout of frustration and headed toward the cluster of guards that must indicate Ton-lal-set's position, gesticulating as he went. Meanwhile, Fel-lar's, Jak-rad-tan's, and Lan-sol's forces moved quietly around the outskirts of the crowd, spacing themselves so as to almost completely encircle it. Jak-rad-tan and Lan-sol had—unconsciously?—converged, separated by only two of the Tofa Jak-rad-tan had brought with him. So close together, they presented all too tempting a target should Ton-lal-set's forces spy them. If Fel-lar tried to move them farther apart, would he only make things worse by attracting their adversaries' attention?

Fel-lar moved closer to Ton-lal-set's entourage. The speaker had reached them and was entreating Ton-lal-set to come forward and recapture the crowd's attention; but Ton-lal-set seemed unaccountably distracted, staring at some hidden object near where his upper left hand must be.

Suddenly the speaker snatched a weapon from one of the guards and strode toward the statute on which Wings Spread Wide had perched. Fel-lar started running, pushing through the crowd, trying to intercept the newly armed Tofa. Off to his left he saw Seth Baruti, unarmed, arms flailing, running forward as well.

But before either reached the statute, the Tofa had raised and fired the weapon. The sound of the shot reverberated around the square; and as it died away, there was silence instead of song.

Then the crowd erupted into every kind of exclamation,

just as Seth Baruti broke through the crush of Tofa and hurled himself in a furious tackle at the armed Tofa's midsection, bringing him crashing to the ground. Human, Tofa, and Glider lay almost on top of each other. Fel-lar reached them just as the Tofa began to pry himself upward, and was able to seize the weapon and bring the butt of it down hard on the Tofa's skull. The Tofa twitched and went limp. Fel-lar pulled Baruti to his feet, but Baruti tugged free of his grasp, sobbing, and knelt by the wounded Glider's side.

Baruti bent over the Glider, his head almost touching the Glider's beak. Fel-lar was not close enough for either his ears or his translator to pick up the Glider's speech; but Baruti listened for several minutes before he bent further and kissed the Glider's crumpled wing. Then he struggled to his feet and, limping, approached the statue, grabbing it as if intending to climb. Fel-lar picked Baruti up and deposited him where Wings Spread Wide had been standing, then turned to stand guard as the old man waved his hands and shouted, "Silence! Quiet, if you please!"

In the emotion of the motion, he spoke in Terran; but the noise of the crowd subsided as its members turned to stare at the human trembling above them. Baruti cleared his throat and went on, this time in Tofar; but his voice was hoarse and weak, and he could not project the nonverbal elements nearly as well as a Tofa would. Fel-lar began echoing Baruti's words, speaking as loud as he could. Baruti, realizing what he was doing and apparently consenting, paused every few words for Fel-lar's repetition.

"I am the appointed voice of Wings Spread Wide. It is my duty and privilege to speak in its place, now that . . ." Baruti's voice broke for an instant before he pulled himself together to continue. "Now that this most honored of the Glider people has sung its last song.

"Wings Spread Wide gives its greetings to you all, and thanks you for listening to it sing. It hopes that it will not be the last Glider to meet, to delight in, and to delight the esteemed beings of Tofarn, from which so many of its friends have come."

Seth paused and looked to one side, evidently tracking some disturbance in that direction. Fel-lar followed his gaze. The cause was soon apparent: Ton-lal-set was finally in motion, heading toward Baruti and the fallen Glider. His guards made as if to follow.

Fel-lar pressed the alarm signal on his communicator and followed it with an urgent series of orders. His and Lan-sol's troops converged on Ton-lal-set's guards, emerging from the cover of the crowd and cutting them off from their leader. The guards, taken by surprise, had not brought their weapons to bear in the proper direction. Two of them tried to aim at the interlopers, but too late. The rising buzz of alarm from the onlookers failed to drown out the report of weapons, and the guards fell bleeding to the ground.

All the while, Ton-lal-set kept advancing, unarmed; but no longer toward Wings Spread Wide. He had turned to face the spot on the perimeter where Jak-rad-tan and Lan-sol stood, with only two Tofa between them.

Fel-lar raced to find a vantage point from which to fire. But when he reached it, he hesitated. Ton-lal-set had paused more than three arm-lengths away from his apparent targets, and stood as if waiting. Fel-lar sighted his weapon on the middle of Ton-lal-set's chest, and waited as well. Jak-rad-tan and Lan-sol both looked around, clutching their weapons but not yet aiming them. Fel-lar guessed they sought some explanation of Ton-lal-set's conduct, some hostile forces still standing to protect their leader; but if any remained, Fel-lar could not see them.

Word of the confrontation made its way in buzzing waves from those closest back through the crowd. In its wake came silence once again, as all strained to hear what the former Eminence would say to the two Tofa against whom above all he must seek vengeance.

*　*　*

Jak-rad-tan trained his weapon on his enemy; but he would not shoot yet, in this most public of confrontations, when Ton-lal-set bore no weapon of his own. He saw Fel-lar nearby, and could only hope that he would see and eliminate any threat beyond Jak-rad-tan's view.

Ton-lal-set faced Lan-sol. "Child of Jak-rad-tan."

Lan-sol pointed his weapon at Ton-lal-set as he replied, "Murderer of children."

Ton-lal-set made a sweeping gesture with his upper right hand. "And yet here you stand, alive and strong. How fortunate your parent! How fortunate any parent whose children survive and prosper."

Jak-rad-tan was seized with a dreadful premonition. Was there a double meaning in Ton-lal-set's words? Had he somehow come to know his connection to Lan-sol? And in another moment, would he tell Lan-sol what Jak-rad-tan had determined never to reveal? Should Jak-rad-tan risk the consequences and shoot Ton-lal-set where he stood?

But Ton-lal-set was speaking again. "Child of Jak-rad-tan, you and your fellows have planned well. I see your forces and how they are deployed. Whether there is more death today or less, the day will end with your victory, and my defeat. I will return to prison, and never leave it. I would rather die, and join . . ." He paused and let out a quiet and somehow distorted whistle that chilled Jak-rad-tan's blood. "I would rather join my children in death.

"But if ever I break free again—"

Ton-lal-set turned to point the stiffened fingers of both upper hands at Jak-rad-tan, then faced Lan-sol once again. But as he spoke, Jak-rad-tan was seized with confusion. Jak-rad-tan had come to know by now the sound of deceit in a Tofa voice. And Ton-lal-set was telling a lie.

"—If ever I escape the prison in which you seek to immure me, I will hunt you down, you and your parent. And even when I am in prison, my followers will know my most heartfelt desire and achieve it in my stead. Unless you flee to the world to which your Twin-Bred fled, then sooner or later, I will rejoice in Jak-rad-tan's death as well as your own.

"If you value your life or that of your parent's, you can save yourselves, and serve that usurper whom you dare to call your Eminence. Shoot me. Shoot me, and live. Or stand there useless, and I will see you die."

Lan-sol turned and stared at Jak-rad-tan, his weapons hanging at his sides. Behind him, Ton-lal-set stood quivering with some unknown passion. Lan-sol looked back toward Ton-lal-set and took one step backward. Jak-rad-tan knew, and Ton-lal-set must know, that Lan-sol was not ready to kill.

Ton-lal-set let out a sudden bellow and reached as if to grab Lan-sol's weapon, reached with apparent clumsiness, failing to even touch it. And Jak-rad-tan, knowing he was acting as a puppet in Ton-lal-set's grasp, lifted his weapon and blasted Ton-lal-set to bleeding bits.

Chapter 29

(Tofarn, including *Star Seed*)

MARA EXITED the head for the fourth time since Fel-lar and his troops had left *Star Seed*, and for at least the tenth time checked the settings on her phone.

("Levi?")

("Right here, Sis. And almost as nervous as you.")

Mara searched for a rejoinder, then started convulsively as the phone finally sounded. She jabbed at it to answer. "Fel-lar?"

"Did Melly arrive safely?"

"Yes! But tell me—"

"We are all alive."

Mara was in the middle of a profound sigh of relief when Fel-lar added, "But Wings Spread Wide is dying. And Ton-lal-set is dead."

The sigh became a gasp. "How?"

"One of Ton-lal-set's adherents shot Wings Spread Wide as it sang. Jak-rad-tan killed Ton-lal-set. There is much more to the story, but explanations must wait. We have an urgent situation to resolve."

("Ah, the Tofa gift for understatement.")

("Hush.") "Is Jak-rad-tan under arrest?"

Fel-lar paused before replying. "His status, and all of ours, is somewhat ambiguous at present. Gen-tar-ten appeared with his own forces after, as the saying goes, the shooting stopped. Some negotiations appear to be necessary."

"Hold on! I have Emily Wilson waiting, in case something like this came up." Mara put the call on the group setting and buzzed Emily as she spoke.

Emily joined the call. Fel-lar briskly repeated his

summary. Emily asked, "Would Gen-tar-ten agree to speak to me directly? Mara could stay on the line—but I would suggest she not interject unless I ask her to do so."

*　*　*

The crowd had first diminished, as many of those attending the rally fled the violent confrontation; and then grown, as word spread that something momentous might be happening. Fel-lar and the other Twin-Bred clustered close to the sculpture where Wings Spread Wide had sung. The Glider lay at the statue's base, and Fel-lar could see no remaining sign of life. Seth Baruti sat on the ground nearby, hunched over with his head in his hands.

In the center of the square, Gen-tar-ten ended his telephone conference with Emily Wilson, then spread out his upper arms for the crowd's attention.

"Jak-rad-tan, whose loyalty to your Eminence has many times been demonstrated, has been of service once again. A former dictator, seeking to regain power, has been prevented from doing so by the only means possible. Jak-rad-tan's child, and this his former comrade, have offered valuable assistance as well. All will now go with me to headquarters, where all the details of this day may be recorded for posterity."

Fel-lar leaned toward Jak-rad-tan and murmured, "And whether any of us leave that establishment in the near future may be determined in suitable privacy."

Fel-lar's phone buzzed again, Mara on the line. "I've got another suggestion. Emily can continue to take part, and is willing to show up in person—though I hesitate to let her. But it might be as well to call on someone whom Gen-tar-ten knows better, and to whom he's listened in the past. Ask him to send for Veda, if she'll come."

*　*　*

Walking as exercise was all very well for people with a functional sense of direction. Stewart had not quite wanted to explain to his doctor—or rather, the ridiculously young woman who had replaced his doctor—how lost he was likely to become if he ran errands on foot, as the woman had so cheerfully suggested.

Following a path through the woods might feel somewhat pointless, but at least he could turn around and make his way out again—and do so sooner if the path insisted on subdividing.

And striding along, legs striking the ground with a satisfying rhythm, lungs taking in the good fresh air, the sun shining after the most recent shower . . . well, it felt good. So far, anyway. He might get tired soon, but for now, he felt something like energetic. How long had it been since he felt like that?

Of course retirement (if he chose to give it that name) had drained much of his vitality. His failure to regain his seat in the Council would have left him hollow, even if nothing more important than his own fate had hung upon it. He was no spell-binding orator. How could he rally the people, make them confront the threat, when no one had to pay attention to anything he said?

But maybe, now that no one paid him any heed, he could find others who saw the danger, others who might even now be working together, a covert company of guerrilla fighters preparing to act. The next time he followed this path, he might be heading to a conclave, with plans to be polished. . . .

What was *that*?

Lost in his dream, he had barely noticed the woods around him. Walking and dreaming, he had somehow walked into a nightmare. Tofa all around him, a Tofa beside every tree—

No. Not beside. *Tied.* Tofa, everywhere, tied to trees, with some sort of cloth around the membranes with which they spoke. Some slumped as if unconscious; and some, now, were stirring, moaning through the cloths, struggling to raise their heads, their great marbled eyes staring. . . .

Who had done this? Could it be some human allies, the sort of force he had imagined assembling? But something about the scene, some detail he couldn't identify, seemed to suggest otherwise.

From behind Stewart came a humming sound, the sound of Tofa grief. He turned, slowly, to find what must surely be a youngster, not much older than that Tofa Veda seemed so fond of—Lan-sing, Lan-san, some such name. . . . The young Tofa seemed to be recovering from whatever incomprehensible event had overtaken him and his fellows. He was jerking his limbs against the ropes binding him, his entire body trembling, and humming louder and louder with every moment.

Who was he? Who were *they*? Stewart turned back toward the others, forcing himself to breathe slowly and calmly as he surveyed one writhing, twitching Tofa after another.

Surely, tied to one of the nearest trees, was the very Tofa who had confronted him in the street a few months ago and hissed an unmistakable insult in his direction, almost knocking into him before stalking on past?

Or was he imagining things? Could he really tell one from another, and after so much time?

And was he imagining, as more of them emerged from their stupor, the wave of hostility, even hatred, with which they stared at him?

They might get loose! Dozens, maybe more, all around him—Was there anything he could use, a branch he could use as a club—

He looked around frantically and spied the glint of sunlight on something reflective, almost hidden in the foliage near the path. He plowed through the undergrowth and saw what looked like the handle, or whatever one called it, of an actual weapon, some sort of gun. Had only one of them been armed? Perhaps they all had been, and whoever removed the other weapons had missed this one. Stewart bent down and gingerly cleared away the plants that had largely concealed it. He knew little about weapons, and what little he knew did not encompass this one, which (he shuddered) might well be of Tofa manufacture. He could not tell just what it would do, let alone how; but protruding at the front, like the bayonet on a vintage human rifle, was fixed a blade as long as his hand, broad and sturdy and sharp.

He stretched out one cautious finger and barely touched the metal handle. Nothing happened; the metal did not burn or sting his skin, and the weapon remained inert. Slowly, warily, he picked it up, holding it by the end of its handle, keeping his fingers away from its cryptic knobs and indentations.

Around him, the muffled moans and hums grew louder, and now became words, the familiar, incomprehensible, alien words; calls, distorted shouts from one tree to another, all around the nightmare grove.

But he had the weapon with its blade; and with all their struggling, none of the Tofa had managed to pull free. Not yet.

Now came a different sound, a sound from behind: not far off and coming closer, the tramp of marching feet on the path. Whoever approached would appear at any moment.

He could not tell how many approached, or even whether they were humans coming to the rescue or Tofa come to the aid of their fellows. Should he run farther down the path? But what other horrors might await him there?

As he looked back, and ahead, and back, his glance fell again on the young one, the Tofa who had been weeping in Tofa fashion but now stood silent and staring at him. Their eyes met; and the Tofa shifted his gaze to the weapon Stewart held, then back to Stewart's face, and then back and forth once more.

The Tofa spoke, his voice audible despite the cloth; and Stewart did not need his daughter's knowledge of the alien tongue to recognize the sound of pleading.

Surely the Tofa would not be asking him for death!—no matter what approached them along the path. . . .

But no, of course. He was asking to be cut free.

Stewart started at the weapon in his hand. Could he grip it securely and use the blade without firing it accidentally?

And if he freed the youngster, what then? How could he even consider it? One Tofa freed, and the entire company could soon be loose, surrounding him; and after dealing with him, what then? What had they been on the way to doing, armed and dangerous?

The young Tofa spoke again, his tone more urgent—and no wonder: whoever approached was just beyond the bend.

They would see him armed! Stewart dropped the weapon, then hopped back, almost falling, as it landed perilously near his feet.

From close to his ear came the sudden and unmuffled sound of Tofa speech. Stewart stared and almost tripped again. While he had been fumbling about, another troop of Tofa had flooded into the grove. Their apparent leader loomed over Stewart, looking down into his face. That word, what was it? He had heard it more than once, surely, during his years on the Council—toward the end, at least. Veda claimed it was some sort of honorific, respect for an elder.

"Human elder?"

Terran! Stewart stood up and arched his back to look up at the Tofa who had spoken. The Tofa might understand him if he spoke, but what could he ask?

"Human elder. You should leave this place."

Stewart had not noticed the silence from the trees all around until a wave of noise rose again, less chaotic than before, more clearly words despite the effect of the gags: shouts and yells and what sounded like cursing. He looked around the grove, trembling, and then back at the Tofa who had spoken to him.

"You can go that way." The Tofa pointed to a narrower path, branching off from the main one a few meters onward. "It will take you back to a street, and the street will take you back where you belong."

Stewart looked one more time at the younger Tofa, now slumped silent against the tree behind him. The urge arose to apologize; but the Tofa would probably not understand, and it would make no difference.

Stewart backed away, one step, then another, before turning and running in the direction he had been told to go.

*   *   *

Gen-tar-ten reclined against his most luxurious leaning post—or rather, Fel-lar noted, the Eminence pretended to recline. The tautness of his muscles, the angle of his body, did not suggest relaxation. But Gen-tar-ten's voice, as he spoke, flowed smoothly. "Your Emily Wilson, and my old friend Veda, have been most helpful in assisting with my response to today's events. Meanwhile, we are tracking down those known to have attended the rally. They will be interviewed in sufficient depth for me to assess their future loyalty. . . . A few more questions, and I believe you and your companions may be on their way."

A young and deferential Tofa knocked at the door of the Eminence's quarters; waited for permission; then entered with a large and intricately carved candle in a gleaming metal holder. It was already lit, and gave forth a soothing, almost intoxicating scent. Fel-lar did his best to gather his wits, and to resist whatever chemical persuasion the candle might contain.

The young Tofa bowed sideways and slipped out the door, closing it behind him. A moment later, Gen-tar-ten waved an upper hand toward the door. "Kindly ensure that no one is lingering outside."

Fel-lar obeyed, looking through the one-way viewing portal in the door. "I see no one. Shall I open the door to conduct a more thorough search?"

"No, that will do. Opening the door might attract attention. Kindly come close again, so that we do not need to bellow. . . . You may use that post." Gen-tar-ten pointed to a sturdy but narrow post facing Gen-tar-ten's, its design obviously intended for something less than comfort.

Fel-lar was tempted to undercut the gambit by disclaiming any need to lean—but it would be foolish to antagonize the Eminence in any nonessential manner. He took his assigned position and did his best to ignore the edges of the post digging into his back.

"Well, young Twin-Bred. No, don't scoff! I still see in you the intriguingly truculent youngster I met so long ago. . . . I require just a few more details of your triumphant return. You landed your ship, collected your companions from the other vessel, and proceeded toward town. Did you encounter any opposition before reaching the square?"

Fel-lar had known some such question might be coming. The pace of events, especially those of the day, had left Fel-lar very little time to consider the best response to such interrogation. It might do little good to temporize, but . . . . "May I ask whether your Eminence expected such opposition?"

Gen-tar-ten whistled softly. "Perhaps my pessimism inflated the numbers of the traitor's supporters, but I had expected to find, at the rally, a larger force than we have already captured. It occurs to me that you may have incapacitated some of the enemy before the final confrontation."

Fel-lar stood up straight, away from the leaning post, and faced the Eminence. "Your surmise is correct. We met a force of Ton-lal-set's supporters moving toward our landing sites, and overcame them before continuing to the square."

Gen-tar-ten did not bother to conceal his excitement. "How admirable! And just how did you accomplish this?"

"There were enough of us, and we were sufficiently prepared . . . . If you move quickly, you may find them where we left them, restrained, in a path through the woods, approximately halfway between the site of the rally and the edge of town."

Gen-tar-ten stood up as well, stepped to where the candle burned, and blew it out. Then he moved to within an arm's length of Fel-lar, and said softly, "You are evasive, and that does not please me. What weapon did you use?"

If Fel-lar allowed himself to become alarmed, his odor would betray the fact. He searched his memory for a calming vision, or at least a distracting one. And both came in one: Mara, the red of the cliffs of home reflected in her face as the sun set, beside a gleaming crystal valley; and her hands in his lower hands, raising an eyebrow at him in mocking inquiry, and then smiling . . . .

He held the image in his mind's eye as he faced Gen-tar-ten and answered, "We used a weapon I have since sent back to *Star Seed*. It is one I hope never to use again."

Gen-tar-ten did his apparent best to loom over him; but Fel-lar had grown to very near his height.

There was a long silence, broken at last by Gen-tar-ten. "You restrained them, you say. Could you do no more?"

Fel-lar chose his words carefully. "We did not wish to kill. I did not think it prudent to inflame the antagonism of those of Ton-lal-set's supporters who would survive. To do so might have limited your future options."

And if he still lacked knowledge of the weapon's destructive potential, and whether it could kill, there was no need to reveal the fact.

"Prudent, indeed." The hint of sarcasm was exquisitely

calibrated. "And you have sent the weapon back to your ship. But I would imagine there were few of its crew present to receive it."

"We did not bring all our forces." He must come closer to speaking plainly, it seemed. "And those remaining include several humans—who are particularly well suited to deploying this weapon if necessary." And for that matter, if truly necessary . . . "The ship itself could be used to increase the weapon's power and reach." Or at least, it might be so.

Gen-tar-ten stepped back and returned to his leaning post. He waved his upper left fingers in an almost-convincing insouciant gesture. "Well, no matter. I am sure our friend Veda will not begrudge me a few details."

"She does not possess them."

Gen-tar-ten tensed again, and let out a short and startling hiss. Fel-lar flinched; then, recalling with difficulty his vision of Mara, he was able to relax once more.

Gen-tar-ten stared at him, the fingers of each hand tapping together; then, abruptly, he let out a sharp whistle of laughter. "Well played, Twin-Bred!" He strode to the door and flung it open. "You may collect your companions and leave. At once."

Fel-lar set as fast a pace as possible. They must reach the ship before any force that Gen-tar-ten might, after all, decide to dispatch against it.

To reach the ship as soon as possible, they must pass through the grove where they had left the vanquished enemy. He suspected that Gen-tar-ten had known, throughout their recent conversation, just where those Tofa could be found, and might well have already removed them. But he could be wrong. And if he was wrong, there was no way of knowing how many of those Tofa might have recovered somewhat, and whether they had been able to free themselves. He had sent Melly and her device back to the ship . . . .

"All of you: weapons at the ready!" He deployed the oldest and strongest Tofa in a circle around those more vulnerable, and marched on toward the grove.

But they found it empty.

Chapter 30

(Aboard *Star Seed* and elsewhere on Tofarn)

AS THE SKY darkened from green toward black and the orange and magenta streaks of sunset faded, *Star Seed*'s proximity alarm signaled the approach of a party on foot. Mara ran to the viewscreen, then to the main entry hatch, whacking the control to open the hatch and extend the ramp.

Jak-rad-tan and Lan-sol came first, inner arms wound closely about each other, Fel-lar's and Lan-sol's forces streaming behind them. As they neared *Star Seed*, parent and child released each other, stood face to face, and then parted, with Lan-sol and his crew trotting off toward *Winds of Home*. Mara craned to find Fel-lar, and was soon rewarded with the sight of him a little ways behind Jak-rad-tan. He walked more slowly than usual, and was carrying something in his upper hands. In a moment she could see what it was, and she squeezed her eyes shut against tears: Fel-lar bore the belt that Wings Spread Wide had worn throughout its adult life, the belt without which a Glider would feel unable to sing.

Mara opened her eyes again, searched the approaching Tofa, and found the two Twin-Bred who had carried Wings Spread Wide from *Star Seed* to Founders Square. They carried him still, swathed in the cloak Melly had worn earlier.

Mara looked back at Fel-lar. And now she had another explanation for his slower stride: a tiny figure beside him, with whom he was considerably keeping pace.

Mara ran down the ramp, clasped Fel-lar's outstretched hand, and then released it to take Veda in her arms.

"So here's the deal." Veda lifted and admired her chocolate muffin before taking a dainty bite. "My, it's good to be eating your chocolate goodies again! . . . Jak-rad-tan is the stated hero of the day—but only if he makes himself scarce. To be specific, New Landing has prevailed upon him to make a long-delayed visit. Whether he'll take ship with Lan-sol, or whether Lan-sol and/or Fel-lar will prefer that he go with *Star Seed*, I don't know."

"So Lan-sol's still coming to New Landing?"

Veda took a larger bite, chewed, swallowed, and nodded. "In his case, it's more or less voluntary and temporary—if he wants to come back afterward. Gen-tar-ten did suggest that he could manage with fewer crew members, given the desirability of having more of those who support Gen-tar-ten's regime available here. However, the more politically connected families have been allowed to decide what their offspring will do."

Mara glanced at the nearest viewscreen, which showed Jak-rad-tan standing alone, gazing at the landscape around the ship. "What about the rest of Jak-rad-tan's family?"

"They're on their way home. According to Fel-lar—and by the way, after all these years, you've managed to utterly surprise me! but I approve. Anyway, Fel-lar thinks the little one, Ved-rad, will come along with his parent. If Jak-rad-tan decides Ved-rad should grow up on Tofarn, Fel-lar has promised to arrange his safe passage back again. The middle ones are rather more attached to their friends at home, so Jak-rad-tan is looking for places they could stay. He'll make a final decision soon."

Mara looked again at Jak-rad-tan, swallowed the lump in her throat, and placed a mug of hot tea next to Veda's plate. "We make this blend in New Landing. It brings out the flavor of the chocolate without diluting it, somehow. . . . What about you? Would you consider coming along? If you'd prefer to travel with Melly, I'm sure Lan-sol would be happy to accommodate you."

Veda raised her manicured eyebrows high, then abruptly abandoned the expression and slumped back in her chair and dug her polished fingernails into her thighs. "It's so *frustrating* to see you again and then have to say goodbye! And it's worse to have Melly dangled in front of me and snatched away for a second time. And the boys . . . ." She sat up straighter and shook her head briskly as if physically banishing the thought. "But Melly and I already talked about this. I think joining the Project used up my lifetime quota of rash and unlikely decisions." Veda picked up the mug of tea and tested its temperature with a small sip, then took a larger one. "There's no way to be sure when I could come home again. I've built a more or less satisfactory life for myself—which took rather longer than I liked. I'd rather not risk having to start over a third time."

("You may as well dangle a little bait, Sis. For the future.")

"Oh, yes! I almost forgot." Mara put down the tea kettle and rummaged in a storage bin, soon finding and pulling out a soft and pliable bundle. "I brought this in case we had an opportunity to get into some trade talks. It's one of the cloths we make from the plants the Gliders grow. I'd like you to have it."

Veda unfolded the cloth, her eyes going wide at the subtle shimmer of blended colors. "Oh, my. My goodness. Does it come in other varieties as well?"

Mara attempted a sly expression. "You'll just have to come and see for yourself one day."

Both ships required repairs before facing the wormhole one more time; but they made only the essential ones, and those as quickly as could be managed. And the crews kept watch, night and day, until the ships could depart.

There was not much visiting between the ships, with their next destination the same. But Lan-sol made a point of meeting those Twin-Bred he had not met earlier, most of whom had featured in at least some story from his childhood, and getting to know the engineer Can-til, the only member of *Star Seed*'s crew near his own age. Lan-sol and Can-til did not immediately find a great deal to talk about. Mara, passing the lounge in which they stood, conversation coming in fits and starts, thought it useful for Lan-sol to realize that not every Tofa of Twin-Bred parentage would necessarily prove a kindred spirit.

Melly visited *Star Seed* several times, coaxing her old friends to tell her tales of New Landing and of the voyage that

had led them there. And one afternoon, Melly sought out
Mara, arriving at her and Fel-lar's quarters with a shapeless
parcel under one arm and with an uncharacteristic manner
about her, as if she had some subject to broach that could
prove awkward.

Fel-lar was absent, deep in conferences with the
various pilots of both ships, discussing the optimal path back
to the wormhole and planning the precautions that should
keep the vessels out of each other's way. As soon as she got a
second look at the shape of the bundle Melly carried, and the
way it yielded with Melly's movements, Mara wished Fel-lar
could be present. She would have welcomed emotional
support when confronting what she guessed it to be.

Mara put off the moment of revelation by offering
hospitality; but all too soon, Melly put down her mug of hot
chocolate, looked at Mara with her brow slightly furrowed,
and, without words, held out the bundle for Mara to take.

At first Mara was confused. The confused tangle of yarn
had too many colors, more colors than Elizabeth would ever
have put in a garment. Was this something Melly herself had
produced?

Melly still said nothing, but reached out and tugged
two sections of yarn in different directions. The tangle
resolved itself into two knitted objects. Mara reached for the
closer one and extracted it: a sweater, as she had imagined.
She held it up. It should fit. She swallowed hard, then turned
to the yarn that remained.

Melly lifted the strip of yarn between her outstretched
hands. "It's a scarf, I think. I'm not sure who it's for. Your—"
She hesitated, then continued. "Your mother said it could be
for a man, if you liked. I'm not sure what man she was
thinking of."

Mara stood up from her chair and turned away. When
she could speak, she turned back to Melly and said, with a
voice she could not make steady: "Melly, dear, would you be
willing to go into town, if Fel-lar sent a couple of Tofa to
accompany you? There's something you can do for me. And
for my mother. And for someone else."

Mara had not been sure where to find Elizabeth; but
when she slipped the sweater over her head, a tag scratched

along her neck. It had her mother's address written in the familiar small script. Hal-tet and another of their tallest Tofa escorted Melly to deliver the invitation. Then all Mara had to do was to wait, and try to breathe; and to listen.

("I'm nervous, Sis. I'm not sure I've ever been nervous. Scared shitless, metaphorically speaking; but this is different.")

("I'll be here. And so will Fel-lar. He's going to be the one to—to make the introduction, so to speak.")

("Why aren't you wearing the sweater?")

("I wasn't sure what it would seem to mean, wearing it. Or what I'd want it to mean.")

They waited.

("I'm glad I didn't have to remind you about my wanting to meet her. You'd forgotten, you know, before Melly came.")

("Yes, I'd forgotten. Events have been distracting, I hope you'll admit. . . . And it was easier to forget. I'm sorry.")

They waited.

("Mara? Shouldn't they be back yet?")

("Really, after all the times you've chided or teased me for impatience? I will never, never let you live this down.")

("Please, don't you tease. Not now.")

If only Fel-lar were here already, and Levi sharing his body fully, so that she could hug him! ("I'm sorry. Just hold on. It won't be long.")

Two tasks to face and surmount: to see Elizabeth again, and then to confront her mother with the presence, the person, whose existence she had once so insistently denied.

But this hesitant, quiet woman seemed unequal to the confrontation for which Mara had steeled herself.

They met each other in a fumbling embrace, and Fel-lar led Elizabeth to a comfortable chair. A chair was available for Mara as well, but she could not imagine sitting: it was difficult enough to stand in one place without pacing. Should she initiate some sort of small talk? But Fel-lar was already speaking. "I have explained to your mother what we hope to accomplish today." Mara noted and admired his choice of ambiguous pronouns: "your" and "we" could include either two or three. "And an approach has occurred to me, a transition which might assist us."

* * *

Long ago, when Fel-lar and his Twin-Bred companions studied carefully chosen works of Terran literature, Fel-lar had been intrigued by the idea of the free-standing and embroidered screens with which English ladies apparently protected themselves from both chill drafts and unwanted scrutiny. In New Landing and even in their current quarters, he had adapted the idea, creating room dividers and painting them with first Tofarna and then New Landing scenes, from sweeping landscapes to piquant details of flora and fauna. He now selected a screen from those that stood folded at the back of the storage compartment: a scene from the border of meadow and forest, one Mara found soothing and perhaps her mother would as well. Then he placed the leaning post behind the screen, hidden from where Mara stood, clenching her arms and vibrating with tension, and Elizabeth sat, bolt upright in the cushioned chair.

"Mara, please move closer to the screen. Yes—that should be the optimal distance. If both of you are ready, we can begin."

Mara, and then Elizabeth, nodded; and Fel-lar stepped behind the screen, relaxed against the post, and welcomed his friend.

* * *

"My thanks to Fel-lar for once again demonstrating his diplomatic skills."

Mara jerked her head around to see her mother's reaction. Fel-lar had explained what would be happening; but would Elizabeth allow herself to understand and accept it?

Elizabeth's face showed more confusion than shock. Whatever fantasies she might have allowed herself of the son she had lost—fantasies entertained, perhaps, even while she so diligently suppressed Mara's own—might have included the sound of his voice. And it would not have sounded like this.

"Elizabeth." The voice behind the screen stumbled on the syllables. "Damn. Excuse me. That's not what I've wanted to call you if we ever met. But what does a son say to his mother, so many years after what his first words would have been? I never had the chance to call you Mommy. I think it's a little late now. But 'Mother' sounds so formal, like a maiden in a melodrama. Would you accept 'Mom'?"

Elizabeth hid her face in her hands. It was hard to tell, with the fuzzy sweater Elizabeth wore, but Mara thought she might be trembling.

"I'm sorry. I tend to be flippant. Mara may have mentioned it. . . . We don't have to agree on a label. You're here, when you didn't have to be. That's what counts. Thank you for that."

Elizabeth looked up, staring toward the screen. Her mouth opened, closed, opened again. Mara could hardly hear the whisper that emerged. "Levi?"

"Here. In a manner of speaking."

Elizabeth spoke a little louder now, almost panting, the words coming in fits and starts. "Are you? What does it mean, to say you're here, to say you're anywhere?"

A shadow, barely visible, shifted on the screen: Fel-lar/Levi must have shrugged in the human manner. "That's one for psychologists and neurologists and xenologists and philosophers and mystics to debate over cups of tea. There's a tautology I could use, something about thinking and existing, but I'm not sure it would add much. In any event, we've all of us agreed not to fret about the question."

Mara looked at her mother's hands, clutching each other, empty. How could she have forgotten to offer her some chocolate? Or was her mother the one guest to whom she could not bring herself to make that gesture?

"Are you . . . are you happy? Or unhappy?"

Fel-lar somehow managed to produce a fair approximation of a human chuckle. "That's quite a good question. It's hard to say from my end of things, but I would guess that my consciousness is not quite as, hmmm, as continuous as what you lot have. I don't think I spend much time lingering in distress, unless Mara or Fel-lar or some other good friend is actively keeping me around at the time." A pause, during which Levi's communication went nonvocal. ("And Mara, don't start worrying about keeping me awake. I'll let you know if I need a breather, to use an inappropriate idiom.")

Elizabeth looked at Mara, back at the screen, and then at Mara again. "Will you—one of you—tell me more about your lives, out there on New Landing? What do you do? What is it like?"

("Levi, is Fel-lar comfortable, back there? This could take a while.")

("We're fine. And we're going to let you carry the conversational ball. Maybe after some unchallenging chit-chat, our mother will be ready for the next hurdle.")

Mara took a deep breath and sat down.

Mara did her best to describe the planet, and the various communities, and her work. It all seemed very far away. Sitting, even in a ship, on the surface of Tofarn, with the familiar gravity gripping her and green sky beyond the portholes, it was hard to believe that she had ever left, that that other life had really happened and was not some long and feverish dream.

Elizabeth asked a few questions, but seemed several times to be stopping herself from asking another. Finally, after an inquiry about the colors of Glider weaving, she bit her lip, sat up straighter, and said: "You haven't said anything about . . . whether you have . . . whether I have . . . ."

Of course. "No, I don't have children. Not . . . ." Could she say out loud, and to her mother, that the possibility might remain open? She could not bring herself to put the thought into words: not now, not weary as she was from the effort to treat this meeting as something like a normal social occasion. Better to move on. "How are you feeling, Elizabeth? Do you think you could manage if we tried to—proceed?"

Fel-lar's voice, Levi's voice, almost startled Mara after so long a silence from behind the screen. "Are you ready? Will you let me look at you, Elizabeth?"

Elizabeth sat very still; it seemed to Mara that she was holding her breath. She twitched her head in what might have been a nod.

The shadow on the screen shifted as Fel-lar stood up from the leaning post. A long Tofa foot appeared at the edge of the screen, and then the fingers of two right hands.

"No, I *can't!*"

Mesmerized by the sight before her, Mara jumped at the cry that came from behind: a cry of panic, such as she had never imagined her mother uttering. She turned to see Elizabeth shoving herself upward, out of the chair, scrambling behind it, then turning toward the door.

Fel-lar stepped forward from behind the screen, with only his left hands still hidden. "Wait, Elizabeth, if you please." It was not Levi who spoke; it was Fel-lar, Captain Fel-lar, and he invested the words with all that he had learned of command. "We are nearly finished. You may, of course, remain standing, if you no longer wish to be seated."

Elizabeth moved slowly back toward the chair, clutching the back with her hands, staring at Fel-lar. Fel-lar looked away, then back; and the change in his posture showed that Levi stood before them once more. He stepped away from the screen, revealing the gold and purple scarf dangling from his upper left hand. Lower hands held close to his body, he took the scarf in both upper hands, then said softly: "I'd like to wear it, just one time." He paused, as if waiting for an objection; then slowly wound the scarf around his neck. One end dangled loose, longer than the other; he lifted it up to rub it against his cheek, and pressed it against the lower half of his face, where a human mouth would have been. A choking sound came from where Elizabeth stood, but Mara would not look away.

Moving even more slowly, Fel-lar/Levi unwound the scarf again, then faced Elizabeth and held it toward her. "It was kind of you, and brave, to make this for me. But I think we both know that you won't take much comfort from the thought of me wearing it in—in the only way I can." Mara had to strain to hear the words: Fel-lar was humming as he spoke, unable to stay completely submerged, mourning his friend's sorrow. "So take it back."

Elizabeth let go of the chair and straightened up. One small step at a time, she walked toward the Tofa, who stood very still next to the screen. When she had come within reach, she stretched out a hand for the scarf; Fel-lar/Levi draped it over her wrist, taking obvious care not to touch her. Elizabeth turned toward Mara and beckoned with her other hand. Mara hesitated, then approached, as slowly as

Elizabeth had done. Elizabeth stepped toward her and draped the scarf around her shoulders. "Levi is within you, isn't he?"

Mara nodded.

Elizabeth sniffed, then coughed, as if tears were running down the back of her throat. "Then this is really the closest we can come, all of us, to my knitting a scarf for my son. Please keep it." Then she turned back toward Fel-lar/Levi. Moving closer, she reached for his lower left hand, and then his lower right, and tugged them forward. Then she opened her own arms and stood, looking upward, eyes wide.

("Should I? Can she handle it?")

("Go ahead, Levi. Do it now.")

Fel-lar/Levi bent down and embraced Elizabeth in his two lower hands, while his upper hands hovered above her head. "Thank you," he murmured above her hair. "And bless you. And goodbye." He let go, stepped back, gave her one more long look, and vanished behind the screen.

Mara looked toward the screen. ("Are you all right? Both of you?")

Fel-lar answered. "We will be all right. But will you take your mother home?"

"Oh, you needn't." Elizabeth came to stand by her daughter. "I don't need an escort. And you should all be together now."

Should she insist? But Mara could not think of anything left to say, or to do. She took a deep breath, then walked over and waited for the clue, the small nonverbal invitation that a daughter's embrace would also be welcome.

When that invitation came, Mara squeezed her mother tight as she had not done since some near-forgotten moment in early childhood. Then, holding her mother's hand, she walked her to the ramp that would lead her back to the world Mara had left behind.

* * *

Once again, Jak-rad-tan leaned in a corner in Veda's living room. The guards who had escorted him remained outside, one on each side of the front door, one near each side window.

Jak-rad-tan looked around at the only human habitation, outside the Project, in which he had ever felt at home. Would he find others, halfway across the galaxy, among those humans he had not yet met, who had come to New Landing on their own strange journey?

Veda tapped a control on her high-end sound system. "You'll probably be hearing this often, on the ship and on New Landing—but we may as well listen to it together before you go. Seth Baruti brought it when they let him out of the hospital, before he went back on board. He pieced it together from some recordings Wings Spread Wide made during the voyage, as well as from that last performance."

The rich intricacies and complex harmonies of Glider song filled the room.

Jak-rad-tan went limp against the wall, letting the music wash over him and through him. A few minutes later, however, some extraneous noise drew him from his trance. He looked up to see Veda opening the windows, and then the front door. She looked back and winked at him. "We may as well give your escort the chance for some cultural enrichment while we're at it."

Jak-rad-tan projected what his Twin-Bred brethren would know to be a smile. Sinking back into the music, he thought how pleasant it would be, soon, to be back among those who would appreciate that projection.

* * *

Two cohorts of Tofa lined the approaches to the park as the ramp slowly raised up and sealed the door to *Winds of Home*. Gen-tar-ten's troops stood watch to ensure that neither Jak-rad-tan nor Lan-sol nor any other member of the crew remained behind. Fel-lar's shipmates in turn kept watch on Gen-tar-ten's forces, lest any last-minute change of instructions be revealed that would prevent the ship's departure. When the fire had dwindled in the green expanse of the sky, and the thunder of the engines had died away, Fel-lar led his companions back toward *Star Seed*, with the Eminence's detachment of Tofa following close behind and setting up a perimeter at a prudent distance around the ship.

Fel-lar strode quickly up the ramp to where Mara stood

waiting. He put his right arms around her waist and shoulders, facing outward toward the fields around the ship. "I at least have revisited old haunts. If you would like to do the same, I can insist."

Mara started to shake her head, then stopped short. "Yes. Yes. I want to stand between streams again, and listen to the water. I want to watch tree-seeds float by. Do you think we can manage it?"

Fel-lar gazed out at the expanse, then headed for the console with which he could reach the planetary communications system. "I have an idea that may prove fruitful."

One hour later, two of the watchful line of Tofa detached themselves to greet and salute their Eminence, walking with a human woman by his side. Mara stood atop the ramp, leaning forward, her body taut with eagerness or strain. Fel-lar, at her side, waited until he was sure she could recognize the human figure, and turned to enjoy the delight that flooded her face.

He gave her a little push with his lower right hand. "Go on. I will keep house until you return."

Mara grabbed his hand, kissed it hard, and rushed down to take Laura in her arms.

The once-familiar stars were appearing in the darkening green sky before Mara returned, Laura by her side. The line of guards still stood, shuffling to ease sore feet, muttering amongst themselves. Laura walked up to the nearest of them and spoke softly. Her words appeared to revive the Tofa's spirits: he stood straighter and called out to his fellows, who stood up in turn and dressed their line. Laura turned back to Mara for a final embrace, then watched as Mara ran lightly up the ramp with an energy defying the unaccustomed gravity. Fel-lar reached out a hand to draw her in. "Are you ready?"

Mara reached up to stroke the side of his face. "Yes, love. We can go home."

Fel-lar punched the code that lifted the ramp, and moved to the porthole alongside it. As the ramp finished closing, he saw Laura start toward town, the line of Tofa falling into step behind her. The sight struck Fel-lar as a comical variant on the habits of Terran water fowl—what had that book been called, read to the Twin-Bred children so long ago?—like oversized ducklings following a small and indomitable maternal figure.

But the matriarch that mattered most, his helpmeet, his lover and inspiration, stood by his side.

He waited until she turned and walked away from the ramp before he turned as well, turned away from the world of his birth, toward the world and the companion of his future.

The End

APPENDIX

Characters (Partial List)

On Tofarn

Randy and Jak-rad-tan (formerly Jak-rad): only Twin-
  Bred pair still resident (separately) on Tofarn
Lan-sol: oldest child of Jak-rad-tan
Ved-rad: youngest child of Jak-rad-tan
Nin-til: a friend of Lan-sol
Laura Hanson: host mother, now a Council member
Veda Seeling: host mother
Stewart Channing: Veda's father, former Council member
Melly: Veda's and Brian's daughter
Gen-tar-ten: former Tofa dissident leader, Eminence of
  the Southern Region
Ton-lal-set: former Tofa host mother, former Eminence of
  the Southern Region

On New Landing

Mara Cadell: scientist, originator of the Project
Levi Thomas: Mara's lost fraternal twin
Fel-lar: Tofa Twin-Bred, co-chair of Congress
Judy and La-ren: Laura's Twin-Bred (La-ren deceased)
Rose: Fel-lar's Twin-Bred twin
Anna: human Twin-Bred, co-chair of Congress
Suzie: human Twin-Bred
Mat-set: Suzie's Twin-Bred twin, spore-parent of
  Fel-lar's twin offspring
Nathan: human Twin-Bred, engineer
Li-sen: Nathan's Twin-Bred twin, sharing household
  with Rose
Kenneth: human Twin-Bred in charge of communications
Elspeth: human Twin-Bred singleton, lover of Judy
Jimmy and Peer-tek: Veda's Twin-Bred

Sin-han: Peer-tek's child
Seth Baruti: former Statistics professor at Project,
    amateur astronomer
Harriet Gaho: former Chief Nurse at Project
Emily Wilson: former Diplomacy professor at Project
Wings Spread Wide: Glider elder
Rides Above Danger: musical collaborator with Fel-lar

Acknowledgments

I give heartfelt thanks to my beta readers, Anthony Herring and David Leek (also my cover designer). Beta reading the third book in a series is especially demanding, and I greatly appreciate their effort.

About the Author

Karen A. Wyle was born a Connecticut Yankee, but eventually settled in Bloomington, Indiana, home of Indiana University. She now considers herself a Hoosier. Wyle's childhood ambition was to be the youngest ever published novelist. While writing her first novel at age ten, she was mortified to learn that some British upstart had beaten her to the goal at age nine.

Wyle is an appellate attorney, photographer, political junkie, and mother of two daughters. Her voice is the product of almost five decades of reading both literary and genre fiction. It is no doubt also influenced, although she hopes not fatally tainted, by her years of law practice. Her personal history has led her to focus on often-intertwined themes of family, communication, the impossibility of controlling events, and the persistence of unfinished business.

Connect with Karen A. Wyle Online

Learn more about Karen A. Wyle by looking her up on:

her author website, www.KarenAWyle.net

the website for her nonfiction reference book summarizing American law, www.cttf.karenawyle.net

or on social media:
Twitter (@WordsmithWyle)
Facebook, at www.facebook.com/KarenAWyle
Goodreads, at www.goodreads.com/kawyle
or her blog, Looking Around, at
http://looking-around.blogspot.com

Like the book? Please tell readers!
Online book reviews are enormously helpful --
and old-fashioned word of mouth is terrific as well!